In Place of Fear

Catriona McPherson

In Place of Fear

HODDER &
STOUGHTON

First published in Great Britain in 2022 by Hodder & Stoughton
An Hachette UK company

1

A CIP catalogue record for this title is available from the British Library

Hardback ISBN 978 1 529 33796 9
eBook ISBN 978 1 529 33799 0

Typeset in Plantin Light by Manipal Technologies Limited.

Printed and bound in Great Britain by Clays Ltd, Elcograf S.p.A.

Hodder & Stoughton policy is to use papers that are natural, renewable and recyclable
products and made from wood grown in sustainable forests. The logging and
manufacturing processes are expected to conform to the environmental regulations of the
country of origin.

Hodder & Stoughton Ltd
Carmelite House
50 Victoria Embankment
London EC4Y 0DZ

www.hodder.co.uk

Facts and Fictions

The geography of Edinburgh is true to life here and the placing of the various offices and treatment centres in the new NHS is as accurate as I could make it, although the personnel are imaginary. The St Andrews Club does not exist and there was never a doctor's surgery in Gardener's Crescent, as far as I am aware.

'No society can legitimately call itself civilized if a sick person is denied medical aid because of lack of funds'
Aneurin Bevan, 1952

'The story of the development of a small, well organized, purposeful, predominantly female, profession would be worth telling for its own sake. . .'
Nottingham and Dougall, 2012

For the NHS, with love.

Prologue

Edinburgh keeps her secrets. She was built on them; the streets of the Old Town slumped in the dark behind close mouths, the sweep to the New Town laid over filth. If anyone knew, striding down the Mound, that underfoot was a midden of effluence, certainly no one showed it. That was Edinburgh's way. Bridges were built not over water, not to join islands, but to lift the merchants' ladies up above the fag ends of the old streets below, still down there, lightless and reeking.

A deacon by day was a thief by night in Edinburgh. A doctor needing corpses could always get them. A sleeping volcano crouched over the city and not a merchant, not a lady, not a deacon, not a doctor, gave it a thought. They called it a park, fed ducks there.

The sturdy new houses for weavers and workmen were built for secrets just the same. Upstairs neighbours with their doors to the back and downstairs neighbours with their doors to the front, they knew one another from creaks, from shuffles. Living inches apart, with only a floor between, hearing water in pipes and the scrape of a coal shovel, they never met. Their secrets stayed as safe as a whisper inside stone walls, as safe as a cat in the shadows.

So of course no one found her. Of course no one looked. She was days there, weeks into months, stiffening and softening, mouldering. Just the latest dark shame in a black-hearted city, unmourned, unmissed, unseen.

Chapter 1

Helen couldn't get a minute's peace up in the house. Her mother was at the sink in the off-shoot scrubbing carrots for their Sunday dinner, but she could do that and nag at the same time. Her father was propped up smoking in the box-bed in the kitchen. After a hard week's work and him the head of the house, who would stop him? But he could scold while he was smoking. Teenie was in the bedroom that used to be Helen's too, before the wedding, but she would come slinking out, hinting and smirking, if she heard her sister's step. That left the big room. But Sandy was asleep in there. Sandy. Her childhood sweetheart, her brand-new husband, her partner in all of life's travails, the minister had said the day they took their vows.

And so here she was, locked in the lav in the middle of the back green, looking sternly at herself in the spotted little mirror, delivering a sorely needed talking-to. 'You are trained,' she told her reflection. 'You are ready. Tomorrow is a great day in this nation and you are going to put your shoulder to the wheel and help.'

The door handle rattled.

'Two minutes,' Helen called out. She leaned close enough to the mirror to fog the glass with her breath and whispered, 'You, my girl, are a qualified medical almoner and at eight o'clock tomorrow morning you will be on the front line of the National Health Service of Scotland.' Her eyes looked huge

1

and scared. 'So take a shake to yourself!' she hissed, then un-chained the door.

'You've not pulled the plug, Nelly,' said Mrs Suttie, who was waiting outside with her box of Izal and her *Sunday Post*. 'Ach but it saves the watter, eh?' She shut herself in without waiting for an answer.

Helen's mother had finished at the sink and the carrots were on to boil. The table was laid with the second-best china, the set she kept on the kitchen dresser and only used on Sundays. Now Greet stood with her back to the range, ironing the very last of the week's wash, finally dry after all the warm, damp days. She was pressing the smell of the dinner into them, Helen thought. It was pork today, a good joint of rolled shoulder, but the fat was mutton like always.

Greet munched her dentures, her eyes darting back and forth across the ironing table. If you didn't know her you'd think she was looking for creases or smuts, waters spots, scorching. But Helen *did* know her mother. She knew Greet could iron a tablecloth with her eyes closed. She had done it in the black-out, when the night was too hot to bear the thick paper pinned over the windows, and she had done it other times too, Thursdays, saving the gas. What she was searching for wasn't crumpled cloth; it was the next point of attack.

'I d'ae trust thon doctor,' was what she landed on. 'D'ae trust either of them.'

'How no'?' Helen said, since straight-talking sometimes worked.

'Of course, you're too young to mind of the *old* doctor,' Greet said at last. It hadn't worked this time.

'Naw, I'm no',' said Helen. 'I mind of him fine.'

'You were a bairn. You knew nocht,' Greet said.

'So tell me now,' said Helen. 'Tell me what the problem is when he's years deid and away.'

'His son's a chip off him,' said Greet. 'What are they think-ing getting a decent lassie like you to work in beside them, just the three of you?'

'Will yese wheesht with all that,' said Mack, from the bed.

But he took it up himself when he sat down at the head of the table for his dinner, an hour later. 'Never thought I'd see a girl of mine stirring a midden for money.' He had poured a lake of gravy over his plate as usual, leaving the rest of them short, and he didn't finish half of it before he had his baccy out.

'I'll be giving out leaflets mostly, to start with,' Helen said. 'I'm no more stirring a midden than the postie.'

'Leaflets!' Mack's voice leapt with the scorn he always en-joyed so much. 'Bad as the bloody war again. Leaflets, leaflets.'

Helen had welcomed the flurry of leaflets at the outbreak. She had just left the school and she missed her books. When they came through the door – How to fit a gas mask, food shortage, petrol rations – she'd consoled herself that the same clever people who knew all this in advance and printed it up for every family would never let Sandy be harmed. They'd kit him out with good boots and a helmet, feed him three meals a day and send him home to her. She had saved the leaflets whenever she got to them before someone else used them to light the fire. She read them and re-read them, in place of letters, until they were as soft as chamois leather and fell back into folds when she let them go.

'You d'ae have to go through with it,' Greet said, with a mouthful of carrot. 'Just swallow your pride. You ken I've got you all set for a job in wi' me.'

It sounded like kindness but Helen knew better.

'I do ken,' Helen said. 'And I'm grateful. If this doesn't wor—' She managed to stop herself from saying her mother's job was a second-best to fall back on. She managed that much.

'It's a lot of strain on you,' Greet tried next. 'Just when you need to be taking good care. You're married now and soon you'll have more to think about than leaflets, Nelly.'

Teenie let out an explosive giggle.

'Mammy, get her telt!' Helen said as her cheeks flamed. She was more and more sure that Teenie knew. Somehow. Maybe she listened. Maybe Sandy had poured his heart out to her. Helen couldn't say which would be worse.

'Och, she just can't wait to be an auntie,' Greet said.

'I *can* wait, Mammy,' Teenie said. 'I'll have to.'

She definitely knew. Helen couldn't help shooting a look at Sandy. He was mopping gravy with a heel of bread, Mack watching him like a foreman. He couldn't charge Sandy with eating too much, given the lake of gravy on his own plate, fag ash floating in it now. And what was a slice of Sunday bread anyway? All of it needing used up before the morning.

'And *you're* sticking, are you?' Mack said at last, as if the sight of his son-in-law had pushed him beyond endurance.

'Sticking?' Sandy said. 'Sticking by Nelly? Aye, I am that. She's stuck by me.'

Greet frowned. And right enough it was a strange thing for a bridegroom to say. *Shut up, shut up!* Helen sent him a frantic, silent message.

'Two good jobs we've got the pair of you,' Greet said, maybe nudging Sandy to understand the point – for she was always ready to keep an argument alight – or maybe just taking the chance to air her own grievance again. 'All oor favours called in to get them and the baith of you thumbing your two toffee noses at it. The slaughterhouse has been good enough for your faither and the bottling hall's good enough for me. Good enough to put meat in your mouth and clothes on your back, Nelly.' She let her knife and fork clatter down onto her scraped plate – Greet, being one of six, had learned to eat quick or starve and

4

decades into adulthood, when she herself was in charge of dishing out, she hadn't broken the habit.

'*I* won't thumb my nose, Mammy,' Teenie chipped in, 'when it comes to me. I'm looking forward to it. I would have tooken a job for the holidays if you'd had one going.'

But it did her no good, for once. Greet wasn't listening. She cleared the plates, ready for pudding. It was trifle and usually they'd put aside any amount of bickering so as not to spoil it. Today Greet served it up in cold silence, banging the jelly spoon so hard on Mack's plate she might have cracked it. The little glass cruet set that was her pride and joy rattled in its wire carrier and, with a glance that way, she tapped a bit more gently to shake off Sandy's portion.

When the girls had theirs too, instead of eating her own Greet went over to the range and pulled the kettle forward. That was when Helen noticed what was laid on the dresser: a tray set with a lace cloth, cups and saucers, and the milk jug with a doily over to keep the flies off.

'Whae's coming?' she said. 'On a Sunday.' Her aunties had been on Thursday night as usual and Greet wasn't one to let the neighbours run in and out.

'Never you mind.' As the words were leaving Greet's mouth though, there came a rap at the door. It sounded like the head of a cane or an umbrella handle.

Helen's eyes widened. 'You wouldnae,' she said.

But her mother was away along the passage already.

'Good day to you, Mrs Downie.' The voice rang out from the bare landing and was hardly muffled when its owner entered their hallway and processed, with heavy tread, to the big room.

Mrs Sinclair! Helen's mentor, her benefactor, her champion all through the years of the war. 'Did you close the bed curtains?' she said, imagining Mrs Sinclair casting her eye over sheets still tumbled at dinnertime. The thought of Mrs Sinclair seeing her bed at all, hers and Sandy's, made

Helen want to shrink her neck into her shoulders and hug herself.

'I closed them,' Sandy said. 'And your ma came in after and had a tidy round.'

Greet was back in the kitchen now. 'Nell? Make that tea when the kettle boils and bring it through.'

Helen pushed her plate away, her appetite gone as her stomach soured and her gullet softened. She closed her eyes.

'Feeling sick?' Teenie said in that way she had. 'It's not the dinner, for the rest of us are fine. What's made *you* grue, Nelly?' It would have worked if Greet was in the room but it went over the men's heads. Helen scowled at her anyway and rose as the kettle started spitting.

If she hadn't the tea things to deal with, the sight of Mrs Sinclair sitting there still in her church clothes might have stopped Helen dead. She was a large woman, her hair teased out in the style of her youth with a hat perched on top of it all, and she dressed herself to look impressive, not attractive, with wide shoulders and box pleats, a fox fur even on a summer's day.

Helen picked her way through the good furniture – so much of it that the place felt more like a saleroom than a home: the chenille-covered table with the thick, turned legs and the four chairs that didn't quite fit under it; another two on either end of the behemoth of a walnut sideboard that was filled with tureens and decanters, never used since they'd been unpacked thirty years before for a present show. Concentrating hard, Helen managed to set down the tray at her mother's elbow and take a seat, doing it all without the unwelcome surge and tingle of her face darkening. That ready flush was the bane of her life. She had got her colouring from Greet, white skin if she could keep out of the sun, freckles else, and orange curls that neither brush nor pin could tame. Anytime she got through an awkward moment like this one and didn't turn as red as a poppy she was glad of it.

So there they were, at three of the four chairs round the gate-leg table in the window, looking at each other through the polished leaves of the aspidistra, Greet pouring tea and Mrs Sinclair unbuttoning her gloves.

'And do you take sugar?' Greet said, in a grating, dainty whine that made Helen's cheeks flame after all.

'Just a little milk if it's quite fresh,' Mrs Sinclair said.

Greet's hand shook as she plied the milk jug and *her* face was a sudden lash of deepest pink, screaming at her hair. Helen felt a moment of glee, but then seeing her mother bend to check the cup for flecks, and even take a quick sniff, sobered her again. Mrs Sinclair had a cold cupboard out the back of her kitchen with slate shelves and a wet floor. Helen had seen it many times as she helped out at children's treats, fetching lemonade. All right for some.

'So,' Mrs Sinclair said, putting her cup back down after a sip. Greet put hers down too. 'You'll know why I'm here, Helen. Your parents asked me to appeal to your better nature one more time before it's too late.'

Helen said nothing.

'I don't think you quite understand,' Mrs Sinclair went on, 'because you're a nicely brought-up girl who has been protected from the nastier side of life, first by your parents' attention, and then by my careful shielding, even while you helped me out with this and that.'

Helen hadn't spent seven years at Mrs Sinclair's side without developing an iron grip on her expressions. She didn't smile or raise a brow. Nicely brought up? She'd spent her early years on Freer Street and if Mrs Sinclair thought *this* room, with all its polish and china, was a place to be wary of Sunday milk, she would have sat on her hanky round there. And as for 'helping her out with this and that': Helen had been her right-hand girl from morning till night, wheeled out as a prime example of Mrs Sinclair's good works, for ministers, masons, doctors and even a judge once.

'But we are in perfect agreement,' Mrs Sinclair was saying, 'that you are not equipped, by temperament, by age, or by standing, to do what you are so wilfully and so very inexplicably set on doing. And if' – Helen had tried to speak, but Mrs Sinclair held up a hand and went on in an even louder voice – '*And if* you are really so unscrupulous as to take advantage of that poor boy having had such a bad war and make hay while he's still not able to exercise proper control of you –' She paused (whether for dramatic effect, from the emotion she had whipped up, to hint that three years on Sandy should be over his war by now, or because she hadn't planned how to end the argument and was lost in it, Helen couldn't tell) '– then I have to say, I have been mistaken in you and I regret lifting you up into prominence out of your proper place.'

'I'm not taking advantage of Sandy,' Helen said. 'I'm doing this to help him. We'd have a job living on his wage alone.'

Greet frowned furiously at her. She had sparse brows for frowning, like Helen's own, but she made herself clear. *She* wouldn't have told the likes of Mrs Sinclair what work Sandy was doing. *She'd* told Helen's aunties he had a milk round, since they lived away down Abbeyhill and Leith way and wouldn't run into him. 'You'll have to live on his wage alone soon enough,' she said. She turned to Mrs Sinclair. 'I was just trying to explain to her that there's no point getting used to a big pay packet when she'll soon be brought to bed and doing what she's made for.'

'Mother!' Helen said. 'For one thing, it's modern times now. We can plan. And for another, isn't it better to save hard while we can, while we're both working?'

Greet was shocked into a rare silence. But Mrs Sinclair sailed on.

'That's another thing I wanted to say.' She was leaning forward, her stiffly upholstered bust straining. She had on a high-necked blouse and a cameo, but there was still a waft of gardenia as she pressed against the edge of the table. 'The best thing all round would be a good wage for your *husband*, Helen. Since even the best-laid "plans"… And I have managed to get a promise of an excellent job for him, with decent prospects too.'

'Where?' Helen said. Because it wasn't as if she *wanted* Sandy sweeping the streets for the Corporation. She wasn't ashamed of it, or of him for doing it, but she wasn't bursting with pride either. And Mrs Sinclair had fingers in so many pies, Dr Deuchar always said, she'd have to start using her toes soon. If she had got Sandy a gardening job down at the Botanics, or even a keeper's job at the zoo, Helen would. . . what? Would she buckle? Would she give in?

'Fleming's,' Mrs Sinclair said. 'A clerk in the ironmongery department. And the under-manager is retiring soon. So. . .'

'But he couldn't do that,' said Helen. 'Fleming's? Inside all day? He'd be with my father if he could do *that*.'

'I thought it was the slaughtering,' Mrs Sinclair said.

Everyone thought it was the slaughtering – the blood or the smell or the cries of the beasts – even though that made no sense at all. If Sandy had been invalided off a battlefield, maybe. If he'd carried a comrade, blown to bits and with the smell of burnt flesh in his nose and the man's guts spilling over his hands, then the slaughtering would be the problem and a nice job behind a high counter at Fleming's with a green apron and a pencil behind his ear would be ideal. But Sandy spent his war in hut thirteen of Stalag 387, captured before the first Christmas and not set free till VE Day. Now, when he wasn't sleeping or eating he was outside. He walked miles when it was dry and sat under the lee of the wash house wall when it rained. Helen could hear him right now, letting himself out the front door. She knew she wouldn't see him again till teatime.

'No,' she said. 'It's the four walls. Not the blood. He needs to be out in the air.'

9

'Pushing a dustcart.' Mrs Sinclair was putting her gloves back on. 'Is that what you dreamed of, Helen? When you were a girl? That you'd be so stubborn, so *thrawn*, you would consign a fine up-and-coming young man like Alexander to pushing a dustcart?'

Consign him? Helen thought. *I* didn't capture him. *I* didn't keep him prisoner. *I* didn't plan that stupid offensive that handed him to the Germans.

'No,' she answered at last. 'I never dreamed of anything like it. But a man's got to work at something unless he's a gentleman of leisure. Here, Mrs Sinclair, what's the wage at Fleming's? *I* could take the job and maybe Sandy could walk in the Pentlands all day instead of behind his cart.' Helen spoke out of something more than devilment, out of a threatening upswell of what felt like hysteria. The combination of what was coming in the morning – her fear and excitement and the surprise of it all – added to the sight of Mrs Sinclair sitting there, feet from Helen's bed, in her high hat and her fox fur, not to mention Greet quivering with indignation but forced to contain it by this battleship of a woman in her own house... it all made Helen feel as though something might burst out of her any minute, all the more unsettling because she didn't know whether it would be laughter or sobbing when it came.

Unbelievably, none of her turmoil showed on the outside and when the mist cleared Mrs Sinclair was answering her suggestion, quite calmly if with a bit of irritation. 'It's a job for a man,' she said. 'And this nonsense *you're* threatening is a job for a lady.' She said the word as if it was the name of an exotic creature that Helen wouldn't have come across before. 'Your own dear mother has a perfectly nice job for a *girl*,' she tells me.'

A 'nice' job indeed, Helen thought. Standing in the clattering racket of the bottling hall all day, in the stink of the malt, learning to lip-read gossip, coming home with glass cuts all over your hands and your pinny reeking. The very thought of it settled her down again.

'Thank you,' she said, out of this new calm. 'I do appreciate your concern.' She was using the words Mrs Sinclair had taught her and the voice too, not her own voice and not Greet's strangled attempt at gentility. But this wasn't devilment. It was practicality. She was going to have to start speaking up and being clear tomorrow. This was a wee practice and it felt good. 'The thing is,' she went on, 'I *am* suited by temperament.' She felt her chest lift as she spoke, her shoulders pulling back. Out of the corner of her eye, she saw Greet put her head on one side, just slightly, like a bird, and regard her with a new kind of curiosity. '*And* I'm suited by training, as you can hardly deny.' Mrs Sinclair's eyes widened so far they seemed to bulge and at the same time her mouth pursed so tight it disappeared. Her rouge, worn high on her cheeks in two circles like the paint on a baby doll, faded into invisibility as a livid flame rose up from her collar and engulfed her face. But Helen still wasn't done. 'I was offered the job because they thought I'd shine in it,' she said. 'And I am determined not to let them down and make them regret their faith in me. They're all going to be stretched thin this next wee while –'

'How would *you* know that?' said Mrs Sinclair.

'It said on the leaflet,' Helen replied, so smartly she was almost interrupting. She had learned it by heart, thrilling at the words. '"If the beneficiaries are to catch up with all their rights, he – that's the doctor – will have to be a guide, a philosopher and a friend".'

'I don't need a lecture!' Mrs Sinclair as good as spat the words.

'And I'm going to help them every way I can,' Helen said. 'Which I couldn't have done without you and your kindness. So, thank you.'

Mrs Sinclair said not another word. She stood, blundered her way clear of the tea table, letting her chair scrape roughly on the lino, and swept out, stumping along like an angry giant after the blood of an Englishman.

Greet, Helen noticed, was crying. Her heart swelled. At last! She had made her mother see. She had maybe even made her mother proud.

'Mammy—' she began.

Greet cut her off. 'For shame. For black shame. I tell you this, Helen Crowther, you can get your airs and graces and your pert, thankless ways and take that useless lump of a husband and get out of this house.'

'What do you mean "useless lump"?' Helen said. Did Greet know too? Was she just better at hiding it than Teenie? Was all this talk of woman's purpose supposed to make Helen break down and tell?

'If you go to that Dr Strasser and his pal the morn's morn then don't come back here at night,' said Greet. 'And when you fall, and your precious job is a fading memory, don't think I'll be at your beck and call for baby-sitting either! Plan! *Plan*, you say, bold as brass! I've a good mind to tell your father how you just showed me up.'

No, Helen thought, she didn't suspect at all, did she? 'Be my guest,' she said, knowing her mother would do no such thing, for Mack had to be protected from the like. She stood and marched to the door, then faltered remembering that her and Teenie's room wasn't her and Teenie's room any more. Instead she swerved, wrenched open the curtain over the box bed and climbed in, pulling it shut behind her. She would stay here until Sandy came back and then she'd have it out with him, once and for all. That's what she would do. She'd tell him she needed her mind on her job, not fretting over him, waiting and wondering. She'd tell him he owed her a bit of straight-talk, plain dealing. An end to it or an explanation.

She rolled onto her back and stared up at the tongue and groove panels of the ceiling, so thick with paint they barely had dents. She wouldn't say anything. She was as bad as her mother. She would just put it out of her mind and be grateful to know she was free to do her job and not worry that she'd soon be boiling nappies instead. Her job. Her wonderful miracle of a job in this wonderful miracle of a thing that would start in the morning, all over the city, all over the country. And her – wee Nelly Downie fae Freer Street – a part of it! That would do.

Chapter 2

Clothes maketh the man, was one of Dr Deuchar's little sayings. He had a hundred of them. Helen was kneeling on her heels with both drawers open, looking over her choices for the day. If it was winter she'd wear grey serge with cream cuffs buttoned on, but she'd stew in that today and have dark rings under her oxters by dinnertime. So a skirt and a blouse. She'd take a jacket with her and put it on a hanger on the back of the door like the doctors with their overcoats. Never a peg through a loop, always a hanger. She used to think it was funny that they brought a coat down to the surgery when they lived upstairs, but after she'd seen them go flying out on an emergency call a few times, grabbing bag and coat without breaking stride, she admired them for the forethought. She wouldn't have emergency call-outs, of course. Would she? The little worm wriggling in the pit of her belly started thrashing at the thought of it. It was the same little worm that had told her not to try even a bite of breakfast.

Get started, she told herself. Dress yourself for the first day. By Christmastime, if someone called her out on this imagined mercy dash, she'd be ready. Get started today. Dress the part. Clothes maketh the man. She had a good pair of stockings with not a single thread pulled on them, as well as a black straw hat she'd never worn on a Monday before now.

'Don't sit like that.' Greet was behind her suddenly. 'You'll get veins.'

Helen shoved the drawers closed and twitched the edge of her eiderdown over the top of them.

'Never mind straightening – I'm going to strip that bed and get the sheets in,' her mother said. She had lived on the stair enough years to have got Mondays in the wash house and drying green and she liked to start her whites soaking before work, not trusting old Mrs Suttie to do them justice. She'd be back at dinnertime, looking over Mrs Suttie's shoulder as the blouses and shirts went in, rushing home to do jerseys and stockings herself before tea. Never mind that Mrs Suttie always said she could manage. 'Them as pays the piper,' was Greet's reply. 'I wouldn't put it past her to bunch mine up and make room.' She 'paid' Mrs Suttie in meat that Mack brought home – liver and bones and the odd fatty knuckle – but you'd never know it from the airs she put on. Even when they were in summer clothes all day and a single sheet to cover them in the hot nights, Greet would scrape up a day's worth of wash-ing and a green's worth of drying from somewhere rather than leave a breath of warm in the copper or an inch of rope for someone else. 'It's my day,' she always said. 'They've got their own days and you don't see me coming begging.' Once, in the war, Helen had pointed out that there were only four of them and no men coming in from the works in boiler suits, seeing as how Mack's aprons got done at the slaughterhouse laundry. Greet had washed every blanket in the press and every mat off the floors, with her jaw set as if it was bound up in a bandage.

'Thanks, Mammy,' Helen said now, bowing her head to hide the smile. Greet must be torn in two, caught between keeping up the pretence of putting her daughter out and the need to fill that copper with linens on this sunny Monday.

'Make it up fresh for whoever's in there next,' Greet said.

You had to hand it to her. Helen even briefly wondered about saying thanks again, because surely the cussedness making Greet keep on with a story of banishment was the same cussedness, handed down, making Helen believe she

15

could do what she was doing. Greet's trouble, one that Helen didn't share, was how to get out of the hole she had dug.

'Aye, fine,' she said, going along. It wasn't her job to make things easy. 'I'll strip them and bring them down.'

'I can do it.'

Helen stared up at her mother. 'What?' Greet said. 'Think it's anything I haven't seen before?' She was in about the bedclothes already, bundling the eiderdown and plucking the pillows from their cases. 'I've not got time to be waiting till you're dolled up for whoever it is you're dolling up for. I need to get this lot soaking before the horn.'

Whoever it is I'm dolling up for, Helen thought, as she stepped into the new stockings and fastened them. That was the meat of it. That was the real trouble, no matter it was a lie. No one – not even her own mother – believed she wanted the job for the sake of the job. But it was true. The only man she'd ever dolled up for in her life was Sandy Crowther. She looked at the dark patch of hair oil on the bare pillow, then turned away before her eyes could fill and streak her face powder.

For a wonder, she didn't pass a neighbour on the stair and it was the perfect time of day to get along the street: too late for menfolk whose day shifts started at seven and too early for any women headed towards the bottling hall and brewery for eight.

Hurrying along Fountainbridge, checking Castle's clock, Helen took the turn onto Gardner's Crescent, and into another world.

Summer in the high tenements, those gaunt chasms between flat cliffs of stone, was no more than dust in the air instead of coal smoke. But to turn this corner was to find summer deserving the name. The lozenge of grass and flowerbeds that formed the crescent meant the sun could reach all the way to the ground, dappling through the trees at the edge of the little park and glinting on the shiny paint of the handful of motorcars parked at the kerb. It was the same in winter, when turning

16

onto the crescent meant leaving behind running walls and deep coughs for sparkling cold light and frosted beech leaves. At any time of year, here was quiet, space and serenity.

Dr Deuchar, always so chatty, had told her the story of the builder away a hundred years ago who thought he could start another posh bit up here like they had down there in the New Town. He'd built just this one crescent of tall houses and sat back waiting to get rich. But he'd reckoned without the slaughterhouse, the brewery, the distillery, the stables, the rubber mill and Mackay's works. 'Still, it's perfect for me,' Dr Deuchar had said, 'that old Dr Strasser settled here, and that my good friend Strasser isn't a married man. I like to be useful but I'm too lazy to walk far.' He'd grinned as he spoke and it had taken Helen a night of thinking it over to find the insult. 'Like to be useful' meant he wanted to cure the impetigo and ringworm of people like her instead of taking care of ladies' nerves up the Braids way. 'Too lazy to walk far' meant he didn't mind treating them but he wouldn't want to live the way they lived. She sometimes wished Dr Strasser *would* get married or just decide he was past sharing rooms. Then Dr Deuchar would have to slog up to Fountainbridge from some other crescent, or hoof it in from a villa somewhere.

Not that she could imagine Dr Strasser putting his partner out on the street. He wasn't as much fun as Dr Deuchar but he was easier in a way. 'Like a bluebell wood in April,' Dr Deuchar would say, standing at an open window and taking a sniff that turned his nostrils white. Helen suspected he was joking, but it took Dr Strasser's straightforward, 'My word, what a pong!' before she was sure enough to reply.

She couldn't blame either of them. No matter whether the rubber, hops, malt or horses was strongest on any given day, there was never just air outside. And then there was Mackay's on top, never mind that a sweetie factory sounded lovely. The women came home sickened with the sugar they'd been breathing, their hair stuck to their collars and their ears plugged with it. Better to be in the abattoir where it all washed off at the first dousing.

Best of all to be on Gardner's Crescent. This morning, though, the usual peace had been sorely disturbed. Outside the doctors' door, which sat halfway round, a crowd was already gathering, even as early as this, with over an hour to go. Twenty people, Helen guessed as she approached, more than half of them with a leaflet clutched in hand, so it looked as if they were waving goodbye to a loved one. She put her head down, glad of her hat brim, and barrelled through them, slipping in at the area gate and trotting down the stone steps to the basement door before any of them could stop her.

'Here!' It was a large woman Helen knew to nod to. She lived in Semple Street and had wheeled a child around in a bogey made from an old box on pram wheels since he'd been a toddler. He was grown now, his twisted legs in stick-and-tape calipers hanging out over the sides of the box and his feet dragging on the ground. His mother was burly from the years of it and sweating already after the journey to bring him here this warm morning.

Helen looked up at her.

'Are you a nurse?' the woman said. 'I cannae get him doon they steps. Will the doctor come up?'

'Don't worry,' Helen said. 'The waiting room and surgery are on the ground floor there. Two steps, just.'

'Here,' the woman said again. 'Are you no' Greet Downie's lassie? I didnae recognise you there a minute.'

Helen smiled and let herself into the dark passageway, feeling a thrill at the bristle of keys on her keyring. She'd had a key to the door of Grove Place handed over on her twenty-first but now there was this area door and the ground-floor door above and even a wee key to the off-shoot up at Mrs Sinclair's where the garden-party trestles were stored. She should have given that back after the last one but the truth of it was this bunch of keys was one of her secret delights. Neither of her parents had four keys. Teenie had not a one.

She stood a moment and took a deep breath. She had always liked the smell down here in the basement of the doctors' house. The dispensary was tucked into what was probably an old pantry and the air all along the length of the passage from the area to the garden door had a nip of cloves and gentian violet about it from the cough bottles and poultices, a top-note of linseed and kerosene and a rumble of sulphur running along underneath.

Braced for what was coming, Helen set off along the flags, the brisk clip-clip of her tipped heels helping to gird her. Those were the steps of a woman who knew her business and wouldn't waste time about it.

It was only to savour the moment, then, that she paused outside the door before pushing it open.

She stopped dead, those same heels making her sway a little before she caught her balance again. 'Good morning, Miss Anderson,' she said. She didn't flick a glance to either side but she managed to take it all in anyway: no boxes, no trolleys, nothing disturbed anywhere in the little room – once a housekeeper's bolt hole, probably – where the clerkess had been making up and sending out accounts for the doctors for the last twenty years. The banks of filing cabinets and shelves of ledgers made a sort of altar around the woman and she sat before it like a statue, with her jaw set and her hands clenched on the bare desk-top.

'Good morning, Helen,' she said and then neither spoke again.

The silence lengthened. Helen knew Miss Anderson was supposed to be out. This was *her* office now. The carters would be on their way to take the patients' notes, ledgers and receipt books off to the Public Health Chambers at Johnston Terrace and Miss Anderson should have been packing her little tin teapot and her locked box of petty cash and sweeping herself out the door. An African violet in a pot left on the desk as a good luck token would be too much to hope for but this was mutiny.

'Oh well,' Helen said at last. 'Maybe I can squeeze in upstairs until you've got yourself sorted.'

Miss Anderson's chin jerked up. 'Upstairs?'

They both knew the only space up beside the doctors was the winter waiting room. Panelled in wood so dry you could taste it, it was unbearable except in the very coldest months, when its oversized fire and the accident of so many hot pipes running round the skirtings made it the cosiest room in the house. The summer waiting room with long windows giving onto the garden was cool and pleasant half the year, but arctic the other half when the frames rattled and any fire in the tiny grate flailed at the chill without denting it.

Still. An office up there beside the doctors, right in the thick of it, was a prize. Helen gave her sweetest smile, knowing but not caring that she'd look like Teenie stirring the pot, and withdrew.

She was halfway to the stairs when she heard a gasp, followed by the bitterest weeping. On tiptoe, she crept back to the office door and hesitated there, flooded with shame, her thoughts darting about like little fish. Should she go in? Would that be a comfort to Miss Anderson or mortification on top of her misery? Would kindness or coldness from Helen be more to the poor woman's taste right now? Paralysed, she stood there with her hand on the doorknob and her knees not quite steady.

Then a flash of unwelcome understanding passed through her and settled low in her belly like gulped porridge: Mrs Sinclair was right. They were *all* right. Helen was too young, too green, too mouse-like for this. She hadn't even started yet and here she was already not knowing what to do.

Hard on the heels of that thought, though, came something steelier. This wasn't the job. This was awkward but Miss

Anderson had done it to herself. Helen would proffer her fresh-pressed hanky and then lend a hand to fill the boxes. She'd be understanding and determined, and she'd be in her office where she belonged by dinnertime.

She pushed open the door. The sobs stopped. Miss Anderson sat white-faced and tight-lipped behind her desk, still with her fists on the blotter. She stared back at Helen with sharp eyes. Dry eyes. This woman hadn't just been crying.

In the corner hidden from Helen's view there was a scuffle. She stepped forward and craned round the edge of the door.

It was dark everywhere down here in the doctors' basement and this room was windowless for one thing, full of those ebony-stained filing cabinets besides, so it was more or less a cave without the lamps on. And that place behind the door was the darkest corner of all. But, despite the gloom, Helen saw – or at least she was almost sure she saw—

'What do you want?' Miss Anderson said.

Helen glanced over at her, startled by the taut twang of her voice, and when she glanced back again there was nothing there. Of course there was nothing there. It was only that the filing cabinet right in the corner was closer than she'd expected it to be.

'Just to say if you need a hand packing,' Helen offered, hating the tremor behind her words and hating the smirk it put on Miss Anderson's face, 'you know where to find me.'

She scurried along to the foot of the stairs and trotted up them with her feet pecking at the steps faster and faster, only slowing when she threw open the door at the top and felt it bang back on its hinges and hit the wall.

It was nothing, she told herself again. There was no door there, nowhere for someone to disappear to and nowhere for them to hide. So that meant no one was there. It stood to reason. She had seen nothing.

But if she'd been looking at nothing, how did she know what colour it was? If it didn't exist, how could it be yellow?

And it was. Helen had seen a scrap of something yellow whisk out of sight as sure as she'd ever seen anything in her life.

'Ready for the advancing hordes?' Dr Deuchar came trotting down the last half flight, ending with a bump on the carpet runner. He had just washed his hair, Helen thought, but forgotten the Brylcreem so it sat up in fluffy bolls on top of his round head. 'Clever of you to nip in through the area and dodge them but you'll have to face them at nine o'clock when the bell tolls. It tolls for thee, Helen. It tolls for thee.'

Dr Deuchar always talked like that, repeating phrases for the fun of the words in his mouth, just like her father when he staggered home on a Saturday. Helen had learned to ignore both of them. 'The thing is, Doc,' she said, 'Miss Anderson's still in her office and doesn't look like shifting.'

'Laying in tins, is she?' Dr Deuchar said. 'Sandbags in the doorway?' He hooked an arm round the newel post at the bottom of the stairs and leaned against it.

'The thing is,' Helen said again, 'that means there's nowhere for the hordes to advance *to*.'

'I think she's probably just making her feelings known,' said Dr Deuchar. 'She has plans to visit her sister at Largs for a holiday.' The light bouncing off Dr Deuchar's wee glasses hid his eyes but his face was an open book. He smiled as he spoke. 'Don't worry about Miss Anderson, Nell. Leave her to Strasser and me. We'll winkle her out.'

The light changed and Helen looked up. Dr Strasser was on the landing, silhouetted against the etched glass of the tall window.

'Not more trouble?' he said, although it was first thing in the morning of a new week and Helen didn't see what could have happened already.

'Miss Anderson's still downstairs, Doc,' Helen said. 'She hasn't packed so much as a book of stamps as far as I can tell.'

'Well, well,' said Dr Strasser, mildly. He had a way of making Helen feel silly, as if she was always seeing trouble and fuss that didn't occur to him. But he bothered about some things that other people shrugged off. Now, as he very carefully didn't look at Dr Deuchar's fluffy hair, he put a hand up to his own to smooth it. As if it could get any smoother. It was already as black and shiny as the polished toe of a policeman's boot, pulled straight back from a widow's peak.

'I was wondering,' Helen said, 'if I could set up in the winter waiting room, just until Miss Anderson gets herself situated and her room falls free?' Dr Strasser said nothing. Maybe she had overstepped and offended him, thinking she could have a room in beside the two of them. 'Or maybe no one will need to see me today,' she added.

Dr Strasser's jaw tightened, pulling his lean face into crevices. 'We have enough referrals waiting to keep you busy no matter who does or doesn't walk through the door.'

'Oh,' Helen said, then felt a surge of heat threaten to climb up out of her collar. She had been pushing so hard against Greet, she had forgotten she needed to be meeker around the doctors, do their bidding.

'I've three convalescing at home that I'd rather see up in the Braids if you can persuade them,' Dr Strasser said.

'Oh,' said Helen again. She'd met the matron of the Braids Convalescent Home while carrying parcels for Mrs Sinclair, but she'd never said so much as good morning to the woman. Still, it would be different now it was all covered and no one asking for charity. Surely.

'Unless you had other plans?'

Helen really did flush now but, since she couldn't help letting her head droop a little at his tone, maybe they wouldn't see it.

'Strasser!' At least she had one ally, she thought.

'Forgive me,' said Dr Strasser. 'Helen, I apologise. The strains of the day.'

Helen nodded and blinked rapidly to clear the shine from her eyes. Nothing about this morning felt ordinary. She had never been here without Mrs Sinclair before, never had one of the doctors snap at her, nor apologise to her.

'Go and have a cup of tea, Nelly,' Dr Deuchar was saying, 'We'll let Strasser here talk Miss Anderson round, get those files out from her lair and off where they belong. You'll talk her round, old chap, won't you? She bullies me dreadfully but she won't say boo to the young master.'

Dr Strasser turned a blank look on his friend. It was true that his father had had the practice before him but he didn't like to be reminded of his father, his inheritance, as if he'd rather be a self-made man like Dr Deuchar than a man born lucky. Mind you, the one time Dr Deuchar had said as much to him, he'd slammed out and stayed away hours. He'd missed a Christmas party.

'One does wonder why the rush,' Dr Strasser said at last. 'I mean, unless they've drafted half the city down there to re-file everything, why the tearing rush, simply to have boxes lie around Johnston Terrace instead of lying around here?'

'Efficiency,' said Dr Deuchar. 'Order. Punctual attendance to the matters of the day. Our brave new world, Strasser.'

'You make it sound. . . Continental,' Dr Strasser said. 'And not Mediterranean.'

'Not at all,' said Dr Deuchar. 'God forbid. Checks and balances are an *American* invention, old man.' He turned to Helen and gave her a smile. She returned the smile but had nothing to add to the conversation, which was far, far beyond her. She missed Mrs Sinclair again, who'd have been tutting and flapping her gloves at the doctors, shutting down their 'boyish nonsense', as she called it, long before now.

'Whatever the provenance,' Dr Strasser said, 'I'm afraid I'm going to need *you* to persuade Miss Anderson, dear chap. I have business with Helen, before we all start for the day.'

Dr Deuchar inclined his head, shuffled past them both and started down the basement steps, walking with a comical dragging gait, like a prisoner headed for the guillotine. Helen smiled but when she turned to include Dr Strasser in the joke, his face was stony.

'Come with me,' he said, but he didn't head for his office to scold her about her insubordination. He crossed the hall and opened the front door.

Down on the pavement, the gaggle of patients turned like a skein of birds in the sky and surged forward. The lad in the bogey craned his neck to see behind him and his mother, from years of habit, hauled on the rope to turn him round.

'Half an hour to go yet!' Dr Strasser said, holding up his hands towards them as he squeezed by. 'Nine sharp.'

'Where are we going?' Helen said, scurrying in his wake before the queueing patients could close behind him again and engulf her with their questions. They'd melt away to let the doctor through but they'd never let *her* get past them if they could help it. 'Where are we going?' she said again, as Dr Strasser strode out over the pavement and straight across the road to the little quarter moon of gardens. 'You haven't a coat on. Or a hat. Are you going on a call? Where's your bag? Where are we going?'

Dr Strasser stopped and pointed through the railings. 'There,' he said.

As Helen stepped close to see what he was looking at, he moved away again down to the corner and round the back of the crescent on its flat side. Then he shot off down the narrow entrance of a side street, not much more than a lane, with Helen trotting to catch up.

Rosebank, this was called. A little knot of dead ends not an eighth of a mile from where Helen lived and yet she had never walked up any of them before, didn't know a soul who lived here. 'Colonies', the houses on these funny little streets were called, a name as mystifying as it was exotic. Helen hurried behind Dr Strasser, glancing around as she passed, at the long solid blocks to the left of her and, to the right, strange wee short terraces, only one house in each, as if the cross street had been put in the wrong place or the builder had done his sums wrong then decided he could squeeze in just one more.

He must have been an inventive sort of builder, Helen reckoned. These 'colonies' weren't like any other kind of house. The upstairs ones were reached by outside stairways on the east side of the blocks; the downstairs houses had their own front doors to the west, and in between these two-faced rows were long stretches of quiet garden, with washing ropes and rhubarb beds, little huts with windows. Helen, rushing by, thought she saw an apple tree.

'Where are we going?' she said once again, like a child. Dr Strasser seemed to be headed, full tilt, towards a blank wall at the end of the lane, ten feet of brick to stop children following a lost ball down onto the railway. If children even played in the street here. Maybe with those long stretches of garden they didn't need to. All that grass. Helen couldn't help pausing to look. It would be like your own private park, right outside your front door. Smaller than the rolling lawns of Mrs Sinclair's house along at Merchiston, but still another world from the bare earth – dust or mud depending – that backed Freer Street, even Grove Place. She turned to face forward again. Where was Dr Strasser?

She was all alone at the dead end, the final long terrace to her left and the last of the stubs to her right. And *there* he was, halfway up the outside stair on that last little house at the far fag end of the street, watching her over the railings.

'A house call?' she said. 'A patient? I've nothing with me, Doc.' All Helen's little store of blank patient sheets were back at the surgery. Sheets for home surroundings, family history, needs and resources, misc. 'Misc.' was where all the really important questions were to be asked, carefully and indirectly, and where all the crucial information was to be recorded, in words so veiled in layers of silky meaning they were like a code. It would pass under the eyes of the patient unseen, but speak its sleekit truth down at Johnston Terrace where her work would be checked by the inspectors. She could cry, she thought. Here she was at her very first call, without a single form, without a leaflet, with not so much as a pencil behind her ear.

'No patients,' Dr Strasser said. 'A decision that's long over-due. This morning seems a good time to grasp the nettle.'

'Grasp *what* nettle?' Helen said, then decided the best way to work out what was going on was to look for herself.

He had the door open before she was at the head of the stairs and he held it for her. Those were his manners. Dr Strasser would no more go through a door before Helen than he would greet a patient behind his desk. He stood every time, and shook whoever's hand. Courtly manners, he had. Not but what Dr Deuchar made them laugh more when they were shamed or scared. Dr Deuchar could stick a needle in an infant and, as he pulled his funny faces, it wouldn't pause in its chuckling.

The passageway behind the door was empty. Bare, pale boards that looked as if they'd just been sanded that morning and smooth walls as white and soft as a powdered bon-bon. Was she imagining it or was there a trace of sawdust in the air? She loved the smell of sawdust, it reminded her of happy days, when Mack would bring a poke of it back from the slaugh-terhouse for her to spread on the floor of the cage where her white mouse lived its quivering little life. Then Teenie decided she was scared of mice and took the vapours, refusing to sleep in their room until Gloria, sweet little Gloria with her pink eyes and matching paws, her white whiskers as soft as Helen's own lashes, had to go. 'To another family two closes up,' Greet said. 'You don't know them.' Helen didn't ask any more and tried not to wonder.

27

Dr Strasser opened a door halfway along the passage, waving Helen through it. It was a kitchen. A big square room just like Grove Place, with a new range in the high fireplace, a bed in the alcove and a white sink standing on iron legs in the window. Unlike Grove Place, though, there was no coal bunker to be seen, only a scrubbed wooden bunker-top on legs beside the sink.

Otherwise, this room was empty too and its sanded floors and freshly distempered walls had not a scuff nor a nail on them anywhere. And so clean! Helen sniffed and could smell – she was sure she could – disinfectant. She started to say, 'It smells like the surgery' but caught her lip in time. She didn't want Dr Strasser to think a clean house was a wonder to her.

He had gone again anyway. She could hear his footsteps out in the corridor so she followed him. There was another room. A big living room, this was, with another bed alcove and a broad high window that looked west across the railway line to the back of Grove Street. More new distemper, more sanded boards, more clean smell so strong Helen wanted to clear her throat.

'Why are we looking this house over?' she said. 'Is it. . .?' but she couldn't think of a way to finish the question. It didn't look fitted for a surgery and it was too small to be a cottage hospital, even if one was needed so near the Infirmary. It was gey tucked away too, except for the downstairs neighbour. Helen glanced at her feet, hoping no one on the nightshift was listening to the pair of them tramping over these hard boards. At last, looking down, she found a flaw. Some of the boards were gone and replaced with a sheet of that rotten pressed chip that had been flung up every time a bomb took out a window.

It might well have been a hospital once then, with a drain in the floor to help them clean it. But that was all done now. No more doctors cobbling together what they could, where they could, to keep sickness at bay. They were all in it together.

And she was a part of it. A small, scared part of it, but whatever *this* was she would manage.

'One last thing,' Dr Strasser said, back out in the passageway. He opened a door half-frosted with glass opposite the kitchen and pointed Helen to go in.

It was a bathroom. A real bathroom, right inside the house: a basin under the window, a bath along the other wall and a toilet behind the door. The distemper in here was shiny and the floor was painted like the sluice-room at the surgery.

'Lovely,' Helen said. 'Handy.' In the night, she meant. Never having to go out in the dark or empty a pot in the morning if you were lazy or it was snowing.

'What do you think?' said Dr Strasser. Unusually for him, Helen thought, he seemed unsure of himself, ill at ease. He was swinging the chain that hung from the high wooden cistern, letting the handle knock-knock-knock against the back of the door. She wanted to reach out and still it, stop the new white paint getting its first mark.

'Lovely,' she said again. 'But why does it matter what I think? Are you. . .?' Again she ran dry. Was he what?

'Good,' said Dr Strasser. 'It's yours. And Sandy's.'

'Has my mother. . .?' she asked. But how could Greet have got to the surgery ahead of Helen to pull the doctors into the story that she was out on her ear?

'Has your mother what?' said Dr Strasser. 'I must say, Helen, I thought you'd be a bit more excited. I know it's small, but it's cosy.'

Small! Two huge rooms and a bathroom, a garden too, just for her and Sandy to suit themselves in? It would have been wonderful, but what would they live on once they'd paid the rent?

'How much is it?' she asked. 'Sandy's wage isn't even what mine is. I'm not complaining about mine! I'm very grateful.'

29

'Shush.' He frowned at her. 'I have no further use for it, and so, rather than see it lie idle. . .we could call it a perk of the job.'

'Why?' she asked, too startled to say thank you.

'Why not?' he said.

She'd known Dr Strasser for eleven years, since the night he came to the Guides, at Mrs Sinclair's begging, to give them a talk on blood transfusion. Half the girls wouldn't sit still or stop giggling, busy pretending to faint, but Helen was rapt and he noticed it. He called on her to answer a question, something about hepatitis, and although she couldn't frame a single word of a sensible response, she understood why not and what to ask to help herself out. That had impressed him. 'We're very proud of Helen,' Mrs Sinclair had said. It wasn't true; nothing had happened yet to cause pride. It started that very night, or soon after. Because Dr Strasser had noticed her, Mrs Sinclair noticed her. Took her up, made a pet of her, then got the bit between her teeth and made a scholar of her. Made an exception of her. 'Made a spectacle,' Greet spat. 'Made a brat,' Mack had said once, just in from Bennet's on a Thursday night. 'Made a fool,' Teenie whispered, in that way she had, that arch way that made Helen forget she was young and didn't know the half of what she was hinting.

This was the first time in all those eleven years Helen had felt the slightest twinge of anything wrong. How could the doctor have an empty house just sitting and why would he give it to Helen? She smiled but it was a tight smile, hiding her teeth, and she stepped back out into the passageway again, suddenly loath to be standing in there beside a toilet and a bath, so close to him.

His face was more of a mask than ever as he came to join her. 'I should apologise,' he said. 'For patronising you. Of course you must be wondering.' But he said no more. Instead he took his watch out of his pocket and pulled his chin hard into his neck as he saw the time. 'We should be getting back.'

But when they were halfway down the stairs again, back in the sunshine, he returned to it. 'You're too bright a girl to swallow nonsense,' he said. 'The thing is, Helen, that you're a professional woman now. You're going to have to be asking some very searching questions. Intrusive questions. Only think of the forms they sent you from the Almoners Institute. And our patients are your neighbours. Do you see?'

Helen nodded absent-mindedly, but truth was all she could see was the stretch of green grass, lush and bright, untouched by kicking-cans or skipping ropes, and the dark earth of the thin border all around it, with flowers besides the rhubarb, the washing rope neatly coiled in a figure-of-eight and hanging from the lug of the pole. This green was for whoever lived in that house, six days a week if she needed it and not if she didn't.

'*Do* you see?' Dr Strasser said again.

'I think so,' she said, realising suddenly that she did. 'You wouldn't be wanting folk fain to speak up in case they met you on the stairs again after tea and felt shamed by it.'

'Exactly,' he said, looking mightily relieved. 'I'm sure your mother's flat is very comfortable, but I'm not taking you far away and I really do think it would be best.'

If Greet could hear him calling their house a 'flat', Helen thought, she'd take a broom to him. She was so proud of living in such a clean stair, after Freer Street. Helen didn't tell him that. What she did say was, 'I used to think you were too good for us, you and Doc Deuchar. Living on the crescent. Doc Deuchar said as much. I thought it was swank but I see now. It's being that wee bit separate that matters, eh no?'

'And Dr Deuchar will have to thole life on Gardner's Crescent a while longer,' Dr Strasser said, with a sadness Helen found mystifying.

'Was he coming here?' Helen said. 'What's he going to say when he finds out—'

31

'I shall tell him about the arrangement,' Dr Strasser said. 'You needn't broach it.' Then he smiled. 'But I take it you accept?'

Helen turned round and walked backwards a few paces, to get a last look. As Dr Strasser put a hand at the small of her back to save her going over the kerb on her ankle, Helen's mind flew back to Greet the day before, hinting darkly about improprieties beyond Helen's innocent imaginings. But she and Sandy were moving into the pretty little house together. She wasn't being installed like a moll off the pictures.

'You'll take it?' Dr Strasser prompted.

'We will take it and gladly,' she said, with a slight emphasis on the first word. 'I'll go and find Sandy at dinnertime and tell him,' she added. 'He'll – You don't know what this'll mean to him, Doc.'

'Ah but I do,' he said. 'I am his doctor after all.' Her cheer dipped a bit at the thought that there was plenty for Sandy's doctor to know. It was right enough that your doctor should be a stranger, really.

Back at the surgery steps, Dr Strasser sealed it. The pavement was empty. All of those people must be packed into the waiting room now, with just five minutes to go. 'Here,' he said, and held out three keys on a loop of tape. 'The Yale, the mortice and. . . I think that little one must be for a shed. Garden tools and what have you.'

He pressed them into Helen's hand and swept off towards his own room. 'Big day today, Helen,' he said over his shoulder. '*What* a day! Exactly the right sort of day to put the past behind us and our best foot forward.'

As Helen looked at the three new keys, and counted up her seven, every worry, every question, every loose end and rough edge and oddness that might have troubled her was quite, quite gone.

Chapter 3

Work would have chased them off anyway. Helen was no sooner settled at Miss Anderson's desk – for Dr Deuchar had indeed winkled her out – than a knock came at her door. It was the burly woman with the son in the bogey. She let herself drop into the wee chair with a groan, like it was midnight after a long day.

'I've had to leave him upstairs,' she said. 'So I'm no' wanting to be hanging about. He gets upset.'

'Have you a note?' Helen said.

'Daft,' said the woman. 'Carrying notes down a flight of steps. As if I couldn't have passed a message on if the doctor had told me.'

Helen took the little chitty out of her hand and unfolded it. 'It's for the filing,' she said. 'For the paperwork. To keep it all straight.' She held it out to show what it said. 'It's not a secret.'

But the woman's face shut like a trap and Helen felt her cheeks flush. The poor thing couldn't read. 'It's just a lot of numbers and letters, mind you,' she went on. 'In the King's English it says you've to be given a chair, for your son. And an appointment to see the specialist up at the Astley Ainslie to fit him out with. . . well, I wouldn't know. Calipers maybe. Or a back brace.'

'And it's free?' the woman said. 'All of it?'

'It's all free,' said Helen. 'I just need your name and address and your number. For the files.'

'Suttie,' she said. 'Mrs Beryl Suttie, and he's Andrew.'

33

'Are you related to Mrs Suttie on Upper Grove Place?' Helen said. 'She's my mammy's—my mother's neighbour.'

'Oh yes. I ken that stair,' Mrs Suttie said. 'My sister comes round to me twice a week and she's a talker.' Helen thought again how right Dr Strasser was, to get her out of the close and away from the gossip. 'I dinnae go round to her, though. It's too much palaver to get Andrew down from our house and back up again.'

'How high are you?' Helen said. 'Because I can put in a word.'

'That's the Corporation, though,' Mrs Suttie said. 'The city. This is the whole country and England too, isn't it?'

'But that's my job,' Helen said. 'To join up schools and hospitals and houses and. . . boys needing wheelchairs.'

'A *wheel*chair?' Mrs Suttie said. 'Is that what like chair you were meaning, the doctor and you?' Helen nodded. 'I wondered. And I was going to say if it's a commode save your bother, for he's too proud. But a *wheel*chair?' She blinked hard, twice. 'And a ground-floor house maybe?'

'If not you, I don't know who,' Helen said. 'So let's get started. What's your number? Have you got it with you? Have you had your card through?'

'One thousand and two,' said Mrs Suttie stoutly. 'I've no need for a card. I've had it off by heart since I was wed.'

Helen held out her hand anyway. That was Mrs Suttie's Co-op divvy number, she was certain. 'Aye, but it's forms and forms and more forms,' she said. 'I have to sign my name to say I've seen it with my own two eyes.'

She copied down the number from the already grubby little yellow insurance card when it finally emerged from inside the folds of Mrs Suttie's shawl.

'And if someone – it might be me,' she took a breath, 'it *would* be me, was to come round and do a wee recce, would that be all right?'

'Inspect my house?' Mrs Suttie shifted her feet, as if making to stand and leave. 'Do I need to let you in to get the chair?'

'See what you need that you've not got,' Helen said. 'And write all the details on my request for a flit. Not. . . run my white glove along your lintels.'

'By Jingo, they'd no' be white after that!' Mrs Suttie said. 'Aye fine, but not this week, for my man's on the backshift and he's in his pit till dinner.'

It might even have been true, or more likely Mrs Suttie needed time to put herself straight before the visit. No matter what Helen said, it was going to feel like the sergeant arriving at the barracks.

There wasn't a minute between Mrs Suttie and the next one. Helen even wondered if she should have a few chairs lined up along the passageway, like her own little waiting room.

The new patient scuttled in with her head down. Helen guessed it was something embarrassing wrong with her: nits or a rash. Not worse than that, surely? Nothing contagious or she'd be up at the doctors, not at Helen's door.

When the girl raised her eyes at last, she stopped in her tracks, lifting a hand to her mouth in confusion. 'Oh!' she said. 'Where's Miss Anderson?'

Not a patient then. But who was she? A friend perhaps? A niece? Helen had never spent much time down here in the accounts office during the years she'd been dragged around after Mrs Sinclair. For all she knew, Miss Anderson entertained guests for coffee every morning.

'Miss Anderson's retired,' she said. 'Gone away to stay with her sister. At Largs, I think. If you wanted to leave a note, I could see she gets it.'

'And who are you?' It wasn't as rude as it might have been, since the girl's bewilderment was unmistakable. She was trying to make sense of a puzzle that so far outwitted her.

'Helen Crowther.' She stood and held out a hand. 'Mrs Crowther. I'm the new welfa—medical almoner.'

'Is that what they're calling it?' the girl said, and Helen felt herself flush for the umpteenth time today. It was partly because she'd slipped and almost forgotten the brand-new title she was so proud of, and partly because the girl had seated herself without invitation and was giving Helen an amused look. A confident sort of look it was, and one you didn't see on girls like this very often. Girls like Helen herself, she supposed. This patient was typical Fountainbridge, with her hair done up in a scarf for a factory floor and inch-thick steel segs in the soles of her work shoes to keep the cobbler away. And yet there was that air about her.

'So you've inherited Anderson's kingdom?' she said, looking about herself as if amused by all the natty little fixtures Helen had been so proud to call her own. She gave the filing cabinets a particularly arch glance and, looking through the girl's eyes instead of her own, Helen saw the dark smudges on the distemper where lamps had been left to burn untrimmed and the score-marks on the polished boards where the char had dragged heavy furniture around to clean the floor.

'Can I help you, since I'm here?' Helen said. 'If you've a bill you want to clear, I think the last of them are all in the post. Or if you're shifting doctors, you should know the records are all going in and then your new doctor can apply to have them sent out again. Too much confusion to do it any other way. But, if you *are* changing, can I give you a bit of advice?'

The girl raised an eyebrow and again it was the sort of look Helen would have expected from Mrs Sinclair's daughters, wry and careless, not from a bare-legged girl with frayed cuffs left to hang, not even darned up to make them practical. She surely couldn't go a machine in whatever works she had her job at like that. Those loose threads would have the hand off her.

36

'Just that unless it's an emergency you should wait,' she said. 'Till the dust settles. It's very organised but there's bound to be a bottleneck a wee while. Little while.'

'I don't know if it's an emergency,' the girl said. 'I hope not. It's a puzzle anyway.'

Helen was reaching for a general intake form off the top of her pile, to get the girl's name and some details at least, when the door swung open after a peremptory knock.

'Customer for you, Nelly!' It was Dr Deuchar, standing back to usher in a tired-looking woman, still with curlers in her hair under a scarf.

'If you could wait outside one moment,' Helen said, before the look on the doctor's face stopped her. He had turned an ugly colour, as deep and painful a flush as any of Helen's own, and his brows had pulled down until his eyes were in deep shadow. 'Not you, Doctor!' she said, although even as she scrabbled to explain she wondered at him. He was always so free and easy with her, much less formal than Dr Strasser. She supposed there were limits.

'Do you have an appointment?' he said, his voice coming clipped and chilly through his clenched teeth. It was her patient he was talking to. It was the sight of this girl that had angered him. Helen doubted if he'd even heard what *she* said.

'I dropped in on the off-chance,' the girl told him, pert as you like. 'But I think I'll toddle off now.' Again, Helen was struck by the tennis-party tone of her voice, as if she'd been too much at the pictures and decided to try it for herself, like poor Heck Driscoll in the next stair, who'd never given up thinking he was a cowboy, even now he was big enough to be working at the Store laundry, with his sister to mind him.

'See that you do,' said Dr Deuchar. 'Miss Anderson is no longer in my employ. And Doctor Strass—' he stopped himself speaking.

When he had watched her to the end of the passage and up the stairs, her segs knock-knock-knocking, he rubbed a hand over his face and put a smile back on it.

'This is Mrs McIrnie, Helen. Mrs Mac, this is young Mrs Crowther who'll be able to help you. There's nothing at all to worry about and no need to feel any reticence. Nelly here is a good girl.'

With that he was gone, and Mrs McIrnie sat herself down on the edge of the chair, her arms wrapped around her like pinny ties.

'What can I do for you, Mrs McIrnie?' Helen said.

'I telt the doctor it was scabies,' the woman said, then bit her lip. Helen kept her smile as warm as ever and didn't draw back an inch, even while she was asking herself why on earth Dr Deuchar would send scabies her way. The patient should be away up to Lauriston to the clinic. Lauriston Place for scabies, the High School Yards for impetigo, Infirmary Street for lice. Unless that was all changed now too. Or maybe Helen was supposed to give advice about boiling linens? Only, Mrs McIrnie at her age would know more than Helen about all of that.

'Are you sure?' she said at last.

'Mind you, it wouldn't be scabies in the summer and all this warm weather we've had, would it? So he kens I'm fibbing. He's sent me down to you because he thinks it's nits. He said you'd a roll of chits for that paraffin shampoo.'

'Ah,' Helen said. She looked about herself, wondering where the packet of chits might have got to. If Miss Anderson had been out of the way, as she should have been, Helen would be able to open a drawer and lay her hand right on whatever she needed. It looked bad, this did: her gazing around, blinking.

'But it's not nits,' Mrs McIrnie said. Again she bit down hard on her bottom lip. And perhaps Helen did pull back a little now, for she went on, 'Or ringworm or anything. It's nothing like that at all. It's my daughter, you see. It's my girl, Betty.'

'You don't need to worry about all that now,' Helen said. 'It doesn't matter who's working.' The old insurance had been cruel, to her mind; just asking for folk to wangle a way round it. So they did too: the workers of the family reporting the symptoms and taking the prescription home to whoever needed it.

Dr Strasser and Dr Deuchar never minded. Even Mrs Sinclair would turn a blind eye, going as far once as to tell a dock-worker to say he'd fainted and get iron pills for his wife, who was having a baby. 'It's half a crown a week he pays, Helen,' she said. 'Why shouldn't they see the benefit?'

Those days were done now and Mrs McIrnie waved the worry away besides. 'She's working,' she said.

'Well, her foreman should give her time off for the doctor,' Helen said.

'Oh aye aye, it's not that. It's just. . . To let you understand, you see. She's married.'

'That's nice,' Helen said. 'A nice boy, I hope? And he's not taken her off?'

'Naw, they're still in with me.'

Helen had almost forgotten the house, waylaid by wheel-chairs and wry looks and the thought, briefly, of mites and lice on her first morning. But she remembered now: the green grass and the coiled rope; the long white bath, with its bright brass taps and little fat feet like a puppy.

'And Stanley's a lovely boy,' Mrs McIrnie went on. 'He's on the railways. Brings his pay straight home and lifts the coal in. He's fine. He's not said a word. Not really. Not yet.'

'About what, Mrs McIrnie?' Helen said, thinking if the woman bit down any harder on that lip she'd draw blood. 'You can tell me anything, you know. I'm just like the doctors that way. Confidential. Everything in your file is strictl—'

'Don't write it down!' the woman burst out. And once she started there was no stopping her. 'She's been married well gone eighteen months and nothing's happened. Not even late.

Not once. And she's a fine healthy girl. She had one bad scare a few years back with her appendix. And she'd bother after. Had to keep having check-ups. But the last couple of years she's been as healthy as a horse. And regular, as I know for my own self, as didn't I wash her rags before she was wed and I still do, if I'm honest with you. Regular as clockwork. For getting on two years.'

'Oh,' Helen said. In at the deep end, she thought. Of course there'd been a lesson on this as part of her course, late on in the last term when all the flibbertigibbets had given up and moved on to their next bit of fun. And of course there was nothing to be bashful about, but still. On her very first morning, to have to tell the new facts of modern life to a woman her mother's age. Once again, Helen felt herself agreeing with Dr Strasser about how important it was to have a wee bit of distance, round at the Rosebank colonies and not up a common stair. 'Well, Mrs McIrnie, I'm sure your daughter will start a family in her own time. Maybe when they've had the chance to save up, get out from under your feet into likes of a single end of their own. It's not such a bad thing to wait, you know. How old is she?'

Mrs McIrnie was shaking her head. 'No, no, no,' she said. 'You're not understanding me. She's breaking her heart on it. She's losing her bloom with the worry. So then she came to me and asked if maybe she should write a letter, only who would she write it to? And I told her to come to the doctor, but she wouldn't. So it's me.'

'Oh dear,' Helen said, then hated the sound of it. *I see*, would have been better. More professional. 'And has your daughter given you any hints about what she thinks might be wrong?' She stared at a spot above Mrs McIrnie's head. 'How are things between them?'

'What do you mean?' Suddenly the woman's voice was sharp enough to set Helen back. 'What are you saying?'

But Helen couldn't even begin to give voice to it. She hadn't seen the trap coming and she could neither climb out nor explain why she'd fallen in. She was well used to her cheeks darkening, but to her horror this time she felt her eyes start to prickle too. She couldn't! She couldn't cry, at work, on her first day.

'Here, here,' Mrs McIrnie said. 'I didn't mean to insult you. Don't be angry. See, this is exactly what *she* said would happen. That the doctor would think she was cheapening herself, letting him cheapen her. Well, she's not. She told me. She said everything was fine. Right as rain. "The birds and the bees, Maw," is what she said. So. There's only one answer, isn't there? But what are we to do?'

One answer, Helen thought. What one out of the many answers she'd studied in that course lesson could Mrs McIrnie possibly be referring to? It could be half a dozen things and all of them medical, most of them surgical, *none* of them anywhere close to Helen's area of operation and concern.

'He was in the Navy,' Mrs McIrnie said. 'And I'm not handing down judgement. Didn't I say he was a lovely boy? But he was all over: North Africa, Italy, you name it. And so he's ruined himself, hasn't he? He's rotted himself. And now my poor daughter's shackled to him.'

'That's certainly a possibility,' Helen said. She had turned this over in her own mind often enough, lying beside Sandy in the dark, like a pair of bookends, two feet of cold sheet between them.

'So I want him looked at. I want him seen to. And I was at that talk thon Mrs Sinclair did last month just. "Wholesomeness," she said. So I know it's your job to make him see.'

Helen opened her mouth to argue, but she had been in the front row that night in the drill hall at the Darroch School and she remembered Mrs Sinclair saying, 'The doctor will give you a bottle of pills or mixture. He might send you to a surgeon. A medical almoner will save you going under the knife and keep the pills out of your hand if you consult her in good time.' Helen thought at the time it was a rousing thing to say. She hadn't seen this coming.

'Fresh air and exercise,' Helen began, 'won't—'

'I remember it as if it was yesterday,' Mrs McIrnie said. 'Well, to be fair with you, I'd heard it a few times in the duration. The Guild and the Rural, the Guides and Brownies, the Mother's Treat.'

Helen nodded. Mrs Sinclair did tend to wheel out the same speech wherever she was invited. It was tailor-made for the Women's Guild, and the WRVS too, although it sailed over the heads of Guides and Brownies and diluted treats considerably, in Helen's opinion. With so many men signed up, however, and so many other women too busy to give little talks on this and that, Mrs McIrnie wouldn't be the only one in the city who could reel Mrs Sinclair's pet performance off by heart.

'And fresh air and exercise wasn't the half of it, as you well know,' Mrs McIrnie went on. 'Wholesome *ways*, Mrs Sinclair said. Wholesome ways and cleanliness in the *habits*. And she distinctly said, for I heard her and so did you, that a medical almoner, when the service was up and running, would be able to point everyone the right road.'

'But she was meaning diet,' Helen said. 'Wholesome food and a good wash every night. Tooth powder and not too much tobacco.'

'But if you can get in about somebody's business close enough to look at his teeth, why not this?'

Helen had no answer.

'So you'll come round?' said Mrs McIrnie. 'Tuesday night her daddy's at the institute seven till nine, for he's on the committee. It's my day in the wash house, so you come round and I'll take my daughter down the back green to scour out the copper and let you talk in peace.'

Helen knew when she was beaten. 'What's Betty's married name?' she asked. 'Elizabeth, is it? Mrs Elizabeth what?' She

42

slid a carbon into a new patient intake form and licked her pencil.

Dinnertime came round after a flurry of expecting mothers needing to be persuaded to have their babies in Simpson's Memorial Maternity, instead of their mammy's kitchen. Then there was a woman in to see if someone could speak to her neighbour about a smell, another woman who needed the district nurse to change the day of her visits but was too scared to ask her, and an old man finally ready to admit he was as good as blind in one eye, now he could get a chit for a pair of glasses. Helen got better with the carbons, re-shuffled the piles of forms three times – she really needed to get them in drawers this afternoon – and said over and again, endlessly, until she was sick of the sound of her voice, 'Yes, it's free. No, there won't be a bill. We're all paying. Like a great big Christmas club nobody ever gets chucked out of.'

She gobbled her piece in two minutes with the door locked, in case of another one slipping in without the doctors' say-so. She'd got so good at chewing slices of National Loaf, she thought to herself, she'd almost miss it when white bread came off rationing and she could pick and choose again. Then she combed her hair and visited the place under the stairs that still seemed so much like Miss Anderson's personal water closet that Helen expected a hammering on the door and a demand to know who was in there. Even knowing Miss Anderson was on her way to Largs didn't help. She washed her hands quickly, as the geyser gurgled and refilled, dried them roughly on the roller – was she responsible for changing it now? Did the doctors' char do in here as well? She would ask, although she didn't relish the prospect. She didn't fear the district nurse but the surgery char was another thing. A silent, gloomy woman of no name Helen had ever heard, she moved as slow and heavy as a hippo in a mud wallow through the rooms upstairs, dragging her mop in its wheeled bucket but never in sight of witnesses lifting it and setting it to the floor.

'And so what did she want, your unexpected guest?' Dr Deuchar said, as Helen emerged into the hall. She stopped short. She was in a hurry but she couldn't ignore the doctor or shout over her shoulder in passing.

'To see Miss Anderson, like you said.'

Dr Deuchar frowned. 'Like *I* said?'

'Sorry.' It came out automatically. 'I'm mixed up. That's what *she* said. That it was a personal visit. I thought that's why you were—' But what would she say? How could she finish the thought aloud? Were annoyed? Were rude? Were angry? She couldn't accuse a doctor of such things.

'Ach,' said Dr Deuchar, like he did sometimes, affecting to be as Scots as Helen. She had tiptoed up near saying it once and it was the only time she had seen him truly offended. 'But I *am* Scots!' he said. 'I was born in Nairn and went to school right here in Edinburgh. Then Glasgow University. I'm as Scottish as a toorie bunnet.' She couldn't help herself; she smiled to hear those words with his mangled English vowels in them.

'Ach, it's a day of obstacles to be overcome,' he was saying now. 'It'll shake down soon enough. I probably shouldn't have minded that some wee sowel slipped through. So don't apologise any more.'

'Wee sowel' was going too far, Helen reckoned. Beyond chummy. It was more like the doc was laughing at her. She half-wished she could take her blurted apology back again because she wasn't wrong and she needn't have said it. He *had* said 'Miss Anderson'. She remembered the swank of the way he put it: 'Miss Anderson is no longer in my employ.' Why would he have said that unless he knew that Miss Anderson was the point? That Miss Anderson was who that strange girl with her segs and her eyebrows had come looking for?

44

Helen shrugged it off as she trotted down the steps onto the street. Now then, where to start? Sandy had told her he was on Lothian Road today. Or rather, Sandy had moaned about going all the way to the depot to pick up his cart only to come nearly back home again. 'You should take turns,' she said. 'You and George. You go in and cover for him if you're bound out his way – down the far end ae Nicholson Street, isn't he? – and he'd do the same for you if you're set for this end of town.'

'Wouldnae work,' he'd said. 'If somebody's off sick or that, they up and change everything. I'd end up humphing the cart away over there to get him and then still have a road back.'

You don't 'humph' dustcarts, though, Helen wanted to say. They've got wheels. She bit her tongue. You never knew what was going to set Sandy off these days, since he'd come home. She'd expected it to change once they were married, or maybe just to get gradually lighter until one day she'd realise it was gone. She knew better now. On that thought, her feet stopped moving and left her stock still on the corner of the main road, all the hurrying strangers buffeting her as they passed this sudden obstacle. What made her think she knew how Sandy would take the wee Rosebank house? What was she doing, chasing all over to land the news on him in the middle of his day, instead of leading him towards it gently-gently later on, after tea? A walk along the old canal maybe. She turned to go back to work and then of course there he was, him and George in their shirtsleeves and their oilskin gloves, coming down from Morningside way. She watched them, George ambling as slow as Sunday with the cart, to let Sandy sweep and dump, sweep and dump, emptying the gutters. She noticed the way no one spoke to them. Sandy was born in Semple Street and surely some of these passersby must know him. Not the women in their hats and buttoned boots, putting a hanky to the nose and turning away. Not the men in bowlers, with rolled umbrellas for the look of it on this cloudless day. But the bairns in their wee vests, the old men, all the rest of them, on their dinner breaks from shops and works. . . Some of them must recognise Sandy Crowther.

Maybe it was her face, the only one staring right at him, that caught his eye. Or maybe – like she'd have said three years ago – love meant he'd always find his Helen on a crowded street. It was what the pictures told you, and the weekly papers.

He was waving his broom at her and George, squinting, raised a hand too. Poor George, with the port wine stain over most of his face and the strange extra teeth like walrus tusks that stuck out even when he closed his mouth. Helen smiled at the both of them and hurried forward to meet the cart.

'This is a nice surprise,' George said. If only it had been Sandy.

'Can you have a wee smoke, George, and let us get a quiet word a minute?' Helen drew Sandy into the shade of an awning, ignoring the haberdasher inside who narrowed her eyes at a street sweeper leaning up against her window.

'Have you ever swept roon' Rosebank?' she said. 'I cannae just mind right now if you've said.'

'The cottages in the wee square opposite your work?' Sandy said. 'Once. It doesnae take much cleaning, quiet streets like that.'

Helen looked up at him, quick as a bird stealing crumbs, then looked away. Was she imagining it, or was that a wistful tone he had?

'I'd never set foot that far side of the Crescent gardens till this morn's morn,' she went on.

'House calls already, is it?' Before she could answer, he went on. 'I tell you what I saw the only time I was ever in there, Nelly, a washing rope coiled in an eight and hinging off a pole.'

'Yes,' Helen said. 'Exactly.'

'And I thought, if we'd kent that rope was there – if we'd dreamed there was ropes hanging – and only two windows for some wee woman to be keeking out and catch us, we'd have had it away and made a swing in the park. There's a currant bush in one of they gardens too, you ken. Times we went all the way out to Merchiston for green apples and made ourselves sick, when there was blackcurrants on a bush, just a step away.'

'Exactly!' Helen said again.

'It's another world compared to here.' Sandy shook his head, looking around. This street, even newly swept, was still shabby. 'But why were you asking?'

'Because it's not another world,' Helen said. 'It's our world now.'

Chapter 4

'Gie us a clue,' he said. 'Gie us a hint where.' Sandy winked at her and elbowed her in the side – nice of him not to touch her sleeve with his mucky glove – but Helen refused to let slip so much as a word.

It was a happy moment, there under the awning on the corner of Earl Grey Street, even while the haberdasher banged on the glass to shoo them off and George, his fag finished, started shuffling in case the depot foreman cycled past to check up on them. It was so different from their usual: Helen's worries pressing on her like a sprung bone in her stays, and Sandy's secrets like a sack of coal on his shoulders.

Still smiling, Helen took herself back to the surgery to an afternoon of filing and a surprise visit from the Chalmers Street supervisor. Bonny was her name, Mrs Isabelle Bonny and never was anyone labelled so misleadingly. She'd never been happy that the doctors wanted Helen 'all to themselves' instead of letting her work at the Infirmary and come out on . . . loan, Helen always wanted to say, until the fancy word stuck in her mind. . . out on secondment as and when. Failing that, Mrs Bonny would even rather have the doctors send their patients, chitty in hand, all the way to Chalmers Street in a procession, and let Helen help them under the supervisor's beady eye. She had come out on this busy day to press her case again.

'Now, now,' said Dr Strasser, who had ushered her in. 'We are indeed in clover with the new service but we mustn't slosh the money around willy-nilly, just because it's not ours. We must be prudent, wouldn't you agree? Helen right here where she's needed, while you fulfill your separate role, makes much more sense.'

He had a good argument at his back. Fountainbridge and Lochrin had enough work for at least one full-time almoner every day.

'But we don't want to set in place a two-tier system,' the woman said, settling into Helen's office as if she meant to stay.

'Heaven forfend,' said Dr Strasser. 'We never intended Helen to give preference to our surgery's patients. I'm very happy to have other GPs send patients this way, and I can't see Helen cavilling.'

Helen didn't know what cavilling meant but she nodded anyway.

'As long as it's not your way of *luring* patients,' Mrs Bonny said.

'Every doctor in the city – in the country! – is set to be overwhelmed,' said Dr Deuchar, who had tagged along. '*Luring* would be madness.'

'Not if you've got your own private almoner to do half the work.' Mrs Bonny wasn't going to give up easily.

'My work isn't doctors' work,' Helen said.

'Your work,' said Mrs Bonny, 'has been rendered obsolete. And I am at a loss to understand why I alone seem to know that.'

Helen nodded, for she had been just as puzzled at first. Lady almoners like Mrs Sinclair had spent their days engaged in a simple, if brutal, sorting of humanity. The indigent and destitute were the business of the Poor Laws and the workhouses. The wealthy had to be sniffed out and sent packing to their own doctors and their own bank accounts. The middling layer, thick and worried, were sent to provident societies, workers' benefit unions or the right charity for their complaint. 'The aim,

Helen,' Mrs Sinclair used to say, 'is to end each month with no ill untreated and no bill unpaid.'

Now that bills and benefits had been swept away on the turning tide, Mrs Sinclair's neat little slogan was useless. Helen's heart banged and she felt a trickle of sweat at the nape of her neck as she prepared to speak her own brand-new slogan out loud in front of people for the first time.

She cleared her throat, but at the last moment her nerve failed her. 'I'm helping save the doctors' time,' she said. 'So many problems aren't really medical.'

'You don't need to answer to Mrs Bonny, Helen,' said Dr Strasser. 'My dear woman, it was the Boards who parcelled out the personnel. You should take it up there.'

'Besides,' said Dr Deuchar, 'there's a practice down in Leith that has *two* almoners working out of it. Did you know?'

'Well, though. Leith!' said Mrs Bonny.

'I wouldn't say that these days,' Dr Strasser chided her. 'Not after the war they've had.'

Helen nodded. Leith was a terrible place by all accounts but no one – not a doctor, anyway – could be glad a slum was gone when it went *that* way. Bodies in the rubble and everyone's best furniture down to sticks, good china away to shards and powder. 'I don't mind showing Mrs Bonny what I've been doing,' she said. 'I've nothing to hide.'

And she made a good showing, with seven patient files already open, three convalescences arranged and a home visit planned. 'Marital,' she said. 'Young wife needs a quiet word.'

Mrs Bonny turned as red as a chimney brick and bent her head over the sheet she was filling in, as if Helen was needing a report written up after half a day. 'Very good, very good,' she said. 'I'm glad to see that you are not shying away from the less pleasant aspects of your new role, Mrs Crowther. And remember you can always ring me up if you find yourself unequal to any task.'

50

'The telephone's in Dr Deuchar's outer office,' Helen said. 'I think I'd rather write a note. And it's better for the files too. To have a copy. Or would there be a special form for requesting supervisory assistance?'

She didn't say it archly, but the plain fact was that no one in the service really knew for sure what forms had come, in all those unpacked boxes, nor knew if more were on their way. Mrs Bonny set to on a lecture as wide-ranging as it was unneeded, to cover her displeasure, and only Dr Deuchar flinging open the door and saying, 'Nits, Nelly! Can I send them down?' got rid of her.

Of course there were no nits at all. 'I could hear her voice droning away,' Dr Deuchar said. 'It comes up the pipes. Why don't you away and get us three cream buns and we'll have ourselves a party when we drop the lock at four o'clock, eh?'

Helen had been upstairs before. At Christmastime the doctors had thrown a wee party like this one, which wasn't a party at all, but just the same few people as every day, only standing around with glasses of nasty stuff and finding out they had nothing to say to each other when they weren't discussing the day book and the hardship fund. Helen had been glad of Mrs Sinclair, that Christmas Eve. There wasn't a silence *she* couldn't fill.

When she'd gone home at last in the frosty night, sucking a peppermint to take the taste out of her mouth and the smell off her breath, Greet had been aghast. 'Upstairs?' she said. 'You went upstairs with they two single men and let them pour drink down you? Oh yes, don't think I can't smell you fae here!'

'I took yin glass to be polite, Mammy,' Helen had said. 'And I never near finished it. Anyway, I wasn't upstairs where they *sleep*. Only where they've got their big room and their rooms they eat in, seeing the surgeries are on the ground floor.' Big room and the rooms they eat in, was a translation for her mother. The drawing room was what the doctors called it. That first visit,

Helen had expected easels and palettes, had looked around for the drawings and wondered where they were. She knew better now. Like she knew there was a breakfast room and a supper room, even if she still thought it comical to imagine the two of them – bachelors, like Greet said – using two different rooms for their meals on an ordinary day. There was no difference, as far as she could tell, beyond decanters of brandy and whisky on the sideboard of one, where there was only a fruit bowl and a letter rack on the other.

Today, someone had brought the decanters into the drawing room for their party. The doctors filled a glass each, and Dr Strasser added a jet of soda from the siphon. Helen didn't know what kind of drink it was you shot soda into and still wouldn't have known if she'd tasted it. She didn't know much beyond a port and lemon at the end of a day on the prom maybe – it had been shyness that made her swallow that Christmas drink the first time. Now, with a kind of intimacy among the three of them, she asked for what she wanted and Dr Strasser went to fetch it. Dr Deuchar seemed to find it highly amusing but Helen always thought a glass of cold milk went better with a cream bun; it stood to reason.

'A very successful first day,' Dr Deuchar said, raising his glass and then chuckling again at the sight of Helen's. 'A few bumps, a few skids, and a few frustrations but I'd say we mucked along pretty well, wouldn't you?'

'It's been a bittersweet day,' said Dr Strasser, 'but it made my heart glad that Mrs Suttie started us off.'

'Bittersweet?' said Dr Deuchar. 'Tosh! Because we lost Miss Anderson? I would say today has been as sweet as Turkish Delight, as sweet as candy floss and toffee apples. But I agree about that benighted "bogey". What better. . . what's the word I'm after, Strasser?'

'Emblem?' Dr Strasser said.

Dr Deuchar raised his glass again, in salute. 'What better emblem of our new beginning?'

'I've started a request for a ground-floor house too,' Helen said.

'Another happy thought,' said Dr Deuchar. 'We're in danger of floating off.'

'Do you think Miss Anderson will be all right?' Helen asked, to bring them back down to earth again. The memory of poor Miss Anderson sitting in her office like King Canute, refusing to believe she had to move, had been pressing on Helen all day.

'Miss Anderson is set for life,' Dr Deuchar said, very coldly. He sounded like when he'd seen that girl. Helen wondered if she could ask again what the matter was or if it would be impertinent to harp on it.

'Miss Anderson,' said Dr Strasser, 'is not our concern any more. We must turn our faces to the future and give up hankering after what's lost. Out with the old! Miss Anderson should really have left years ago. Likewise Mrs Sinclair, God be praised!' That was a very strange thing for him to say, pairing up two women with nothing to connect them. Not to mention bringing God up like that, bald as a frog. He kept off matters of church and religion usually. Right off them. Never so much as tipped carollers.

'Mrs Sinclair will be missing it all,' Helen said. 'She must be rattling round like – well, she'll be at loose ends, is what I'm saying.'

'She'll find another pie,' Dr Deuchar said. 'Her fingers won't be flapping in the summer breeze very long.'

This was by far the rudest thing he'd ever said about Mrs Sinclair, to Helen's recollection. She should feel chummy and proud, she supposed, to be in the circle this way, sitting chatting and sharing buns with them, hearing their thoughts. Strange then that what she wanted was a way to make it stop and put them back where they had been on Friday: polite and kind, but separate from her, on good behaviour.

'Now we've got Mrs Bonny instead,' she said, thinking she would change the subject.

But that made it worse. Dr Deuchar hooted with laughter, and Dr Strasser said, 'I hope I live to see stones on her bones,' which was even ruder and really quite nasty when you stopped to think it through.

'The funny thing is,' Helen said to Sandy as they climbed the stairs to her mother's house, 'Mammy threw a fit this morning and threatened to put us out. I'll need to mind and make sure she knows this is just a fluke, us flitting the same day. I ken she didnae mean a word of it.'

'A fit about what?' said Sandy. He'd been dog-tired, worn out with the heat of the day and breathing in dust and dirt until he was gravel-voiced, but his tone lifted and sharpened now.

'Ocht, my job.' Helen almost felt the breeziness of her words. 'She'll come round.'

But Sandy was a good bit taller than her and he saw over the banister first. He stopped short and stared. There, out on the step, were the two new board cases they had got for their wee trip after the wedding. Beside them sat a bundle of clothes done up in an old sheet stained with fire-black. And Helen's sewing machine was there too.

'Didnae mean a word of it, eh?' Sandy said. He strode forward, with his fist up to hammer on the door.

'Stop,' Helen said. 'Leave it. That's what she's expecting. Us begging and clamouring to get loten back in. But we don't have to.'

Sandy grinned. Then he picked up the bundle and the sewing machine and stood aside. 'Can you manage twae cases?'

'If it kills me,' Helen said. The thought of all the neighbours traipsing past, seeing 'that Nelly Downie's been put out', put iron in her. Greet would never have dared if Mack was due in, for Helen's father was a man who liked his private business kept that way. The only time Helen had ever seen him angry enough to clench his fists was when Greet sent it round the wash house that he could do with some extra work and was willing to dress tripe and sell it cheaper than Meldrum's ready-cooked was going. That was back before his promotion and before the war brought jobs to everyone. A man with Mack's pride wouldn't thole his daughter's traps sitting out on the dusty landing, and wrapped in a floor sheet too. As if to say her and Sandy had no good sheets of their own and Greet had none to spare.

Helen hoped the sets they'd got as wedding presents were in one of these cases. They were heavy enough and she couldn't see the stiff corners of the card wrappers making points in Sandy's bundle. She thought of asking him, but sheets – anything to do with their shared bed – were not to be mentioned between them.

Or maybe not any more. She looked up and smiled at him.

'Flitting, Nelly?' Old Mrs MacEwan was hanging out her ground floor window as she did every day the rain didn't blow in.

'We've our ain place noo,' Helen said.

'And where are you aff to?'

'Ask my mither,' said Helen, badness leaping up in her. 'She'll tell you a' aboot it.'

'You'll turn into her if you keep that up,' Sandy said when they were out of earshot. 'It's not like you to be sly.'

But nothing could put a dent in Helen's happiness. She fairly skipped along Grove Street, ignoring the strain in her shoulders. Her feet couldn't carry her fast enough to the mouth of their wee secret lane, to the far end, to the cottage with the steps all their own, dying to see what Sandy would make of it.

'Is this our bit green?' he asked, letting the bundle drop onto the grass and setting the sewing machine down beside

55

it. He knuckled his back and looked around as he stretched his neck out.

'All ours and just ours,' Helen said. 'That's our coalhole, Sandy. No bunker in the kitchen! No black dust!'

'We'll need to start calling it a "draining-board" instead of a "bunker" then,' Sandy said, putting on a pan-loaf voice.

'And we need to work out what you call the steps up to your door when it's not a close,' Helen said, pointing to them.

Sandy nodded but he didn't look. He was facing the farthest corner of the garden. 'They've kept it then,' he said.

Helen turned. Three years after the war had ended, the Anderson shelter still sat half sunk in the ground with a few stairs leading down to its padlocked door. The turf had been taken off the top, leaving the rusting roof open to the weather. 'We can soon have that up,' she said. 'Use it as a wee shed. Mrs Cameron says she put tatties and carrots in a clamp in hers all winter and they kept lovely.'

'Who?' Sandy said. 'What?'

'Mrs Cameron. At the four-in-a-block houses. But they've got a great big stretch at the back. We'll not be growing store tatties in here. You're no' digging up *my* nice green!'

'They take them away for scrap,' Sandy said.

Helen turned her lips in and kept quiet. Nothing was going to sour this first visit to their new home. But if he thought she was going to give up a garden hut for scrap money and then save up and buy the wood to make a new one, he was mistaken. She was tempted to say he didn't have to go inside it. She was even tempted to say that, if it ended up getting used as a Wendy house for weans, he'd not be *allowed* inside it, for that was the best of a gang hut; no grown-ups admitted. Her lips were turned in so far from the effort of saying nothing that they had disappeared. And if Sandy could read the look, he was choosing to ignore it.

'Come on and see.' She held out a hand to him as she started towards the bottom of the steps. He ignored the hand, but followed.

It was shady in the garden as late as this in the afternoon but when Helen fitted the key and threw the door open, sunlight poured along the passageway. Again she noticed that there was not a single mote of dust moving.

Sandy stepped inside and whistled. He opened the door on the left and disappeared into the kitchen. Helen heard his feet on the boards and a second whistle, and she followed him. She hadn't expected him to pick her up and carry her over the threshold. Not really.

'This is braw,' Sandy said. 'And nae rent?'

'Nae furniture neither,' Helen said. 'That's only just struck me this minute. I never thought we'd be flitting the night.'

'Ach, furniture!' Sandy said. 'We can get a few crates from Fleming's back door, see us through to Saturday, then we'll away to the sales! What like's the big room?'

He was off again. Helen followed.

'There's a bench chucked out at the yard behind Tommy Lang's,' he called back to her. 'Geordie and me saw it this afternoon. It needs a wee buff but it's sturdy. If it's still there tomorrow I'll get George—'

'Who am I?' Helen said. 'Lady Muck? I can carry the other end of a bench if it means we get it before some other scrounger that doesnae need it like we do.'

'And this is another bed, is it?' Sandy threw open the doors – real doors that folded in half on hinges like the tall shutters at Mrs Sinclair's windows – and clicked his teeth. 'Just as well you're not Lady Muck, hen. There's nae mattress. We either sleep on our coats the night or we go doon the Store stables and pinch some straw.'

Helen felt her nose wrinkle before she could stop it. 'We could get into Fleming's before it shuts at eight and buy a half-bolt of buckram to cover it at least,' she said. 'It wouldnae waste, for I'd make it a quilt back once we got a mattress proper.'

Sandy nodded. 'Is there a cupboard anywhere? It would be a sin to bang nails into these nice walls to hang a rail fae, but it'll be a while till we stretch to a wardrobe.' He was walking back towards the door. Helen hugged herself.

'What's in—?' he said, opening the door with the clouded glass, before the sight of the gleaming white bathroom took his breath away. Helen let out a gurgle of delight at his face when he came back to her.

'This is too good to be true,' he said.

'I ken,' said Helen. 'It's a – I was going to say a boon, but it's beyond that. It's a—'

'It's a new life,' Sandy said. 'Look out that window. You can see a mile. We'll be able to watch the sunset. It's like you said at dinnertime, hen. It's a new *world*.'

She should have left it there, their happiest moment for months, left it like she'd left the question of the shelter. Instead she said, 'It could be a new start.'

'What do you mean "could be"?' Sandy said, turning, still with that big grin on his face. She half thought he was going to grab her arms and start dancing. There was room in here, what with not a stick of furniture. They should get going to the back of Lang's for that bench and on to the stables and Fleming's for straw and ticking. That was another good reason to say no more.

'I mean a new start for you and me,' she said. And this time he caught her meaning. His eyes darkened. How did he do that? Without squeezing them shut or lowering his brows, all the light went out of those warm brown eyes.

'It could at that,' he said, sounding so reasonable. 'All this space. Two big rooms. We've nae need to pack into the same wee box bed the two ae us, have we?'

Helen could feel her eyes filling. 'Why?' she said, and now the gates were open there was no stopping her. 'Why, Sandy?

58

What's wrong? Do you think I've forgotten you pestering me before you went away? What's changed?'

'Before I went away,' he said, his voice as black as his eyes now. 'You'd think it was a trip to the seaside the way you say it.'

'Teenie knows,' Helen shot back. 'She's laughing at the both of us. And my mammy's started asking.'

'Well seen they've fell out with you then,' Sandy said. 'They'll never see the set-up, will they? They'll not ken where you are and where I am. So that's that sorted. No more laughing. No more asking.'

'*I'm* asking!' Helen said. 'And you should be glad I'm not laughing.' He winced and she knew she'd struck him somewhere tender, but the sudden flare of pity only made her angrier still. Why should *she* creep about caring how *he* felt? Damn sure he wasn't bothered whether she was curling up inside and trying every day not to cry.

'You know nothing about it,' Sandy said. 'You've not the first clue.'

'So tell me!' Helen said. She knew she should try to talk more gently, get some kindness in her voice or on her face, but the devil had entered her and she stood back and let it choose her words. 'Talk to me about it,' she said. 'Tell me what happened "when you were away".' She was speaking for Mrs McIrnie's Betty as much as herself now. 'I'd like to ken what you got up to and what you've done to yourself that means you're like you are now with me. And why you didn't tell me before the wedding if this is how it was to be.'

'Don't you dare!' Sandy flashed back. 'You think I'm going to stand here and let my wife speak to me like that?'

'I'm not your wife!' Helen said. 'We're not married. If I went back to the church and told them what my "married life" was, Mr Clough would rip up that bit paper and burn the scraps in the grate. And that's all it is too. A bit paper. It's nothing!'

Sandy looked down at the floor then. Not at his feet. At the floor. 'This is a nice introduction to the neighbours,' he said. 'You screaming like a fishwife.' He walked away, his stride steady and determined. This was no show to make her beg and say sorry. He was leaving.

With every drop of blood in her body telling her to run after him, Helen kept her two feet planted on the bare boards and let him go. Only once the front door clicked shut – he didn't even slam it – did she go to the window, jump up on the bunker – the only place to sit in the whole room, and let the tears flow.

Chapter 5

She had cried herself out, cheered herself up a bit by splashing her face with cold water in the bathroom basin and actually started pacing out the rooms, thinking about a table and chairs, a wee settee if there was maybe a nice one to be had second-hand at the shop in the Cowgate, and a stool to set by her sewing machine. She had almost lost herself in daydreams when she heard him at the door. A faint rap.

'You d'ae need to knock, you big—' she said, opening up to reveal Mrs Sinclair standing there. She stared at Helen.

'I heard this but I didn't believe it,' she said. 'And so it's true, is it?'

'Heard that the doctors have got us a house?' Helen said. 'Yes, it's true. Would you like to come in?'

Mrs Sinclair shuddered. 'I've no wish nor any desire to cross this threshold again.'

Again? Helen frowned. 'Did you know the last people?' she said. 'Here, thinking of that, Mrs Sinclair, do you know the people downstairs? I've not heard a peep but I'm thinking it's a shame us clacking over bare boards in our shoes. I wondered if I should go down and say we'll have linoleum just as soon as we can and I'll make some rugs if I can get wool. Somebody said wool was coming off rations, but I've not had a minute to check.'

'You're babbling, Helen,' Mrs Sinclair said. 'But you can stop worrying about "people downstairs". There's no one there. The downstairs house is. . . riddled with rot and not safe. Uninhabitable.'

'Are *we* safe?' Helen said, putting out a hand and grasping the railing on the landing. Which was stupid, for wasn't the railing built on the same crumbling foundation as this uninhabitable downstairs house?

Mrs Sinclair flapped a hand at her. 'You're fine,' she said. 'You're fine up out of the damp. It's the floors that are away, not the stone.'

'But *our* floor's away!' Helen wailed. 'There's a patch of pressed board in the middle of the big room.' She felt sick. To have seen this place then have it snatched back again was more than she could bear.

'There's no damp up here!' Mrs Sinclair said. 'It's rising damp. Rising from the ground. It can't jump up to the floor of an upstairs apartment. Don't be silly now.'

'How do you know all this?' Helen said. 'I never really heard how the doctors had this place anyway, but is it connected to the Foundation?'

'It is not!' Mrs Sinclair drew herself up so sharply the feather in her hat trembled. She was proud of her Foundation. She had every cause to be. And Helen had reason to respect it too, for hadn't it educated her and set her on her path. But if she was living in a house the Foundation wouldn't touch with a pole…

'Not that there's any reason we wouldn't be, you understand,' Mrs Sinclair said hastily. It wasn't like her to explain herself and, far from it setting Helen's mind at rest, it made her all the more rattled. She might even have frowned, because Mrs Sinclair went on, 'I would fain take credit for good works that aren't mine.'

'Good works?' said Helen.

'I know you're a good girl who doesn't chatter,' Mrs Sinclair said, 'despite this wilfulness about the job. And that will be over soon enough. When it is, I shan't crow. I shan't mention it again. I shall welcome you back to be my good little Girl Friday the same as before. For you really are a very good girl, Helen. And I know I can trust you.'

'Of course you can,' Helen said. She had proved it time and again. She had listened to Mrs Sinclair tell one story to the lady volunteers at lunch and another, quite different, story to the trustees in their office at teatime. She had listened to Mrs Sinclair boasting about her daughters in the VAD and the Land Army and then tried *not* to listen to her on the telephone to them, whipping herself up into such a rage at how they'd shamed her, commanding them to come home.

Helen wasn't a fool. She knew Mrs Sinclair had taken her on to rub her daughters' noses in what they'd given up – her patronage, her attention, her influence. All of it, from the classes at George Square to the course at the Almoners' Institute, was supposed to bring the Sinclair girls to heel.

Oh, she'd felt special for a while. Plucked out of the Guide troop and given extra tasks. It wasn't until Christmas 1942 that the penny dropped. Standing in the 'flower room' at the end of the long passageway off to the side of the Merchiston house, wiping the bottles of ginger beer that had been standing in cold water all afternoon before the party, she'd heard Fiona Sinclair whispering at her mother, the sound hissing along the bare stone passage to Helen's ears better than a shout would have done. 'Do you think we *care*, Mother? Do you think we weep over it? So you've got yourself a little side-kick, a little tag-along, and Caro and I are supposed to feel wounded and come back, jealous in case she... what? Replaces us in your affections? I go out dancing three times a week and Caro flies a plane! Do you think we'll give that up to be back under your thumb and doing your bidding? You sicken us, don't you see? Judging us for the work *we* do while you barge on without a care.'

Now that Helen had twisted out of Mrs Sinclair's grip too, she could almost pity the woman. Except that begrudging a young couple a nice wee house was sour beyond reason and it turned Helen obstinate and shut the pity down.

63

'The thing is,' Mrs Sinclair said, sidling in and pulling the door shut behind her, 'that this place isn't generally known about. And it is never talked about.'

'What is it?' Helen said, looking around as if the bare rooms and clean walls might suddenly reveal something. 'I mean, what was it?'

Mrs Sinclair nodded. 'The thing is,' she said again, 'you and I know, Helen dear, that there's no shame in illness. None at all. Not even those complaints that we see so many of in these streets. For it's not the poor's fault they are poor.' When Mrs Sinclair got on to The Poor, saying it straight to Helen's face like that, it took a lot of patience and reminding herself about the good work and the helping hands not to snort. 'But there are people who don't see it that way. And, as you know, the City publishes their patient lists.'

Of course Helen knew. The City Hospital lists weren't something to glance through at the breakfast table for *her*. They seldom saw a paper till it was wrapped round fish the next day. Whenever someone they cared about was up in the isolation wards they waited for the daily report to be pinned up in the Chambers' window. It didn't get much more public than that.

'And the best little private hospitals,' Mrs Sinclair was saying, 'well, they don't take contagious cases at all. So, Dr Deuchar and Dr Strasser decided they would offer an exclusive service. A very *small* isolation ward – just these four rooms – and in such a tucked-away spot. It worked very well.'

Helen gazed around herself. That explained the sanded floors and the new distemper. Explained too the neat white bathroom, tiled and sparkling.

'It's all been gone over since the ward closed,' Mrs Sinclair said. 'There's no need to worry.'

'*Four* rooms?' Helen said. 'So the trouble with the downstairs flat is recent, is it? They'd never billet a consumptive where there was rot or mould.'

'Of course not,' said Mrs Sinclair.

'Is that why they closed it?'

'Not at all,' Mrs Sinclair said; she sounded flustered, which wasn't like her. 'What it is is that the rates are dropping. You've seen the charts, Helen, in your studies. Diphtheria is almost vanquished. Scarlet fever will be next to go.'

'Scarlet *fever*?' Helen said, startled. 'Were there *children* here?' She thought of those will-o'-the-wisp children of her own that she used to dream about, that she was trying to keep believing in. She'd not let them near a secret wee four-bed fever ward with who-knows-what in the other rooms.

'I'm not sure who was in and out,' said Mrs Sinclair. 'As I told you, it wasn't connected to me in any way. I only knew about it from the doctors asking if I cared to be involved. Which I declined to do. You're the first soul I've told.'

'And it stops here with me,' Helen said. Then she paused. 'If it's still as secret as all that. Seeing it's over.'

'It most certainly *is* secret,' Mrs Sinclair said. 'If a man of standing was seen coming here years back, no one could say then or can say now what his business was. But if it leaks out what this place was used for, and someone remembers – just think of it, Helen. They paid for privacy. They have a right to expect it.'

'Would they be walking though?' Helen said. 'If they were as sick as all that? Wouldn't the neighbour across the way see ambulance vans and start to wonder?'

Mrs Sinclair gave her a considered look before she replied. 'You've been studying so long, Helen,' she said, 'that you've made a virtue of curiosity. But in real life discretion is the better part of valour.'

'I see,' said Helen. 'Let sleeping dogs lie.'

'If you must put it that way,' Mrs Sinclair said. 'I'd say wholesome thoughts are better than nasty suspicions. Now, I've taken up more than enough of your time. You'll need to get the place ready for your furniture arriving. They're very late. You should admonish the men when they get here. Is it the Co-op you used?'

Helen smiled and said nothing. Mrs Sinclair prided herself on the matter-of-fact way she went in and out of what she called 'slums' with soup and blankets. She thought she was so courageous and long past being shocked. But she believed there was a motorvan full of furniture on its way.

In fact, as they went out onto the step again, Helen could see Sandy coming along the street, with a chipped deal bench balanced precariously in some kind of barrow, and a pair of fruit crates awkwardly under his free arm. He stopped and ducked down the next street when he saw Mrs Sinclair. Helen gave him a wee wave with her hand down at her side, and hoped he could see her smiling.

'Thanks,' Helen said, as she met him and the cart at the garden gate, when Mrs Sinclair was safely off along the lane in her motorcar.

'Sorry,' he said, looking up at her from under his brows. 'About storming off.'

'Ach, you're fine,' said Helen. She was too tired for any more tonight, no matter what the rights and wrong of it were. 'Here, gie me the crates and you steady that bench. It's a good one. It looks like a church pew. I wonder how come Tommy Lang disnae want it.'

Sandy shrugged. 'I went in to Fleming's,' he said. 'They're holding a wheen of good stiff buckram for you, said you can pay on Friday. It's in three bits so it's cheap but you can get it stitched together, can't you? As long as you're in before they close at eight tonight, it's yours.'

'Thank you,' said Helen again. She lifted the crates over her garden wall and let them gently down onto the grass. Then she opened the gate and held it for Sandy. 'Here,' she said, 'you'll never guess what Mrs Sinclair told me. We've naebody underneath us. The downstairs house is empty.'

'Not for long,' Sandy said, giving its windows an appraising look.

Helen decided not to tell him they were living over damp and rot. You never knew what would set him off. Even she would be happier once she'd had a good go at her place with hot suds.

'But while we're on bare boards, I mean,' she said. 'We d'ae need to be tiptoeing for fear we're getting on anybody's nerves. And I'll have rugs made soon enough. I could ask about scraps when I pick up the buckram. Might as well get started, eh?'

Sandy had been walking backwards, lowering the bench until it balanced on the side of the cart like a see-saw. Now he lifted the other end and set it down square on the grass.

'Nice,' Helen said. 'Do you want a hand up with it now or do you need to get the bogey back? Whose is it, by the way?'

'Oors,' Sandy said. 'I found it dumped in a midden on Spittal Street when I was cutting through. It saved my bacon tonight and I thought it would come in handy. Save a bus fare when we're kitting out and buy too much to carry.'

'Spittal Street?' Helen said, giving it a closer look. 'Here, I think I ken what this is. I think this is that Mrs Suttie's laddie's cart. Ken who I mean? A big boy with tapes and boards on his legs?'

'Andrew Suttie! Have I pinched his bogey? It was sitting at the midden and there was no one there.'

'He's getting a wheelchair,' Helen said. 'I wrote his note this morning my own self, but she's gey quick chucking it away. Unless she's been down already and they had one sitting.'

'Would they?'

'Only for looking at. Like a. . . a sample. They'd never have given it to the first buddy that rolled up.'

'They must have,' Sandy said. 'Given it away and then ordered another sample? If they saw Andrew in this, they might well have. Like somebody gave us a house. Like somebody gave you a job. Things are changing, Nell.'

He sat down on the bench then, right there in the middle of the grass, and reached a hand out to invite her to sit beside him. 'I'm going to plant celery,' he said. 'It's too dear to buy and it disnae give you the strength to blow a feather an inch, but with a pinch of salt and if it's good and fresh, there's nothing like it.' He let his gaze travel over the strip of earth as if he could see the trench already. 'What will I plant for you, hen?'

Helen cocked her head and gave him a look. Had she not said to him he wasn't digging her green up? Was this his sleek-it way of saying who was boss? That had never been Sandy's style before but what did she know about him now? Well, she would fight him. This lovely green grass felt so good under her tired feet with her shoes kicked off. She wriggled her toes until her stocking seams were all any way. If he would take his boots off and feel it for himself he'd forget about celery.

But a stretch of green needed a couple of fat babies to roll about on it and she didn't want to start off all that again. 'Strawberries,' she said.

'That's my girl,' said Sandy. 'I want to spoil you. And speaking of straw. . .' He clapped his hands down on his knees and got to his feet, ready to take up his burden again. He looked older than twenty-nine sometimes. Older than Mack.

'Look,' she said, pressing her advantage. 'I'm not asking *you* to go in, but I've a key to that padlock on the Anderson shelter, I reckon. At least, there's a key I can try. I'm thinking the bogey would go in no bother. Keep it safe.' She held her breath.

'You check,' Sandy said. 'And I'll away for the straw. Don't forget Fleming's shuts at eight. Or we could go together?'

'I'll not forget.' Truth was, Helen wanted a look inside the shelter on her own, to see if she could get back some of the feeling from the morning, the bubbles of hope and happiness she'd felt when she walked through the rooms with Dr Strasser. Whenever they were together, fetching straw the same as walking in twilight, it was Sandy's precarious happiness that mattered and her job not to shoogle it.

The keys were on the bunker where she'd dumped them to sit and cry. One day without crying would be grand, she found herself thinking, and made a promise to herself that tomorrow she wouldn't shed a single tear from morning till night. Unless at work, maybe. She'd seen a child's coffin one time, when Mrs Sinclair had her tag along on a visit to sort out a funeral, and only a cold-hearted monster could stay dry-eyed at that. Even Mrs Sinclair had a lump in her throat when they came away.

Seven keys. She let them rattle in her hand as she came back out onto the step. She could put a pot of marigolds here at her front door. She could get a sprig of mint and see if it would root. Her spirits were lifting already as she trotted down, over the grass, and took the three steps down again to the shelter door. She hadn't been in one since VE Day, when she'd stripped the bunks with Greet and been shocked to see the black mould on the feather pads they'd all been lying on, night after night. But there wouldn't be bunks left here; not when the house itself was pared back to the boards and as clean as a pin. She was hoping for a lantern. Garden tools would be a boon, for she had no idea how much they might cost, her the grandchild and great-grandchild of a tenement dweller. The last of her family who'd turned earth was long gone and forgotten. She squared her shoulders, ready for anything between a shed as neat as the house, a treasure trove of tools, and a swamp of filth, then bent to tackle the padlock holding shut the low wooden door.

It wasn't locked! Oh, the shackle was fast in its solid wee brass body but the whole hung uselessly from the hasp, not through the sturdy loop on the door-jamb. Helen faltered. A quiet shelter would be a find for any tramping man, and she didn't want to see what lay behind the door if one of them had made the place his own for more than a night or two. Dinnae be daft, she told herself, then tugged on the door and peered into the darkness.

Her first thought, coming up out of a pool of calm she didn't know she possessed, was *I shouldn't be here*. Every step on the way to this moment, standing at the mouth of this stale black cave, was a fluke. Helen had heard her whole life about how they thought she was going to die the night she was born – 'so small you slept in a boot box'. And then a few years later the scarlet fever nearly carried her off; *did* carry her brother off. Then the war.

Right now, since she'd survived, she should be at home, getting fat with her second one, hugger-mugger in with Mack, Greet and Teenie, saving Sandy's wages for a wee single end up a clean stair.

She shouldn't be *here*. Who would ever have thought she might be? Not her teachers, not her chums, none of them at home. Not Sandy.

She heard Greet's voice, thrilled and bitter, saying 'Aye, see, you *would* go where you didnae belong, wouldn't you?' and Mack with his lazy 'no daughter of mine,' and even Mrs Sinclair so determined to warn her how poorly it would end if she persisted. 'Had it coming,' Helen heard, although who knows what voice it was sneaking *that* thought into her mind. She shook her head.

The voice was wrong. No one had this coming. No one had *that* coming. Helen shook as she stood there, unable to drag her gaze from the sight before her. It wasn't a tremble shaking her, not a shiver; she shook with great juddering spasms, as if her whole body was retching. It took her six sore breaths, hauling air into herself like swallowing a solid lump of misery, before she could make herself be still again and think.

The poor soul, was her first thought, as she dropped down out of shock into pity. She didn't deserve to end like this. Whoever she was. Whoever she'd been. Huddled there on the bare ledge of the bunk. The mattresses were gone, just the four wooden shelves stacked two to a side, and this lost wee lassie washed up in the corner of one. The poor, poor, soul.

And then the pity too receded and anger came. No one deserved an end like that. An ending like that was everything that was wrong with this world, unfair and rotten and wrong. Helen fumbled in her skirt pocket for a match and struck it on the rough face of the bare brick retaining wall, the sulphur working on her like smelling salts so she gasped even before the flare settled and gave a ready light to let her look.

The eyes weren't shut, but they were dull, like a scoured pot, and the mouth looked dry, though the pale hank of hair still gleamed. She wasn't in her nightie, as Helen had thought when all she could see was a white billow. Now, by the match-light, it was clear that the dead girl wore a hospital gown. Helen had seen that rough, sturdy cotton and those tape ties every time she went with Mrs Sinclair to visit a patient on a ward.

She looked down. The feet were bare. How far had she come on those bare feet? How could she have flitted through the streets in that gown with its ties gaping and no one seeing her?

And why was she dead? A fine, well-grown, young-looking thing like that. Her skin was smooth and her hands, curled in soft fists in her lap, were as white as little mushroom caps and as spotless too. Even her feet were clean, each toe curled as neat and pink as a cockle shell, with not a callus or corn about them.

How *could* she be dead? There was no taint of sickness nor tang of blood in the close air and not a speck of red on the gown. Not a speck on the *front* of the gown, Helen found herself thinking, and crouching she lifted the hem to check under it.

Just as the match burned down to her fingertips and she let it go, she saw the girl's face clearly for the first time. The

Chapter 6

All the while she was running, she kept thinking she was doing the wrong thing. Go back, Helen, get a penny from your bag – her bag! Lying there in the empty kitchen and the front door wide open. Run to the kiosk at the road end, Helen. Tell the operator. Go home, Helen, get your mammy to sort it for you same as a scraped knee. Go to the doctors, Helen, ask them what to do. Run to the stables, Helen, and get Sandy to see to it all like he should. Her husband. He should tell her to look away and never mind and let him make it better.

But instead of any of that she was running, and she knew she was, to the blue light over the door at the Torphichen Street station, never mind her bosses and betters, her elders and her dearest. It was like the black-out again, like the lessons she'd learned in 1940: look for the uniform, run to the uniform, whether it was the ARP warden, the Home Guard, or a fireman. They had all turned into such good little citizen soldiers in the bad times and here it was coming up again.

She didn't make it as far as the door. Maybe it was a shift change or a dinner break, but for whatever reason there were police all over, coming and going in pairs, a couple with their helmets off leaning against the barred windows for a smoke.

'Help!' She couldn't slow down on the slope. Although she pulled back, her feet carried her on, slapping hard against the road. 'Help me. There's a dead girl. There's a dead girl.'

The police were more like a flock of birds than a group of tired men. They turned as one and as one they straightened and came to meet her, one of them putting his cigarette in the corner of his mouth to free his hands and offering up a buffer to her headlong pelt. He gripped her securely, not quite tight enough to leave marks, and pushed her back until she was steady.

'Dead?'

'On the tramline?'

'At the railyards?'

'A wean, is it?'

'No.' Helen caught her breath at last. 'Not a wee one. A girl, like me. A young woman. Young lady. Her name's Fiona Sinclair and she's lying deid in the Anderson in my garden.'

'Have youse been out, the pair of you?' said the policeman who had caught Helen so expertly. 'She's maybe passed out.'

'I don't think so,' Helen said. Then she shook herself. 'I know she's deid,' she insisted. 'She's cold. Who knows how long she's been there.'

'In your shelter? Are you sure it's not a bag of rags or a coal sack, hen?'

Helen, in answer, turned and started walking away, sure that at least one of them would follow her and just as sure that, when they saw Miss Sinclair, then she could go upstairs and close the door and let a bobby ring for a sergeant and the sergeant send for an inspector, who would get the Chief Constable of the city to go round to Mrs Sinclair's house while a doctor put Fiona on a stretcher and took her away and Helen would never have to think about her dull eyes and dry lips again.

'We've just moved in,' she said over her shoulder. 'My man's away to get. . .' she hesitated, 'a few bits we need for the night. I was looking round and I found her. Miss Fiona Sinclair. I've met her. At her mother's. I know her mother.'

'Sinclair!' There were three of them following Helen and one had put a face to the name at last. 'Sinclair from up Merchiston?'

'I know her poor mother,' was all Helen could say in reply. Then they were on the crescent and were turning away into the side street, the police ahead now, bit between the teeth.

'Up at the end,' she called after them, sinking down to lean on a low wall. 'Turn right at the end there.'

She would wait here for Sandy. She glanced up at the sky, wondering how long it had been since he left. It felt like a day's labour, but it was really only skipping up the stairs to fetch the key and opening the door then racing to Torphichen Street and walking back again. Sandy could be a while yet, between the stables and Fleming's. Or was *she* going to Fleming's? The whole exchange between them had the feeling of a dream now.

Helen had been drunk once in her life, on VE Day, and this felt just like that, like remembering laughing crowds and strange lips kissing hers in the thronging streets.

'Helen?' It was Dr Deuchar. He was standing in front of her in his shirtsleeves, frowning. 'What's going on? I saw—I thought I saw policemen.'

'Oh, Doc!' Helen said. 'There's a body!'

Dr Deuchar stared at her. His mouth hung open, making his cheeks sag, but his eyes were busy, pinching up and blinking, darting side-to-side. 'Where?' he said. 'A person, do you mean? A human?'

'Yes,' Helen said. 'A girl. Downstairs.' After all the news of the war years, given and received, offered and accepted, you'd think people would be better at voicing concise reports and drawing sensible conclusions. But it wasn't so. Trying to tell Dr Deuchar and make him understand was like running in a dream, held fast and not knowing how to break free.

'Where?' Dr Deuchar said.

'At my house,' Helen said.

'At your mother's house?' said Dr Deuchar. 'In Grove Place?' He looked up and down the street. 'What are you doing here?'

'No,' Helen said. 'Dr Strasser has let Sandy and me move in to the wee upstairs house that used to be the fever hospital.'

Dr Deuchar was staring utterly blankly at her. 'The fever . . .?'

'Rosebank,' she said, pointing. 'Along at the end. We just moved in tonight. And I found her. I went down to see if there was space to— Oh it doesn't matter. And I found a body!'

'You're saying,' said Dr Deuchar, 'that there's a dead body downstairs from the little flat at the far end of Rosebank?' He was as bad as she had been, not hardly able to take it in. 'And you found her?' he repeated. 'You found her?'

'I found her. I just opened the door, looking for space to store the bogey or hoping maybe to find something handy.' Talking through it was bringing it back and Helen scrubbed at her eyes. When she looked back at Dr Deuchar there were dark spots dancing. She could barely see him.

'I can't believe it,' Dr Deuchar said. 'Is it, I mean can you tell how long. . . Or is it a skeleton?' He was still trapped in *his* dream, like a fly on sticky paper.

'No,' Helen said, and at last she managed to say the worst of it. 'Doc, it's Fiona Sinclair. She's huddled in the Anderson shelter down in the garden as dead as anyone who ever died.'

Tottering, Dr Deuchar moved until he sat beside her, shoulder to shoulder, hitched – as she was – on that narrow ledge on the gable wall. He let his head fall back and didn't so much as twitch when it hit the brick with a dull smack. His shoulder, Helen could feel through his shirt and her blouse, was flickering like the dairy horses on a hot day when the flies bothered them.

'Fiona Sinclair is dead in your garden shed,' he said at last, his voice sounding dull and flat, like the voice of a survivor plucked from a bombsite that Helen had seen on the news-reel one time, saying, 'I'm fine. I'm fine,' and everyone in the pictures weeping. But there was a knock of acceptance in the sound of it.

76

'Oh Doc,' said Helen. 'She is.'

'How did she die? Could you tell?'

Helen hesitated. 'I think she's done herself away. I can't say *what* she did, for I don't just quite seem to. . . I didn't see that, I don't think. But she's not right, that's for sure. She's not in a good state, bare feet and her hair down and she's not dressed – she's covered!' – for he had flinched – 'but she's not in her clothes. What are we going to do? What's her poor mother going to do? This will be her end. This will break her into pieces. And who's going to tell her?'

They both turned at the sound of heavy footsteps advancing briskly. The sun had gone down behind the rooftops while the two of them were perched there, washed up and too drained to move. The policeman came trotting out of the shadows towards them, only slowing when he was almost past.

'Is it—?' he said. 'You're the one who found her?'

'Is she breathing?' said Dr Deuchar. 'I'm a medic. If you're running to get help.'

'She's cold, Doc,' said the bobby. 'Long gone. I'm running to get the sarge to ring the Fiscal.'

'And the police doctor? Or *I* could do the deed. Pronounce. Would that be any help to you?'

Helen glanced up at him. He had recovered. There were still patches of ill colour on his neck and a sheen above his lip, but he sounded like himself again.

Something passed between the two men that she didn't understand. Not even a word, but some code that men use, or at least men who see the worst of life as doctors and coppers must. Before she could catch the sense of it, she found herself hurrying along behind Dr Deuchar as the young policeman set off again at a faster run for the station, to hand his worry over.

The two of them left in her wee garden looked like sentries, standing one at either side of the half-open shelter door.

'Deuchar,' said the doctor, striding forward. 'I'm from the surgery on the crescent there. Let me have a look and then I can slip back for a certificate. Get this nasty business over and done with.' The two coppers shared a glance and then a nod.

'I can go for the cert, Doc,' Helen said. She had no wish to see Fiona's body again. 'Tell me where they are and I can easy fetch one.'

She trotted up the stone steps and in at her door to get her keys and her jacket; no more running around the streets in her sleeves, no matter what the trouble. She even stopped in the gleaming white bathroom to smooth over her hair and pat her cheeks. If only she hadn't, she'd have been downstairs and away when Dr Deuchar threw the door wide, instead of perched up where she was with a bird's eye view.

The second look was worse, somehow. The first had been a shock, but Helen knew the whole point of shock was to protect you. This time the sight of the girl was a heartbreak. It was pitiful to see such a youngster, healthy and strong, sprawled there in that gaping gown – someone had pulled it clear of her and it hung like a pinny between her knees, making Helen think of Mack at the slaughterhouse tucking his apron down when he sat, to let the blood drip off the hem and not pool in his lap.

When one of the policemen looked up, Helen came back to life and pattered down the rest of the steps just as Dr Deuchar came out from where he'd been leaning over the girl. He pushed the door closed.

'Silly fool,' he said, shaking his head and taking out his handkerchief to wipe his hands. 'Stupid girl. Whatever it was, it can't have been that bad.'

'So that's right?' Helen said. 'She done this to herself?'

'Her poor mother,' said Dr Deuchar. 'I'll have to tell her. Just as soon as I've signed the cert. I'll get up there and break the news. Somehow.'

It wasn't meant to be a rebuke but Helen ducked her head and darted away. Out at the gate and along the quiet lane, not so quiet now. Even the settled rows of houses that made up

Rosebank weren't immune to the rumpus of three police at a quick march and then one running. Neighbours that Helen might have hoped to meet on a Sunday, tidy and in a good hat, were hanging over their garden fences as she came towards them. It wasn't Grove Place, where they'd have been jostling as close as they could get without the police driving them off, but it wasn't seemly.

'What's to do?' said a man collarless in a waistcoat, still with his evening paper folded under his arm.

'Someone's died,' Helen said, to the evident thrill of the three women who stood just behind him, happy to let the man speak but eager not to miss a thing. 'Along at the end house there.' She pointed.

'No,' the man said. 'That house is empty long since. War effort it was and then not used after. Here, it's not a tramp, is it?'

But Helen had no more time to give him. She hurried away across the gardens and in at the surgery, laying her hand on the right form in a minute and taking the time to feel proud at how she managed it. She sped even faster on the return trip for, as she turned off the crescent, there was Sandy halfway home, three bales of hay balanced on the bogey and a paper parcel that must be the ticking sitting on top. She raced to catch him.

'I went myself,' he called as he spotted her. 'Save you, I thought, seeing you'll be sewing till yon time.' He was in higher spirits than Helen had seen him since Christmas, when a cigar and a brandy had made him smile and even Teenie cheating at cards couldn't flatten him. It didn't last. 'What?' he said, as Helen drew close. 'What is it?'

'Something's happened,' she said. 'Something awfy's happened. And I d'ae want it to upset you. So gies those reins and you get along to Bennet's and have a pint. Mack'll not be in on a Monday. Here.' She scrabbled in her bag and pressed a half-crown into his hands.

'What are you on about?' Sandy said. 'I'm needing my din-ner, Nell, not ale. I'm perishing hungry from all this running aboot. What is it that's wrong?'

But, before she could answer, the police klaxon was upon them and past them and Sandy could see, like all of the neigh-bours could see, the van draw up at their own gate. A sergeant leapt out and held the door for a tall man in an overcoat and soft hat, who stepped down like a grandee and entered the garden.

'Nell?' said Sandy.

'Come away,' she whispered, keenly aware of the neigh-bours bending over the fence as if a wind was behind them. 'While our house was empty,' she said, 'while it was quiet there, a puir sowel crept into the Anderson shelter and decided to die there. I found her body. Doc Deuchar's there and now some big polis too and it'll all be done in no time, but it's nasty. It's not nice, Sandy, and I d'ae want it set before you.'

Sandy stood with his hand still balancing the tottering pile of brown-paper parcel and bales of hay – so ridiculous, so undignified, all heaped up on a child's old bogey. Helen could have wept for him, for the both of them, and for their life that all these neighbours were seeing.

'Her?' Sandy said. 'A woman?'

'Fiona Sinclair,' said Helen, quieter still, and watched his eyes widen. He shook his head as if he'd been clouted and needed to clear the ringing.

'Fiona Sinclair – Mrs Sinclair's Fiona – has kilt herself?' he said. 'In the howff of an empty house. How did she know it was there?'

But he'd had enough, Helen reckoned, without news of fever wards too. '*I've* seen her already,' said Helen answering his tone, if not his words. 'There's no point you having the sight in your head too. So gies that bogey here and get off. I'll come and find you when it's all done. We can get chips,' she added, wheedling at him as if he was a bairn. 'We should be treating ourselves anyway, big night like this. It won't spoil it. It'll soon be done and then we'll start again. Eh?'

Sandy narrowed his eyes and stared at her. It took her a while to see anything *except* those eyes, nearly black as he pinched them up in the low light, then she blinked and saw that he was smiling. 'You're a nice woman, Nell,' he said. 'You were always a nice wee girl. I never saw you pull a pigtail or say a mean word about anyone. And now you're a nice woman. Kind. But why do you think I need to be tret with kid gloves?'

Helen couldn't speak. The question was so unexpected and so bizarre, that if she wasn't close enough to smell his breath, she'd think he'd been drinking already. Fighting with all her confusion was a burning little nub of anger. Laugh at *her*, would he? For wondering if the man who couldn't work inside a building, and couldn't so much as kiss his wife without weeping, might wilt at the sight of a corpse in his new house where he'd been hoping to be happy.

'Right,' she said. 'Sorry. I thought you'd be. . .' but she couldn't finish the sentence. Not to Sandy, not to anyone, and she never had. She had never said any of the words. Upset, unnerved, set back, cowed, scared, broken. She knew there was no way to say any of them. Because of all the other words she couldn't say either. About how strange he was, how lost, how odd and ill and changed he was. And how *hard* it was. How cold and exhausting and endless it was. And the shame of it. The shame was buried deepest of all.

And now here he was smiling and asking why on earth she'd dream him unequal to this latest.

'Fine and well then,' she said. 'Let's get back and see what they're saying.'

There was one thing she needn't have worried about: Sandy wheeled the bogey in at the gate, parked it out of the way, and none of them – the three constables, the sergeant and the man in plain clothes, Dr Deuchar – gave it mind. Maybe hay meant ponies or at least rabbits to them and they weren't shamed for Helen. She whisked the paper parcel off the top and ran away upstairs with it, setting it down on the bunker and then going back outside to join them.

'No question,' Dr Deuchar was saying, as she handed over the death cert. 'Suicide, the poor misguided wretch. It's a sin, isn't it? When you think of what so many of you went through to give her the life she's thrown away.'

That set them off, the whole hand of them: the inspector, as he turned out to be, had been at the landings. The oldest constable had been in Egypt, the one who'd run for reinforcements had got no further than France but that three times, in between recuperating from shrapnel in Perthshire. The youngest had missed it and hung his head.

'I was reserved,' Dr Deuchar said. 'But I'm no less keenly aware of the sacrifice. And the waste.'

Helen said nothing. She'd heard the same line from Greet the last three years. 'Stop complaining. Men died so you could live this sweet life.' She had learned to bite her lip, for the few times she'd tried to argue she tied herself in a knot.

'You never know what troubles a buddy has.' It was Sandy speaking. All five of the other men turned to stare at him. 'Who's to say why anyone does anything?'

'Rather a nihilistic outlook, Crowther,' Dr Deuchar said. 'This young man was a POW,' he added, sweeping out a hand as if Sandy was a side of meat on a butcher's hook. 'My partner Strasser keeps telling him he was still part of the effort, wearing them down, making them feed him. But nothing shifts the melancholia.'

Sandy barely noticed, Helen reckoned, for he was staring in the shelter door, but *she* couldn't help rounding on the doc and sending a silent appeal. What was he at, blabbing private business, private sadness, to a set of coppers? 'How did she do it?' she asked, to cover the look that the doc hadn't missed.

'Poison,' said Dr Deuchar. 'No question.'

'Is that right?' Helen said. The thought of it troubled her deeply and she didn't know why. Perhaps because with poison, unlike a knife to the wrists or a pistol to the head, there would have been time. If only someone had found her.

'Absolutely,' said Dr Deuchar. 'Characteristic discolouration around her mouth and jaw and an unmistakable smell.'

Helen looked back at the girl. It seemed to be getting easier every time. She'd smelled nothing, but then she didn't know what smell it was she should have caught. And as for the discolouration, Fiona's head had fallen even further forward and there was nothing to see but the parting in her hair and the two golden hanks of it falling down.

'What a long, lonely death,' she said. 'To come and sit in a dark place all alone and drink poison.'

'Don't dwell on it,' Dr Deuchar said. 'I need you to be strong, Nell. I'm going to Mrs Sinclair's house to break it to her and I'd like you to come with me. I think that would be best for her when she hears the news.'

'And best for you too, Mrs. . . Crowther, is it?' the inspector said. 'Best to be away when we move her. You don't need to be seeing that.'

'That's right,' Sandy said. 'You go, Nelly. I'll have the place to rights by the time you're back. Leave it to me.'

'He's a good sort, your Sandy,' said Dr Deuchar as he and Helen made their way back to the surgery. He opened the door of his little car and stood back. Dr Strasser would have handed her in, courtly to the point of awkwardness. Dr Deuchar was easy, treating her like one of the girls that came to his parties of a Saturday evening. Helen had seen them, standing at the open windows on the drawing-room floor, laughing and smoking, with gramophone music drifting out onto the street. 'Two minutes till I get my bag,' he threw over his shoulder, bounding up the steps and disappearing through the door.

'In case she needs a powder,' Helen said when he returned, and got a rueful nod as he pulled away from the kerb and set off to the top of the crescent. She hugged the big black leather bag he had handed her, drinking in the smell of the saddle oil he used on it and comforted by its weight. There would be something in here to help poor Mrs Sinclair get through this first dreadful night, until maybe a relative could come and stay. Of course, Helen had no idea what relatives there were or how far-flung, or even whether the immediate descent of family was how things were done when a woman like Mrs Sinclair found herself in dire trouble, the way it was at the Downies' – aunties gathering at the first rumble of thunder.

'How will you break it to her?' Helen said, after a while. They were getting towards Holy Corner now. The lighted shops and evening bustle of the main road had cheered her briefly. When she saw the spires that heralded the turn into Merchiston, though, their errand settled on her again like a fire blanket.

'I wonder if I shall have to,' said Dr Deuchar. 'You saw what she was wearing, didn't you? She'd obviously been a patient somewhere in recent days. Perhaps Mrs Sinclair knows already that the poor girl is missing. Perhaps our news will be a strange sort of relief.'

'Relief?' Helen said. 'Doc, for the rest of time Mrs Sinclair's going to know she was right there, visiting me, and Fiona was lying dead yards away.'

'Mrs Sinclair came to see you?' he said. 'That was nice of her, Nelly. So she's forgiven you for being such an upstart then?'

'Something like that,' Helen said. 'Doc? How do you think she could have got through the streets dressed in that gown?'

'Middle of the night. Small hours. And it's so quiet at Rosebank.'

It *was* quiet at Rosebank, Helen thought to herself, and on the crescent, but take a turn out onto the thoroughfare at either end and then to the main road itself where they were now and even in the small hours there were people aplenty: by the time the last of the late workers were home, the bakers were up and the newspaper men, the carters, milkmen and cleaners, and then the deliveries began. Perhaps Dr Deuchar, living quietly where he did, wasn't thinking of all the other people.

'Mind you,' he said, as if Helen had spoken her thoughts aloud, 'when I'm called out to a confinement or a fever, it's rare not to pass someone or other.'

'Maybe she walked along the railway lines and scrambled up over the wall,' Helen said. 'If she was running away. I mean, if *I* was running away in a goonie I'd go on the railway, not the streets.'

'And here we are,' said Dr Deuchar. It was darker again now and the spreading trees that sheltered the grand houses on Mrs Sinclair's road made a bottle-green gloom like a stagnant pond. Helen had never been here in the evening before. So many unlit windows, so many unused rooms. Mrs Sinclair lived alone in a house that had dazzled Helen and made her mouth drop open the first time she'd seen it on a garden-party afternoon. She wouldn't swap places tonight, and be hearing the worst news a mother could ever hear, all alone in that mausoleum. She decided if Mrs Sinclair asked her to stay, she'd agree. She would even pat the woman's shoulder, make her tea, bring her blankets.

Dr Deuchar was out of the car and Helen hurried after him. Together they ascended the few stone steps to the open vestibule, where he knocked smartly on the inner door.

No one answered, but then it was gone eight o'clock and Helen could imagine Mrs Sinclair starting, taking a moment to regret the days of a live-in maid, then tidying herself before coming to see what had disturbed her evening.

Dr Deuchar had stepped back to look up at the façade, as if he was thinking of scaling the ivy. Helen stepped down too and scanned the windows: a deep bay on either side and a sort of turret above, as square as a Norman tower and slightly looming as she craned her neck to take it in. 'Maybe she's in the garden, taking a turn,' she said. 'Or shutting up the chickens.' Mrs Sinclair had been proud of her little flock of bantams in the war years, counting the tiny bright eggs like a miser with his gold and making sure she was out for the day whenever one was killed for stewing.

But the door, at last, was opening. Mrs Sinclair was still in her high-necked blouse and pleated skirt, but had a shawl round her shoulders and soft shoes on.

'Alastair?' she said. 'Helen? What – oh! Have you come to your senses? Well, good, but it might have waited until morning.'

'Can we come in?' Dr Deuchar said. And perhaps something in his voice sent a signal, for her face grew grave and she stepped back without another word to let them enter.

'I was sitting in my little library,' she said. Dr Deuchar turned left and headed along a short passageway. Of course, Helen thought, he would know the house, from meetings and soirees, or perhaps all these big houses were the same inside, just like the tenements were.

There was no fire, but the lamp was lit and a basket of fancy-work sat open by a comfortable chair, the silks laid out neatly in the pool of light. Helen sat herself as unobtrusively as possible behind the door, tucking her feet in and folding her hands in her lap.

'Have you heard from Fiona today?' Dr Deuchar said.

'She's staying with friends,' said Mrs Sinclair. 'In Brighton. And no, thankfully. I say thankfully, because it would be just like her to ring me up and reverse the charge, just to tell me she had found a lovely hat or won at some silly card game.' Then she caught herself. 'Why do you ask?'

'Brighton,' said Dr Deuchar and Helen understood him perfectly. That was the story her mother was putting about to cover an absence. 'And none of her friends has been in touch with you?'

'Should they have been?' said Mrs Sinclair. 'What is this?'

'The most dreadful news I have ever had to break,' said Dr Deuchar. 'Poor Fiona has left wherever it was she's been staying. And she has met with misfortune. With the most grave misfortune.'

'Are you saying my daughter has died, Dr Deuchar?' Mrs Sinclair was sitting up as straight as ever and her voice was even steelier than usual, as if news like this was an effrontery and she would not have it.

'I'm desperately sorry,' Dr Deuchar said. 'But I'm afraid I am. She has taken a way out of her troubles.'

'Nonsense!' There was a telephone on a little writing desk quite near where Helen sat and Mrs Sinclair strode towards it now and snatched up the receiver, rattling the wee thing in the cradle and barking at the girl on the exchange. She was staring at the table-top and Helen turned to follow her gaze, seeing a framed photograph propped on a stand there. It showed both Sinclair girls after they'd joined up, giddy with defiance in their uniforms. So Mrs Sinclair had finally forgiven them, had she? For running off to the war instead of staying at home with her? A distant ringing broke into Helen's thoughts and a man's voice came tinny and faint down the line.

'Teddy? Alvia Sinclair. That's right. Her mother. Yes, yes, look. Is she there? I need to speak to her urgently.' There was another long silence and then Helen heard the quacking, chirping sound of a girl's voice on the other end. 'Darling? It's Mother. I've just heard the most startling piece of gossip about you.' Helen thought the quacking got even more high-pitched, but it was no match for Mrs Sinclair when she was determined. 'Apparently, you're dead!' she said. 'Yes, you've reportedly done away with yourself here in Edinburgh. Someone who should know better has just come to my door to regale me.' She shot Dr Deuchar a withering look.

Helen felt her gullet sink as a terrible notion took hold of her. She stood and scurried over to the doctor's side. 'What if it's Carolyn?' she breathed into his ear. 'I've only ever met them twice and both times they were together, at a party. Oh God in heaven, Doc, what have I done?'

'Stop whispering!' said Mrs Sinclair, taking the receiver from her ear and holding it against her chest. 'What are you muttering about?'

'Can you hang up, Mrs Sinclair?' Dr Deuchar said. 'And try Fiona's sister instead? Do you know where *she* is?'

Mrs Sinclair's face turned a shade of putty from her brow to her chin as though the colour was draining out of it. 'Her sister?' She stared at Dr Deuchar. 'Is that what you're trying to tell me? Is that what you've brought Helen here to tell me?'

'I was sure it was Fiona,' Helen said. 'I'm so sorry. I've mixed them up. It was definitely one of them and I'm so sorry I didn't know which one. They're just very alike, you see?'

Mrs Sinclair's grey face shone like wet clay. Her eyes fluttered and, letting the telephone fall from her hands, she slumped against the desk as she fainted away.

Chapter 7

'I'm sorry, I'm so sorry, I'm sorry.' Helen couldn't stop the words spilling out of her mouth as she settled Mrs Sinclair on her side with a cushion under her head and tugged her skirt down over her stocking tops. 'I'm so sorry.'

'Wheesht, Nell,' said Dr Deuchar. He was rummaging in his bag and soon plucked out the little bottle of ammonium to wave under her nose. She came round spluttering and rolled onto her back.

'I have to see her,' she said, and put her hands over her face. 'I have to. Where is she? What happened?' She was struggling to her knees and then to her feet, hauling herself up by the edge of the desk. The telephone was still emitting chirps and quacks. Mrs Sinclair reeled away. Helen lifted the receiver.

'Miss Sinclair?' she said. 'I think you had better come home. Your mother is. . . Your mother needs you.'

The arguments began without a pause but Helen hung up. She glanced at the photograph of the sisters, which had fallen flat on its face as Mrs Sinclair gripped the table. Perhaps that was better just at the moment. Helen left it to lie there and turned away. Dr Deuchar was quizzing Mrs Sinclair about getting help: relations, friends, even neighbours.

'Neighbours?' she said, her voice rising to a shriek. 'I'm not in the habit of having my neighbours running in and out at *any* time, Dr Deuchar. I would hardly turn to them now.' She sounded exactly like Greet. 'I need to be taken to see her and I need someone to tell me what happened. What *happened*?'

'Shush now, shush,' said Dr Deuchar, as if he was talking to a child. Helen would never have dared speak to Mrs Sinclair like that. 'The thing is that I don't know where she'll be. Everything's in a state of flux with the start of the new service. The hospitals were careful not to have any minor ops and consultations on the docket—'

'Minor ops?' said Mrs Sinclair. She was standing four-square again, although still breathing raggedly, and she drew herself up with crossed arms under her bosom until she seemed to swell to twice her size.

'I was merely expressing the level of uncertainty expected, in advance of the day,' Dr Deuchar said. 'To persuade you not to spend the night chasing around trying to find where they've taken her. I can dispense you a soothing draught to help you sleep, then come back in the morning once we know what's what.'

Helen bit her lip. She was almost certain that the mortuary in the Cowgate was trundling on the same as ever. She had read every letter and notice the Corporation and Regional Board had put out, readying them all for today, and nothing in her own papers or the checklists for doctors, nurses, manipulators and other aides had mentioned the Cowgate or the police doctors. Helen couldn't see why the new service would affect them. But she wasn't about to correct the doctor in front of another person, especially not *this* other person. She would tell him, gently, when they were back in the car and then double check in the morning.

Because maybe, she thought as they made their way back through the streets, full-dark now, she had let her eyes pass over those details, thinking they would never be in her basket. A medical almoner surely couldn't have a reason to visit that dark place, deep in the guts of the city. She always hurried past even on the sunniest day, coming home from a walk up Arthur's Seat or whatever, trying not to think about what lay behind the high blank wall.

'Wouldn't the inspector know?' she said, opening the matter gently. 'Where Miss Sinclair has gone, I mean. We could stop off and ask him. Don't you need to tell them that the name's wrong as soon as possible anyway? Write a new cert?'

'That,' said Dr Deuchar after a long pause, 'is a very good point, Helen.' Then he drove in silence, chewing at the ends of his moustache the way he did whenever he was lost in thought over a tricky diagnosis, or a treatment not responding, or even a hardship case as she had seen more than once. On the thought, Helen's spirits lifted again. Hardship case! This was a terrible evening for Mrs Sinclair and a rotten start to her and Sandy's new home, but they shouldn't forget that it was still a grand day overall for the city and beyond.

They had passed their turn; he must be going straight to Torphichen Street right now. That was Dr Deuchar's way. Get it over with, even more so if it was a task to dread. She had always admired that about him. And he was certainly dreading this. His hands gripped the wheel hard enough to make the leather squeak.

'They won't make trouble,' she told him. 'It wasn't you said "Fiona". If it's on anyone, it's on me. And here it'll be set right before they had a chance to. . .' But she didn't want to think about what came after a suicide, in place of the undertaker's skill and a nice neat coffin to lay in the front room.

'I hope you're right, Helen,' was all he said in reply.

On Torphichen Street, he parked his car at the end of a row of police vans, all sitting nose to the kerb and back doors out in the road, taking up as much space as they felt like, she supposed, for what carter or drayman would let his horse clip one of those shiny bumpers? Dr Deuchar shot her a haggard look as she stepped down but she repeated, 'It was me said it,' and he nodded and even smiled at her.

It wasn't her first time in a police station. She and Mrs Sinclair had been forced to visit this very waiting room once before. They had been drafted to collect a squalling toddler, whose mother was under arrest for petty theft. She wouldn't let the child go to her *own* mother, owing to some age-old family feud that made no sense at all. Or not when both the prisoner and the granny were screeching their versions, the baby topping both of them for yells.

But that had been a bright spring morning. It was a different place on a hot summer night after dark, even a Monday. It was stale and close for one thing, smelling as if the mop used on the floor hadn't seen bleach for years. Helen hadn't smelled that sour reek since the wee school, when they were all supposed to wet their slate sponge every night at home and no one ever did, just only spat on them as and when, so the whole classroom stank and the teacher sniffed and sniffed and sometimes even checked their feet for dog dirt, but never did work out what it was, her not knowing the smell of a damp towel in an outside place probably.

The waiting room was empty tonight, except for two young women, girls really, garishly dressed and smoking with a big dollop of bravado as they waited for their fate to be handed down. Of course! They were a stone's throw from the notorious 'back of Haymarket'. Though Edinburgh folk liked to say you had to go to Leith for the likes of that, here was the evidence proving them wrong.

Helen tried not to look in their direction bur Dr Deuchar said 'Ladies,' and lifted his hat as they passed the bench, making for the high desk.

The girls tittered and Helen felt her colour rise. Then she caught herself. The needs of everyone, Mr Bevan had said. *Everyone.* Rich and poor, grateful or complaining, nuns and girls like these, just the same. She turned as Dr Deuchar cleared his throat to attract the attention of a dozy sergeant, and marched back towards them.

'I'm Helen Crowther,' she said. 'Medical almoner at the Gardner's Crescent surgery.' That made them prod one another and giggle again but she pressed on. 'Do you have a doctor sorted out yet?'

Both of them gaped at her. The younger was surely not twenty-one, with a rash of spots in the crease of her chin and still with silky eyebrows like a baby. Her friend was nearer thirty, Helen guessed, and a hard thirty.

'We get seen when we must,' the older one said. 'We're no' needing charity.'

'It's not charity,' said Helen. She opened her mouth to give her little speech, the one she had been reciting up closes and on landings for months now, then she opened her bag and took out a leaflet instead. 'Dr Strasser is full already,' she said.

'Strasser?' said the older one. It came out like a squawk. 'I thought he deed years back.'

'His son,' said Helen. 'But like I said, he's full. Dr Deuchar has space on his lists still but it won't take long.'

'Dr Deuchar has space for *us*, does he?' said the younger one, with a sneer. Her teeth were as short as milk teeth, little stumps set far apart in dark gums. 'Have you asked him?'

'At least get a dentist,' Helen said. 'Before your teeth rot in your head.'

'Push off,' said the older girl. 'Cheek of you. Think *you're* such a pin-up, dae ye? Think you'd make a living if you came oot wi' us?'

That hit home, but before Helen could conjure up a reply or even get her expression back under control, Dr Deuchar hailed her.

'Helen!' He sounded as if he was trying to bring a dog to heel.

'You should be more careful who you talk to, lass,' said the sergeant as she joined them. 'Those are bad girls.'

'Mrs Crowther is my medical almoner,' said Dr Deuchar. 'She's fearless in the face of vice and squalor, aren't you, Helen? But not so adept at identifying lost souls. As I was just telling the sergeant.'

'And as I was just telling the doctor, nobody's been back here. It's the first I've heard about it. So wherever your certificate is, Doc, it's not been entered into any file yet. You're in grand time to sort it.'

'Are you sure?' Dr Deuchar said. 'It's five minutes up the road. Where have they got to?'

'I'll check,' the sergeant said. He reached behind him and lifted the receiver of an old black telephone worn dull from age. He dialled two digits with the end of his pencil and spoke tersely to whoever answered. 'Did a mort van go out? An hour since? And Inspector. . .' then he put his hand over the phone and raised his brows at Helen and Dr Deuchar. Helen shrugged. 'Tall with a good coat or round with hair like a sheep?' the sergeant said. He surely wouldn't have described the inspectors like that in their hearing but it was efficient, at least.

'Tall,' Helen said.

'Inspector Nunn,' said the sergeant into the phone. 'They're none of them back yet, eh no? Aye, right well can you ring up the Cowgate and tell them to stay put for the certifying doc coming. There's been a wee hitch.' He hung up. 'This phone doesn't ring out,' he said. 'Helps me delegate to them through the back playing cards, else I'd be a one-man show.'

And so they were off to the Cowgate now, were they? Helen wondered if Sandy would be worrying. Or maybe he'd think they were still at Mrs Sinclair's making her cocoa and putting cushions under her feet.

Helen would rather be back in that looming crypt of a house trying to coddle a woman made of scrap iron than be headed where she *was* going. The mortuary! She had never admitted to her chums, as she pelted past just how much the place scared her, but she piped up to Dr Deuchar now.

'Will we have to go in?'

'In?'

'To where she's laid out. To where they're all laid out?'

'Are you frightened, Helen?'

'I am. Laugh all you want, but I am. I've never seen such a thing and I don't want to start.'

Dr Deuchar nodded thoughtfully. They were crossing the Grassmarket, as raucous on a Monday night as a Saturday, with beggars and rascals darting in and out between the swaying drunks, and the pie men with their boards doing a roaring trade. There was even a hurdy-gurdy going at nearly ten o'clock, trying to sell toffee to crowds who were only after beer. 'Give me the mortuary any day,' said Dr Deuchar, waving out of the window at the scene. 'Breathe through your mouth and you'll be fine.'

Breathe through your mouth and then you're eating it. Teenie's voice came into Helen's mind. She had a pert wee saying for every occasion, each one meant to do someone down and bring Teenie herself out on top. But at least the thought of her sister's scorn bolstered Helen as they headed for the narrow neck of the cave-like Cowgate, leaving the brash lights of the Grassmarket pubs behind them and entering the very barrel bottom of Edinburgh. Even to someone from Freer Street, the Cowgate was a place to put goosebumps on you. The rag and bone emporium was the best of it; the hostels for men and the pitiful hostel for women the very worst. Helen thought fondly about the new straw and ticking waiting for her tonight behind a locked door inside a clean house.

'Aye, right,' she said. 'Through my mouth. But just as well I've not had any tea.'

It looked like the police station from the outside, except that, set discreetly back from the street behind trees, it had the look of Mrs Sinclair's house too. The door, when they knocked, was opened by a caretaker who put Helen's mind at ease. He wasn't the goblin she'd been imagining, but a well-built, well-groomed man in his early forties maybe, only the empty pinned-up sleeve of his coat to explain why he had this job instead of something better.

'We're looking for the girl that was brought in by Inspector Nunn,' said Dr Deuchar, once he had introduced himself. 'Not even an hour since.'

'There's been no delivery tonight,' the man said. He had the lilt of the Highlands in his voice and a clear blue gaze to go with it.

'We've beat them to it, Nell,' said Dr Deuchar. 'Even better,' he added to the attendant. 'I put the wrong name on the cert, you see. Two sisters and I mixed myself up between them. Can we wait? And will you tell them when they get here? I'd rather set it right tonight, you understand.'

'Wait where?' Helen said. There was no bench. And why would there be? This place didn't get passing trade.

'If you go round the back, you can head them off,' the man said. 'They'll be driving in that way if they're depositing. That would be your best bet.'

Round the back of the mortuary was even worse than the front. The lane that disappeared along the side of the building was narrow, half choked with weeds, and so dark it obviously appealed to men wending home from the Grassmarket pubs. It stank, and skittered with rats as they passed by.

'What do you think's kept them?' Helen said. 'Should we maybe go back? Maybe they're still at Rosebank.'

Dr Deuchar shook his head. He was lighting a cigarette and Helen saw him in the flare of the match. 'They won't be long now,' he assured her. 'There's nothing to keep them as late as this.'

'Will they have to open her up?' Helen shivered at the thought of it. She could almost be calm if she concentrated hard on a polished coffin set in Mrs Sinclair's front room, lilies turning the air rank and a candle burning. In this picture, Mrs Sinclair was sitting on a hard chair with a handkerchief pressed to her mouth and Fiona was standing behind her with a hand on her shoulder for comfort. But the truth, the fact that Carolyn Sinclair would lie on a slab in this hulk of a

96

building while orderlies joked and cleaners sluiced the floor...
She shivered again. She was beginning to feel light-headed
from hunger and upset. And, as time passed, she couldn't
get Carolyn's face out of her mind. The dull eyes and the
dry mouth and the photograph on the side table of both
girls laughing in their uniforms. The victory roll of one and
pin curls of the other. She had been so sure it was Fiona.
Fiona in her sparkling-buttoned tunic and her VAD cap
pushed back on her head. Carolyn in her canvas dungarees
and scarf, each of them proud and defiant. One of them now
lying on a stretcher in the back of a police van, who knows
where in these city streets.

'Here they come,' said Dr Deuchar, throwing his fag to the
ground. The lane was so dank and the weeds so lush that it
hissed as it went out. Being the man he was, the doc searched
around with his foot and stamped at where the dout had landed
to make doubly sure. So the car was almost away in the gates
before he stepped forward.

'It's not the van,' Helen said, at the same time as the driver
caught sight of them and braked sharply.

'Who's that loitering there?' came a voice from the back
seat of a long motor-car as the driver unbuttoned his window and pushed it aside. 'Take your dirty business away from
here!'

Helen drew back into the shadows, shame flooding her.
Well, what else would someone think, seeing a man and a
woman huddled at the edge of this black little lane?

'We're waiting for a van bringing a case in,' Dr Deuchar
said. 'I'm the doctor who wrote the cert – Deuchar's the
name; Gardner's Crescent – but no sooner had I done it than
I realised I'd written it down wrong. I've come to set matters
right before it goes any further.'

'Gardner's Crescent?' The voice was what Greet called
plummy. Helen had heard it from her instructors at the university, and from some of her fellow students too, rolling

words around like sweeties in their mouths and always with a threat of laughter at the throat, no matter what the topic was. 'You don't mean the Rosebank Colonies case, by any chance, do you?'

'Exactly!' said Dr Deuchar. 'Excuse my boldness, but how do you know of it?'

That wasn't bold, Helen thought. It was a roundabout way of asking who the hang the voice belonged to. Bold would have been demanding a name straight out.

'All done and dusted, my dear boy,' the voice was saying now. 'I happened to be having a little dinner for some friends – shop-talk with no one to hear it – and the news reached me. The lads on the scene rang the Glasgow lads and they rang my chief superintendent at Gayfield Square, who rang me, as I happened to be dining with Mr Brodie. Very irregular but not inefficient. Rather a rude ending to a charming dinner, mind you; my wife is most put out. But the end of a long man-hunt for our friends in the west. Woman hunt, one should say. So a good night's work all round.'

'Mr Brodie being. . .?' said Dr Deuchar, inching even closer to the question he really wanted to ask.

'My Glasgow counterpart,' the voice said. 'I'm Duncan Pyne. Didn't I say?'

Dr Deuchar said nothing, merely took in a sharp breath and shifted his feet in the muck of the lane as if to get set for running.

Helen stepped forward at last. 'Why did Miss Sinclair have Glasgow polis after her?' she said.

'What?' The sweeties and the laugh were both gone. 'Who are you to be bandying that name about. The poor wretch was a Miss Maggie Dickson. The notorious Maggie Dickson, scourge of the Gorbals, who has met the end she'd been courting for many a long year. What on earth made you say "Sinclair"?'

'She was her dead spit,' Helen said. 'Oh Doc, can we go and tell her mother? Can we go right now?'

Dr Deuchar patted her arm as if to tell her 'Patience, patience' and said to the shadow in the back of the car, 'But whatever her name, sir, where is she?'

'Glasgow,' came the answer, 'or halfway by now, at least. No need for you to trouble yourselves any further. By all means, let the mother know that her daughter is alive and well. That's a very pleasant task, I should think.' Perhaps he tapped the driver on the shoulder, or perhaps the man had learned when his boss was done and wanted to be going. Either way the window flap fell and the long car passed through the open gates and into the covered place at the back door where the business of the mortuary was conducted so very discreetly.

'Who *was* that, Doc?' Helen said. 'Who's Duncan Pyne when he's home in his vest?'

'I'd have to look him up in the directory to be sure,' said Dr Deuchar. 'Bigger than a sheriff. Much bigger than a JP. A judge of some stripe and not a lowly one, Helen.'

'Aye, he sounded like Lord Muck, right enough.' They were picking their way back round to the Cowgate, to what now seemed like decent lamplight and good clean air after the noisome back lane. 'What's he doing here, do you think?' Helen added. 'A judge.'

'Ocht, they're all on the same boards when you get up into that thin air,' said Dr Deuchar. 'You heard what he said about his little dinner where they could all gossip and no one the wiser.'

'I bet his wife's raging,' Helen said. 'I would be if I was scraping my cooking into the pig bin after they'd all gone away to shift a corpse and left me spinning. Not as if there was any hurry. She wasn't going anywhere.'

'Poor girl,' said Dr Deuchar.

'I'm only glad he never said what she'd done,' said Helen. 'To be a "scourge", I mean. I'd rather not know, seeing she met her end in my Anderson. Not that I believe in ghosts. But still.'

'I wonder which of those coppers suddenly took a second look and recognised her,' Dr Deuchar said.

'Oh don't, Doc!' said Helen. 'I'm mortified. If I hadn't jumped to conclusions, poor Mrs Sinclair wouldn't have had that terrible shock and gone down like a sack of spuds. I'm sure she hurt her ankle on the way. Didn't you think she was limping?'

'Not at all, Helen,' he said. '*I* thought it was Miss Sinclair too. I was convinced, just as you were. And, besides, we're going straight there to let her know. Unless you'd like me to drop you off? It's getting late.'

'I'd love you to drop me off,' Helen said. 'But I couldn't live with myself. It was me made the mess and it's me should clear it up.'

For the rest of the journey she stared out at the emptying streets, watching the pools of light and stretches of darkness flash past in turn, trying to compose an apology and getting nowhere.

But when they pulled into the sweep at that looming house again, it was to find lights on upstairs and down. And, before they could ring the bell, Mrs Sinclair came out onto the step and met them.

'I've had the most marvellous news!' she said.

'Already?' said the doctor. 'Who rang you?'

'Oh. . . Inspector someone or other,' Mrs Sinclair said. 'It wasn't her! It wasn't my Carolyn.' Helen had never seen her so giddy, not even at the Christmas parties when the sherry and the noise had everyone else fizzing like stomach powders.

'Mrs Sinclair,' she said. 'I don't know how to tell you how sorry I am—'

'Shush now, none of that! She must have been awfully like my girls for you to have made such a blunder. Don't give it a thought. And now I must get on with my packing.'

'Packing?' said the doctor.

'I'm going to see her. Carolyn. I'm going to London to stay with her. She has a little flat in Bayswater, with another couple of modern girls. And how I scolded! How I scorned! Well, all of that is done now.'

'But Mrs Sinclair,' Helen said. 'It's awful late and you've had a right night of it. You could sleep and go in the morning when it's easier driving.' She had caught a strong whiff of port on Mrs Sinclair's breath and shuddered to think of her setting off alone in the dark.

'I'm catching the sleeper! Heavens, I'm far too old to take off to London in a two-seater. Those days are long gone. But perhaps when I get there, I shall hire a little car and take Carolyn to Brighton, get both my girls together and have a holiday. Now, I really must go. I'm not half packed and the train leaves at midnight.'

Dr Deuchar grinned at Helen as they both climbed back into the motorcar. She couldn't grin back, although she saw that she should be happier now. It wasn't Carolyn Sinclair. It wasn't Edinburgh's problem. And if Maggie Dickson was as bad as Mr Pyne said, she maybe didn't deserve solemnity.

Sandy was out on the step with the door open behind him when Helen came along the cobbles ten minutes later, weaving from tiredness and half-wishing she could go home to Greet and the box bed, porridge on the range in the morning.

'You've been donkeys',' Sandy called. 'I thocht you'd run away and joined the fair.'

'You wouldnae believe where I *have* been,' Helen said, climbing the steps and sitting down beside him.

'You wouldnae believe what's gone on here either. More polis turned up. And two men in penguin suits. There was nine for a while. All standing roon the shelter door peering in at the poor soul. It was like they were watching a dog fight, Helen. The time they stood there.'

'That was two judges,' Helen said. 'One Glasgow, one here. They kent her. Seems like every polis in the country must have kent her. Pity they never had a good look before I went and said it was Miss Sinclair. Her poor mother's had the right run-around because of me, Sandy. I would kick myself if I could reach.'

'So it's not Miss Sinclair?'

'It's not.'

'Well, that's good, isn't it?'

'It is.' Still, Helen couldn't account for the way she felt. 'You might even say that the thought of losing a daughter has healed a rift.'

'More good news.'

'It is,' Helen said again. 'It's made me think I'll speak to my mammy the morn's morn anyway. Just listen to whatever she needs to say and then let it lie. Life's too short.'

'For that poor lass it was,' Sandy said. Then he put an arm across her back. 'But it's nocht to do with us, now she's gone.'

Helen turned it over in her mind a few times before answering. 'I don't agree,' she said in the end. 'You should have heard that Duncan Pyne, drawling out the window of his big car. "The notorious Maggie Dickson, scourge of the Gorbals," he said. He reckons she met the end she was asking for. So what I'm thinking is. . . it's hard to get it in just the right words, Sandy.'

'Have a try,' Sandy said.

'What I'm thinking is. . . we just missed her. Only just.'

'Who missed who?'

'Us. The service, the almoners, the doctors. I'm thinking, whatever turns a girl into a scourge and makes her notorious? Whatever starts her off to that end? That's exactly what I'm trying to stop happening.'

'But you d'ae even ken what it was she did or what happened in her life. You're adding two and two and getting five there, Nelly.'

'I d'ae ken *which* thing it was,' Helen said. 'But I'd bet you our straw bed and the mattress ticking it was *one* of the things I've got on my docket.'

102

Sandy said nothing for a while. Then he gave Helen a quick squeeze. 'Speaking of our straw bed, how about we put an end to this day?'

'Gladly! It's about the worst one I can remember.'

'We've still got a new hoose though,' Sandy said. 'And each other.'

Helen bit her lip and counted to ten. 'We have at that,' she said at last. 'Ach, I'm just tired. And I've not had a bite.'

'I've kept you a fish and took the batter off so it's not gone greasy. There's a roll too. And I got doughnuts for the morning.'

'Doughnuts and a swallow out the tap,' Helen said. 'I'll get out on my dinner and get us a kettle, at least.'

'It'll all look bright again in the morning,' Sandy said.

As Helen lay beside him on the ticking thrown over the hay and listened to the rain that came sweeping in, she hoped he was right. She needed to turn her face to the future, like Dr Strasser had been saying all day. She shouldn't let the dead girl haunt her, even if she knew that, from now on, she'd always be working, at least partways, in Maggie Dickson's memory, in honour of her name.

She started to turn on her side then realised the rustling straw would wake Sandy, so instead she bunched her jersey up to make a more comfortable pillow and tried to reassure herself. The shelter door was still open. Perhaps that rainwater would sluice in and wash away the dust of the girl's feet and the air of her last breath. Perhaps the grass would spring back up and the footprints of all those coppers would be gone. And perhaps if she was lucky the fresh damp dawn would brush away all the questions that were hounding her thoughts and continued to hound them long into the night as she stared at the black square of window and tried to let Sandy's easy breathing quiet her own.

Chapter 8

She was woken by the sunlight pouring in the bare window and lay cosy in the dent her body had made, like a spoon snug in a velvet slot inside a walnut box. Greet had a box like that, a set of spoons and servers that had come from her own mother and were marked for Helen. They hadn't been in the bundle Sandy lugged round here last night though. Maybe they were Teenie's now. The dignified thing would be to shrug it off, but as Helen lay there she remembered more and more that was rightly hers: a layette of snowy white blankets, edged with broad satin and done up in a ribbon, that sat on a high shelf on the big press, 'for when you've your own place, Nelly'; a creepie stool with a drawer in the end for tapers, that sat at one side of the range but which her Granny Downie had given to her, to Helen by name, when she'd come to spend her last years with them. And there should be a fat bag of remnants and other odds to go with the sewing machine. A bag she had made herself from a camelhair coat when the cuffs and collar were worn but the back and two fronts were still as plush as ever. She had wound brown wool round embroidery hoops to make a handle and was proud of it.

'You've woken me up breathing like a bull,' came Sandy's groggy voice. 'What's to do? Is it still aboot last night?'

Helen propped herself up on her elbows. When you weren't lying flat you could feel the floorboards through the straw. 'I'm lying here thinking on all the bits my mammy never put in that bundle.'

'To bring you back round,' Sandy said. He'd lived long enough with Greet to learn her ways.

'Fine and sure I'll be back round! I'm not spending good money to buy blankets and spoons and a creepie when I've already got them. There's enough to get anyway.'

Sandy was rolling away, onto his knees and then up onto his feet. He looked as if the night had left his back stiff. 'She knows you,' he said. 'That bale of blankets is like cheese in a mouse-trap.'

Helen got up too then and tried a laugh. 'I'm away to have a wash,' she said. Nothing could kill the pleasure of padding through in bare feet to her own clean white bathroom and running cold water into her own clean basin, without a wipe-round in case some clart had been in there last. By tonight it would be hot water, if they could get the range lit and running. If they could get a quick delivery or a borrow of some coal. She dried her face and went back to the kitchen, where her hairbrush and pins were set on the mantelpiece.

'You'd think this place would feel bad,' she said as she scraped her hair up. 'A fever hospital, doonstairs empty and rotten, then after last night and that poor soul, it should be. . . I d'ae ken the word. But it's not.'

'Oppressive,' Sandy said.

'Aye, it should be. No' cheery like it is.'

'We'll make it oppressive if you're dead set.' Sandy caught her round her waist and kissed her cheek. 'We can put velvet curtains up and paper blinds. An aspidistra in a brass pot at every window and thon stuff on the tables. What's it called?'

'Chenille.' Helen was giggling. He had described exactly Greet's big room, where their box bed had been. 'I'm only getting paper blinds if we can set them halfway down. Keep the sun off.'

'Keep the aspidistra half deid.'

They were still smiling when they parted ways at the gate, Helen to stretch the rope across the green and air the buckram before she could make a proper bed that night, Sandy to the depot to pick up his cart and start another day. He kissed her cheek again and Helen flicked a glance to the hedge that set their garden off from the next one down. If a neighbour was looking they'd see a nice young couple who'd not been beaten down by the sad start. But no one was looking, not from the upstairs anyway. And the hedge was too high for the down-stairs to see over.

Helen turned away and tugged the rope to make sure it was taut. It twanged when she plucked it; the poles must be good and firm, not like the cleats set into brick in the back green at Grove Place, overworked and always threatening to let go like bad teeth, sending a wash trailing in the glaur. For some reason to do with the rules of childhood – not so different from the rules of the high seas that let pirates flourish – whenever a set of sheets and shirts hit the ground they were fair game. Weans would swarm and make forts, until some woman finally looked out a window in the stair and saw what they were up to.

Helen eyed the Anderson shelter. Sometimes she envied them as could have lit a candle in the dark and said a prayer, making it all better. All she had was a plan to keep a bogey and a lawnmower stowed where that poor girl had breathed her last.

'I'm sorry,' she said, laying her hand briefly on the weath-ered panels of the door. 'I promise you I'll never let another lassie end this way if I can help it.' Then she turned away. For Maggie and every other girl like her, for those two at Torphichen Street last night, and for that pert miss yesterday morning in her working clothes and her party manners, Helen had a job to do.

A noble calling, Mrs Sinclair used to say, before her nose got put out of joint. But if it was noble for her, volunteering, it was still noble for Helen drawing a wage. She nodded firmly.

It wasn't her job that filled her head as she headed for the crescent, though. A table, two chairs. A bedstead. Shelf paper.

A kettle. A big pot with a thick bottom. She would go to the Bread Street junk shop on her dinner and see what she could pick up. Or should she try Greet first, see if things had thawed out there and her mother was in a sharing mood?

She stopped, almost tripping over her feet. As if she'd summoned her like a godmother in a fairytale, Greet stood at the foot of the surgery steps, and her mood might as well have been written on a banner waving above her. She was angry and scared and annoyed and defiant and determined. Angry that she'd been outwitted, that her ploy of putting Helen's traps out on the stair hadn't brought her daughter to heel. And scared about where the two of them might have spent the night, or rather what they would have said to whoever had taken them in. Annoyed with herself for giving in and coming here to wait, defiant still about the fight she'd started, and determined to triumph somehow.

'Mither,' Helen said, walking up and surprising Greet, who'd been looking the other way.

Greet turned. Her eyes were wet and her cheeks white. It took three ragged breaths for her to recover enough to speak. 'Where did you spend the nicht?' she said. 'Where did Sandy go? Do you even care? You were baith seen, let me tell you.'

'Had your spies oot, eh?' Helen said. 'Well, tell them to look a bit closer next time if they've left you with questions.' She expected a sneer or even a slap for being cheeky. Odd, she thought, that Greet seemed to be pleased.

'You were seen in his car,' she said. 'After dark. Your Auntie Linda's old neighbour saw you. Everything you told me about this "arrangement" put to the lie on the very first day! Everything I knew was true, *coming* true! And poor Sandy walking the streets with a cart, hawking junk. I never thought—'

'Mrs Sinclair's,' Helen said. 'That's where we were going, if we were seen from Auntie Linda's old stair. Or coming back. I was at the Torphichen Street polis as well and through the

Grassmarket to the Cowgate, but only to the mortuary, and I wasn't home till after ten.'

'You weren't home at all,' Greet said. 'You're not telling me Teenie let you in, are you? She would never.' Then her brain caught up with her ears. 'Polis station? Mortuary?' And her face paled to the colour of a candle.

'Not *your* home, Mammy,' Helen said. '*My* home. Sandy's and mine. We got moved in but we're right roughing it, so I'll be round tonight for my blankets and spoons and the creepie and my scraps bag. And I'll have a look through the big press and just remind myself what else I've got stored away there.' Member early on, when we were saying "over by Christmas", you and me put all sorts on that high shelf for Sandy coming back and us getting set up. So I'll see you tonight. I'll not expect my tea. But once you've got your face straightened, maybe you and my daddy and Teen could come to me on a Tuesday and we could come to you on a Thursday. See the aunties. That would be nice.'

Greet's mind was a long way off from any of that. 'Mortuary?' she said again. 'Police? Oh, Nelly. And running around in a car with another man and Sandy walking the streets, hawking—'

'Sandy was hawking nothing,' Helen said. 'He went to get something to sleep on. We've a hoose, Mammy, but it's as empty as a scraped stall the day after the market. So we lay on straw.'

'Shoosh,' Greet said, looking up and down the street, as if straw hadn't been good enough for the baby Jesus. 'Who's renting a hoose, on a Monday night, without a scrap of a mattress? You've no need to be hiding away in a fleapit, Helen. You've a good home.'

'Mammy, you put my traps out on the stair,' Helen said. 'Or some of them anyway.' She pushed her cuff back and glanced at her watch. 'Like I was saying, I'll be round later for the rest of it. Now, I'm late for my work and you're that late you'll be getting docked. So I'll see you later. On you go.'

She trotted up the steps and in the door, leaving Greet standing with her mouth open.

'Good morning, Helen. How are you?' Dr Strasser was padding downstairs, knotting his tie although he still wore his slippers. His smoking slippers, he called them. He had what he called bedroom slippers too. Helen had learned not to laugh at his ways, since he didn't find himself funny and didn't take kindly to *her* smirks.

'Raring to go, Doc,' Helen said.

'That is excellent news. None the worse for yesterday evening?'

Helen shrugged. She wouldn't go that far.

'Deuchar told me all about it, of course,' he went on. 'A terrible thing. As if we lacked evidence of how much all this is needed. How much *you're* needed.'

'That's exactly what I—' Helen began, then changed tack. 'And you, Doc. Needed, I mean.'

'Hm,' he said. 'My father was a great comfort and solace to... lost souls. And I've always tried to carry on his work in the face of ignorance and opposition. But you, Helen, are what they've been missing.'

'It's the minister takes care of souls,' Helen said, loathing the tremor in her voice but unable not to quake a little at the size of the task when he put it that way.

'Hm,' said Dr Strasser again. 'Is that really what you think? Because you don't need to mouth piety to me of all people.' Helen said nothing, lost again, the way that Dr Strasser often lost her. 'Today,' he went on, when he'd given up hopes of an answer, 'you'll be stepping in for Mrs Sinclair since she's been called away.' He smiled at her surprise. 'Ten o'clock at the Lochrin Nursery, addressing young mothers on childhood nutrition.'

'Right,' she said, grabbing onto this task instead of the bewildering conversation.

'You could do it in your sleep. Take pamphlets and remind them the milk's clean. They'll adore you.'

Adore me, she thought, running downstairs to her office. That was a smoking slippers kind of a word and no mistake. Then she sat down at her desk and to gather her thoughts. She'd heard Mrs Sinclair give this talk a dozen times. The last few times she'd been thinking what she would say instead. Now was her chance.

She took a sheet of paper and made it into a grid, then printed carefully at the top in block letters: I AM AWAY FROM MY OFFICE THIS MORNING. SIGN UP FOR A SLOT AND COME BACK THIS AFTERNOON OR TOMORROW. IF IT IS URGENT TELL THE DOCTOR WHO REFERRED YOU. She tacked it firmly to the outside of her door, added a pencil on a string and locked herself in to get some peace while she made her preparations.

Clean milk, she wrote on a fresh sheet of paper. *Tuberculin testing now nationwide.*

Orange juice. She underlined it three times. Mrs Sinclair had never been clear enough about the orange juice. It was ideal if mother's milk was thin from a bad diet, but she'd caused no end of confusion and a fair few sore wee tummies. *You* drink the orange juice and all the goodness will filter through, Helen planned to tell them.

Sunshine, she wrote, with more underlining. *It's free and it's full of goodness.*

Should she try and get them off rosehip syrup and back onto fruit again now it was easier to find?

Rosehip syrup, she wrote. *Still worthwhile if the bairns are used to taking it.*

Prunes, liver, malt, greens.

Helen's head was a whirlpool of Woolton menus, ministry slogans and hedgerow jam recipes. Mrs Sinclair had been right gung-ho for sending families out along the hedgerows but she was adamant they should bring the harvest home. *Let the bairns eat the brambles*, Helen wrote. She'd never manage to persuade Mrs Sinclair that scoffing the berries as you picked them straight off the briar was better than handing them over all squashed and rotting then using up your sugar ration to make them edible, but she was in charge now.

Skim the fat off the stew. That was another Sinclair special, and it made sense for a woman in her fifties, fighting with the tape measure, but not for growing weans running about the back courts all day, just one burnt pot from going to bed hungry. *Skim the fat off the stew*, Helen wrote, *if it's tasty enough without. But use the fat to fry bread at breakfast-time.*

Scores settled, she tapped her pencil against her cheek with her mouth open. What would they want to hear? Not 'If they won't eat it, serve it up again next time'. One of the Callan boys had got a bad case of dysentery from a stand-off over a mound of boiled beetroot tops that appeared morning, noon and night until he gave in and swallowed them, slimy, mouldy and only fit for the midden. *If they won't eat it*, Helen wrote, *all the more for the rest of you and they'll have a sharper appetite for the next mealtime.*

Pepper covers the taste of burnt meat.

A whole peeled potato fixes over-salting and is good to eat after.

Pastry over wet fruit and under dry. Then she crossed it out. It was true. It was one of Greet's rules. But she'd look a fool if anyone asked her why, for she had no idea.

She took a stack of vitamin pamphlets from her shelf, and stowed them in her satchel. Maybe she would go round by the Store fruiterer and get some fresh bits to lay out on the table, hand then out to the mothers that asked the best questions. If anyone at all asked *any* questions. If they didn't all sit there with their arms folded and stare at her. Or whisper. She hoped there was no one she'd been at school with.

'Doc?' she said, putting her head round Dr Strasser's door. 'Have I got a budget?'

He had been sitting staring out of the window into the garden. The high blue of the early morning was gone and the day had turned, a heavy sky threatening more rain by lunchtime and a tang in the air that spoke of thunder even. When he looked round at her, his face was drawn and so pale in patches he might just have been struck.

'Sorry?' he said.

'I was thinking I might buy some cabbage and apples to… illustrate my talk.' Helen still felt daft when she trotted out the words she'd learned in her classes. 'And maybe I would give them out at the end…' Dr Strasser was facing her now but seemed to be staring right through her. 'Are you all right?' she said.

'Just ghosts,' said Dr Strasser, which was rich. He'd never fought a day of the war, nor even had to see the dead girl yesterday. What ghosts haunted *him*, Helen would love to know. Then, 'Budget!' he said, snapping back as if slapped. 'Yes, yes, why not? Ask Miss Anderson to let you have some petty. . . oh.' He rubbed his jaw with a finger. 'It's going to take a bit of getting used to, isn't it? Here.' He had drawn his wallet from his jacket pocket and plucked out a ten-shilling note.

'I'll write you a receipt,' Helen said. 'Only, I really did want to know if there's a proper budget, else I don't know where to pay you back from. Do you see?'

'Call it quits,' said Dr Strasser. 'Call it a bonus, a tip. Don't worry about it.'

Call it a copper-bottomed kettle, Helen thought, as she skipped down the steps half an hour later. Or a feather bolster or that aluminium dustpan and stiff-bristled brush she'd seen hanging in the ironmonger's window.

But she wasn't that type of girl. She bought a punnet of raspberries, a bag of new apples and a red summer cabbage from a barrow lowering the tone outside the Palais de Danse and had enough left to hand in at Fleming's accounts desk, square away the ticking and keep them on her right side. She would try her best with Greet tonight, but there was still plenty needed and nowhere better to get it.

The young mothers were everything she had dreaded. Seventeen women, with prams and pushchairs and older weans tagging along, were sitting, smoking and knitting, in the bentwood chairs in the wee nursery drill hall. Most of them seemed to know each other and had plenty to murmur about from the corners of their mouths as Helen set out her stall on the trestle table along the front. At least none of them looked all that familiar. In fact, with a flush of unwelcome realisation, it struck Helen that they were a good bit younger than her. She shoved the thought out of her mind and turned to them with a bit of a smile, but not too much of one. Mrs Sinclair had always said it was more important to be heeded than liked when you were telling people things they might not want to hear.

'Good morning,' she said. 'My name is Mrs Crowther and I'm the medical almoner at the Gardner's Crescent surgery. I'm here to talk to you about food and health for you and your babies.'

'Here and I thought Edinburgh was meant to be pan-loaf and toffee-nosed!' It was a mountainous woman, none too clean, who lay sprawled over two chairs, with a baby of about a year lolling and drowsing under an enormous pregnant belly. Her voice was like the bark of a sea lion, and the tune of it – the sing-song of the west coast – made Helen remember that mermaids and sea lions were cousins, supposedly.

'Are you new here?' Helen said, with a smile for the woman.

'Aye. I'm Gorbals since they poured the foundations. Only *he's* got work at the basin yards. So I'm in exile.'

'Ocht, it's not so bad,' Helen said. 'Exile' had set the others bristling. 'I'm Fountainbridge born and bred, Tollcross Primary School and Caledonian Baths. You'll soon get used to us.'

She should have been a politician. As soon as she claimed these streets as her own, the Edinburgh girls started smiling and turned all their scorn on Glasgow.

'And I can give you some news from the Gorbals, as it goes,' Helen said. 'It'll not be in the papers yet, but I heard it last night. In return, you could answer a question.'

'Are they clearing the sites?' the woman said. 'My wee-est sister got a septic leg from playing in they bombsites and it was all still lying when *I* left.'

'It's about Maggie Dickson,' said Helen. 'The "notorious" Maggie Dickson, you know. She died last night. And I'd like to make sure her family – if she's got a family – have been told. Whatever she did no one should learn that on the radio or in a paper.'

The fat woman was frowning. She waved a hand back and forth in front of her face – from the straining and reddening, Helen guessed that the toddler draped over her breast had filled his nappy. 'Who?' she said. 'Who's Maggie Dickson in her curlers?'

'Oh,' said Helen. 'Well, never mind. Maybe it was Govan.' Or maybe, she thought, Dickson was so far underground, such a shadowy character, so very lost, that a normal girl like this one, married and decent if a bit grubby, knew nothing of her world. 'Anyway, we're here to talk about sunnier things this morning. Health and happiness without bursting your purse! Yes, happiness,' she said at their look. 'Because feeding your family and sitting down to share food together is at the heart of family life, like breaking bread in church.' She was parroting Mrs Sinclair. She couldn't help it. She held up a cabbage in one hand like an actor with a skull, making them all titter. 'Guess how much I just paid for this?'

When all the pamphlets had been handed out, and the apples too, and each of them had had a raspberry and agreed they were better than barley sugars – 'not that a sweetie dissolved in hot water is a bad thing. It can settle a stomach quicker than bicarb' – Helen dismissed her class. They trailed out, pushing their prams and dragging their toddlers, but the large Glasgow woman came to the front. She really was filthy when you saw her close up and caught a whiff of her. Her ankles were swollen and dark, too, and Helen couldn't help herself.

'Are you getting a chance to lie with your feet up at all?' she said.

'Aye, aye,' the woman said. 'Leastways I sit on my step with them stretched straicht oot. I'm better on my step with a bit of company, than lying on my lone upstairs. Never mind that my stair's full of snobs.'

'Well, above your head ideally,' Helen said. 'Are they not uncomfortable as tight as that?'

'Uncomfy? Aye, like my piles and my veins and these too.' She slapped her prodigious bosom, making it shake, then hefted herself around under her dress until she was settled again. 'He's still dragging at me unless I'm quick,' she said, jerking a thumb at the toddler, who had fallen asleep during the talk and was now draped over the mound of her stomach like a sheet over a budgie cage. His nappy was turning the air thick and yellow-smelling.

'What is it you would like to ask?' Helen said. 'It goes without saying, it's in confidence. And any way I can help I will.'

'It was that name,' she said. 'It's went out my head already. Only, *he's* a Govan man – on the docks till his back went – and he'll know her. A madam, was she?'

Helen hesitated. The girl had looked far too young to be a brothel-keeper and the startling likeness to the Sinclair girls got in the way of the notion too. Besides, wouldn't she be pretty small beer in a city the size of Glasgow? Those two girls at the Torphichen Street station last night had sat there as if they were waiting for a late bus, no urgency about whatever fate was ahead of them. The desk sergeant barely looked the road they were on. Maggie Dickson, the scourge of the Gorbals – or Govan – must be something much worse than that.

'I'm not sure what Maggie Dickson was,' Helen said. Someone whose life had taken her far from ordinary folk, she was thinking. So far that she had decided to come and die in a treatment gown, in the garden hut of a shut fever hospital in a different city. It made no sense, but then real life didn't have to make sense.

Helen smiled at the woman, still waiting, standing planted four-square in front of her. 'Would you like to get his nappy changed here before you go home?' she said. 'If you've got one with you. He'll be more comfortable.'

'Cheers,' the woman said, holding the wean out with hands under his oxters. He was deeply asleep and hung like wet washing on laundry tongs. 'And ta for the bit gossip to serve him with his tea.' Her face clouded suddenly, lips and eyelids both suggesting that tears were close for some reason. Kindness, Helen reminded herself, is for everyone.

Dr Deuchar came upon her when she was scrubbing her arms in the wee place under the stairs. 'That looks determined,' he said.

'I'll need to go out on a visit,' Helen said. 'I just peeled a nappy off a wee boy of eighteen months and near about boaked. But they're new in their house and *it* can't be that bad yet. I want to nip it in the bud. Soon. Before she has the next one.' Dr Deuchar said nothing. 'Right, Doc? I don't need to get her in to see you to get referred to see me, do I? I can just. . .'

'Take a shortcut over the allotments,' said Dr Deuchar. 'Oh, absolutely, and I applaud your initiative.'

'Thank you,' Helen said. Now all she had to do was decipher the pencilled names on the sheet she had handed round the chairs and work out which one was which. 'Did you want me for anything?' she said. 'I was going to take an early dinner and do a bit of shopping for the new place. It's still making me smile every time I remember.'

'That's what I came to tell you,' he said. 'The Strassers have all manner of bits and bobs upstairs, never used and never will be. And Dr Strasser thought you might like first refusal. We could drop some of it round and you can keep it if it suits, or put it out for the rag and bone man if not. We need the space in the attic, you see. For old files.'

'Files?'

'Rubbish really. Nothing surgical, nothing current, nothing worth sending to Johnston Terrace. I took far too many notes when I was wet behind the ears and didn't know better. Still can't quite bring myself to put it all in the ashcan.'

'Well, that's very kind of you,' Helen said. 'We'd be grateful for anything Doc Strasser can spare. But not family heirlooms. And not a sewing machine, for I've got one of them.' She bit her lip in case she was hoping for too much. Maybe he meant old blankets and the like.

'Good girl.' It was something Dr Deuchar did tend to say at odd times, often leaving Helen wondering what exactly she had done to deserve it.

'And I can go through those old files for you sometime when it all settles down,' she said.

'Oho! You think this is just an opening flurry, do you? You think it'll all settle down and give you spare time?'

'Or I could do it at night. It won't be hard. We got it dinned into us what to send and what to burn. I was that scared of missing something I've near got it memorised.'

'No need for a nightshift!' said Dr Deuchar. 'There's no rush.'

'I'd be glad to! I'd take a guilty pleasure in finding some sort of miscellaneous paper they haven't foreseen. It would be revenge for sitting there all those nights in that draughty hall, choking on the paraffin and trying to stay awake.'

Dr Deuchar smiled at her. 'You really did put in the time for this new posting, Helen. Didn't you? I don't know how anyone could query my decision to employ you. Well, well. Let me ask Strasser and get back to you on that one.'

Despite the hot water still in the basin sending plumes of steam up to fog her hair and melt her waves, Helen felt a coldness creep over her as the doctor went on his way. She nearly called him back to tell him on no account ask Dr Strasser anything and please tell him she didn't want his cast-offs either. In case the anyone who was doing this 'querying' was Dr Strasser himself. For Dr Deuchar had definitely said 'my decision to employ you'. Not 'ours'. Definitely.

Chapter 9

The smell was different. When Helen put her key in the door at the back of five that afternoon, that newly cleaned and disinfected smell was overlaid with something dustier and more homely. There was a carpet rolled up and tied with string, sitting half in and half out of the big room door. That would account for it. But when she stepped over the roll and walked into the room, she saw a table and four chairs, old-fashioned things and all the varnish worn off round the feet from someone mopping the floor and not moving them. As well, there were two Rexine-covered chairs with long wooden arms sitting side-by-side under the window, ready for her and Sandy to place by the fire and then sink into.

A packet of dried-out paper tied up with some string that smelled about rotted through broke open at her touch and revealed a bale of curtains. Not the brown velvet Sandy had joked about but pale things with big roses on them and a sheen to their surface when you turned them in the light. They looked like bedroom curtains from forty years ago, but they were lined and interlined and still had good brass hooks in the tapes. Helen shook one out and held it up, gauging the length against her nice tall window. It trailed on the ground. She could make pelmets. Or cushions. And there were three more pairs in the parcel. Strange curtains for a kitchen, but maybe she could dye them plain. In the bath, with nobody in the wash house to say peep if it didn't work. For there was nothing the Grove Place women liked better than to watch a neighbour try her hand at dyeing and fail. She had seen it many times.

She carried one of the folded curtains through to the kitchen to check the length and stopped dead in her tracks. Five tea chests sat in the middle of the room, with their tops tacked down. Were these the records? Had Dr Deuchar maybe misunderstood her and brought five chests of old files round here for her to go through? She tried to wiggle her fingers under the edge of a lid, but the tack heads were pounded in hard and she could feel her nails bending. When Sandy got back he could—

She heard him open the door as she had the thought.

'What's this?' came his voice. 'How much has all this cost then?'

'Nocht,' Helen said. 'They're having a clear-out at the surgery and we got first refusal.'

Sandy was crouching at the rolled carpet, turning back one corner. 'This is good wool, Helen,' he said. 'Look. Knots. Nae glue. This would have been dear when it was new.'

'Funny colour,' Helen said. It was green and orange and looked like frogs, but he was right about the quality. 'And when I say "nocht" that's not quite right. We've got to give houseroom to five chests of papers for me to sort through. See if you can't get the lid off them with your knife, eh? I'm crossing my fingers they're in they banker's boxes, and maybe not so many as all that. If it's solid paper, that's the rest of my year.'

'I'll help,' Sandy said. 'For that carpet under my toes at the end of a long day.'

Helen smiled as Sandy reached his knife out of his pocket, unfolded it and set about the nearest chest. This was what she thought it would be like when she had borrowed Mary Lowe's wedding dress and taken her vows. The two of them against the world, working hard and getting on. The squeak of tacks giving up drew her attention back and Sandy lifted off the lid, stepping back sharply with a 'Faugh!' of disgust. He put his hand up and over his nose and then threw his knife down on another case and reeled away to let up the sash and stick his head out into the fresh air.

Helen felt her legs turn to rubber. What was it? What had he seen nailed down in a case and right here in the kitchen? She stepped closer and peered. It wasn't. . . anything. Of course not. It was napkins and tablecloths and, under them, was no more than a set of china.

'Sandy,' she said. 'It's fine. Look at this!' She started lifting the pieces out. Blue and white dinner plates, soup plates, wee bowls, tea plates and then, after a thick layer of straw and some more tablecloths folded into pads, there were glasses too.

'Sandy, *look* at all this!' she said. 'It's not the bill for the carpet at all. It's more. It's china and glass and linen and – oh my goodness – a willow-pattern teapot. I've always wanted a willow-pattern teapot. I'll keep it on the mantel for best. And a sugar bowl with a lid! Sandy! What's wrong with you?'

'I cannae stand the smell,' he said. He was bent right over the sink with his head and shoulders outside. 'It's the mothballs, Nelly. I cannae bear it.'

'Have you baccy?' Helen said. 'Light a fag. You need to *see* this.'

But Sandy took a huge breath and then sprinted across the room, along the hall and out the door. Helen went to the front window and watched him sink down on the top step of the outside staircase. She weighed his knife in her hands and swithered between going to comfort him and prising up the rest of the lids to see what more treasure lay in store.

In the end, she went halfway. Sidling out beside him, she said, 'I'll open them up and find the mothballs.' 'I'll chuck them out the back window. Nae downstairs neighbours to mump about it.'

Sandy managed a smile. 'They put them in the Red Cross parcels,' he said, 'if they were sending socks or jerseys.'

'I didn't know you minded them.'

'I didn't. Until one bad winter when we thought we might get a heat off the things if we burnt them in the stove. I can't even tell you what it was like. I thought we were poisoned. I thought we'd all dee of it if we kept the doors shut, and perish from cold if we opened up to clear the air.'

'You burned mothballs?' Helen said. 'Scootery wee things like mothballs? How many did you have to make it worth a fire of them?'

'Six,' Sandy said. 'But nothing else.'

She sat beside him a while looking at the last of the sunshine before moving.

It was only a minute to Caledonian Place if you were a crow, but the railway line cut it off so completely that it might as well have been an entirely different bit of the city, one of those places that always startled Helen if she found herself there after a bus or tram had picked her up and set her down again. The sun in the wrong place and pale light off the river, or a view of hills instead of the works.

Had she ever been on Cally Place before? It wasn't an obvious route to the baths and she reckoned she'd only ever passed the street end. Greet had once sold a mangle to someone near here, years back when they moved out of Freer Street and into where they were now, with its well-appointed wash house, but Helen's only memory of that night was bumping the monster up two flights of steps and checking out each landing window that none of the wee boys playing peevers had taken a fancy to the pram. This didn't look like the kind of street where you'd worry about a pram vanishing. The tenements were flat-fronted, same as Grove Place with no bay windows for the tenants to be proud of, but they were set back behind wee stone walls, a foot high, still dotted along their tops with the stumps of the railings sawn off and taken for the war. In between the railing stubs and the downstairs windows lay four feet of garden, obviously out of bounds to the weans, for there was grass here and earth, flowers even. Helen passed a rosebush that took up the whole expanse of one garden and hung over the pavement. It was going over, its blooms browning and nodding, but its scent still filled the air.

The McIrnies lived in one of these ground-floor houses, their two windows giving onto a strip of grass as manicured as a bowling green and edged with monstrous waxy mounds, looking more like fungus than plants and sticky with insects. Helen let herself into the stair and knocked at the door.

'It's yourself!' Mrs McIrnie sang out as she opened up, then she reached behind her and grabbed the arm of a young woman who had come to have a nose at what visitor might be calling. 'We're away to the wash house. In you go. In you go.'

'Mammy, what—?' Helen heard, as the door was pulled sharply shut. She stood in the wee lobby, breathing in traces of mackerel left over from their tea, wondering how to begin. She couldn't even remember his whole name.

'Sir?' she called out at last and heard a scrape of chair legs as he reacted to the surprise – and who could blame him? – of a stranger in the house when he thought he was alone. The door right opposite opened and three feet away stood a young man in his vest with his braces dangling. His feet were bare, long and yellow with purple patches on either side from boots that didn't quite fit.

'Who are you?' he said. He wriggled himself back into his braces and cast a glance behind. His shirt must be nearby.

'Don't worry about that, Mr. . . Stanley, isn't it?' Helen said. 'You've had a hard day and you're needing to sit back now. It's been hot, hasn't it?'

'Who *are* you? My wife and her mammy are at the copper.'

Helen said her name and held out a hand to shake. He stared at it a moment but, when he took it in his, he had a ready enough smile and a polite nod. He stepped back and ushered her into the kitchen.

The mackerel was stronger in here and Helen took a seat next to the open window. 'Now then,' she said. 'We've never met and we never have to meet again so we could just decide not to be bashful.' She beamed at him but felt no surprise when she was met with a frown.

'Is it Bibles, is it?' he said.

'I'm not after you to sign the pledge, no,' Helen said. 'I'm from the Gardner's Crescent surgery. I work with Dr Deuchar and Dr Strasser. Are they your doctors?'

'Me?' the man said. 'I'm no' needing a doctor. I never ail, me.'

'That's good. You can still sign on with one, though. For the new service. Have you been keeping up with the literature?'

'What are you on about? What service is this?'

Helen managed not to let her astonishment show. She had been steeped in it, stewing in it like a pudding, since before Christmas. How could anyone in this city – in this country – not have heard what was changing?

'And the reason I'm here is that your wife is worried and so is her mother,' Helen said. 'And I'd like to encourage you to come for a check-up. Absolutely free of charge, of course. You're with the railways, right?'

He nodded. 'Goods yard.'

'So you'll have seen the stamp for the insurance and by Thursday night you'll see it off your pay packet too. You might as well get the benefit, eh?'

'A check-up?' he said.

'Your wife is worried,' Helen said again. It was all very well to announce that they wouldn't be bashful. It was quite another thing to say what she'd come to say. 'She's looking forward to a baby, you know. Well, I'm sure you do know. And I'm sure you are too.'

'Betty is?' He blinked and then beamed. 'Is she? Is she really? She's never said. But how come it's you sharing the news? And how come you're after *me* to get a check-up? Should it no' be her that's getting checked if she's that way?'

'Oh!' said Helen. 'No! I'm sorry. I've said it wrong. It's absolutely the opposite of that. I've said it all back to front. She's not. . . expecting. She's *hoping*. She's yearning and she's unhappy that it never seems to happen. So she's asked me to have a wee word and get you in to be checked over.'

The man sat back – flump! – against his chair, making it creak. 'You want to check me over to see if I'm not right?' he said. He was swarthy-skinned and that complexion could usually hide a blush but this was probably the blush of his life and it turned him the kind of purple that Helen had only seen on an old, old man with a bad heart.

'If necessary,' she said. Of course her own treacherous complexion had turned on her and she was beeling as shiny and red as a new gobstopper. 'But the first step is to ask a few questions. I believe you were in the Navy? Did you have any worrisome times while you were away?' It was Mrs Sinclair's phrase and it covered a multitude.

'Worrisome times?' he said.

'Rashes or discomfort of any kind?'

'You're sitting there,' the man said. He was forward again, with both hands clamped on his knees, and his bare toes were gripping the lino under his feet as if he wanted to make four fists instead of two. 'You're sitting there, a stranger off the street, asking me if I've had a dose of the clap and brought it home and passed it on to my wife and spoiled her life for her?'

Helen took a deep breath and nodded. 'I don't say it to be offensive—'

He cut her off. 'Go on and tell what you'd say to be offensive then!' Helen let a shaky breath go as she realised he was laughing. 'No, Mrs whoever you are from whatever it is service, no bit of me got painted with sulphur while I was off fighting for King and Country.'

'Sulphanamide powder is taken internally,' Helen said. 'Not painted on. You ingest it.'

'I wouldn't know,' he said.

'Left untreated—' she tried, but he held up a hand.

'Listen, you're barking up the wrong tree. I went to the church to wed my Betty as innocent as a newborn babe. And I'm fond of her. We walked out from when we were bairns. So I wasn't gonny queer the pitch from the off, kicking up a fuss about what didn't concern me. But I'll tell you this. She knew more than me when we went over to Kinghorn for our week at the seaside. You get my drift? She knew a gey sight more than me. And she'd forgotten that she shouldnae. She never even hid it.'

Helen was transfixed. She believed him. The fondness and the gruffness over shame in his voice were unmistakable. But then why would the girl turn to her mother with an act of innocence? Or had her mother misunderstood? Was Mrs McIrnie maybe learning the truth right now in the dim of the wash house? Helen put her head in her hands and let out a soft groan.

Then she raised it. 'But *you're* fine?' she said. 'No symptoms? And you're having a normal married life?'

'Till tonight!' said the man, making her laugh in spite of everything.

'Well then whatever happened in the wartime, she came through it,' Helen said. 'It's not the sort of thing you can keep to yourself.'

'And this is your job, is it?' he said. 'Going round nebbing into beds and underdrawers.'

'No!' Helen said. 'At least, I bloomin' hope not. It better no' be.'

So it was that they were laughing together when the two women let themselves back in.

'Betty?' Helen said. 'Can I have a quick word? Why don't you and I take a wee toddle to the road end and back. Bit of air.'

'Aye, that mackerel's awfy,' Betty said. 'And I want to have a wee "word" with you too. Eh I do, Mammy?'

126

Whatever had passed between mother and daughter in the wash house had deflated Mrs McIrnie quite a bit. Her shoulders were rounded and she looked at the floor as she edged her bundle of damp sheets towards the fire and let the pulley down.

'See when we get our own place?' Betty said, as they left, 'I'm no' roasting fish on wash day. I love my maw and I wouldn't hear a word agin her but she's no' got the sense she was born with whether it's drying the fish stink into the linen or flying away to tell tales to you when nobody asked her.'

Helen said nothing, aware of all the open windows just feet from where they were passing on the pavement. They had reached the street end and turned along the main road, to make a circle of the walk, when she finally began.

'But everything's working right?' she said. 'No pain? No obstructions? Nothing unpleasant? And you're regular? Uh-huh? Well, see I think all you need to do is relax. Stop thinking about it. Let nature take its course.'

'Nature's taking its damn time,' Betty said.

'What do you work at? Is it active and healthy? If you're sitting all day you might need some exercise. Have you a bike? Or are you too proud to skip? Skipping's rare for staying fit. We none of us should ever have stopped it.'

'I'm at the Buttercup,' said Betty.

'Good,' said Helen. There was no sitting about in dairy work.

'And I am "relaxed". Why wouldn't I be? I used to worry every month that I'd get caught out, but I never did. And I've been relaxed ever since.'

Helen walked a good ten paces before she spoke again. The young man had hinted as much and here was Betty confirming it. It was delicate work, this. 'So you were experienced,' she said. 'Before he came home and you wed?'

They were away past the baths now onto a bit of street Helen didn't know at all, but she let Betty lead her up a lane and round a corner until they arrived at a high wall and a tall gate. 'Where are we?' she said.

'Back of the Orwell Street church,' Betty said, pushing on the gate and passing into the graveyard. 'I was never out of here in the wartime. Trying to get a bit of privacy. When they were all still at home and we had a lodger too, the house was fair heaving. I still come sometimes.'

'Because if you were experienced,' Helen said again. 'Maybe...'

Betty said nothing for a while, speaking volumes. 'Maybe I'm being punished for my sins?' was what she came out with in the end, as the gate clanged shut. 'Is that what you're saying? I suppose *you* were white as snow, were you? For six years?'

'We all got through it our own way,' Helen said at last, thinking back to herself then, knitting and praying, 'Please send him back, safe and sound.' That had been her first prayer. Then when Douglas Bader went back to France, waving in the newsreel, she started praying, 'Bring him back any way at all, God. Just bring him back.' And her prayer had been answered. Helen shook it all out of her head.

'Can I speak frankly?' she said. 'Did you ever have to... seek treatment?'

'That's what you call frank?' Betty said. 'I'd hate to hear you mincing. Sorry.' Helen waved it away. 'I've aye been the same. I scratch like a cat when I'm riled. Been the same from a bairn. Did I ever have to "seek treatment"? No. Never. Not for what you're insinuating. I had a spell of no' being well but I'm fine now.'

Helen let her breath go. She wouldn't have relished telling this girl she'd ruined her life for a fumble in some alley. A fumble right here in this graveyard probably. But if she'd got away with it and never needed to go skulking off to a clinic in a different bit of town, giving a false name, then there was no reason to connect then and now.

'I don't think God hands out punishments like that,' she said. 'Not any more. How could anyone still think it after what we've seen. It's the luck of the draw, I reckon.'

'Luck!' Betty said. 'Aye, I used to feel lucky. Getting away with it, like I said.' From habit she had led Helen to one of those graves like a low stone table – a coffee table, Mrs Sinclair called the one she had in her morning room – and now she sank onto it and shuffled back until she was propped against the railings around the next grave over.

Helen sat beside her, after a quick look round to see if anyone was there to witness their disrespect. 'Don't keep on like that,' she said. 'There's no "getting away with it" and "being punished". You're just taking a while to get started. Same as me. I've been wed more'n two years and there's no wee stranger in sight for me either.' She felt a twinge of conscience, but she told herself she was helping Betty. She ignored the voice telling her she was having a treat, acting like another wife in the same boat, awarding herself a break from her real life, like a cup of tea mid-shift or easing off her shoes under her desk on a hot day.

'Is that right?' Betty said, looking round with a new light in her eyes.

Helen smiled and kept up the chatter inside her head. She was doing her job. She was cheering Betty up. She was making the girl's life a wee bit brighter. 'What do you bet by Christmas, we'll both be out to here?' she said, pouching her hands out and rubbing the imaginary swell in front of her neat waist.

'I'll bet you the drawerful my maw's already knitted,' Betty said, 'against the drawerful your maw's already knitted. Am I right?'

Helen laughed and, for once, the thought of all those little bonnets and mittens, the matinee jackets in rose pink and the roll-collared cardies in powder blue didn't make her eyes fill. She was deep in the daydream where she and Betty had every reason to hope. 'So drink plenty milk in that dairy when you're on your dinner,' she said. 'Start putting cold cream on your stomach now and get a head start on they stretchmarks. And no more trips to this gravestone, eh?'

'Eh?' said Betty. 'How no'?'

'Ocht, fine if you're really coming just for some quiet,' Helen said. 'But no meeting anyone, right? The last thing you need is to fall and be wondering who—'

Betty scrambled to her feet. 'What are you saying about me?' she said. 'You think I hung around the streets and brought men *here*, do you?'

'I-'

'Little Miss Perfect. So nicey-nice to me, pretending we were pals and that's what you're really thinking?'. Betty had bent down and was spitting the words out. Helen drew her legs up and hugged her knees, feeling her eyes fill. 'Maybe *you'd* have waited under a lamp-post and lain on a grave with your skirt up, but some of us got to be more choosy.'

Then she turned and marched off back down the lane, seething with grievance from her tapping heels to her shaking curls.

She took the daydream with her, and left Helen back in reality. She stretched her legs out again and leaned against the railings. They dug in and she could feel the cold of them through her blouse and thin jacket. What a mess she'd made of that. Stanley laughing had made her bold and she'd breenged in with Betty where she should have tiptoed.

She had been telling herself she could have helped Maggie Dickson of the Gorbals if she'd been in time, had she? And there Betty McIrnie from the Buttercup Dairy had left her shaking!

What would Mrs Sinclair say? Helen drooped. For the first time since she'd been picked out for special treatment she'd let her patron down.

Then she tried to drive the thought away. She owed Mrs Sinclair a lot less than she once believed. The pair of them were evens.

That day in the flower room, when she was supposed to be wiping dry those bottles of ginger beer, she had stood frozen in horror as Fiona Sinclair went through her mother like a hot knife. Droplets of water dripped into the sink from the stone bottle she held, the plink sounding awfully loud and sure to bring one of them along here to see what was leaking. How could anyone talk to her own mammy that way and not get a skelp? That was all she thought there and then. Later she started to unpick the knots of meaning. 'Little sidekick'. 'Little tag-along'. That was *her*. Mrs Sinclair had taken her up to make a point to her daughters, not for Helen's benefit and not for the city, not for "The Poor". So they were quits.

And, Helen was the winner whichever way you sliced it. If she hadn't overheard Fiona that day and learned what Mrs Sinclair really thought of her, she mightn't have had the guts to stick up for herself now, take the job and *do* it. Pick herself up even when she got it wrong, like she just had with Betty.

She got up from the gravestone, brushed herself down and prepared for a long tramp home, going over and over the memory of that day in the flower room, partly to keep out the wicked thought of a lamp-post and a stranger that Betty had put into her head. But partly too because something about it was troubling her suddenly. There was a thorn in the memory, digging into her like a feather end poking through a pillowcase. Or a spike of straw through the buckram as it was last night. But not tonight, with all that bounty in the tea chests and no need to go wheedling round—

She stopped.

She'd forgotten, in all the excitement, that her and Sandy were meant to be at Grove Place for their tea. Oh, she'd pay for that when Greet got a hold of her! The prospect of the scolding to come drove the thorn, the feather, the spike of straw, clean out of her mind.

131

Chapter 10

'Where would I get Glasgow news?' Helen asked, when the shop bell brought a woman to the counter of Yarrow's on Earl Grey Street.

'The *Herald*,' the woman said, as if Helen had asked who the king was. But then she had a west coast twang to go with her smart turn-out and it maybe seemed unthinkable that a person wouldn't know the name of her city's paper. Right enough, Helen had never bought anything but the *Evening News* in her life.

'A *Herald* it is then,' she said, and handed over her tuppence.

'Are you moving through?' the woman asked. There was a bale of newspapers still in their string on the counter in front of her and she took up a pair of scissors but then leaned her elbows, settling in for a chat. Without waiting for an answer, she went on, 'You won't be sorry. I've been here ever since I fell in with my husband and agreed to follow him east but I miss the dear green place every day of my life.'

Helen knew there was another refugee from the beloved city not a quarter mile away, but the very thought of this neat woman and that sloven from yesterday being pals made her bite her cheeks not to smile.

'I'm not moving,' she said. 'I've a good job here.' Then she faltered. How could she explain it to this stranger when she didn't understand it herself? For all her resolve to face the future, like Dr Strasser was saying, she just *had* to know more about Maggie Dickson. Dr Deuchar had squashed her flat late the day before when she tried to winkle more details out of him. And truth be told she wasn't keen to offend him by pushing any harder. There was so much treasure in those tea chests – a set of clothes brushes on a mahogany paddle to hang in the hallway, ten sundae glasses like you'd get in an ice-cream emporium, only too shallow for a knickerbocker glory and the wrong shape for a banana split so maybe they were jelly glasses. There was a phonograph with a long-reaching horn like a nasturtium blossom and a leather box of crackly dance records. Sandy had put one on the night before when she got home and they'd made up the steps of a kiddy-on Charleston until their pounding feet made the needle screech over the wax and leave a score in it.

'I'm following a story,' she decided to say, in the end.

The woman behind the counter pushed her tongue up under her top lip and ran it along her teeth. Helen had always believed that vamps and starlets had a special ability and it was only when girls like her tried out that thick, dark-red lipstick that they had to keep checking it. But maybe she was wrong and this woman was forever looking in the mirror and licking her teeth all day every day. She finished the exploration with a loud smack. 'Following a story?' she said. 'Are you a. . . what are you?'

'Oh! Just out of interest,' Helen said. 'I'm not professionally involved in anyway. I'm an almoner.'

'A what?' said the woman. She looked affronted.

'A relieving officer, more or less,' Helen offered next. 'I work with the Gardner's Crescent doctors.' She waved vaguely towards the surgery. 'I help out with anything that's not medical. Or surgical.'

'Like a district nurse?' the woman said and, before Helen could answer, she turned and called over her shoulder. 'Robert! *Ro*-bert! Here's handy. There's a district nurse come in for a paper.'

'I'm not—' Helen said.

'We're expecting the patter of tiny feet,' the woman said, simpering a bit and patting her curls. She still wore her hair in two high rolls so her head looked like a gondola and what with the lipstick – such a deep red it showed as black in the dim light of the shop with its magazines pegged on strings in the window – she appeared too old, or at least too old to be coy about it and asking for advice.

'Congratulations,' Helen said. 'When is it due?'

'Any day now. Tomorrow maybe.'

Helen couldn't help but glance – the pile of newspapers hid the woman's middle. 'And you had a question?' she said.

'I've a hundred questions!'

A man had appeared at her back through a kind of stile formed from half walls off-set one to the other. 'And we can get to the library and answer them all,' he said. 'There's no need to be blabbing our business over the counter instead of getting on with your work.'

Helen had smiled at him but now she felt her face falling. What a way to talk to your wife in front of a customer and im-agine making her work when she was days, or maybe hours, away from her confinement. 'Don't worry about me,' she said. 'I was just saying I'm from the Gardner's Crescent surgery.' He reared back at that as if the news was displeasing to him. She pressed on. 'I'm surprised you're not a patient there. We must be the closest. Have you registered yet? Did you get your letter?'

'We've no need,' the husband said. He was a dashing sort, black hair combed straight back, showing off his temples and his cheekbones, but there was a coldness about him. 'Neither one of us ails a day and I'm not needing to be paying a big stamp for every other scrounger that's scared of hard work.' He scowled at his wife. 'Papers,' he said, jabbing a finger at the bale, and he disappeared again.

Helen felt her cheeks flame in sympathy for the woman, but *she* managed a twist of a smile. 'He's het up,' she said. 'About the baby.'

'*He's* het up!' Helen said. 'What about you? Are you seriously saying you haven't been under a doctor all nine months?'

The woman blinked twice and then threw her head back and let out a peal of laughter. 'Get away!' she said. 'Naw, we're adopting. We've a baby boy coming any day.'

'Ohhhhh!' said Helen and her face continued to darken even as the rest of her recovered. 'Well, I must say, I think you're exactly what I'm for then, Mrs. . .?'

'Yarrow,' the woman said. 'It's above the door.'

'Why,' said Helen, 'only yesterday I gave a talk on infant nutrition. And I can tell you all about what check-ups you'll need. Anything you have to ask, I'll do my best to answer. You should pop round with the wee one, when he gets here.' She dropped her voice. 'There's no connection between the stamp and the service, you know. I mean, yes, we all pay but it's not like a savings bank. It won't put Mr Yarrow's stamp up if you bring the baby to see us at the clinic or down if you don't. Has he a name yet?'

'We're going to call him Gordon,' said Mrs Yarrow. 'Distinguished, don't you think? The nuns have given him Mortimer but I was worried that was his mammy's name. I wouldn't want her finding him and causing bother.'

'The nuns?' Helen said.

'Aye, that's upsetting him too. That's not to be spoken of. But it's not to say *he* is. Gordon, I mean. And they've promised they won't baptise him. They'll let us christen him at Fountainbridge Free. But it's all a strain.'

'Worth it, though,' Helen said. 'And you know what else? This is the best way to get your own started. If I had a pound for the number of times I've seen Irish twins, one adopted and one following hard on its wee heels. . .'

'Wheesht case he hears you!' said Mrs Yarrow. 'Irish twins! You'll get me tawsed.' Helen hoped she was joking. 'Naw, this is it for us. Gordon Yarrow.'

'Lovely,' said Helen, thinking to herself that anything would be better than Mortimer, the poor wee scrap, and not wanting to dip a toe in the rest of it. 'I can't wait to see him,' she went on. 'Bring him round. No need to make an appointment. Just stop in one day when you're pushing his pram.'

Mrs Yarrow gave her the *Herald* free, refusing to keep the tuppenny bit and then, under duress, putting it in the collecting tin for the Sick Children, which felt about right.

So Helen was buoyant – that was the word – as she came swinging back out onto the street. She had dealt well with a tough customer and she had done good to a woman in need of advice. When she bumped into a trio of girls and let her newspaper go in the kerfuffle, she assumed it was kindness that made one of the three stamp down hard to stop it blowing away. Friendly, she thought, and smiled at them.

'Helen Downie,' said the girl whose stout boot was on top of the newspaper.

'Mary Terry,' Helen said, and glanced at the other two. They were a pair of twins and although Helen had told them apart fine when they were all pals together she didn't dare take a guess now. They had been identical, two thin girls with long brown plaits and gaps between their front teeth. Now one was stout and beefy-looking, with a tight perm that didn't suit her peeking out from under her yellow headscarf. The other had had her teeth done, and now showed a brilliant white top-set, like a tooth-powder advert in a magazine. 'Sorry,' she said. 'I never saw youse. I'm run off my feet.'

'Aye, you look it,' said one of the twins, giving Helen that sweep up and down, taking in every detail: her high heels and her fine stockings and the fact that she was wearing a hat on a Wednesday, instead of a head square. The three of them were in overalls, feet in short boots for a hard shift on the stone floor of wherever it was they were working.

'I thought you were engaged to that Sandy Crowther,' the other twin said. 'And he was cleaning the street at my granny's last time I clapped eyes on him. Did you chuck him over and get yourself a sugar daddy, did you?'

'I'm a working girl,' Helen said. 'Same as you.' She glanced at her watch. 'And I'm late.'

'Oh, late by your *watch*, are you?' Mary Terry said. 'No factory bell for our Nelly, eh?'

'Ocht,' said Helen. That was all it took in the playground when someone was out with someone over a skipping rope or a smashed marble, but it didn't work now.

'I didn't think "working girls" started so early,' said the stout twin.

'And that doctor's too young to be a sugar daddy,' said the other.

Mary Terry lifted her foot and toed the folded paper across the pavement towards Helen, who refused to stoop and pick it up while they were watching. So they knew exactly where she was working then, or they wouldn't have mentioned the doctor, would they?

'You could take evening classes,' she said – a remark met with three frowns. 'If you're not suited where you are. Better than trying to set me down just to make yourselves feel better.'

'Who the hang do you think you are?' said the stout twin, muscling forward.

Helen stole one glance at the sturdy forearms above the bunched fists and felt her feet telling her to move out of the way, but she stood her ground. 'It's who *you* think I am,' she said. 'I think I'm the same as ever, but you've got your knickers in a twist about something.'

'You're giving your mind a treat,' said Mary Terry. She took an arm of each twin and dragged them away.

Shaking slightly, Helen bent and picked up her newspaper, now with the dusty print of Mary Terry's boot on the front page, and hurried away.

And so she was aghast when, an hour later, Dr Deuchar set a brown Gladstone bag down on top of her nice neat papers with a thud, nearly spilling her cup of tea.

'I'm not a nurse!' she said. 'I can't go swanning about the streets, in and out of folk's business, pretending to be a nurse!' And it was definitely a nurse's bag, like a smaller version of the doctors' bulging leather bags with the brass rods across the top, so stuffed with bottles and bandages that they struggled to close them.

'You need a good bag as much as I do,' Dr Deuchar said. 'And it's fitting that I should present you with one. Mine was a present from old Dr Strasser. We graduated together, as you know – Strasser and I – and the dear old thing knew there would be nothing coming from the Deuchars. So he matched the gift to his own son with one to me. Splendid old gentleman.'

'That was very kind of him,' Helen said. It always tickled her when Dr Deuchar got on to his 'humble beginnings' and how lucky he was to go through medical school with the son of a doctor, how if he hadn't hitched his wagon to his friend's, he'd never have got a practice of his own. 'But you were a doctor. If there's such a thing as an almoner's bag, why not get me one of those, Doc?'

'Ah but this one shouldn't go to waste,' said Dr Deuchar. 'They are built to last, you see. Mine will see me out. I'll set it on a shelf the day I retire. Or perhaps take it fishing. It cost twenty guineas, you know.'

Helen only just managed not to gasp, and she looked at the nurse's bag with new eyes. It was much smaller, a soft donkey-brown colour instead of the black of the doctors', but the same shape and smelling of saddle oil and Brasso like theirs. But she couldn't! What would Mary Terry have said? What would Mr Yarrow have made of it?

'It's bad enough that no one knows what a medical almoner is, Doc,' she said. 'I can't pretend I'm something more, toddling about with a medical bag. I'll lose their trust before they even start. And I can't go about looking grand. I've got to be someone they think they can talk to.' She moved her saucer to the top of her cup to keep her tea from getting any colder as Dr Deuchar settled into the other seat as if for a good long chat.

'Oh my dear Helen,' he said. 'I sweep in with a bag twice that size and a regimental tie and cufflinks and they tell me every thought in their head. Marital, financial, spiritual. One chap last week asked me for help making the soup more tasty when I was there to treat his bedridden wife. I shouldn't worry if I were you.'

'But what will I keep in it?' Helen said. 'There aren't enough leaflets in the world to fill a bag that size.'

Dr Deuchar mugged shooshing and checking over his shoulder for eavesdroppers. 'Don't let them hear you. I've a feeling the leaflet game is just getting started. Don't encourage them. Apples.'

'Apples?'

'For the kiddies. It's perhaps a bit too obvious, what with the old saying. But you could keep lollipops too. Take the necessary out of petty cash and stock up. What about bath salts?'

Helen considered it. 'That's a good idea,' she said. 'I'm going to have to tell a woman from my infant nutrition talk that she needs a scrub. If I say she needs. . . to relax her muscles and I give her salts, that'll take the edge off it. I was worried she might punch me. But honestly, Doc, you should have smelled her, and the baby's bottom had a pie-crust round it, poor wee mite.'

'There you go then,' said Dr Deuchar. 'Apples, lollies and bath salts. Your charges will come to love your nurse's bag. You'll be like Mary Poppins.'

Helen smiled. She had never read it but at least she had heard of it, which was more than she could say about most of what Dr Strasser dropped into conversation.

139

'What about the fathers?' she said. 'A quarter of baccy would go down well but it's not the same thing.'

'Beggar the fathers,' said Dr Deuchar. 'They do well enough between the pub, the track and the bookies.' He stood up and smacked the bag with the flat of his hand. 'Onward, Nell.'

Helen put her hand on her cup and thought it was still warm enough to be worth drinking, so the last thing she should do was stop him leaving. 'Whose was it, Doc?' she said, despite that, as he disappeared around the door.

He stopped. 'Old Doc Strasser's nurse left it behind her when she retired. So mind and keep it well-polished or she'll be back and haunt you. She was a tartar. She had a bottle of castor oil and she used to clack her dosing spoon against it, heaven knows why. It was a sound that played in the nightmares of many generations of Edinburgh children, let me tell you. No one better when you were truly sick, but woe betide a malingerer.'

And at last he was gone. Helen took the saucer off her tea and drained the barely warm cup in one gulp, then opened the bag to inspect its interior – both capacious and natty – and scrupulously clean except for one ripped pictures ticket in the document pocket. She smiled at it and tucked it back in place, liking this tartar of a nurse all the better for that scrap of humanity.

She had a busy morning coming up, with a visit planned to the staff room at the wee school to have a chat to the teachers about referring pupils for a helping hand before the dirt or the lice or the malnutrition got bad enough for the Corporation to step in. She just had to work out how to phrase it, and she was hoping that none of her own teachers would still be there. Surely not, after all these years? They had seemed like old women – solid and vital still, but not young by any means – when Helen had peeled out of the gates for the last time and moved to the big school.

So there was that and then she was going back down to Torphichen Street to try to broach the subject of those two girls with whatever bobby was on duty there. She would leave some leaflets behind and hope one or two of the coppers were soft-hearted enough to hand them out. Helen tucked *these* leaflets well down inside an inner pocket and folded the flap over them carefully. She had spent that lesson of her course scooted right down in her seat with her blood beating in her ears and, although she knew she would have to become tougher eventually – a tartar, even – she didn't want to be letting leaflets with words like this on them go fluttering around the streets.

Perhaps to put it all off as long as possible, or maybe just to mug up on the latest news and not be such a daisy at the police station, she started flipping through the *Herald* for the story – the one that had to be there, surely – about the death of Maggie Dickson. She was distracted by the adverts for the big Glasgow stores. They were surely no better and no worse than Binn's and Darling's here in Edinburgh but it was a true poet who had written the tales of wonder that went with the drawings of ladies in their wraps and children sleeping like angels. Tearing her eyes from them, Helen leafed through from the small advertisements to the racing results and found not a mention of Maggie Dickson, or even of the death of an unnamed wanted criminal. She folded the paper over thoughtfully and went to rinse out her cup.

At the basin, she ran into Dr Strasser, who had been out in the back garden, probably at the wee incinerator there, for he had rubber gauntlets on still. Helen looked away from them in case traces of whatever had needed instant burning were still clinging.

'Is it really all right with you if I use your father's nurse's bag?' she said. 'It just struck me that Dr Deuchar gave it me, but it's yours by rights. Same with all the bits from the attic really.'

'My father's nurse's bag?' he echoed. 'Oh! You mean the bag of my father's nurse. News to me any nurse from my father's time

141

left a bag behind her. So have at it. No one else is clamouring for such a thing. And a cleared attic is an unearned favour, Helen. Thank you. I have no use for any of the gewgaws up there.'

There it was again: that way he had of making her feel daft for minding wee bits of nonsense he never even noticed. Dr Deuchar knew this nurse was a tartar and Dr Strasser couldn't remember her at all and couldn't care less what happened to her leavings. Helen went upstairs to use the main door, feeling obscurely as if she had to reclaim some dignity.

'I'm nipping out, Doc,' she said, seeing Dr Deuchar leaving the cloak room en route for his surgery. 'It's work,' she added. 'Not. . .'

'Buns and hairpins.'

She smiled. There! He was so chummy and easy to talk to. There was no need for Dr Strasser to be the way *he* was. 'Exactly,' she said. 'I just found out there's a couple adopting an infant and they've done nothing. Well, they might have a cot and a bottle but they've no doctor and nothing set up with a visiting nurse, So I thought I would maybe try and. . .'

'. . . reel them in for us?' said Dr Deuchar. 'That's the spirit. Drumming up business. Good girl.'

'I don't think they'll be a lot of bother,' Helen said. 'Nice respectable people, you know. They run a newsagents.'

Dr Deuchar stopped dead in his tracks and stared at her. 'What?' he said.

Helen stuttered and cast her mind about for what might be troubling him. 'I'm sure they'll not leave him to cry in his pram while they're in the shop,' she said. 'Or is it me saying "respectable". I didn't mean harm to the rest of our. . . Sorry. You're right. I shouldn't have said that where the patients might hear me.'

'The name, Helen. What's the name of this pair adopting a child on a whim?'

'I never said that!' She felt close to tears now. 'It's emm. Ocht. They're going to call him Gordon. And their name is... Mortimer? No! It's Yarrow. Yarrow, with the newsagents round on Earl Grey Street. The one with the magazines all strung up like washing on wee strings in the windows.' Dr Deuchar gaped at her. 'They're not long married but they're not spring chickens,' she said, babbling a bit as she tried to get back from wee washing ropes to something an almoner might say. Spring chickens wasn't right either. Why was she in such a flap? She took a breath and tried again. 'I think it's very sensible,' she said. 'If they're family-minded. I told Mrs Yarrow that there might be another along soon.'

She had managed it. Dr Deuchar had settled down and was smiling again. 'Ah yes,' he said. 'I know the chap you mean. He has a very healthy turnover of cherrywood flake. It's always extremely fresh. Not like the sawdust from Malcolmson's. Well, you go ahead and reel away, Helen. With my blessing.'

'Right.' Helen gave the best smile she could muster.

'And don't worry about mincing your words,' he went on. 'Boils, by-blows, bubonic plague: as long as you don't name names, they never think you're talking about *them*, you see. They always think they're overhearing gossip about a neighbour and drink it in. It's human nature.'

He grinned at her and disappeared into his surgery. Helen could hear him slapping alcohol onto his hands as he always did after he had washed them. Goodness knows what they'd feel like if he had to examine a tender bit of someone.

'Needing Aberdeen's now?' said Mrs Yarrow, looking up from the counter as the shop bell dinged. She must feel like a trained pigeon by day's end. She'd finished with the papers and had a block of tablet out on a waxed sheet. She was paring away thin slices with a large knife.

'How's that?' said Helen. Then she nodded furiously at the blade, to make the woman look back at what she was doing.

'Glasgow's news bored you already, has it?'

'Oh,' Helen said. 'Right. It was one story in particular I was following, see? Or trying to. But then I thought maybe it would a better idea to get it from the horse's mouth.' Mrs Yarrow was twisting the slices of tablet up in brown paper, making them look like giant toffees instead of folding the ends in. 'Nearly two years you said you'd been here? Not long enough to fall behind with the local news. Or gossip, maybe.'

'And my mammy rings me up from the kiosk at her road end every Saturday night,' Mrs Yarrow said. 'As soon as my daddy's away to the bowls. What is it you're after?'

'That's nice,' Helen said. 'Keeping close even when you're away.'

'Ach, her and me get on a sight better with a few miles between us,' Mrs Yarrow said. '*What* is it you're after?'

'Maggie Dickson,' said Helen, watching closely for any spark of recognition in the woman's eyes. 'She died in Edinburgh a couple of nights ago, but she was a Glasgow girl.'

'Oh, uh-huh,' said Mrs Yarrow. She was plying her knife again and spoke with the bare minimum attention she could give without rudeness.

'A notorious Glasgow woman,' Helen said. 'A wanted criminal. Or a lost soul, depending how you look at it.'

Mrs Yarrow laid down the knife. 'Someone's been pulling your leg,' she said. 'Ah, that's my home town! Always a laugh and joke. Not like here, no offence. But everybody's that dour, till they've a drink in them. Then there's as many signed the Temperance pledge.'

Helen ignored this slight on her city and pressed ahead. 'So you've never heard of a Maggie Dickson, wanted all over the country for notorious crimes?'

'I'm not saying there's none like that. I mean, there's Billy Fullerton, for a start. And Patrick Carraher, to keep things even. Although they've hanged him, or so I hear.'

Helen stared. She felt a very faint, very distant, stirring of a memory but before she could chase it and catch it, Mrs Yarrow was talking again. 'I can ask my mammy when she rings me on Saturday. Or if she comes through. To see the baby. She might get on a train and come over for a few days.' She beamed and, lifting another stack of wrapped tablet, she hugged it to herself, even patting the bottom slice as if soothing an infant, before she turned to pile them on the shelf behind her.

'Lucky wee boy,' Helen said. 'Coming to live above a sweetie shop. You'll need to mind and get him on a dentist's books as well as a doctor.'

'Aye, aye,' said Mrs Yarrow. 'I'll talk Robert round. He's just. . . He's a proud man.'

Helen puzzled over that for a moment – why would pride get in the way of a doctor for your son? – then she caught it. 'But it's like I said, Mrs Yarrow, it's far too early to be giving up. My mammy would take her hand off me if I laid a bet, but I meant it: if you've not got two bairns by this time next year, I'll be surprised.'

Mrs Yarrow's face clouded. 'Shhht,' she said. 'He's upstairs putting a cot together, but he's in his slippers and he could easily nip back down again. The thing is, you see. . .' But she ran dry. 'The thing is. . .'

'You've no need to tell me anything,' Helen said. 'But there's nothing you *couldn't* tell me. Like I said. It's my job.'

'I'm the second one,' Mrs Yarrow said, the words tumbling out of her. 'He was married before, see? A local lass, young and healthy, and a beauty, despite all her nonsense. A hypochondriac, she was. Always wanting to take herself off for check-ups. She'd had endless bother with herself before she was wed and she'd got into the habit, you know?'

Helen did know. They'd had a presentation during the training about how to stop a hypochondriac from swamping the doctor.

'I mean, I say she's a beauty,' Mrs Yarrow went on, 'but I've never seen her. I daresay she took all her photies with her when she left. But I've heard she had hair as black as coal and skin as white as snow.'

'And lips as red as cherries?' Helen said. 'They're having you on.'

'Except I found one,' said Mrs Yarrow. 'Well I mean, you don't expect a man on his own to give a house a proper do-ing. I found one of her hairs on the back of a chair by the fireside. The one I sit in. Ken that stiff stuff, halfway between velvet and a shoe brush?' Helen laughed; it was the perfect way to describe those scratchy settees. 'It was right there,' Mrs Yarrow said. 'Two foot long and as fine as silk.' She gazed at nothing, rubbing her thumb and forefinger together, re-membering. 'But anyway,' she went on, at last, 'for all she was bonny, nothing happened. So he put her out. Sent her away. And took up with me, who's still got her tonsils and her wis-dom teeth and her appendix, to go with my coarse hair and all the freckles you'd see if I didn't have my face on. But, there! There's nothing's happened again, so he knows it's him now. I think he feels badly about Marion. That was her name. Sending her off like that, ken? Seein' it wasn't her fault.'

'He sent her away?' said Helen. The rest of it was under-standable but that was cold.

'Or something,' said Mrs Yarrow. 'I've never got the full sorry tale off him. I just know she was here then she was gone. Mind you, it might be for the best. Robert took no nonsense from her, but if she's managed to convince the next man she was at death's door, she might be able to spend the rest of her life in a sanatorium.'

The word caught at Helen and the memory of that white treatment gown blazed in her mind. 'She'd like to be in a sanatorium, would she?'

Mrs Yarrow nodded. 'So I hear.'

'But she's got black hair?'

Mrs Yarrow frowned. 'What?'

'Ocht, nothing,' Helen said. She shook her head and smiled. 'I haven't come across a true hypochondriac on my books yet. They can't be easy.'

'I thought he was a bachelor, you know,' Mrs Yarrow said. She had finished her wrapping now and turned to fill the shelf behind her. Maybe it was easier to talk that way. 'All the time he was through and back to Glasgow, courting me,' she said, 'it wasn't till I was stood right on this spot behind this blessed counter that the local mouths came coiling round, dying to tell me.'

'I bet,' Helen said. 'I mean, I can imagine.' It was true. She could easily imagine how Mrs Yarrow felt, her new beginning soured and spoiled, everyone laughing. And the man she married revealed to be a stranger. Helen only had Teenie hinting and smirking but that was bad enough. 'What a sadness,' she said.

'Aye well, there's a lot of it about,' said Mrs Yarrow. Then she twisted the big sheet of waxed paper up into a poke and offered it to Helen. 'I'm not a lover of tablet. You take this and eat the flakes when there's no one about to see you lick your finger.' Helen smiled and tucked the little package into her pocket. 'And as for sadness, the little stranger will soon drive that away.'

'Gordon,' said Helen.

'Gordon Yarrow. A name to be reckoned with. He sounds like a teacher, doesn't he? Or a painter.'

'Or a doctor,' Helen said, since her imagination tended to run along those lines these days.

'Why not a lawyer? Or a poet?' Mrs Yarrow was beaming again.

'A judge!' said Helen, thinking here was someone who wouldn't laugh at the highest reaches of a daydream.

'A cabinet min—' But she heard the soft footsteps of Mr Yarrow's carpet slippers and bit her lip on the final flight of fancy.

'Who are you talking to?' His voice was as cold as his face.

'I'll not keep you then, Mrs Yarrow,' Helen said.

'You!' He came forward, jostling his wife out of the way and planting his fists firmly on the counter. 'I'll not tell you again. You're not welcome in this shop.'

Helen was already walking backwards to get away from him and was glad to hear the bell ding to announce another customer arriving. 'Rather you than me,' she said, out of the corner of her mouth to the startled elderly gent who was probably only after a packet of pipe cleaners. Then she fled.

Chapter 11

Helen had seen some poor-looking houses in her time, but tonight beat the band. When she was a wee girl in Freer Street, there were pals she wasn't allowed to play with when it rained, because Greet would no more let Helen inside their doors than she would let them bring their grubby hands and lousy wee heads inside hers. She couldn't stop the weans from palling around the back greens and the front streets, although she told Helen not to give killycodes if she could help it, but there were limits. Helen used to cry and ask her mammy why she wasn't allowed into the Mortons', when Mrs Morton didn't mind and it was fun there. You were allowed to jump on the bed and make burrows out of the blankets, sacks and coats piled up. Greet shuddered and took Helen in between her knees, holding her like a crab holds its prey, till she'd combed through her hair from root to tip, raking her scalp.

Only gradually did Helen begin to connect the grey hands and brown earholes of Annie Morton, the foosty smell of her jersey in winter and the oniony reek of her bare skin in summer, with Greet's mysterious rules that threatened the friendship and put big trembling tears in Annie's eyes. By the time they were at the school and the Downies had flitted to Grove Place, Helen was as like as all the other girls to pull back from poor wee Annie. 'Naw, naw,' she'd say. 'You skip and I'll caw.' It seemed like kindness but the other girls smirked their understanding. Helen didn't want Annie Morton to touch the painted handles of her good new skipping rope.

Since then she had followed Mrs Sinclair into the dormitories of the men's hostels in the Grassmarket, inspecting them for the church. She had watched the newsreels of the camps being liberated, weeping into her box of caramels in the dark, unable to let the images fade and enjoy the big picture when it came on. She had helped clear a house where the children were trying to keep going after both parents left them, a ten-year-old making pieces out of blue bread and an eight-year-old washing clothes in cold water at the scullery sink with nothing but a bit of pumice to rub the dirt away. 'You've a lady's natural grace,' Mrs Sinclair had said to her that day. 'No retching and staggering. I'm proud of you, Helen.' Then, all in her furs and her good leather gloves, she had taken the littlest child onto her knee in the back of the motorcar as she drove them all off to the nuns at Lauriston. 'Thank God for the Sisters of Mercy at times like this,' she said, shocking Helen at the time.

Helen was thanking God for something much more shocking now. She slipped out of her drawers, undid her brassiere, let both drop onto the pile of clothes already on the bathroom floor, then kicked the whole lot out into the passageway before locking the door and stepping gingerly into the deep bathful of hot water, sinking under until every inch of her was submerged and only the ends of her hair waved on the steaming surface.

Thank God for this bath, she thought to herself, and shuddered. Shields, they were called. Mrs Shields and her wee boy, still in the nappy Helen had put on him hours before, had a dog that hadn't been outside for days, as far as she could tell, from the smell and the puddles half-soaked into the bare boards. Mrs Shields had at least snatched up the solids in a handful of paper, but only to put them in the slop pail alongside Mercy knew what – well, Helen knew exactly what – leaving smears behind for the wee fella to crawl through and sit in. Unbelievable as it was, Mrs Shields had evidently spruced him up for the infant nutrition talk that morning. Even dirtier now, he was sleeping curled up on the hearthrug with a black thumb plugged in his mouth.

'Tea?' Mrs Shields had said, stretching out a hand to bring a kettle forward over a fire of what looked like rags and meat bones and smelled like scorched hair.

Helen's lady-like control of her gullet nearly deserted her then and there. 'What are you burning?' she said, unable to help putting a hand to her nose.

'Don't look at *me*,' said Mrs Shields. 'It was her downstairs told me I wasn't to drop my leavings out the window because something caught on her sill and she's too stuck up to lean out with a wooden spoon and flick it off again.'

Helen didn't ask for details, but she was still thinking what 'leavings' might be hours later, lying in her bath, as she let the air trickle out of her lungs and watched tiny bubbles break the surface above her.

'If you don't start letting your dog out, windowsills are going to be the least of her worries,' she had told the woman. 'That'll seep through, Mrs Shields. It'll rot the ceilings downstairs before it harms your floor here and you'll be out. I know the factor for these houses because he's the same as my ma-in-law round at Grindlay Street and he's a brute. Word to the wise.'

Mrs Shields was leaning back in her box bed with her shoes up on the covers, owing to the fact of there not being a second seat anywhere in the kitchen, what with dirty clothes and old newspapers and a box of kindling sticks that could as easy have gone on the floor but was installed on the Windsor as if it was an honoured guest. She scowled and Helen, perched on a three-legged stool, knew she had a fight on her hands. 'I don't say that to shame you, but to help you. Just open the door and let the dog out to run in the back green. It's good exercise for him and it'll help you keep on top of things up here too.'

'You don't know my snobby neighbours,' said Mrs Shields. 'Of course, I let him out. I've had dogs all my life and I know what they need, but that pernickety lot over by took the huff with him.'

'Well, that's just daft,' Helen said. 'The poor wee pup's got to go somewhere. Tell them to write to the factor if they've got wasps in their stocking tops. They won't but it'll shut them up.' She smiled. 'Now then.'

'Here we go!' The woman was a sloven but not a fool.

'How about a week, Mrs Shields? A week from today for you to get on top of this? What day have you got in the wash house?' A shrug. 'Or can you stretch to the steamie and get it all done in one? If you've someone to mind the wean. You need to get ahead of it before the new one comes along, you know.' The woman's face was setting into stubborn lines, with her jaw sticking out and her eyes narrowing. So, Helen thought, she's got some steel about her somewhere, even if she looks like a dropped pudding. 'Because it won't do,' she went on. 'This is unsanitary. Even if *you've* got used to it, it's no place to have a new baby.'

'You're just like the rest—'

'I'm not,' Helen said.

'Aye, you are. You don't care what or why or how. You just want to—'

'I don't "just" anything. That's where you're wrong. Because I'm giving you a week to sort it, instead of calling in the inspector today.'

'What inspector? Are you threatening me?'

'Yes!' Helen said and was happy to see the other woman blink. So often that question was supposed to make you back down. 'Well done for seeing clearly.' Helen held up her hand to stop a threatened tirade. 'Never mind your excuses. Your man's in work, isn't he? At the basin yards, you said? So you can afford a bar of soap and a cloth. You just need to stir yourself. This isn't safe, Mrs Shields. You're lucky none of you have gone down with the cholera before now. So. Put your dog out for a run and shout down to the weans in the back green, see if there's a big girl'll take your wee boy for a penny – I'd have done it gladly. We liked nothing more than a wee one to drag around and play at houses. Then you get stuck in. And I'll come back a week today. You can't bring a bairn into this.'

'So you're saying straight out you'll have my wean off me?'

'Yes. How many times do you need to hear it?'

Mrs Shields seemed to collapse then, subsiding into the pile of blankets until, enormous as she was, she all but disappeared. It must be a sprung base and stretched to uselessness.

'The new one just or the both of them?' she asked after a long pause.

'Why?' said Helen. 'That's a queer sort of question.'

'I love my wee boy,' said Mrs Shields in a low voice.

'Good,' Helen said, deciding to ignore the implication. Greet always said the babies brought the love with them no matter how you might feel before they came. 'I'm not saying you don't. But unless you turn your love into soap and elbow grease it's not much use to him.' Then she softened. 'This is my job. I can advise you and answer questions. I can see about more classes if you need them. But I can't close my eyes to it now I've seen it, can I?'

She stood and took a long look around the room, finishing up with a sniff. 'I've a husband of my own,' she said, 'and I ken no man wants to finish his shift and walk into this. Come home to that!' She pointed at the chaos of dirty blankets and stained pillows. She didn't mean Mrs Shields herself.

But maybe she should have been clearer. 'I know,' Mrs Shields said, in a small, broken kind of voice. 'He's left me.'

Helen bit her lip on 'I don't blame him' and said instead, 'When?' then at last, 'Why?'

'It's not his,' came the same tiny voice, as if a much smaller woman was speaking from inside the mound of Mrs Shields.

Helen formed her lips to ask what wasn't whose, but the woman went on. 'I used to keep myself nice. Never went out in my curlers and baffies. Never wore a darned stocking. Lipstick and lash black before I'd go over the door.' It was hard to believe, looking at her now, but Helen said nothing. 'Then he lost his job and off he went looking for work. Carlisle, Lockerbie, Doncaster! By the time he got sorted here and sent for me, I was three months gone. I hid it. I lied and I would have said it was early no matter what size it came out, but he's fly. He knew, size of me. By the time I was six months in, he knew. So he left me.'

'But that's no reason to let yoursel—' Helen said.

'That's not why!' Mrs Shields had found her voice again and it rang out. 'That's not why I'm filthy and lying in filth.' The wee boy shifted in his sleep. When she went on she spoke softly. 'I would never have looked at another man. *Did* never. But high heels and straight seams? Lipstick and lash black? I didnae have to.' Helen caught her lip. 'It was dark and naeb'dy came when I screamed. Naeb'dy cared.'

Helen stood and went over to the bed, shuffling herself into the heap of blankets and reaching for Mrs Shields' hand. 'Some devil forced himself on you?' Mrs Shields nodded, turning her face and wiping tears on the pillow ticking. 'And you fell?' Another nod. 'And Mr Shields doesn't believe you?'

'He – He – he asked me why I was all dolled up when he was away to Lockerbie.'

'Says more about him than you,' said Helen.

'Aye. But after he said it I telt myself I'd never doll up again. Keep myself safe, I would. Naeb'dy'd come at me now, nor tell me I was asking for trouble.'

'But the house?' said Helen. Mrs Shields' greasy hair and clothes stiff with dirt made some kind of sense but not the wean's sore bottom or the bucket of dog mess.

'It just. . .'

'Of course it did,' said Helen. 'You're a wee soul. You're a poor wee scone, aren't you? So!' Mrs Shields turned to look at her. 'One week.'

'*Whit?*'

'It changes nothing, Mrs Shields. I've got bath salts here for you. That's a nice way to get started. Get a big girl to take the wean and get yourself down to the baths for a good steep. Then buy some soda on your road back and get cracking. I'll be back a week today.'

'You heartless article,' Mrs Shields said, but she was almost smiling.

'I'll take the dog with me when I go down and let him out the back, eh?'

There was a terrier and a wee skinny tan-coloured thing like a whippet already out there. Both greeted the Shields' dog like a friend with wagging tails and happy barks. Helen called over one of the bigger girls, who seemed to be organising a game of chasey over by the wash house railings. 'Here,' she said. 'How'd you like to earn tuppence? Go up and knock Mrs Shields' door, get her wee boy to look after till teatime.'

'Wee Stinky Shields?' said the girl, tossing her plaits over her shoulder as she turned away. 'Nae chance, missus.'

'Thruppence,' Helen said. 'And just to keep an eye on him. You don't need to be cuddling.'

'Sixpence,' the girl said. 'That'll get liquorice for all of us, a bite each.'

Helen scrabbled in the big nurse's bag that had swallowed her purse whole, and headed home to this long gleaming bath and these gallons of piping hot water turning her as pink as bubblegum.

She needed to breathe, so she pushed her feet against the tap end and brought her face up into the air, pulling in a deep steamy lungful and settling her head against the glossy slope of the enamel. It was warm against her skin. She had never had a bath so deep that the enamel above the water line was warmed through. And she'd never had a white bath either. The family tub that hung behind the big cupboard door was bare tin and the private baths at the Cally were painted dark green. This was like bathing in. . . Well, it was like bathing in a blood trough from the slaughterhouse if she was honest. Helen closed her eyes and promised herself she would buy some of that 'bubble bath' to hide the view when she got a minute. Once life settled down.

Because, with a family fight, poor dead Maggie Dickson, a night chasing about the dark streets with Dr Deuchar in his motorcar, a flitting, and the little bit of drama here and there from Mrs Sinclair to round it all off, this week would have been a lot to take, even without a new job, home visits, talks, interviews, endless paperwork and the worry of Mr Yarrow's coldness and Mrs Shields' helpless misery. Under the water, Helen rubbed her fingertips together, hoping the ink from those blessed carbons would lift off without too much scrubbing.

Count your blessings, she said to herself, as she so often did. Sandy. Sandy was kind and friendly. If she told him she was going out to the pictures with Greet or her aunties, he'd not mind. Her job. So much harder than she'd dreamed but still a happy miracle that Helen Downie fae Freer Street had her own office and ate buns with the doctors. And this house, where she could lock the door and run a bath on a Wednesday teatime, lie in luxury and know that no one would be telling her her hour was up or banging on the door needing into the kitchen before she was clean.

She was concentrating as hard as she ever had on her blessings, but it wasn't working. Because there was something else there, lost under patients and carbons, rugs and glasses, upsets and scoldings. It was more than her vow of 'never again' to poor dead Maggie. It was more than her wish to find out exactly who she was and why she'd died. It was something deeper than plans and convictions. Smaller maybe but deep,

156

deep down. Helen let her mind drift, seeing if she could bring it to the surface.

She didn't hear the feet on the stairs. Or maybe she was so used to neighbours four to a landing and folk climbing steps through the wall from her that she didn't think it strange. Either way, the first she knew was the rat-a-tat-tat on the front door and she flailed in the deep water, sending a spout of it over the side. She crouched with her hands gripping the roll on the edge of the bath, her eyes darting and her heart picking up as the knock came again. Or rather as another knock came, firmer and faster, more like a pounding. Her thoughts flew to the top step out there, gauging how far it might be from the railings to the window, and whether whoever it was could lean over and peer in. The glass was scoured but surely you'd still see an outline. And the steam curling out of the propped-open top pane must tell whoever was out there that someone was feet away, naked and vulnerable.

Whoever was out there. Sandy had a key. Her mother would shout her name, her father too, and it didn't sound like Teenie. She'd not come alone and she'd be giggling by now. Could it be one of the doctors? Why would they be here after the end of the day? A little worm started wriggling in her. What if Mrs Shields had complained about Helen breenging in and Dr Strasser had come round to sack her and take the house back? Or Dr Deuchar had come round to reprimand her and put her on warning. *That* would be justice! After her doing the very same to that poor woman. A third time whoever it was pounded on the door and a third time there was no shout to go along with the barrage. A salesman with a suitcase full of cloots would have given up by now. Even a copper would shout 'Police!' Who *was* this, spoiling Helen's first soak in her lovely new bathroom?

She stayed there, still and silent, until after a fourth and a fifth assault at last she heard the scrape of boot heels on the top step and the sound of someone walking slow and halting back down the stairs. He had a limp, whoever it was, dragging one foot and landing heavy on the other. She strained to hear the gate and then the sound of those awkward steps receding on the lane beyond it, but there was nothing.

Maybe it was someone from before. From when this was the wee hospital. Ordinary door-to-door salesmen might not carry on like that but maybe it was one of those pushy travelling reps the doctors got sick of, always handing out wee bottles of something or other and pestering for an order. By the time she had scrubbed herself, climbed out, wiped the bath, wound her hair round rags to dry and put on her summer nightie and a cardigan – for the cotton was worn thin and showed the shadow of her body if she stood against the light – she had got as far as scorn for this heavy-handed medical rep, who thought knocking down doors and frightening your customers half to death was how to fill an order book.

The one thing that hadn't entered her mind, hadn't crossed the farthest reaches of it, was that this desperate stranger was anything to do with the corpse. It was when she was standing by the front kitchen window, ten minutes later, with her damp towel over her arm, wondering if she could go down to the garden in her nightie to sling it over the line, that she saw something.

The door to the Anderson shelter was opening. Slowly the door swung open and a hand appeared around it, gripping the edge. Helen drew back out of the light and held her breath, watching. The hand was white and bony, long fingers and long dirty nails, and maybe her mother was right – 'Full of nonsense' she'd always said. 'Away with the fairies' – because Helen couldn't think of anything except that she couldn't remember Maggie Dickson's hands. They had been white, and soft, but were they bony like that? And even if they'd been soft on Monday, wouldn't they have changed by now? And wouldn't those little shell nails have grown dirty clawing through dirt to escape a grave?

Here came the rest. Grey in the shadows as the sunlight died, a person was edging round the door. But not – Helen let her breath go and set a foot out wide to steady herself – a figure in a white treatment gown, or even a shroud. It was a man, in flannel trousers and a collarless shirt, his hair plastered to his high-domed forehead with the sweat of fear or illness. He came up the cut-in steps to the grass, staggering. Maybe he was drunk and had gone inside the shelter for relief. Helen would take a bucket down and check it over once he was away.

Except he wasn't going. He had stopped in the garden and was staring up at the house with a murderous look on his face, his jaw clenched and his fists tight as he held his arms rigid at his sides. Finally, Helen realised: *this* was who had pounded on the door. He had battered the daylight out of her good sturdy door then hidden in the shelter all the time she finished bathing. Now he stood there like a pillar of fire, his eyes flashing and his body shaking with pent-up rage.

She was transfixed, as frozen up here looking down on him as he was down there staring up, one caught in fury and the other in mounting terror. For suddenly it seemed to Helen there was only one thing to bring a stranger to the old shelter at this tucked-away house at the end of a quiet lane: he had come to gloat over the corpse and was enraged to find it gone. He had murdered the girl and left her here. He had thought the house empty, the corpse well-hidden, and believed he could visit it anytime. His wrath at being wrong showed in his glare and his rigid stillness and Helen would have cowered if she hadn't feared that the movement would alert him.

It must have been nigh on ten minutes they stood there, caught up together in a spasm. Heaven knew what *he* was thinking but Helen's thoughts raced as if a newsreel was playing behind her eyes. She imagined a poisoning, like the doctor said; imagined that rigid, staring man forcing a bottle between the girl's lips as she struggled.

Just as that vision began to fade and Helen felt a new idea rising, suddenly the man broke the spell and lurched away, dragging his bad leg and stamping on his good, as if pegging hard with the one could make up for the other and keep him steady.

Helen drew a hand over her forehead and wiped away a film of sweat, then tottered over to sit at one of the bulbous chairs that looked so odd and out of place in her bright kitchen. She sank back and let her head rest, waiting for her breathing to settle. There was no settling her mind. It was as if drops had been falling into a jug all week, covering the pattern there, ever since she opened the Anderson shelter door and found Maggie. And she'd held the drops, good little jug that she was, ignoring the level rising, until one too many fell and now she had overflowed, letting it all stream out again.

As it poured away, there at last was the truth! The thing she had looked at and yet not seen. The thing deep down that was still plaguing her without her even knowing, because the shock of finding the dead girl, and of being so sure she was Fiona Sinclair, had driven everything else away.

Just as she was looking about herself for a pencil and a scrap of paper she knew weren't there, she heard the fleet, even steps of Sandy coming up the stairs and the sweet sound of his key in the lock.

'Nell?' His boots hit the floorboards as he toed them off.

'I'm in here. In the kitchen.' As he arrived beside her she did her best to smile at him, but knew from his look that she'd failed. 'I need you to listen to me,' she said. 'Sit doon and let me make you a cup of tea or bring you some water, but promise me you'll listen. Because something's wrong and I cannae keep pretending it isn't, see?'

Sandy stared at her a long while, chewing his lips, but in the end he nodded and pushed himself up from where he'd been leaning. 'Aye, fine,' he said. 'But I'll bring *you* the water or try my hand at a pot of tea if you'd rather. As soon as I've had a bit of a wash. For you look like you've seen a ghost. You sit and tell me and I'll do the rest of it, eh?'

'I haven't seen any ghost,' Helen said, managing a bit of a laugh. 'I've seen something worse, I think. Compared to this, a wee ghostie would be nothing.'

Chapter 12

If things had been different, this would be a moment to treasure. Helen lifted her feet as Sandy put a wee stool under them, then watched him draw water and fill the kettle. While he washed, she tried to gather her thoughts but, on his return, still she opened with, 'I scarce know where to start.' Then she drew a breath, told herself it didn't matter where she started as long as she covered it all in the end, and began.

'For one thing, that girl in the shelter was no Glasgow moll, wanted all over the city. I ken that for a stone-cold fact because there's nothing in the Glasgow papers about her getting her comeuppance and I've asked two west coasters today and they've never heard of any Maggie Dickson. So that's for starters.'

'Maggie Dickson?' Sandy echoed in a wondering sort of voice.

'Aye, me too,' Helen said. 'Just the same. It rang a bell but only a faint one. But listen. That's not all. If she wasn't this notorious Glasgow villain then why was she not took to the mortuary in the Canongate there? And why was that bigwig, Duncan Pyne, coming in the back way in his fancy car saying his pal from over there was on the job? Why was he *there*, see? Even if it was true that she was away to Glasgow to be nailed down under a lead lid to make sure she was gone – and it's not true, Sandy; I swear it's no' – why would an Edinburgh judge be at the mortuary back door the same night?'

'Aye but, Nelly—'

'Hear me out, like you said you would,' said Helen. 'Next: Mrs Sinclair. I told you how it went with her, didn't I? She was annoyed when we said the body was Fiona. Went straight to the phone and started jabbing at they wee holes as if they'd offended her. But then, when I said Carolyn, she hit the ground in a deid faint. I was that upset and feeling guilty, I never thought on how strange it was for her to do that.'

'Stranger to be annoyed, if you ask me,' Sandy said.

'Strangest of all to be one then the other though.'

'Right enough,' Sandy said, over his shoulder. He had filled the kettle so full it would be morning before it boiled but he stood at attention with a cloth over his hand to lift it.

'But even that's not the worst thing,' Helen said. 'The worst of it all is. . . Oh, Sandy, I don't even know how to tell you; I cannae account for it except maybe to say that it was the job, and then the hoose, and my mammy putting us out, and not wanting to argue with him in front of the coppers and then all the chasing about, the polis station and those poor girls—'

'What poor girls are these?'

'At Torphichen Street. Working girls. I d'ae ken if they were in trouble or just sitting in for a warm. On a tea-break, I should say; it was a warm night outside too. But there they were and one of them was a girl, just. What a life.'

Sandy had been distracted from his watched pot. 'No concern of yours,' he said. 'You're no' going to be in about folk like that, are you, Nelly?'

'Wheesht!' Helen said. 'I'll go where I'm needed. It's not catching. So there was them and then Mrs Sinclair fainting and the mortuary. Polis in the garden and a night on straw, then away back in in the morning and standing up giving a talk, then that poor wean and the filth of his mammy's house. . .'

'What's that got to do—?'

'Nothing! That's what I'm saying. It was nothing to dae wi' it and it distracted me. Mrs Shields' sad tale, Mrs Yarrow waiting to adopt her wee Gordon and poor Mrs McIrnie's daughter and me with the bare-faced cheek to say what I did

163

to her man. . . none of it was anything to do with the girl in the shelter and it filled my heid and knocked me off my bar. Until just now when I finally managed to knock myself back on again.'

Then, just like the thing, when Helen needed a word of encouragement for what she had to say next, Sandy was finally silent, concentrating on the water, which had boiled at last. He spooned tea and poured. Of course, he hadn't warmed the teapot and he'd used too many leaves, so it would stew before they could drink it, but Helen took the cup from him gladly.

'Dr Deuchar made a mistake,' she said, after the first scalding sip. 'This is the thing. He said that Maggie poisoned herself. He said her lips and her jaw were discoloured and it was a classic sign. But he was wrong. Her lips *were* a funny colour but that's because her *face* was a funny colour. And her face was a funny colour because the blood couldnae escape doon past her throat. Because. . .' Helen drew in a breath and let it slowly go '. . . her neck was crushed.'

Sandy started to speak but she held up a hand. 'I saw it. And yet I didnae see it. All I could take into my heid was that Fiona Sinclair was deid. I was so sure it was her. The rest of it flew out my mind until tonight. Or more like it got covered up . . . oh, it's hard to explain. But tonight everything else drained away and I finally got a haud of it again.'

'What are you on about?' Sandy said.

'It doesn't matter. The thing is she wasn't poisoned. She was—'

'But Dr Deuchar wouldnae make a blunder like that!'

'I don't know what to tell you. He *did* make a blunder exactly like that. Her lips and her chin were purple and red, but it wasn't from poison spreading a stain out round her mouth. It started up under her jaw. At the bend of her jaw. I saw it. She'd had all the life choked out of her at her neck and the colour had spread up. Up into her face as far as her mouth. I saw it, Sandy. I was holding a match and I saw her

164

face – recognised her; thought so anyway – and kent what had happened. But it was all so sudden. Fiona! Choked! And then I was running and then it all started up and it's tooken this long to stop.'

'But – I'm not arguing, Nell, I'm just saying. If she'd been strangled, the marks would be halfway down her neck wouldn't they? Bruises and marks where someone would grab her.'

Helen could feel all her certainty starting to dissolve. Was he right? 'Let me think, Sandy,' she said. She squeezed her eyes shut and instead of trying to banish the vision as she'd been doing all week, she forced it closer and made it sharper until she could see it as plain as she'd seen it on Monday. 'She had not a mark from where I was standing looking doon,' she said. 'I 'member thinking how white and soft her skin was in the neck of the gown. But there was something about her ears. Or not exactly her ears. It was the marks. The marks. . .' her eyes were screwed so tight now, she could feel her head start to ache with it '. . .the marks were away up there!' Helen touched herself behind her earlobes. 'Dr Deuchar was right to say her jaw, but the marks were *here*.' Then her eyes sprang open. 'She was hanged.'

'Hanged?' Sandy set his own cup down on the hearth ledge, using both hands as if he didn't trust himself with one. 'But. . . so did the rope break? Was it round her feet and missed in the dark?'

'She didnae hang herself in our shelter,' Helen said. 'Wherever she was hanged, she got cut doon and moved to where I found her. And' – Helen held up her hand – 'if you're going to ask why somebody would do that rather than call the coppers and get her seen to. . . my answer is I d'ae think she hanged herself. I think somebody else hanged her. Because here's another thing Dr Deuchar said: an unmistakable smell. I think I smelled it too. Sweet and strong, like vinegar. I think she was knocked oot with ether and *then* hanged. I think it was murder.'

165

'And then hidden?' Sandy said.

'And would have stayed hidden if the doctors hadnae given us this house.'

'Are you sure?' said Sandy, after a long silence. 'Aboot any ae this?'

'I'm sure it was murder,' Helen said. 'Even if it *was* poison and a stain spreading from round her mouth, she didn't sit and poison herself where I found her. Because where was the poison? Where's the bottle? Or the packet?'

'But she could have. . .'

'Poisoned herself somewhere else and then come away through the streets in that goonie and her bare feet with no one seeing her, to dee where she was found? Why? If she was in a quiet place with the peace to swallow poison and no one to stop her, why no' stay there? Or if she wanted to dee in our shelter, why not bring the poison and drink it there? And if she wanted to do away with herself wouldn't she make sure and be tidy for when someone found her? A vest and knickers at least. A pair ae shoes. No' like that. Why *would* she?'

'Whae kens what goes through someone's head when it gets that length?' Sandy said, very sombre. It brought Helen up short to hear him. She was so carried away with things falling into place she was forgetting the girl herself. Her feelings. And how scared she must have been at the end.

'There's one last thing,' she said. 'They do say, don't they, that a criminal will return to the scene of the crime. Well, this is the thing that finally convinced me. He did.' Sandy frowned at her, not understanding. 'I think the man that kilt her came back again. He was here an hour ago. He was in the shelter and he was up pounding on our door too. And – oh, Sandy – if you'd seen the look on his face. I've never seen anyone look like that in my life. Not even on the pictures. He looked murderous. Nae other word.'

Sandy leaned forward and spoke quietly. 'You're telling me there was a stranger here, in oor garden and up banging on oor door?'

'And in the Anderson shelter too,' Helen said. 'Terrible-looking. I thought maybe he was ill. Or drunk. And I still think maybe he's mad, the way he stood there with his fists clenched and his face set, shaking all over, and just staring. He must have stood ten minutes staring before he went staggering off.'

'Staggering? So he *was* drunk?'

'No, he's got a limp. A bad leg.'

Sandy leapt to his feet. 'And what else does he look like, besides a bad leg?' he said. 'For if I see him again, he'll feel my fist.'

'Thin,' said Helen. 'Bony as anything. And his hair going backwards aff his heid, ken that way? He'd have looked like an egg if I hadn't been up above him. Long bony fingers like a skeleton.' She shuddered and Sandy was over beside her suddenly, rubbing her arms and dropping a kiss on her head.

'Shh-shhh,' he said. 'Dinnae upset yourself. It sounds like he's given you a proper turn, Nell. Listen to what you're saying. A skeleton, lurching about, murder in his eyes? I mean, it's understandable. You were up to ninety thinking aboot Maggie already. But, hen, I have to tell you, it sounds more like he got the wrong address and got caught short. Had to nip into the shelter before he disgraced himself. I'll go down with a bucket of water and see, will I?'

Helen shot back that he'd not been there to witness it and he wasn't *listening* to her, but Sandy was filling a pail and scooping in a handful of soap. Helen thought of asking him what he'd wash so's not to waste it, if the shelter was clean, but she bit her lip on it. There were more important things to worry over than a scoop of soap flakes. Like the fact that a girl had been killed and everyone who should be trying to find out why was covering up, was *lying*. The police on the scene,

Duncan Pyne, and even. . . She stalled. Everyone involved was either covering up or had *made mistakes*. Serious, if not grave, professional errors. The question was, did she have the courage to knock on Dr Deuchar's door and tell him?

And the even bigger question was what to *do*, since the very people who should be getting to the bottom of it all were the ones kicking dust and telling fairytales. Coppers and lawyers, who should be pillars of rectitude. If you couldn't turn to them then where could you?

Sandy was back. She could tell from the way he swung it that the bucket was empty and she felt her mouth pull down at the corners to think of a mess left behind in her lovely new shelter. Well, her nasty old shelter at her lovely new house, anyway. On the heels of that thought, it struck her that Sandy, with a task in hand, had gone quite happily inside the place that he'd hated the sight of only yesterday. She smiled at him, glad to see any wisp of him getting better in any way. He smiled back but it was a most uncertain kind of a smile, with a question behind it.

'I cannae leave it,' she said. 'I d'ae ken who she was or what she'd done but I cannae let them get away with it. Him that did for her and them that's trying to sweep her away like yesterday's dust. I'll not stand for it. I already vowed as much to her memory when I thought it was a shame and a sin. I promised I'd never let it happen again to another girl. But if it's a *crime*? Well, I ken fine what I owe her now. I care not one whit what you say to me.' She was ready for Sandy to put his foot down, come over like the head of the household. She was ready for a fight, if he was minded to start one.

'But what *can* you do?' was all he said.

'Plenty,' said Helen. 'I've been sitting here thinking it over. This was a hospital, right? This place? In the war. And that girl was in a hospital goon. There's a start.'

'What are you talking about, Nelly? You think they only got rid ae the patients the day before we moved in, you and me? And the last one of all went no further than the garden?'

168

'No,' Helen said. 'Of course not. Just that it's likely not a coincidence. Maybe she was a patient here. And something that happened here led to Monday.'

Sandy screwed his nose up. 'That sounds like suicide again,' he said. 'Coming back to where something bad happened, trying to lay demons to rest. Failing.'

'It wasn't suicide,' Helen said. 'Believe me. But maybe whoever killed her didn't know the wee hospital was closed and they thought they'd dress her up in a goonie and plant her here to throw everyone aff the scent. Well, *you* tell *me* then!' she added as Sandy's face twisted up so far his eyes were nearly closed.

'I'm not the one setting myself up like Sherlock Holmes,' he said.

'Jane Marple,' said Helen, then shook her head, saying it didn't matter, when Sandy shrugged. She didn't like to remind him of the years she'd had to read library books by the fire while he lay in that cold hut and did nothing. 'I've got an advantage she never had, though.'

'How's that?'

'Because it's my job to go in and out folk's houses and ask nosy questions. And I work at the surgery.'

'What's that got—?'

'Because we've only got all this,' Helen said, sweeping an arm around the room, 'owing to the docs needing to clear the attic and store records there. Dr Deuchar said it himself: nothing surgical, and not current patients, just notes he made when he was new at the game and feart to miss anything. Not worth sending up to Johnston Terrace. I think it's the records from here he's meaning. From the wee hospital. All sitting there in the attic of the place I work.'

'And what would they tell you, even if you're right?'

'They'd tell me if Maggie Dickson was ever here.'

'If she's even called Maggie Dickson,' Sandy said. 'Seeing as how she's nothing else they called her.'

Helen considered this. 'Still,' she said, eventually. 'The records would tell me what young girls *were* patients here and their right names.'

'And you'd whit? You'd track them all doon except one would be missing?'

He was laughing at her and she could feel her cheeks warming. But she wouldn't be cowed. 'It's only four rooms and it's only a few years,' she said. 'And you ken how long folk stay in the isolation wards, from when it was your auntie and your mammy had all they cousins to mind.'

'But even so—'

'And Mrs Sinclair was talking on important *men* being patients. "Men of standing", she said. 'It might only be a handful of girls.' Sandy was still frowning. 'I've got to do something!'.

'Does it have to be poking about in attics?' Sandy said. 'You'll get the sack. And we'll get pit oot. And I know it's only a day or two but I could get used to this, Nelly.'

Helen looked around, at the solid table, the china stacked in the open press, the fire irons, and lampshades and those blessed jelly glasses that she couldn't imagine ever using. Sandy was right, wasn't he?

Nevertheless, she stuck her chin out and said, 'That's nothing. I'm going to have to tell Dr Deuchar he made a mistake with the cause of death too, mind. But dinnae worry. He was fine when I realised he'd put the wrong name on the certificate. He just set to to fix it. He wasnae angry.'

'But that was *your* mistake, Nell. No' his. That was him being polite, so's not to hurt your feelings.'

'Chivalrous,' Helen said. 'That's what Mrs Sinclair calls it. Like a knight, it always makes me think. That would be like Doc Strasser, but it's no' Doc Deuchar's way.'

'He'll still no' like you setting him straight.'

'If I tell him everything – about Maggie Dickson and that strange man down there too – the mistake he made will be the least of it.'

'That man down there was a drunk needing a widdle,' Sandy said. 'As I should know since I've just sluiced it away. You'll make a fool of yourself if you try to fly that kite, my girl.'

Helen glared at him, and deep inside she still disagreed, but she took the easy road and nodded. 'Aye, fine then. But I still need to find out who she was. And I'd dear like to find out who killed her. She should rest in peace. And how can she with all this still going on?'

Sandy drained his cup and lifted the pot to refill it. Right enough, the tea was stewed black, not a wink of evening light showing through the stream as it poured. 'The years we've kent each other, Nell,' he said, when he was done. 'And the things I still can't put hand on heart and say I know about you.'

'Likes of what?' said Helen, coming back to the room from what felt like a long way off, where she was out of a job and out of a home, back at Greet's begging for the box bed in the big room again and scouring the paper, hoping for a shop or an office, not a factory and not the brewery with everyone smirking.

'Likes of if you believe in ghosts,' Sandy said. 'Likes of what you'll say if I tell you what's in my mind this minute. On account of what you just said about her needing to rest and not getting to. Unquiet.'

Helen's eyes moved to the window. She couldn't see the garden from her seat but she felt her pulse quicken anyway.

'I didnae *see* her,' Sandy said, 'but just there, there in the dark, I felt her. And I think I heard her. Heard something that sounded like gasping, anyway.'

'She would be,' Helen whispered. 'Choked with ether and then her neck crushed the way it was. Oh, Sandy!'

'So you believe me?'

Helen chewed her lip for a moment before answering. 'This flew out of my mind too with everything else. Monday had more in it than any day I can mind of. But early on, in the morning when I first went in, *I* heard something. In the basement, at the doctors. I thought it was Miss Anderson greeting about having to leave her office and all her ledgers. Sobbing, she was. Crying sore. But when I went back her eyes werenae red, and her cheeks werenae wet. And she hadnae gone blotched the way you do when you cry that hard.' Helen took a mustering breath. 'And I saw something, in the dark corner. It was nearly out of sight, but I caught a glimpse of it. And when I turned back to Miss Anderson again, it was like I saw *her* more clear too. I'd only noticed that she couldnae have been crying, ken, with dry eyes and pale cheeks. But, second look, I saw it was more like *wide* eyes and *white* cheeks, because she'd seen it as well as me.'

Sandy swallowed hard and tried a laugh, one that came out very shaky. 'Maybe it was her,' he said. 'Trying to show the way to the answer. Back roon where the record of her life's sitting in a drawer.'

Helen shook her head. 'She'd be in her goonie, wouldn't she? All in white. And the flash I saw was yellow.'

'And this is your office that you sit in all day every day?'

'It's no' there noo!' Helen said. 'I was fine when I got in later and fine again all day yesterday and today when I was in and oot.'

'Because she's back in the shelter,' Sandy said. His voice made Helen think of stories they told on winter nights in the back green, before their mammies called them. Thrilled to be out in the dark, scaring themselves with tales and peering into the blackest corners as they listened. That's how he sounded, half laughing at himself for it but the other half not able quite to push away the dread all set to come creeping. Then he sat up and cleared his throat. 'I'm putting a new padlock on that shelter, Nelly. A stout one. Just till this is all squared away.'

Squared away, Helen thought later as she lay in bed looking at the inky square of the bare window. The novelty of no

172

black-out had worn off now and she wanted the comfort of closed curtains between her and the outside world where strange men lurched about as stiff as peg dolls. Shame there were no curtain rods in Dr Deuchar's attic to go with the swanky curtains that were still sitting in a heap. She could nail them up, maybe. But it would be a pity when they were so well-made and had hooks in the tapes. And it might bring down the plaster. Since the house was free they had even more of a duty to care for it, she reckoned. That thought led back to Mrs Shields and the threat Helen had made about a report to the factor, before she knew what the woman's troubles really were, and it was while that thought occupied most of her mind that a plan of sorts began to form in its recesses, while she wasn't looking.

Chapter 13

It was a busy surgery next morning. In the old days, Mrs Sinclair would take tea at Gardner's Crescent on a Friday afternoon and write down the details of the worst hard-luck cases the docs had uncovered in the week preceding. Or at least the cases they couldn't decide how to deal with anyway. If it couldn't be shunted onto a closed ward or a nit nurse, it would land in Mrs Sinclair's lap. 'Iodine, isolation, or Iolanthe,' Dr Deuchar had said once that spring. 'Between the three of them they can solve most difficulties.'

'Iodine for ringworm,' Helen had said. 'I understand that. And isolation for contagious illness. But what's Iolanthe got to do with anything?'

'Don't listen to him, Helen,' Dr Strasser had said. 'It's his nickname for Mrs Sinclair. And very unkind.'

'She called herself a Fairy Godmother more than once in my hearing,' said Dr Deuchar. 'She's only got herself to blame.'

Helen had opened her mouth then to share the clever little saying she had dreamed up, all set to take the place of 'no ill untreated and no bill unpaid'. But her nerve deserted her and the conversation, as it always did when Dr Deuchar was in the room, moved swiftly on.

This morning Helen had a young mother, overwrought to the point of tears, who needed either a line to get off work so she could visit her convalescing child at the allotted hour, or a different line, from Helen to the nursing home, to let her visit after the workday was done, for if she didn't see her bairn soon she would pine herself too sick to work anyway.

Then there was an old woman who needed help of a kind she couldn't mention to the doctors and could barely mention to Helen either.

'If I come round on a visit,' Helen said. 'Will I see for myself?'

'Would you do that?' the woman said. 'Would you really? And then I won't be breaking my vows, will I? Better or worse, I promised fifty years ago, sickness or health.'

The third patient needed advice about a dentist who 'Wasn't a butcher. For my weans are all feart after that Pelham had the face off their daddy, getting a tooth out of his head. State of him.' Helen managed to maintain a front of professional loyalty, but inside she was nodding. Dick Pelham was renowned for his savagery. A year or two back one of the elephants from Corstorphine Zoo had broken a tusk and it was in the *Evening News* how it had taken three vets to pull the root out of the sleeping animal's jaw. The photograph showed two of the vets stripped to the waist like navvies and the other standing on the elephant's neck straining against a stout rope. The joke went round that Dickie Pelham could have done it without unbuttoning his cuffs.

And, as the morning passed, Helen assured a succession of worried faces that there was no bill coming. 'Else I'd wait till October,' one woman said. 'Seeing I've missed April.'

'Ocht, the doctors would always have held the bill for you,' Helen said. 'You needn't have waited.' It was true. Old Dr Strasser had started it and his son carried on: sending bills for co-op divvy time when folk would have the cash to pay them. He over-billed the rich ones too. 'Five shillings Robin Hood surcharge,' he called it.

After a flurry of milk tokens, vaccination schedules, two requests for a hearing test, and a query about whether Helen would witness a will – which she reckoned she should mention to the doctors when she got a minute because surely that was nothing to do with an almoner – at last she heard the front

175

door upstairs closing behind the last of the morning patients. She washed her hands and, trying for a look of innocence, climbed the stairs to the ground floor and kept on going.

The smell of pipe tobacco from Dr Strasser's office told her that he was writing letters of referral as he usually did at this time of the morning, while Dr Deuchar did his home visits in the motorcar. Maybe they'd be able to afford two cars now, with all the extra patients and none of them paying with leeks and shortbread. So maybe, soon enough, Helen would find herself alone in the building regularly. Maybe she should wait till then.

She knew she wasn't going to. If Maggie couldn't rest until her murderer was brought to justice, Helen shouldn't put off what she had to do.

Once she had climbed the first flight of stairs, she paused on the landing of the drawing-room floor. This far she could explain away her presence without too much difficulty. But when she set her foot on the bottom step leading up to the bedrooms, she was crossing a line. All the insinuations of Mrs Sinclair and Greet came back to her, along with Teenie's smirks, and she made her way as quickly as she could without any noise, up to the next landing and in at the little door that concealed the steps to the attic. She considered taking the key and locking herself in, but what if Dr Strasser came upstairs and noticed it missing? How could she explain that? Better to act as if she had nothing to hide. So, not only did she leave the key where she had found it, but she left the little door ajar too, as a claim to innocence.

The steps were dustier than she expected, considering that all the presents now arranged around her house had come down them two days ago. The attic at the top was dustier still, with so many motes dancing in the shafts of sunlight that the air dazzled. And it was stifling hot, here at the top of the house. Helen crossed to the skylight and jiggled the rusted sickle that was supposed to hold it open but she feared the noise of it moving would filter down to Dr Strasser and so left it closed.

Turning round slowly, she wondered where to start. She had expected a pile of boxes dumped for ease in the middle of the floor or stacked near the entrance, but there was nothing so obvious. Towards the rear she could see a tailor's dummy with a bustle attached and the mounted head of some kind of beastie. So all that back there had to be from the old days, when the Strassers lived in the whole house. She took a moment to be grateful that the stuffed head hadn't made its way to Rosebank, even if the tailor's dummy, stripped of its bustle, might have been welcome.

Leaving that back section, Helen still had a lot of searching to do. She levelled her gaze at the floor, thinking there would be marks in the dust, showing which of the many boxes had been shoved into place recently, but there were too many crisscrossing footprints, too much general disturbance.

Her next tactic was to grip each of the many crates and chests in turn and shake them. Stored ornaments would surely have a very different feel from stored documents, she reasoned. And indeed the first little box she applied herself to rustled and rattled. She lifted it down and opened the top. This would be her alibi, if one of the doctors disturbed her.

Inside, all she could see was a nest of crumpled paper, cushioning something or other. She left it in the centre of the floor and turned back to the pile she had plucked it from. The next box sounded just the same, the muffled clink of glass when she shook it, and the one after that and the one after that. But once she had piled them up behind her, she found a larger box, silent and heavy, at the bottom of the heap. This could be papers.

But could it be papers that were moved in here from Miss Anderson's office on Monday afternoon? Surely not. Unless, in the great switching over of fire irons, kettles and rugs for files and records, everything had ended up in a jumble. Worth a look, she decided, and prised up the lid.

It wasn't papers. On the top of the box, spread over and tucked in around the sides like an eiderdown, was a fur coat. Helen stroked it.

She had seen fur coats a plenty on Princes Street when Greet took them down to look at the Christmas windows, and she had hung up Mrs Sinclair's short rabbit jacket once at a meeting up Swanston way, but she had never felt the full satiny smoothness of a long fur coat under her hand and she had never felt what it was like to wear one. With half a glance behind her, she stood and swept it over her shoulders, pulling it in around her face.

She sneezed and shrugged it off again in an instant. It was far too close in the attic to thole a fur, and there was nothing to feel when you were inside it, with the plain lining next to you. If she ever had one of her own, she'd have it inside out, fur to her skin and satin for everyone else to look at. She let the coat fall behind her and scratched her neck, trying not to think about mites and moths and whatever further kinds of insects might have set up home – for weren't you supposed to store furs at a shop in a special bag or something? Didn't the poshest big department stores have a place where ladies dropped off their coats in spring for cleaning and left them there till it was cold again? She was sure of it, because there'd been a fire in Forsyth's one midsummer and the news said thousands of pounds' worth was gone.

Helen's skin was crawling now and she bundled up the coat ready to stuff it back with no thought about covering her tracks. But, as she knelt at the open box again, the next thing she saw snagged her attention. It was a photograph album, a bright red Rexine cover and red velvet ribbons holding it closed. On the front in flaking gold writing it said not 'Photographs' or 'Memories' like the album that Greet kept wrapped in chamois cloths under her bed but '1946'.

Imagine, Helen thought, having such a life that you made a new album of photographs every year – for underneath that one was another and another: 1945, 1944, 1943. From the depth of the box, Helen guessed that they reached back well into the twenties. It went with the fur coat, and the box after box of glasses. She lifted the top album and tugged at the velvet ribbons until they gave way. Then she opened the stiff cover of the album and the flimsy sheet of tissue paper guarding the first photograph inside.

It wasn't at all what she was expecting. Not a wedding, nor a christening – although, she supposed it couldn't be a wedding every year, actually – but it wasn't a picnic, or a carol concert, or a family gathering either. It was a... scene from the pictures, as best as she could make out. '*Destry Rides Again*,' she whispered to herself, looking at the little tables with stubby candles and those funny wee jelly glasses on them, men smoking cigars and holding up playing cards. They weren't dressed in cowboy hats and chaps from the films, though; they were wearing black bow ties and stiff fronts or striped ties and dark suits. The girls were just like Frenchy though. They wore those corsets with the fringe along the bottom that made Helen think of curtain tops, and they had on mesh stockings too. Their hair was in curls, under feathered headpieces, and their lips were dark. And, just like those Wild West girls, they sat on men's knees or stood hanging over their shoulders, watching the card game. The jarring note, though, was that they were Scottish.

Helen knew it as sure as she knew the beauty spots and long lashes were pasted on. These were Scottish men, with their whiskers and spectacles, Scottish girls with their sharp noses and rosy cheeks. She hadn't known there was a Scottish face, the way there was an Italian one or an Irish one, but she knew it now; some of them looked so familiar she might even have thought she recognised them.

She turned a few of the stiff pages, but it was the same scene over and over. A set made up of dark-papered walls with a glittering bar at one side, the little tables, the men – ties undone and ash falling from the fat cigars – and the girls – perched on laps, draped on shoulders, always smiling.

Helen went to put the album back in the box but stopped as she caught sight of something shoved down the side of the box, glinting. She hauled it out and couldn't help chuckling. It was one of the costumes. Part of it anyway – a headdress of feathers and glass beads. Helen had never seen anything so fancy in real life, not even the seed-pearl coronet her chum Mandy wore at her wedding. She dug even deeper down, pulling out one of the satin corsets with the lacy pelmet along the hips. She held it up to herself and turned it this way and that, laughing, blushing even though she was alone. The thought had stolen into her head, that maybe if she took it home and put it on, Sandy would look at her and. . . turn into Jimmy Stewart or Gregory Peck. She chuckled again and set the corset back in place, thinking she would look as daft in it as those other Scottish girls did. She hoped whoever made the film – if it was a film – was happy with it and that somebody had gone to see it and clapped. She herself couldn't bring it to mind. Greet, Teenie and her had been to the pictures three times a week all through the war, happy to watch whatever was showing, and she'd never seen a picture with all those monocled men and freckle-faced girls pretending to be in a saloon. Even the roll of tickets, unused and taped over, that she spotted down the other side of the box, seemed to say that this had been a bit of a flop.

As Helen replaced the fur coat, her thoughts started to re-order themselves. Why would the same people – whoever they were – who stored the costumes after a picture was made also have the roll of tickets from the picture house? They wouldn't.

And now that her brain was turning, the questions came thick and fast. Why would a doctor be involved in storing costumes and props? He wouldn't. Why wouldn't the money men – the producers, they were called – get folk a bit more glamorous to play the dancing girls? They would. So what *was* this she was looking at?

Obviously, she reckoned, it was a play. An amateur dramatic show got up in some church hall somewhere by a friend of the doctors. If she opened another photograph album it would be a different year and in another box would be the leftover costumes of nuns, or soldiers, or Regency princes. Helen lowered the lid on top of the fur and turned to the wee open box of crumpled paper, ready to close it too and set it back in place behind her.

But someone was coming. A pair of feet was climbing the attic steps. Helen started unwrapping a glass just in time as Dr Strasser came round the door and stopped dead, eyes wide, at the sight of her.

'Oh no,' she said. 'You've caught me, Doc. Red-handed.' She finished unwrapping the glass – it was another of the shallow jelly glasses.

'I certainly seem to have,' Dr Strasser said. 'What are you doing?'

'Looking for glasses,' Helen said. 'Taking a mile, since I got an inch, you could say. In among all that stuff that got given to Sandy and me to make space up here for the files, there was a set of these funny wee things.'

'Coupes,' said Dr Strasser. 'They're for champagne.'

'Oh,' Helen said. She hoped the light was too low to show him that she had flushed. 'I thought they were for jelly. And so maybe there'd be knickerbocker glory ones too. And banana boats. Make a set.'

'Banana. . .?' said Dr Strasser.

'But right enough, champagne makes more sense.' Helen was thinking of the photographs. Of course, a club with men in bow ties and girls in their corsets wouldn't be laying on sundaes! 'And so I thought maybe they were still up here and I could come and see. It's a right old jumble sale though, isn't it?'

181

'And when you say "space for files",' Dr Strasser went on. He had lost interest in the question of glasses, making Helen feel greedy and shallow. 'Which files would these be?'

'From clearing Miss Anderson's office,' she said.

'Ah!' he said. 'Well, after some discussion, we had a change of heart about those, actually. We decided to send them up to Johnston Terrace after all.'

'Oh,' Helen said. 'Lucky me it wasn't until after you'd cleared out ready for them! I'll not have to give everything back again, will I?'

'Not at all,' said Dr Strasser. He sounded friendly enough but his face was solemn. 'I told you I had no use for any of it. Help yourself to brandy balloons and whisky tumblers.' He waved his arm as if he was conducting an orchestra. 'Red wine, white wine, water, sherry, port. Fill your boots.'

Helen couldn't work out of he meant it or if he was scolding her in that sideways manner of his.

'Ach, I'll never use the ones I've got,' she said. 'A tumbler for milk and a toothmug is all I need really. I'd be better to bring back the six.' For it suddenly occurred to her that there were probably no sherry and port glasses here at all. It was more than likely champagne bowls in all of these wee rustly, clinking boxes. Enough to give everyone in that dancehall scene a drink of kiddy-on champagne in the play. And so it was a pure mistake that the one lot had come to her at all. They weren't cast-off household items from the days of the old doctor. They were props from 1946, stored for the drama club in case they put it on again, or did another one with plenty drinking.

'Will I get out your way then, Doc?' Helen said. 'Let you get on?'

'I was looking for you,' he replied. 'I heard you come up.' At her startled glance, he went on, 'I know this house's noises very well after a lifetime here.'

'And what did you need me for?' Helen said.

'Blood drive! I've had that holy terror Sister Armitage on the telephone saying we're not doing our bit here in Fountainbridge. She wants you out recruiting.'

'How's she got that notion already, after three days?' said Helen, outrage at the ready. Sister Armitage was a little bull who charged in, gave orders and charged out again, leaving everyone reeling but somehow always determined to do her bidding in case she charged again. 'There's no way there's any reports in about practices or parishes or wards or however they're going to do their counting. We're only just finding our feet, for goodness' sake.'

'Be that as it may,' Dr Strasser said, 'and between you and me I think you've hit the nail on the head, but can I tell her you'll pitch in?'

'Tie a broom to my bahookey and I'll sweep the floor while I'm at it,' Helen said. 'Tell her *that.*' Then she clapped a hand over her mouth. She couldn't believe she had actually said that out loud in front of the doctor. In front of *this* doctor! She hardly dared look at him.

But when she finally raised her head, he was smiling for the first time all day. 'I'll pass it along,' he said. Helen let her breath go and scuttled for the attic door.

As they neared the ground floor, they met Dr Deuchar and Helen felt her cheeks threaten yet again to darken. If Teen had seen her and Dr Strasser coming down from upstairs together, she'd have put her tongue in her cheek and lifted her eyebrows, but Dr Deuchar didn't turn a hair.

'Did you manage to dragoon her, Strasser?' was all he said.

'Of course,' Helen said, calming down. 'Of course I'll help. I want to, so I can report to Sister Armitage and have a few words while I'm about it. She needs to understand you can't give a pint of blood and go back on a factory floor to a big machine, so it's not safe always. She needs to get up to Morningside to her ladies that only have to lie on a couch and turn the pages of their picture papers all afternoon.'

'Yes, it starts innocently enough,' Dr Strasser said. 'Stratifying humanity, coming up with the notion that hardy, working people can take a needle in their stride and spare a pint of claret, while the gentry might swoon. But we know where it can end.' His face had clouded. Helen didn't know what to say when he got that way, working everything back round to the worst of the war. She knew what had happened, same as anyone who didn't live in cloud cuckoo land, but Dr Strasser seemed to find reminders in places no one else would. He went into his surgery without another word, leaving Dr Deuchar frowning at the closed door.

'Is Doc Strasser all right?' Helen said. 'He's been that keen for the service but since it started his face has been—' She paused. 'He seems sad.'

'I hadn't noticed,' said Dr Deuchar. 'He's never exactly juggling and tap dancing, is he? Poor chap.'

Why was he a poor chap, Helen wondered. 'I was up in the attic, Doc,' she said, to lighten the atmosphere. 'I might as well tell you before Doc Strasser clypes on me.'

'The attic?'

'I thought since you put the files up and brought all my lovely stuff down—'

He cut her off. 'Ah, but I didn't in the end. In the *end*, I decided to burn them. A lot of rubbish really when I went through the top one or two.'

'Oh,' said Helen. She wondered whether he'd said to Dr Strasser that he was sending the files in and then decided on his own to burn the lot. Or if Dr *Strasser* had told her the tale of sending them in, in case the thought of burned files shocked her. Whichever way it was, they needed to get their story straight; it was a good thing she trusted them. 'Well,' she went on, since he was looking at her with a curious expression, 'maybe if folk are burning papers instead of sending them in, Johnston Terrace really *has* finished the filing and got as far as blood drive league tables, after all.'

184

Dr Deuchar laughed, clapped her on the back and went on his way, whistling.

But Helen stood her ground, and cleared her throat. He turned back with a look of enquiry. 'Can I say something?' she asked.

'Anything, Nell. Always.' He opened his door and ushered her in, settling behind his desk with a smile for her.

'It's about the girl in the shelter,' she began. 'Maggie.'

'What about her?' said Dr Deuchar. 'Are you still upset at the memory of what you saw?'

'Not upset,' Helen said. 'Troubled. And it's funny you said "memory" because – it's hard to put it into words but – I was fuddled. The shock and everything. I mean, when I saw her I thought, "I know who that is" and then it turned out I didn't know who it was at all and all that terrible business of saying to Mrs Sinclair that Fiona was dead, then saying it was Carolyn. It put it out of my mind. Then all of a sudden last night it popped back in.'

'What did?' said Dr Deuchar.

'About the poison,' Helen said. She hadn't trod this carefully since playing Grandmother's Footsteps when she was wee. 'The smell of poison, you said.'

'Yes?'

'And marks.'

'Yes?'

'It was her ears, see?'

They sat opposite one another for a moment in silence and Helen thought someone looking in the window would be reminded of two strange cats meeting on a wall at night, neither one wanting to start the fighting nor back away.

'You said the marks were round her mouth,' Helen said at last. 'And I did see *them*. I crouched down to look and saw those marks. But I saw the marks at her throat too. At her jaw. Up behind her ears.'

Dr Deuchar sat back, slumped really, as if the air had gone out of him. Or as if all his tailored clothes – his jacket and waistcoat and stiff collar and firmly knotted tie – had gone soft and stopped supporting him. 'We didn't want to tell you,' he said. 'When we realised the mistake I said there was no need for you to know. It seemed so much worse that the poor benighted fool hanged herself than that she drank poison. To me, anyway.'

'Not to me,' Helen said. 'Because that means, surely, she didn't die where she sat. Or where was the rope?'

'Didn't. . .' he echoed. 'What do you mean? How else could she be there?'

'Someone must have—'

'But she did, Nelly,' he said, leaning forward again. 'She died right there in the shelter. I just didn't want you to think about it. She put a rope around her neck – a simple loop – then she inhaled chloroform to make her slump down in a faint and she died. The rope broke and fell down behind her. We found it when we moved her.'

'Oh,' Helen said. 'Oh! If only it had broken sooner. She might have survived.' She had a vision of a fraying rope and a sinking weight, the breathing stopping seconds before the last strand let go. 'Oh Doc. That's awful.' Then she frowned. 'But where was the chloroform bottle?'

'Behind the door,' said Dr Deuchar. 'She must have dropped it and then when you opened—'

'But the door opens out,' Helen said. A flicker of annoyance crossed his face then. He wasn't used to all of this from her. From anyone, probably.

'It must have rolled sideways. Under one of the bunks.'

Helen remembered the tented gown and the little white feet with their pearly nails. If the girl had let a bottle fall from her hands as she passed out it would have rolled down her gown and landed at her feet. And from there it should have rolled, if it rolled at all, straight to the front of the shelter.

The memory was fresh of Teenie bawling and sobbing one filthy night because her baby doll's glass eye had come out and rolled away under the shelter door into the mud that was puddling outside at the bottom of the steps like it always did. So many mornings Greet had lifted Teenie over that puddle into Mack's arms, and more than once she had said, 'Think yourself lucky your daddy's such a clever man. He's set us on a slope, see? None of this muck is round our feet all night. Not like Mrs Scobbie. She's sleeping in a duck pond over there, for her man's got the hands of a haddie on him.'

Maybe another handless man had put in the shelter at Rosebank.

'All I know,' Dr Deuchar was saying, 'is that the policemen found it after they'd moved her. Now, let's put the whole sorry episode behind us, shall we? Onwards, Helen! To the blood drive!'

'Onwards, Doc,' Helen said. To answers, she thought. And to justice for Maggie, whoever she might be.

Chapter 14

Whether the patient notes from the wee hospital were up at Johnston Terrace waiting for the filing clerks to dig down to them or were ashes round roses by now, or if – a possibility Helen should bear in mind – the notes in question were nothing to do with the wee fever hospital at all, her bright idea of finding the key to Maggie among them was a bust. So what should she do instead?

Need she do anything, she asked herself yet again. The vow she had made to the girl was never to let it happen to someone else. She hadn't promised to untangle what had happened this time. And only one of those two tasks was her job.

Besides, if the poor thing really did put a rope round her own neck and then knocked herself out so she'd slump into it and hang, there was nothing to be solved. It was just a pair of coincidences that the rope broke and the chloroform bottle rolled sideways. And a third coincidence that Dr Deuchar made that mistake.

Helen took up a pencil and idly drew a sketch of the shelter on her blotter. She marked with an X where Maggie had been sitting, and then closed her eyes, trying to call to mind the wall behind and the curved ceiling above. Was there a hook there, or a beam? Something to throw a rope around?

The pencil was in her hand again. This time she drew a noose, or tried to. She had her knot-maker's badge from the Brownies but she had only ever seen the hangman's knot on the films and it was far too complicated to render in blunt pencil on thick blotting paper. Helen looked up.

It was no easier to render in *rope*, surely, in the dark, and in extremis. And hadn't the Doc just said 'a simple loop'? And wasn't that why the rope didn't stay around Maggie's neck, but unravelled and slithered down behind her?

Helen had a wee sewing kit in the top drawer of her desk; a present from Teen, embroidered for her birthday, back when a big sister was the most precious treasure in the world. She opened it now and unwound a length of darning thread. She looped and knotted one end of it, then made a noose by drawing the other end through. Then she let the little contraption dangle from one hand while her other thumb sat in the belly of the loop, resting in it, pulling it down. Helen opened her clasped fingers and let the free end go, watching as the noose slipped down her thumb, the way a rope noose would have slipped down the girl's neck, coming to rest at the top of her gown, where there was no chance – none at all – that it could have gone unseen. Helen remembered the white skin and the gaping cotton, how clean she looked and how soft.

What if she had made an even simpler loop, hooking the top of it over the beam or nail or whatever and putting her chin into the bottom of it, like resting in a hammock? Then when she slumped. . . she would have fallen free, wouldn't she? And wouldn't the broken rope have been left hanging from the ceiling?

The only way it could have happened was for Maggie to make the kind of noose no one determined to die would ever make, and then for her to fall backward, out of the rope, just before it gave way. But that would put the thing in her lap. Or, if she fell forward, how would the rope unhook from under her chin? So she must have gone just far enough back to escape the rope but not too far to stop it coming down behind her, hidden by her body, until the police moved her. And the bottle of chloroform rolled sideways.

If Sandy hadn't locked up the shelter she could go in with a marble and at least try that bit for herself. For, in the light of day, talk of ghosts seemed foolish. She glanced at the corner of her office where she'd seen the flash of yellow on Monday morning, as Miss Anderson sat stony and determined, at this very desk. There was nothing to see today, beyond the squat block of the corner-most cabinet, now lightened of its load of files, holding only the very few she had managed to produce in four days. For a while, Helen thought, the char would be able to shift them and mop underneath without scoring the good wood floor like she'd been doing.

As she stood and went to fetch her coat and hat, she rubbed at the scores with her toe. It was a shame to have spoiled these polished boards, dragging furniture. But there was only one char and full cabinets must have been far too heavy for her to lift alone. Helen decided she'd offer to help when she happened to catch the woman, as long as she could do it without seeming to criticise. She'd say, 'My boards in my house are a midden. All spoiled and patched. These are lovely though, aren't they?' They'd never had a carpet on them to let moth droppings eat away at their smooth surface. And they'd never had lino nailed down round the sides either. If the cleaner was the usual lazy sort who'd never dream of shifting furniture to mop behind, they'd be perfect. But facing the surgery char was a job for tomorrow. She had something even harder to face today.

She tugged the front of her jacket down, as she'd seen soldiers in dress uniform do in the war films, then she pinned her hat firmly to her head as if to arm herself against blows. If ghosts were helpless to scare her on a fine summer's morning, what better time to go where she was going, to do what she was sure she had to do? For she'd be a pretty poor champion of the needy if she let them down any time they slipped through the cracks, if she washed her hands of them whenever their precarious lives finally unravelled. If angry Mr Yarrow harmed his wee Gordon, Helen would be on him. If the filth in Mrs Shields' clarty house harmed her new baby, Helen wouldn't just shrug and close the file with thon pink tape tied in a bow. Maggie was no different. She'd died of her troubles, one way or another, on the very day that help finally came. And Helen wasn't having it.

She stood on the Cowgate looking at the mortuary's front door, wondering whether to march right in or go round the side lane again and wait for an orderly coming out on his dinner break. She was an official medical almoner with bona fides she could call on. But why would anyone on her books need her here, asking questions? Better, she reckoned, trotting across the street before an oncoming caravan of traffic stopped her, to get in with one of the working men. She was Edinburgh bred and buttered, her daddy in the slaughterhouse and her mammy in the bottling hall, both grandpas with time served at the Pilrig works and both grannies with years in service in big houses all over the city. There was bound to be some connection she could pull on, if the orderly she happened upon was a local laddie.

The goodness of the bright morning had already been dimmed by a walk along the Cowgate, more like a tunnel than a road, and once the string of vans and carts had clattered by behind the slow pony and cart that was holding them up the silence all around joined to the gloom of the side lane and made Helen regret the entire adventure. But she was committed now and, daft as she felt lurking here, she'd feel dafter to have come all this way only to leave again.

She didn't have long to lurk anyway. After a few minutes of shifting from foot to foot, and constantly checking over each shoulder in case some stranger using this lane as a cut-through found her standing there, the back door of the building opened and a dapper little man stepped out. Helen, watching him through the railings, thought him too neat to be a worker. He was surely a doctor or professor, with his bright little boots shining like conkers and the leather buttons on his tweed suit winking like teddy-bears' eyes. As he emerged from the gates, he lifted the cap he'd only just clapped on his head and gave Helen a little bow before going over to a red van parked on the slope of the side street ahead of her and opening the back doors.

He bent over, reaching inside, then emerged again, a paper-covered tray in his hands. Helen glanced at the side of the van and read: *Henry Barbone and sons, since 1903.* He was a butcher! Or maybe a baker. But that, unless she was very much mistaken, was a tray of pies. She swallowed hard against a sudden flood of bile and only just managed to hoist a smile onto her face as he came back towards her.

He did not return it, but looked at her with concern. 'You all right there, hen?' he said.

'Aye,' she said. 'I'm waiting on my felly.'

At that his eyes twinkled again. 'Billy, is it? My, my. He's done well for himself. But he's nothing like ready for coming out. I've just seen him.' Helen couldn't help her eyes straying down to the tray. 'Looks bad, doesn't it?' he said. 'But I take my apron off, at least. I couldnae thole wearing it the rest of my round if I'd worn it in there.'

'I'm used to it,' Helen said. 'Well, used to hearing about it. From Bill, you know. But I ken what you mean.' She grinned at him. 'Anyway, it would look worse if you were bringing them out.'

He frowned and then gave a shout of laughter as her meaning reached him. 'Aye, you're right!' he said. 'Sweeney Todd's given the lot of us a bad name.' He gave a theatrical shudder. 'I could never. . .' he said. 'Walking in that door's enough for me.'

Helen, as a brainwave hit her, said: 'Well, how about killing two birds with one stone? I'll take the pies in for you and that way I get to see Bill a bit quicker.'

'You would do that?'

192

'Tell the truth, I've got to see him. I'm in a wee bit of trouble and he's been avoiding me.'

Mr Barbone's eyes pinched up as he took in this news and for a moment Helen thought she'd queered her own pitch. She imagined the little man bursting into the morgue to demand that poor innocent Billy make an honest woman of a complete stranger.

'I thought you looked peaky,' was all he said in the end, however. And then, 'Is this tray not too heavy for you, though?'

Helen tested the weight and assured him she'd be fine then, once he had opened the gate for her, she trod with a fair bit of apprehension up to the mortuary door.

Wedging the tray hard between one hip and the wall of the wee porch, she banged on the door and shouted out in the gruffest voice she could muster, 'Pies!'

'Too good to erse open a door now, are you, Harry?' As the door swung wide to reveal Helen on the doorstep, though, the man inside shut his mouth with a smack and turned a deep painful brick red. He had the same ginger-and-freckles colouring as Helen herself and she felt for him. 'Pardon my French,' he said. 'I thought you were. . .' Then he glanced at the tray. 'Where's Harry?'

'I've been seconded,' Helen said. 'Harry's called away.'

The young man – was this Billy? – reached out to grab the near side of the pie tray and take it from her, but Helen held fast.

'Sorry,' she said, 'but I promised I would take the tray back. So if I can just come in and unload it. . .'

'He usually picks it up the next day when he's delivering again,' the man said.

'Are you Billy?' Helen said. 'Maybe that's what he meant. I said I'd take the tray back and he said Billy would keep me right.'

They were inside now, walking along a corridor distempered dark brown and with a floor of red linoleum that came up either side eight inches like a skirting board. Helen didn't want to think about why. And she didn't want to breathe too deeply either but, even with her mouth open, there was a sharpness about the air that, added to the thick fatty aroma of the warm pies, threatened her gullet. She felt it soften, felt that sinking sensation of everything between her stomach and her mouth falling open to give clear passage to what was coming. She swallowed hard and while her lips were pressed shut, inevitably got a noseful of everything the corridor had to give: soap and chemicals and damp and Billy's sweat and a low slink of decay under everything, making her remember a rat under the floor at Freer Street and a box of ancient eggs in her granny's house when she had grown forgetful, and poor old Mr Something or other neglecting his leg until he had to lose it, after Mrs Sinclair and Helen found him in his chair, merry as a robin on gut-rot whisky, watching the maggots without a care in the world.

A moan escaped her lips.

'Dinnae you boak on oor pies!' Billy said, making her laugh and feel a bit better. He opened the door to what looked like a wee staff room, with old chairs and piles of newspapers and the doings for what looked like ten pipes all heaped up on a table against the wall. 'You can set them in the meat safe,' Billy said, pointing to a wire-fronted cabinet.

When the pies were stowed and Helen had wiped her hands, she sat down on one of the seats at the table, not waiting to be asked. Billy raised his eyebrows.

'I'm nothing to do with Mr Barbone,' she said. 'I've got myself in here under whatsit.'

'False pretences,' Billy said. 'How? What are you after? A loved one? A look-see?'

'Neither,' said Helen, shuddering. 'Is one of those pipes yours? Can you light it before I lose my porridge?'

'We never notice it unless it's a bad one now,' Billy said, but he clamped his hand on a baccy pouch and clay pipe and set about producing some comfort for her. 'So *what* is it you're after?' he said, after a few deep puffs had filled the air with the wondrous scent.

'Duncan Pyne,' Helen said. 'Monday night.'

Billy took the pipe out of his mouth and pointed the stem at her. 'Are you from the papers?' he said.

'I'm not,' said Helen. 'I'm a medical almoner, but that's not the point. Someone died in my Anderson shelter, you see. Maggie Dickson, supposed to be a notorious Glasgow criminal, except she's no'. She never came here, because the Glasgow fiscal or whoever he was was having dinner with Duncan Pyne and scooped her away west. But what was Mr Pyne doing coming in your back door? That's what bothers me.'

'What were *you* doing at our back door watching him?' said Billy. 'If it comes to that.'

Helen thought about lying but she wasn't quick enough and didn't know what a good lie would be. 'I was with the doctor that signed the certificate,' she said. 'It needed changed, so we were trying to catch the van before it came in. Only it went to Glasgow.'

'Aye, that's the second time you've said that.' Billy sucked his pipe a while but it had gone out on him. It turned Helen's quaking stomach to imagine the taste of ash instead of smoke in his throat. 'Someone's been telling you tales, whoever you are.'

'Helen. Sorry.'

'The doctor on call here signed that cert. on Tuesday morning. Nobody took her to Glasgow. Mr Pyne dropped her here on Monday, like you said. You seen him.'

Helen stared. 'Mr Pyne. . .' she said. 'She was in his *car*?'

'When I saw her she was on a trolley wrapped in a sheet,' Billy said. 'But aye. That's what the rest of the nightshift said. Special delivery. I thought we were away back to the old days.'

'And what had happened to her?' Helen said. 'Do you know? Did you see her? She wasn't poisoned, was she? She was hanged. I know she was. But did anyone try to work out what knot was in the rope? Could you tell? Did you even see her, before she went away? Where did she go? Is she buried? Cremated?'

'Slow down,' said Billy. 'Steady on. What are you talking about? She never went anywhere. We d'ae even ken who she is yet. So she's still here, waiting for them to decide what to do.'

Helen felt her leg muscles tense the way they used to when the teacher raised her wee flag on sports day and all of them in their vests and knickers prepared for her to drop it and send them away down the field. 'She—Maggie's still here?'

'Jane Bloggs is still here,' said Billy. 'I d'ae ken where you're getting "Maggie" fae. Do you want to meet her?'

'I've already "met" her,' Helen said. 'It was me that found her. But I'd like to see her again, aye. Get a better look at her, and put away this notion I cannot shift.'

'You think you know who she is?' said Billy. 'Because that would be no end of help to us here, Helen my lass. Give her her name and get her away to the undertakers, before it gets any worse.'

'Is it bad?' Helen said. 'I'll need to take a bucket in if it's really bad.'

'See now, you're my kind of girl,' said Billy. 'If the coppers and medical students and the rest of them that make all the mess would just ask for a bucket!'

She didn't need it. For a start, Billy gave her some Vicks to smear on her top lip and breathe through, and for another the shock of seeing the girl again was a blow to the heart, not the stomach.

Of course, her knees were knocking up to the minute. As Billy led her along the passageway deeper into the bowels of the building, the temperature dropping and the light dimming, Helen knew she was turning pale and she wiped her hands on her skirt to dry her palms.

Another orderly poked his head out of a side-room. 'Has Harry been?' he said. And then 'Whae's this?'

'She thinks she kens Jane Bloggs,' said Billy.

'Mr Pyne'll no' like that,' the other orderly said, coming out into the corridor. He wore an oilcloth apron over his tunic. It reminded Helen of Mack at the slaughterhouse and she turned her face away.

'Mr Pyne can whistle,' Billy said. 'What's he gonny dae to us? We know too much.'

'That's right,' Helen said, turning back. 'You said something about the "old days". So this isn't the first corpse Duncan Pyne has dropped off with you? Why does he get his own hands dirty if he's as much of a high heid yin as you're saying?'

'Say nothing, Billy!' the other orderly called back over his shoulder as he beetled along towards the staff room.

'Is he going in there like that?' Helen said. 'To eat a pie with those hands?'

'Ach, you get lazy,' Billy said. 'We all start out boiling our ovies and dipping our hands in soda. But you get easier as time goes by.'

Helen was planning to put every stitch she had in the sink when she got home and have an even hotter bath than yesterday. But that was for later. Now, Billy was opening a door that revealed itself to be lead-lined on its other side. He led her into a drab grey room, the walls lead too and the floor tiled in dark-red and sloping towards the middle. All around were panels that Helen slowly realised were drawer-fronts.

'Are all these drawers. . . ?' she said. She clutched her bucket in both hands.

'Not even half,' said Billy. 'Summertime, see? In the winter, it's different. But not in July. Right, then.'

He had found the drawer he was looking for and he un-locked it with a key from the ring hanging off his belt. 'Ready?' he said.

Helen nodded.

Billy pulled it open, revealing a shrouded shape lying on a long tray. As it came out, a prop dropped down from the underside, like a gate-leg table. Billy kicked it square and let go of the drawer, allowing the weight of the body to settle with a creak. The shroud wasn't linen, Helen saw, but some kind of waxed canvas. It was probably meant to keep odours in and insects out. It crackled as Billy lifted it and sat tented over the girl's chest when he folded it back.

Helen let out a small moan but managed not to look away. At least the eyes were closed. And the lips. But the soft white skin was yellow now and wrong-looking over the bones, not plumped out by a living body. It sagged and melted down-wards towards the lead shelf she lay on and the nose had grown beaky as the face around it slid away. Honestly, she could have been anyone. That likeness Helen saw to the Sinclair girls in the dark of the shelter had faded as the mask of death settled. Only the hair was the same, singing like silk, coiled in a golden roll at one side of her neck. It looked false, but then locks of hair inside lockets still shone years after the mourning. The lock of hair from her brother, Greet and Mack's lost boy, still shone in the wee snuff box on the kitchen mantel where it sat, unless Mack took it out when he came home late and sat over it, sighing. Helen hated him for that. Buffered by drink he'd sit, enjoying his wallow, while Greet went about with her face turned the other way, really hurting.

There was no point staring at her hair, Helen told herself, and – thank heavens – no need to look again at that wooden, slipping-down face. What she really needed to look at was the neck. But as she moved her gaze she was struck by the little hole in the girl's earlobe. She had pierced ears. Of course, lots of girls had pierced ears, no matter what their mothers and fathers thought about it. Helen might even pierce her own ears now that she wouldn't have to listen to Mack nagging her about it after it was done. And if she did, at least she had a nice round earlobe for the needle. The dead girl had no such thing. The thin rim of her ear went straight into her jaw and the wee hole for the earring looked out of place.

Helen saw the flash of memory behind her eyes as if she was at a picture show. The first time she'd seen that thin rim instead of an earlobe was at the Christmas party at Mrs Sinclair's. She had touched her own ear and thought she might not be able to afford diamond drops, but she'd look better in them if she could.

So it was true. Helen was certain now, more certain than she'd been on Monday night, even though days of death had changed the face. It made no sense and it left her reeling but she couldn't deny it.

'I would still have sworn it was Fiona,' she said. 'But I've mixed them up. She probably borrowed her sister's earrings the day I'm remembering. Same as Teen and me. Anyway,' she drew a huge breath, 'that girl is Carolyn Sinclair.'

Billy was silent a moment and then he whistled long and low. 'That explains Mr Pyne and the hush job,' he said. 'I thought it was the same old story but it's not. It's making sure no scandal touches them and such as them. It's *that* same old story.'

'What do you mean?' Helen said. 'You never did explain what you meant by the old days.'

'Nocht you need to know,' Billy said. 'The dark side of life. No business of a nice girl like you.'

'Well then,' said Helen, 'can you at least help me decide what made these marks on her neck? I'm no' too nice for that, am I?'

She had bent low and was scrutinising the weal that had rubbed the underside of Carolyn's jaw until it wept. The burn carried on around the back of her ear and disappeared under her hair.

'How d'you mean?' Billy said. 'Sisal rope from a chandler or a carter. Just rope.'

'No, not the rope. I'm asking what knot. A loop? A slipknot? Or like a proper hangman's knot? Is there any way to tell?'

'You've some stomach on you, I'll gie you that,' Billy said, shaking his head in wonder. 'Why are you asking?'

Helen tried her best to explain. About the rope slipping down behind the corpse, out of view, and her attempts to imagine how it happened.

'But if it was just the one big loop, she could easy get out of it,' Billy said. 'She'd no' be deid.'

'But that was what the chloroform was for,' Helen said. 'To knock herself out in case she lost her nerve.'

Billy was staring. 'Her*self*?' he said. 'You think she did this to herself?'

'Don't you?'

In answer he rummaged under the canvas and drew out one of her hands, holding it in his as if they were about to dance a reel. Helen felt a wave of faintness wash over her. 'What are you showing me?' she said.

'Look at her nails,' said Billy.

'I've seen them,' Helen said. 'They're lovely.'

'Look closer. Look under them.' As Helen crouched, she saw what he meant: a rime of short spikes and flakes, wee crumbs of brown and yellow. 'Is that fur?' she said. 'Dog hairs?'

'It's rope,' Billy said. 'She fought hard but she couldn't escape it.'

'So,' said Helen slowly, 'there's no way it was a loop she slipped free of as she passed out. If she had changed her mind while it was still happening, she could have got out of a loop. And a better knot would have stayed round her neck. Until someone took it away.'

'And moved her,' Billy said. 'From wherever she deed to wherever you found her. A shelter, you said? Like an Anderson shelter, you mean?' As Helen confirmed it, he shook his head. 'See, there's no way. If she was struggling in an Anderson shelter, she could have got her feet up on a bunk. They're too wee. That'll maybe help you set your mind at rest, eh hen? Wherever she deed it wasnae in your huttie. Someone moved her there.'

'Unless she kept slipping,' Helen said. 'Trying to get her feet up and falling and that's when she started scrabbling at the rope.'

'I'm *sure* somebody moved her,' Billy said. 'Somebody definitely put that goonie on her anyway.'

Helen frowned at him.

'It's no' pretty, dying,' said Billy. 'Maybe you know that if you've sat by a deathbed yourself. But if you've only seen the pictures where someone shuts their een with a wee smile on their face and it's like they're sleeping, maybe it's news.'

'What's news?'

'Everything lets go,' Billy said. 'Gravity takes over when all your muscles give up what they're doing, see? It's no' dainty.'

'Oh, poor Carolyn,' Helen said. 'I mean, I know she was past caring but she was right perjink when she was alive. She was in the Land Army. And that proud of her overalls.'

'Aye well,' Billy said. 'She died naked. And everything was dry before that goonie went near her, because it was pure white and still in its folds from the laundry. But she was maukit inside it.'

'She looked so perfect,' Helen said. 'Her bonny wee feet and her wee white hands.'

'Oh, she was perfect,' Billy said. '*Virgo intacta.* That was a first, too.'

201

Chapter 15

If she was a man, or the kind of woman who didn't care, or even just if she wasn't born here and odds on to meet someone she knew at every turn, Helen would have headed into the nearest Cowgate pub for a brandy to still her nerves and jolt her brain back into working order. She was reeling. She all but staggered away from the back door, with Billy calling out after her, offering her a cup of tea or one of the pies. She closed her mouth firmly and tried to ignore the sloshing that felt too high to be in her stomach. Port and brandy. That was what she needed. Maybe the nearest pub to the morgue was used to respectable people washing up there, after they'd identified a loved one or looked at a face and seen a stranger, when they'd half-hoped and half-dreaded that a wait was over. She knew it was worse before they knew about Sandy. 'Missing' was the blackest time of all. 'Presumed dead' was sadder but less exhausting. 'Captured' should have been a horror but all she could think was that he was safe. He was inside, fed and clothed, and no one was shelling the POW camps, not the Germans and not their boys, so he'd come home. And then he came home, to his mother and to Helen and the two women stared at each other, aghast, both of them flooded with shame for thinking he was safe and fed and clothed and fine.

The Sandy who came home was emaciated, his cheeks sunk so far you could see his teeth through his skin and his shoulder blades showing like open shears through his shirt. Teen roared with grief and rage, kicking her heels and shrieking at Helen. 'You lied! You lied! You told me big fat lies!' She'd been young and didn't know the difference between a POW camp and the other kind and had cried sore, until Helen told her about cosy huts like Brownie trips and Red Cross parcels and games of cards and football. And then Sandy came home and looked just like the newsreel ghosts. It was the one time Greet was hard on Teenie. 'Wheesht your nonsense!' she'd said. 'This isn't about you, you wee besom. It isn't even about Helen. It's about our Sandy, come home at last, and you've not to let on you can see a change in him.'

'Or you'll feel the back of my hand,' Mack said, his usual contribution, always threatened, never carried through. Still, Helen had bitten her lip. There had been enough of all that. Threats and attacks and tantrums. The world had gone mad and, now it was over, people should try to be better. Or it would only happen again, in another twenty years, like last time.

Remembering had distracted her from Carolyn Sinclair at last. Now she needed to get away from here, back to work or even home, but definitely out of the Cowgate gloom and the squalor of the Grassmarket. She needed to be up in the light and get a lungful of good fresh air.

She dithered at the bottom of Blackfriars Street, undecided about which route to take. Neither was ideal. That was what came from having a castle plonked in the middle of the city. She could head north for Chambers Street and Lauriston Place, then into the crescent from the top end, be done with cobbled closes for the day. Or she could go up to the High Street and all the way to Johnston Terrace, straight past, no need to go poking in records now.

For if that was Carolyn Sinclair – and it was – then whatever had happened to her was none of Helen's concern and the patient files were nothing to do with her dying. Carolyn and Fiona had a doctor up in Blackford somewhere. They'd never set foot in the Gardner's Crescent surgery. And they'd certainly never been patients of the wee hospital. For one thing, neither of them ailed a day in their lives. 'Rude health', Mrs Sinclair called it, as if she was pining for the days when girls in tight corsets fainted on couches. And for another, Mrs Sinclair would have said as much on Monday. Wouldn't she?

Mrs Sinclair! She had believed the corpse was Maggie Dickson. Late on Monday night when Helen and Dr Deuchar went back to her house, she'd still believed both her daughters were safe and she'd been bustling about buying railway tickets and packing. But she'd know better by now. She'd have discovered long since that Carolyn was missing. Why hadn't she been in touch? And, given that she couldn't be visiting in London, where was she?

None of it made any sense. Mrs Sinclair's daughter Carolyn who lived in London had been killed, her body dressed in a treatment gown and dumped in the garden of what used to be a fever hospital, run by the doctors her mother helped as an almoner? Why? And why on earth did a bigwig like Duncan Pyne take her body to the morgue and lie about Glasgow? Why did a bigwig like Duncan Pyne *ever* do the dark work of moving bodies? Like those old bogeymen they used to sing about, skipping in the back green.

'Doon the close and up the stair.
Into the hoose with Burke and Hare.'

And then how did it go? Something something, Burke's the butcher, Hare's the thief. Knox is the man who buys the beef.

'But who's Pyne?' Helen muttered.

'You all right, hen?' The voice made her jump and she wheeled round. 'First sign of madness, talking to yersel.'

Maybe he was just being nice, but the gap-toothed grin that split his dirty face was more of a leer and the burst of laughter that followed as she sprinted away from him sounded anything but friendly. Helen lifted her eyes to the bridge high above, with bright omnibuses passing and ladies bound for the good shops shading themselves from the hot sun with parasols and straw hats. If they had looked over the parapet they might have seen her running away from that wheezing, cackling tramp. But why would they look? That was the whole point of the bridges: to carry the quality across these streets without them having to see what happened down here.

At the bottom of Niddry Street, still sure she could hear footsteps behind her, Helen darted to the right and pelted, hell for leather, up towards the Tron. Here were cobbles still, and narrow close mouths, but also light and people and then the cathedral and ahead the esplanade, and then she could bob down round the castle and get back to Fountainbridge that way, shake all that Burke and Hare nonsense out of her head. It was just the mortuary making her daft, and the talk of ghosts. Attics, old photographs, old clothes – they always spooked her.

She paused at the big junction where the bank building faced up to the court and the libraries, with only one pub on the fourth corner to lower the tone. Or maybe it didn't, for this pub was a long throw from Bennet's where Mack spent his wages and where he'd tried to get Sandy to join him before he gave the boy up as a 'jessie'. This was a burnished Victorian drinking emporium, the brass and crystal visible through the high windows. It was probably full of advocates and bankers from opening time on. Helen looked at the name picked out in gold against the smart green paint, like livery, and as the words sank in, she missed a gap in the carts and trams and got buffeted and tutted at by the other pedestrians flowing into the street around her.

'Deacon Brodie's Tavern,' she said. 'Deacon Brodie.'

She had no proof but she was sure of it. It had happened again. Not Burke and Hare after all, but William Brodie, the picture of respectability by day and breaking into folks' house at night. Edinburgh loved him for it too. Called a pub after him and devoured the book about him, where Dr Jekyll turned into

Mr Hyde. 'The old days,' Billy had said. And 'we know too much'. And then, at the end, 'virgo intacta. That was a first, too.'

Duncan Pyne was *worse* than Deacon Brodie. A murderer, not a thief. Maybe he didn't know the wee hospital was closed down. Maybe he thought a girl in a goonie would throw suspicion in another direction. Or maybe he knew fine well the place was empty and reckoned she'd sit there with no one knowing until. . .

Until what, though?

And why should Carolyn be untouched if other, earlier girls had been degraded before they died? Why would Carolyn be in his sights at all? A well-protected girl from a rich, powerful family was the last person a devil like Pyne would make for. Helen shivered, remembering an afternoon in the King's Pictures, watching a jerky, silent melodrama all set on foggy nights in London, remembering coming out blinking into the grey day, glad to be in Edinburgh with Greet's arm about her waist as they hurried home.

Now she really *did* wish she had the nerve to walk into a pub and demand that port and brandy. She'd get put out of Deacon Brodie's though. Those bankers and lawyers would never thole a chit of a girl standing at the bar beside them. Not when they were dressed for the day in their wigs and bowler hats. If she wanted a sit-down while her thoughts skirled she'd have to perch on a wall or find a bench.

She started to head for Lauriston Street, needing to be away from the old places where it suddenly seemed nothing good had ever happened, newly loath to skirt the castle walls and have to think about hundreds of years of sieges and beheadings.

Then, as she was halfway over the bridge, high above the dark tunnel of streets below, she remembered the central library. She could sit, rest and recover there, same as anyone. There, in the quiet, perhaps she could bring herself back down from these spinning notions that surely had to be fancy.

Or, she told herself as she entered the tall glass doors, perhaps she could find out if any of it was true.

Just walking through the hall calmed her. She had never been here before and it was much grander even than the lovely new branch library at Dundee Street, the one that looked so much like a picture house it had been disappointing Fountainbridge weans since the day it opened. This place was as fancy as a museum, just like the big Glasgow gallery they'd all ended up in one day when it rained hard on a Girls' Brigade picnic.

'Help you?' said a wee woman in a cardigan with her specs on a chain, as Helen ventured into the soaring room at the top of the stairs.

'Have you. . .?' she began. Then she thought hard.

'Probably,' said the librarian, with a twinkle.

Helen smiled. 'Have you pictures? Portraits, I mean. I think. Of the big men in the town?' she said. 'Judges and bishops and the like? Doctors,' she added to make it less obvious who she was after.

'Certainly,' said the librarian. 'How far back are you going?'

'Oh,' Helen said. 'No. I mean today. Not likes of. . .'

'George Drummond and Sir Arthur,' said the woman.

'Exactly,' Helen said. 'Duncan Pyne was one of the names and the bishop, like I said.'

'Rev. Warner,' the librarian supplied. 'Hmmm. He's new last year. You might be better in the newspaper room. I'm not sure he's had a portrait done so soon after his investiture.'

Off she went, at a bustle, as thrilled to be searching for pictures as Helen would be to write up forms and hand out leaflets. She felt a flare of guilt since she should be doing that right now, instead of chasing ghosts.

If the librarian had been less efficient, sulky or lazy even, Helen might have left the table where she'd taken a seat and hurried back to her duties. But the woman returned almost before she had left, with a thick book, bound in cloth, open at a page near the beginning.

'Transactions of the St Andrew's Society of Edinburgh,' she said. 'Mr Pyne is the president.' She laid the book down and beamed at Helen before trotting away again to fetch more. She was like a collie.

Helen stared at the glossy page. It was a photograph, but it was posed like a portrait, with Mr Pyne in robes, holding some kind of sceptre or mace. She peered intently into his eyes and felt a flash of recognition. Strange that— she wouldn't have said she'd got a good enough look into that car in the dark. But he definitely seemed familiar and she knew, when she'd seen his face before, it hadn't been this frozen solemn look for the camera.

She stared at him. Was that a good man? Or was there a chance that, underneath his robes and watchchain, he was the kind of creature she suspected?

Her helper was back. 'Rev. Warner, and if you turn the page back that's his predecessor. Now. Doctors. Doctors.' And she was off again.

Rev. Warner was wearing a robe that looked like a table-cloth, lace and all. And the retired bishop on the page before him wore the same garment, or its twin. Helen thought she recognised this one too and was relieved. It must just be the Scottish face, she reckoned, the same face in portraits of important men everywhere in the country.

And probably you *couldn't* tell a bad man from his picture. She turned to ask the librarian, as another thick book hit the table. The woman was puffing a bit as if she'd been running, or climbing stairs.

'Thank you,' Helen said. 'And sorry, but – it's what you said about going back – have you got portraits of men like Deacon Brodie and Dr Knox?'

The librarian twinkled even more. 'Ah, we've got you now,' she said. 'We've got you hooked on Edinburgh history. Of course we do, dear. I'll not be a minute.'

Because, Helen surmised, that would work as a way of checking. If William Brodie and that terrible Dr Knox who took the bodies from Burke and Hare looked as blameless as Mr Pyne and the bishops, then she'd learned nothing from seeing the bland, dignified faces, had she?

And they *did*. They looked every bit as innocent. 'Are these good likenesses, do you think?' she asked the librarian as a book of coloured illustrations was presented. 'They seem so. . .'

'Rather romanticised,' the librarian said. 'Or maybe sanitised. But better that way. The pictures of half-hingit Maggie and Sawney Bean are too gruesome for words. We have to keep them away from the children.'

'Who are *they*?' Helen said.

The librarian tsked. 'And I can tell from your voice you're a local lass,' she said. 'I've long pestered the schools to tell our wee ones the history of our city but it's all kings and queens as far as the Education Board is concerned.'

Helen agreed with a rueful nod. History at the school had been as dull as mud. The same as times-tables only with names instead of numbers.

'I tell you what *is* livelier,' the librarian said. 'The St Andrew's *Social* Club. I'll see what I can dig up in their minutes, will I?'

'It's a lot of work putting it all back,' Helen said, astonished at how quickly the table had filled up with heavy books, all to let her glance at one picture on one page. So she turned a few more as she was waiting, and saw pictures gruesome enough to be kept from any children right enough. Half-hingit Maggie was horrific in the engraving of her, her neck bent like a knee and her face dark and stricken. Helen had just averted her eyes from the picture to read the caption below it when she heard the librarian approaching. She closed the book, not liking to be thought a ghoul, and turned with a smile.

'Here you are,' the librarian said. 'Just to show they can let their hair down sometimes. This is rather an old volume but it's to give you an idea. That's Mr Pyne and the bishop and there's Mr Grossart – he's a surgeon – and oh mighty – lots of them. All St Andrew's Social Club, dear. You see?'

Helen did see. She saw them all in their black jackets and bow ties, with cigars and glasses of drink, all sitting at little tables with candles on them, in a sumptuous room with rich velvet wallpaper, and all wearing expressions of eager antici- pation. As well they might, for there were enough girls, either still to arrive or waiting out of the view of the camera lens, for each of these ministers, lawyers and doctors to have a floozy on his knee for the rest of the night.

It *wasn't* a film, *or* a play, and Helen blushed for herself, thinking it was.

'Thank you,' she said to the librarian. 'Can I ask one more question? Where is the St Andrew's Society? Do you know?'

'Down in the New Town but it's very – I mean it's a gentle- men's club, you see, dear. It's not like a public reading room. They won't let you in.'

'I'm sure,' Helen said.

'No offence intended,' the librarian said. 'Nothing pers—'

'Who's that?' Helen said suddenly, pointing. The face shone out of the old photograph as if it had a torch pointing at it. He was standing by the fireplace, leaning one elbow against the mantel and staring straight at the camera. It if hadn't been for the thinning hair, the starched shirt, the wink of cufflinks on the wrist of his bent arm, Helen would have sworn it was 'Maggie Dickson' lounging there. He was Jane Bloggs' spit- ting image. He even had poor Carolyn's ears on him.

The librarian bent close. 'I don't know,' she said. 'He's probably a private gentleman, not involved in any profession. He could be anyone. But as I was saying. It's nothing personal. They don't admit ladies, you see. It's gentlemen only.'

That's what you think, Helen muttered to herself as she made her way back to the street. They most certainly do let women in; women in corsets and net stockings. But ladies and gentlemen were another matter entirely.

She needed to talk to someone. And it would have to be Sandy. She would wait till after tea tonight and, over a bottle of beer, she would tell him everything. Even better would be if she managed to get back up into the attic to sneak that photograph album out of its box and take it home to show him.

But she was out of luck. She knocked on Dr Deuchar's surgery door halfway through the long afternoon. 'Have you got any biscuits, Doc?' she said. 'I'm ravenous and I've too much to do to go out for buns.'

'Not on me, Helen,' Dr Deuchar said. 'But slip up to the dining room and help yourself from the box on the sideboard. Any time. You don't need to ask.' Helen was halfway out the door when he said, 'Money's all right, isn't it? You're not saving pennies till payday or anything?'

She stopped and frowned. 'No, I'm not going hungry,' she said. 'I just didn't get round to packing a piece this morning and I thought I could work through.'

'Because if there are unforseen expenses I haven't thought of, with the move and everything, you can always have an advance.'

'We're fine,' said Helen again. 'Between what I had in my bottom drawer and what my mother gave me, added to everything Dr Strasser donated, we're laughing.'

'I'd hate to think of you struggling,' he said. 'To make ends meet.'

'We're fine,' Helen said again. 'Do you want one?'

He quirked a look at her.

'A biscuit. If I'm getting one for me.'

He shook his head and waved her off.

She clomped up the first flight and then, on her toes, flew as quickly as she could up to the next floor, crossing swift and silent to the attic door and reaching for the key.

It wasn't there. Helen stared at the empty lock, then, hearing a noise from below in the house, she flitted down to the drawing room and, from the biscuit barrel, helped herself to a couple of wheaten crackers that she could no more swallow than she could juggle. Her throat had closed over and her mouth was desert dry.

'I was mortified!' she said to Sandy once they were both home. The plan to have tea first and talk later over a friendly beer had gone out the window. Helen had pounced as soon as he was in the door and right now she was talking to his bent head as he washed off the dust of the day at the kitchen sink. He was too mucky for the white bathroom, he had told her. Helen reckoned it was just old habits. 'He must have thought – one of them did – that yon time I was up there I was grubbing about for bits to hawk. Or pawn! I even said it myself – "like a jumble sale". And so they took the key away to keep me oot, as if I was a. . . and Dr Deuchar asked if we were all right for money and did I need an advance. Oh Sandy, I could have died on the spot.'

'Wouldn't hurt. An advance,' Sandy said. 'Another night of wersh tatties is nothing to hurry home to.'

Helen bristled, but it was true. She had laid in a sack of potatoes and a bit of butcher's mince to see them through, but she'd never got round to salt and pepper and tins and that; the sort of things you never think about not having till you've not got them.

'I can go round to my mammy's and ask,' she said.

'I'd rather eat them as they are,' Sandy said. 'Go and put in a big order on Saturday once we're both paid, eh?'

'And some browning, too,' Helen said. 'Grey mince willnae make your mouth water.'

Sandy shrugged and smiled at her. He had the scullery towel round his shoulders, catching drips from his hair. 'It'll blow over at work,' he said. 'They ken you for who you are, Nell. And, when you get right down to it, if they want to lock a door to keep you out after they found you raking through their stuff you cannae really blame them. But it'll die doon.'

'But that's not what I wanted to tell you,' Helen said. 'Not really. I was going to sit you doon and lay it all oot after the

212

grey mince and wersh tatties.' She grimaced to acknowledge the point. She had been so busy she'd barely thought about the water porridge, paste pieces and plain boiled dinners. Maybe if she tempted him more at the table. . .

'I'm going oot efter,' Sandy said. 'Tell me now.'

Helen felt a storm of conflict at that. Sandy never went out. He wasn't like so many other men, spending what they had and coming home angry to their wives when their pockets were empty. But on the other hand, if he was starting to go out at night, maybe he was getting better. 'You peel and I'll talk,' she said, and then she proceeded to tell him everything.

He listened without interrupting as she reeled off about the rope and the knot, the marks on the neck, the chances of a bottle rolling where it had. Only once did he put the scraping knife down to stare at her, when she told him she'd been to the morgue.

'It's Carolyn Sinclair,' she said. 'I'd have said it was Fiona but it's one of them and I spoke to Fiona on Monday night. So it's Carolyn. Even though I don't see how it *can* be.'

'It can't be.'

'But that's not all. The mortuary orderly told me straight out that it's no' the first time Duncan Pyne has brought a body in after dark. He might not have said after dark, but he meant under cover, ken? So I went to the library to see if I could get a keek at him – Duncan Pyne, this is – because I thought, it would show in his face if he was that kind of devil. I saw his picture.'

'And did it?'

'No,' Helen had to admit. 'But I was right. He's not a good man, Sandy. He's not an upstanding man like he pretends to be. It's Deacon Brodie all over again. It's Jekyll and Hyde. I saw a picture of him and some doctor from the hospital – a surgeon, I should say – and a bishop, if you can believe it! From St Mary's, this is. And they were all in a nightclub, or worse.'

213

'Nelly,' Sandy said. 'You've led a lucky wee life if you think—'

'But you didn't see them,' Helen said. 'The girls. They were in their corsets and they crisscross stockings and chokers round their necks and beauty spots painted on. Like the pictures. I thought at first it was a play.'

'And this picture was just in a book in the reference library for the world to see?' Sandy said. 'So there's the proof that it's innocent, you daftie.'

'No,' Helen said. 'The picture in the book was just the men. There's a Society and a Social Club. They're two different things. And I think they're maybe two different places. Who knows what posh bit the Society's in – George Street, Queen Street, somewhere – but I think the Social Club was here. I mean, right here. Wi' wallpaper and wee tables and a plaster fireplace looking like stone. Maybe a drinking room upstairs and private rooms doonstairs, or maybe the other way on. Not a fever ward at all, see? Not a bit of it. But for sure private. Secret. Shameful. Like Mrs Sinclair said to me.'

'Well,' said Sandy. 'Private. Embarrassing, maybe.'

'Sandy, if you'd seen them! They were all grinning and smirking, laughing at whoever would ever see the photo, like that poor wee librarian that called them gentlemen and leaders of the city. Then they took a picture with the girls to put in an album. I reckon old Dr Strasser must have been in the club and took their bits into store when it all shut down. But, by accident, one of the boxes got mixed up with the stuff that came here to us.' She went to the press and took down one of the champagne glasses, holding it up to the light. 'These self-same glasses are in the picture.'

'I'm no' saying I d'ae believe you,' Sandy said. 'I'm saying a man having a wee bit fun of an evening doesn't make him Jack the Ripper.'

'Well, why's it all under wraps then? Why was Mrs Sinclair saying on Monday that no one was ever to know who came here? Why was she so pit oot at us moving in? Telling me that daft tale about a top-secret fever ward and downstairs riddled with rot and mould.'

'Nelly,' he said, 'just because this social club isn't all Burns' poetry and eightsome reels, just because they're discreet, that doesn't mean Duncan Pyne kilt someone.'

'So why did he take her body to the mortuary back door?' Helen said. 'And say she'd gone to Glasgow, and cry her Maggie Dickson when that's not her name?'

'I can tell you why he called her Maggie Dickson,' Sandy said. 'And that's nasty enough. It came to me just the noo when you were talking. Half-hingit Maggie—'

'Oh!' said Helen. 'That's horrible! What a devil he is. Half-hingit Maggie? He killed her and then he called her the name of a. . . what was it she did anyway? To get herself hanged.'

'Murdered her baby,' said Sandy. 'Threw it in the river. And they hanged her but the shoogling of the bier when they took her body away fae the gallows woke her up and she ran off.'

'That's a terrible thing to do to a poor lass,' Helen said. 'Giving her that name. Like a joke.'

'It is,' said Sandy. 'But it doesn't mean he killed her. It's just means he's got a black sense of humour. Our girl from the shelter was half-hanged and half-poisoned so she got a nickname.'

'But why would he move her and hide her and lie, if he didn't kill her?'

'You're lovely, Nell,' he said, 'Too innocent to think of the things men do to cover each other's backs. Shocked at a night-club! I hope you never change, in a funny way.'

'And whose fault is that?' Helen said, lashing out as he laughed at her. 'Me being innocent?'

His face shut as if he'd pulled down a black-out blind and they spent the rest of the time waiting for the mince to boil in cold silence, then ate the tasteless meal the same way.

Chapter 16

'Where are you going?' Helen said, finally, reluctantly, when Sandy was halfway out the door. She cringed to hear herself sound so much like a nagging wife with her man on a short rope.

'You needin' something in?' Sandy said. He would make time and bring her a sweetie or a poke of chips if she asked him.

'Just wondered,' Helen said.

'Pint with a pal,' said Sandy. 'You're no' scared to be left, are you? All that fretting on the lass and what happened.'

The true answer was 'not till you mentioned it' but she didn't want to carp so she shook her head and told him she'd mats to start if she could find her big shears to cut scraps. Still, she turned the key in the lock after him and listened to his feet going down the steps. She was waiting for the sound of the gate and his boot heels on the lane then she'd turn all the lamps up to settle her nerves. When she heard nothing, she moved to the front window and stood just to the side, out of view. Was he lighting a fag, was he looking with pride at the grass and the rhubarb? Was he counting his money, maybe worried he couldn't stand a round?

None of those things. Helen forgot to hide as she took in what he *was* doing. He had unlocked the padlock on the Anderson shelter and was letting himself in, pulling the door to at his back. She kept watching, waiting for him coming out again, sure that whenever he reappeared it would all make sense. He'd have a new coat on – one he was embarrassed to admit he'd bought; or he'd have a ball under his arm – heading for a kick about and wanting his wife to think he was past such things. Or maybe he had a bit of cash stashed in there, safe from her prying. She would tell him he had no need to skulk about. She wasn't a battle-axe in training. She wasn't his mother, who'd worn his old dad see-through with her sharp tongue. She would go down and tell him he'd no need to brave that dark hole with its ghosts, no matter what he was keeping there.

Only, he didn't come back out.

Helen turned away from the window and leaned her head against the wall, trying to make sense of it. He wasn't meeting a pal for a pint. He had left his nice new cosy house to go and sit in a cold dark shelter, where he said he'd seen a ghost. It made no sense. Sandy said he had to work outside because of the camp. He wouldn't let her close the curtains of the box bed. So why would he put himself through something that would be nasty for anyone and would feel like torture to him?

Was he trying to get better? Forcing himself to face down the demons? Was he doing it for her?

Helen decided to leave him in peace, whatever it was. She tidied the kitchen then put a scarf over her hair and slipped back into her shoes. She'd go to Greet's and make her apologies, see if she couldn't get round Teen while she was at it. Pick up her scrap bag too.

At the bottom of the stairs, though, she couldn't help herself. She tiptoed over the grass and leaned close to the shelter door. All was silent, but she could smell the smoke of his fag. She thought about knocking, offering to help. But as she studied the door handle, gathering her nerve, she was sure she could see a glint between the boards and the lintel. He'd bolted it shut on the inside. That was a brand-new brass bolt, bought – no doubt – at the same time he picked up the padlock.

Well, that was clear enough and she wasn't going to scratch at a locked door like a puppy. Umbrage carried her all the way to Grove Place.

Greet let her in with hardly a word of scolding, since she had no anger left over from Teenie, who was in some kind of trouble. Both Greet and Mack were shooting black looks and muttering but not saying much about why.

'You speak to her, Nelly,' Greet said. She was washing pots, scouring them hard enough to leave marks. They had had a pie – steak and kidney from the lingering smell of offal – and the white enamel of the dish was coming off in flakes under Greet's knuckles, floating on the scummy water. 'See if you can talk some sense into her. I'll leather her if I have to put up with more of her cheek the night.'

Mack had lifted the paper in front of his face. He wasn't reading it, because his glasses were all the way over on the windowsill. He was just hiding.

Helen knocked on the door of the room that had been half hers for all those years. 'Teenie, are you in there?' There was no response, which was as gracious an invitation as she was likely to get, so she entered.

There were still two beds in the room, side by side with a cloth-covered box between them. Teen had taken over Helen's bed for sleeping and used her own old one like a table. It was covered in comics and the toys of a girl who thought she was a woman, meaning curlers and scarves, bangles and belts, half-knitted jumpers and half-made skirts still pinned to the patterns.

'What have you done now?' Helen said. 'Mammy's trying to kill the pie plate seeing she cannae kill you.'

'I've done nothing and I'll never get to do nothing either,' Teen said.

So that was it. 'Where did you ask to go?'

'A wee dance,' said Teen. 'Me and some pals and just because Mammy doesnae know all their grannies I'm not allowed.'

'What pals? And when's the dance?' Helen said. 'I could maybe take you. That would sort their faces oot for them.'

'You?' said Teenie, too bumptious to see what side her bread was buttered, as usual. 'It's not your kind of dance, Mrs Crowther.'

Helen opened her mouth with a retort – right back to sparring, the same as ever – but then a thought struck her. 'Where is it?' she said. 'It's not like Mammy and Daddy to mind a knees-up. What's sticking about this time?'

'It's in a posh place down in the New Town. You'd think it was the moon.'

'Who do you know that's invited yo—' Helen got out before a terrible idea stole over her. 'Where in the New Town?' she said. 'Not the St Andrew's Society? Oh, Teenie!'

'The whit?' Teen said. 'Naw, it's at a school doon there that Bessie McNulty's cousin goes to. Her cousin that stayed with her when the rest of them had the 'flu'.

Helen remembered. It wasn't the flu but no one talked about it. None of them in Fountainbridge knew to this day whether it was TB or scarlet fever, only that it was something that should have had them all in the closed ward, except Bessie's auntie knew they'd get put out their house by a hard-hearted factor. Mrs McNulty had taken the weans out into the street, holding them over the tar barrel to make folk think it was the whooping cough. It was a wonder she hadn't killed the lot of them.

'But how did you hear about this dance?' she asked Teenie. 'Bessie McNulty flitted years back. Do you keep in touch with her?'

'Why shouldn't I?' said Teen. 'Just cos you've dumped all your pals!'

Helen smiled at her sister's ready belligerence. She was like a little bull, maybe a terrier. 'And what makes Bessie McNulty's cousin such a draw?' she said. 'For you to be traipsing halfway across creation?'

'Half an hour's walk and all downhill,' Teenie said. 'There's life beyond Fountainbridge, you know.' Helen waited. Eventually Teenie snorted and spoke up. She never could keep a huff going; she was too much of a show-off. 'If you must know, it's because she likes the finer things in life, same as me.'

'Likes of what?' Helen asked. As far as she had ever seen, Teenie liked chewing the sweet meat off a soup bone and mashing a slice of bread into her gravy. She liked picking the bobbles off her flannel nightie. She'd a soft spot for liquorice water and comics.

'Champagne for one thing,' Teen said. 'Champagne glasses anyway.'

Helen couldn't help another flare of fear from leaping up in her chest. 'But this party's definitely at a school?' she said. 'Honour bright, Teenie?'

'*Whit*?' Teenie scowled and flapped a hand at her sister. 'What are you on about? Stop nagging me!'

'When did you ever taste champagne?' Helen said.

'Stop going on at me!' Teenie said. 'Never, if you must know. I just like the glasses. Bessie's cousin's got one she stole from her work. Don't look like that! It was broken. The wee stalk bit had snapped off so it was just the bowl bit left. She had it when she was laid up after her appendix. It went wrong, see? Or leastways, she kept having to go back. She's fine now. But that wee glass was right handy, because she could drink lying down.'

Helen beamed. The girl was so innocent, thinking a broken glass brought home was a scandal. 'I'll tell Mammy to let you go,' she said. 'You're a good girl.'

'How?' said Teen. 'What did I do?'

'Well, you're not a bad girl,' Helen said.

'Chance'd be nice,' said Teen, launching herself off the bed and landing on the lino with a smack of her bare feet. She started sorting through the clothes on the other bed and was holding a white jersey with puffed sleeves up in front of her when Helen stepped away.

'Let her go, Mammy,' Helen said, sitting down in the kitchen. Greet had finished with the pots and was scrubbing the bunker. She always cleaned her own kidneys, despite being married to a slaughterman. It was a point of pride, but it took some sluicing after. 'It's at a school and it's Bessie McNulty's lot that have heard about it. Mind of her cousin staying?'

'Aye, that's what's worrying me,' said Greet. 'I wouldnae trust her as far as I could throw her.'

Helen had no idea which 'her' couldn't be trusted: Bessie, the cousin, or Teen, but this was what passed for peace in the family home and she wasn't going to threaten it with more questions. 'Sorry about Tuesday,' she said. 'Work's busier than I thought it would be. Even without everything else that happened.'

'The sooner you've got a baby in your arms the better,' Mack said from behind his paper. 'Settle you down and get that lad to step up to his responsibilities instead of mumping about.'

Helen said nothing. What was there to say? She glanced at Greet, hoping for a bit of sympathy, but the look she saw on her mother's face stilled her heart. She felt it stop and hitch before it started up again. Greet knew. Teenie had told her. Nothing else could have put that mixture of shame, pity and exasperation there.

'Have you tried—?' Greet managed to get out before Helen was on her feet.

'That's me away,' she said. 'I'll see youse all on Friday for your baths, eh no? And you don't need to be waving towels in the street, for I've plenty to go round.'

'Have you now?' said Greet. 'Where have you been getting five towels? You're not in the tick book, I hope.'

'A house-warming present from a friend,' Helen said.

'And we'd have them in a duffel bag anyway,' Greet said. 'Since when did I traipse the streets with a rolled towel?'

It was true. Wee boys away to the baths never bothered, but Greet would fain bring down Mack's wrath by displaying any item she was moving. When she took a slice of Christmas cake up a flight to Mrs Suttie she put a paper bag over it, in case someone saw their business.

'And we can get chips after,' Helen said. 'Friday night. For a treat.'

'No off they greasy clarts at Bread Street,' Mack said. 'That would turn your wame inside out.'

Helen left them bickering about the best fish fryers, and headed home wanting nothing more than to make a cup of tea and sit with her feet up in the quiet. She knew she should be lining shelves or sweeping her floors, still stoury from unpacking, but she quailed at the thought of it. She'd never had a big carpet before and couldn't believe how much work they were to sweep clean instead of whisking a hard brush over the lino. She could understand why maids in big houses lifted the edge and shoved the dust under. Maybe she should roll the carpet back up again and say to the doctors she didn't want it. But the floor underneath was ugly, patched with that square of board in the middle of the polished planks. 'Ach, Helen,' she told herself. 'As long as it's clean for Greet on Friday. Take your ease tonight after the day it's been, eh?'

But as she reached her garden gate a moment later her heart sank, for there was Sandy, letting himself out of the shelter again, edging round the door with a guilty look on his face. He caught her eye and his cheeks drained. There was no chance of the pair of them pretending now. Helen shook her head and climbed the stairs, feeling herself move like an old, tired woman as Sandy came trotting after her.

'You werenae meant to see,' he said. 'Where have you been? I thocht you were going to sew, through in the back room.'

'I was at my mammy's,' Helen said. 'Look, let's get in and sit down over it, eh?'

'Don't sound so black,' said Sandy. 'There's nothing wrong.'

It took all her strength not to turn on the step and shove him. *Nothing wrong?* She managed, gripping the banister tight and clenching her jaw, simply to keep moving.

'Right,' Sandy said, as they settled on either side of the kitchen table. 'I owe you this much.'

'Can you go and put your nightshirt on before you get tore in,' Helen said. 'And hang your claes on the bathroom door hook. The smell of you! Have you been sitting in there lighting one fag from the end of another? You're like to choke me with it.'

With no more than a look of injured surprise, he moved away.

'Sorry!' she shouted after him. 'But it smells so much worse than your baccy does usually. You're not supposed to smoke in shelters, anyway.' That was in all the leaflets that came at the start of the war, urging the adults to think of healthy air; not to stop up the ventilation flaps and never to smoke down there. Of course, between the mothers fearing gas attacks and the fathers needing a pipe to get through the night, the shelters were usually sickening. The reek coming off Sandy's clothes tonight had taken Helen right back.

When he returned, wrapped in a blanket off the bed over his goonie, he said, 'No need for you to be sorry. It's me that owes you.'

'Too right you do,' Helen said. 'You've offended Mack turning down his job, saying you cannae be inside, and yet you'd rather sit in that wee hole than spend an evening with me in our lovely house that's dropped out the sky for us. You owe me making sense of that, for sure.'

'The shelter's nothing like the hut was,' Sandy said. 'Our hut, Helen, hut thirteen, was the size of a barn. If the ceiling had been low we could have kept it warmer, but even the top bunks couldn't get the best of what came off the oil stove. They're nothing like. Nothing at all.'

Helen nodded and waited. That was more than he had ever said before tonight, but she could tell he wasn't finished.

223

'It's the other men,' he said at last. 'In the slaughterhouse, or a factory, or even Fleming's. It's too many other men all in thegither, see? I could work in a typing pool with a load of girls, if I could type. Or I could stand on the bottling line with Greet and the rest of them.'

'You cannae—' Helen bit her lip.

'I know,' Sandy said. 'I'm kidding. I'm fine where I am, with just George. He understands what it's like.'

'*I* could understand what it's like, if you'd tell me.' Helen had never thought about George much. A strange wee man was as far as she'd ever got. She didn't like this leap of envy she felt in herself. 'I understand more now than I did half an hour since. Do you talk to George about it all? You could talk to *me*.'

'I don't need to talk to George,' Sandy said. 'He kens. He was the same. Different stalag, same do. Non-compliance. Too much time to think, see.'

'What's non-compliance?' Helen said and then reared backwards as Sandy's face darkened in sudden anger.

'Aye, see that's it,' he said. 'Naebody kens. *We're* not heroes! We never jumped a fence and escaped and got medals for it! And you know the truth, Nelly? They'd have loved us if we did. The guards would. We'd have given them a break from the grind of it and let them run aboot like wee boys playing, getting us all back in again. But naw, we just sat there. Lay there. And ground them down.'

Helen had once seen a rabbit, when the Brownies were on a picnic in the Pentland Hills and she'd stepped away a quiet place to spend a penny. She was balanced with her Brownie dress bunched up in one hand, her a yard wide so's she didn't topple, and it hopped up to within a yard of her, sat quivering, watching her out of one shiny black eye. She'd have died if someone came and saw her like that but as long as the rabbit sat still she kept still too, knowing as soon as she moved it would be gone and when would she ever see one as close-up as this again? It was half-grown, with long silky baby fur that let the sun shine through the tips. Maybe it wasn't old enough to be wary yet. Maybe its mammy would come along any second and grab it by the scruff to drag it to safety, far from this monster, but while it lasted it was magical.

She felt the same now. He was *talking* to her. She needed to be as quiet as she'd been in that clearing in the Pentland Hills, not frighten him away.

'If you worked for them,' he said at last, 'farming or logging or whatever they needed done, you got three square meals a day. We could smell it: stew and ham and porridge. But if you didnae work for them – if you were as big a burden as you could be – you got NC. Non-compliance rations. Potatoes to cook yourself on the oil stove and bread to share. Oor hut was all NC. Six years nearly. Building roads or breaking out would have been easy. But nobody's ever going to put on a parade for lying on a bunk with your belly griping, are they?'

'They should,' said Helen. 'Maybe they would, if they knew.'

'Oh, the brass knows!' said Sandy. 'They knew all along. But they don't *want* to know. Dr Strasser explained it all once, only I cannae mind the word he used.'

'Doc *Strasser*?' said Helen.

'Old Doc Strasser,' said Sandy. 'He knew what life was like. It made him kinder than most to them as needed it worst.'

Helen said nothing. She barely remembered the old man and all she knew of him lately was he stored the bits for that social club and kept his nurse's bag off her when she retired. That wasn't kindness. And anyway, what Sandy was saying made no sense. The time was wrong.

'But he was dead before you got back,' she said. 'Did you write to him? Did he write to you?'

'Why would I write to a doctor?' said Sandy. 'It was hard enough getting a stamp and a sheet of scrap to write to my mammy and you.' That was true. Whenever Helen saw Mrs Crowther coming with that look on her face, she knew there had been a letter, sometimes a postcard just. A stamp from the Red Cross and a note that said nothing, a note the pair of them would pore over for hours as if it was a crystal ball. The first one had come after more than a year. A whole year when all they'd had was three words in ink on the bottom of the notification from the camp. 'He is well,' some German soldier had written in his odd, curly writing. They'd say it to each other, Mrs Crowther and her, like a prayer. 'He is well'. So Helen – although she'd never say this to Sandy's face – felt she knew all about living on scraps longer than you dreamed it was possible to.

'I wasnae meaning the war, Nelly,' Sandy was saying now. 'Not particularly. Dr Strasser was just kind all round. That's what everyone says. Anyone who's ever needed a kindness anyway.'

The sun had sunk as they sat and, when it was clear he was done talking, Helen moved to light a lamp. 'Dinnae for me,' Sandy said. 'I'm away to my kip. I'm going to the bed through by and you can have this one, Nell. Or the other way on, if you'd rather.'

But that was the choice. She was to sleep in one room and he was taking the other. As he left and she listened to him opening the hall press to get more blankets out, she felt herself leave the imagined hut where she'd followed him and come back to now. He had finally spoken and it had only made things worse. And when she turned her mind to it, nothing he'd said had actually explained why he'd cowered in the shelter all evening, smoking his head off. She felt for him – she did – but she was bewildered. And what did old Dr Strasser have to do with anything?

When she heard him come out of the bathroom, she went to cut him off. 'For tonight,' she said. 'But not forever.'

'Not forever,' he agreed. 'Just give me some time.'

'Can I ask one last question?' Helen said.

'I'm tired, hen,' he said. Me too, Helen thought. She'd rather push a dustcart through the summer streets than look

226

at corpses and hear people's secrets. 'Go on then,' he added at last, with a sigh.

'Did you really think there was a ghost in the shelter? Or were you just trying to get it for yourself? Stop me keeping my peg bag in there?'

'I d'ae believe in ghosts,' Sandy said. 'No' that kind. Do you?'

'Me?' Helen said.

'You were the one saying there was ghosts in your office,' Sandy said. 'Hiding behind your blessed filing cabinets. Dressed in yellow.'

It was the strangest feeling. To know two things and keep them in separate places in your mind, like two odd socks, one in the drawer and one on the pulley, not actually odd at all but useless till you paired them. She hadn't said where the ghost was hiding. Sandy had just added a touch to mock her gently. But that wee touch had done the trick.

Helen had seen a flash of yellow in the corner of her office and heard a sobbing unearthly enough to chill her blood. Then she had seen the scores in the floorboards from the filing cabinets moving in the same grooves, time after time.

No one shifts a cabinet full of files to mop behind it. She saw that now. With a quick good night for Sandy, she went quite happily to her own bed to try to sleep until she could get into work bright and early. Even if Duncan Pyne and the St Andrew's Social Club and poor Carolyn Sinclair were still the mysteries they seemed to be, she would solve this one puzzle in the morning.

Chapter 17

On Friday morning every patient in the whole of Fountain-bridge and Lochrin conspired against her. Every mother wanted advice about the best shoes for a lad's fallen arches, or help making a wee girl with a lazy eye agree to wear her patch, or someone to visit a sister-in-law and say the unsayable. 'She's a midden, Mrs Crowther. It's unsanitary and my brother willnae lift his head and get her telt.'

'Are there young children?' Helen said.

'Six. She runs a wee nursery on the quiet like.'

Helen nodded as her heart sank. These 'wee nurseries on the quiet' let women get out to work and earn enough to keep decent when their menfolk wouldn't hand over the house-keeping. That was her experience. When matters were above board, likes of a low wage and saving for a place of their own, the bairns were farmed out to grannies and aunties. But when it was all hush-hush – and sometimes not even the husbands knew their wives were working – the babysitters got away with murder. Got away with enough filth to cause harm to a deli-cate child, anyway.

'I'm no' wanting her shut down.'

'I'm not *getting* her shut down,' Helen said. 'I'm just getting her telt. Like you said she's needing.'

The patient looked across Helen's desk with a twist of a smile. 'You don't talk like Mrs Sinclair even if you've got her job.'

Helen laughed and blushed. She was slipping. 'I wish I *could* talk like her,' she said. 'I wouldn't need to be wheedling round folk. I could just lay down the law.' It gave her an idea, an excuse to get into the Merchiston house for another look at the pictures of Carolyn and Fiona and assure herself of what must be true, earlobes or no earlobes: that Jane Bloggs was nothing like either of them really. She started composing her plea: a wee girl with flat feet and a wee boy with a lazy eye would be easy, she would say to her old mentor. 'I could talk about high-heeled party shoes and pirates. But this way on, I'm struggling.' Would Mrs Sinclair see through it? Was Mrs Sinclair even back from London? Maybe the house was lying empty and Helen could peer in the big back window at the photographs on the table.

As a thought struck her, she let go of the drawer she'd been holding. It rattled back into place and closed with a snick. She didn't have to peer in windows. If the Sinclair house was empty, she could let herself in with a key. She glanced over at her big leather bag where her keyring sat in one of the many compartments and her heart started to bang at the very thought of such a transgression.

Start small, she told herself. Do this first and work up to the Sinclair house. She turned the little silver-coloured key to lock the four deep drawers of the cabinet and then took a hold of the top handle and pulled. As she had been hoping, as she had deduced, but as she had hardly dared actually to expect, the lock held and instead of the drawer sliding open again, the whole cabinet began to move forward. It was rolling on hidden castors, Helen guessed from the sound, and they sat snugly in the grooves on the floorboards, like tram wheels on tracks.

When the cabinet was out as far as it would come, Helen squeezed round the side and peered behind it, catching her breath to see a short, narrow door set in the wall there. Just as she reached out to turn the handle, though, she heard feet on the basement stairs, one of the doctors approaching. She was sure of it, for not only were most on her list women but

229

none of the few men strode about the surgery with those confident, ringing steps. She froze as he approached and rapped on her half-open door. Without knowing why, but knowing for sure it was right, she sank down to hide. She could have said, 'Come in, Doc,' and then, 'Look what I've just found. What do you think of this then?' There was no reason not to sing out to him – whichever one it was – and share this odd discovery. But still she sank down, hiding, silent, and holding her lip in her teeth to quiet her breathing.

He pushed open the door. 'Nell?' he said. It was Dr Strasser. But when no one answered he clicked his teeth and went away.

Helen was shaking, unnerved by her own actions. Why had she behaved as if she couldn't trust the doctors? Where had *that* come from? Did she think they would scold her for exploring her own office? Hadn't they always praised her enterprise and her. . . what was it Dr Strasser called it?. . . her verve.

She shook it off and turned again to the little door. It opened smoothly, on oiled hinges, and behind it lay a brick-lined lobby with a few steps leading down to a longer passageway. Helen took off one shoe and wedged it against the door-jamb. There was no way she wanted to be trapped in here. Then, limping a little now she was lopsided, she stole into the cubbyhole and followed the passage away from her office, towards. . .

Well, it had to be out along the side of the area and, around another corner, into the stores set under the pavement. She had never wondered before now about the three arched doorways, locked and bolted. She'd assumed they were never used. Now she saw different. There were three little bays all facing out onto a passage along the front, like the horse boxes in the dairy stables, or cubicles at the baths. Very like cubicles at the baths, actually, since there had been curtains along the fronts of these bays once upon a time. The rods were still there.

230

Otherwise, all three were empty. The walls had been painted and the floors tiled, but there was nothing left behind to suggest what they had been for, when they were in use. Helen made her way back to her office, deeply puzzled by what she had found. The doctors could surely find a purpose for three big box-rooms like that. And if not, *she* certainly could. If one of the bolted doors was thrown open, Helen could have her own waiting room for her own patients. If she moved the filing cabinet, that could be the public entrance to her office. It made no sense to have a handy wee passageway like that blocked off and hidden.

She had just put her shoe back on, pushed the cabinet against the wall, and seated herself, when she heard the doctor coming back again. This time he opened the door without knocking and then, startled to see her there, he dropped the sheet of paper he was carrying.

'Nell!' he said. 'I – where were you?'

'When, Doctor?'

'I just came down to say— And then, when you weren't here I went to write a note instead. Now here you are like a genie.'

'I stepped away a place,' Helen said. It was true, technically. 'But you could have taken a wee bit paper off my desk, Doc.'

'I didn't like to assume any piece of paper wasn't important,' he said. 'Anyway. Here you go. Mrs Sinclair is home again and wants to see you. That's the message, I'm afraid. You are summoned for tea.'

'I'm glad,' said Helen. 'I was needing to speak to her.'

'Oh?' said Dr Strasser. 'What about? You should be asking us or Mrs Bonny whatever you want to know now, Helen.'

'Well, can I ask you this then?' Helen started to compose a question about the secret corridor to the three bays, but she couldn't form the words. Everything sounded like an accusation. Instead, she touched her hand to the side of her head and said, 'It's about earlobes.' He blinked. 'How common is it for folk to just not have them. You know what I mean? I know it sounds daft.'

But Dr Strasser was frowning. '"Daft" isn't the word I'd use,' he said. 'Superficial physical differences are just that. There's nothing to be learned from the size of a skull or the shape of a nose, Helen. And it's not a harmless exercise to keep wondering.'

Helen's face flared the deepest puce. 'I wasn't saying it meant anything,' she said. 'I was just asking how many.'

'And for all I've ever said about Alvia Sinclair, I don't think she has any interests in that area.'

'No,' said Helen, agreeing to who knew what. 'No, I'm sure. It's a matter of. . . It's another matter I need to speak to her about. She taught me a lot, but there's still plenty I could learn.'

'As could we all,' he said. Helen was sure he glanced towards the back corner as he turned to leave, and just as sure he stopped in the corridor outside for a moment, halfway back to the stairs. She knew why, too. If she had really been 'a place' as she'd claimed, the cistern would still be filling and the wee geyser tank above the sink still gurgling as it re-warmed after her washing her hands. She sat and listened to the silence along with him, then his footsteps started up again as he walked away.

So did Dr Strasser know about the passageway? The bays? Did he hope that Helen didn't know? Why would that be? Perhaps she was making something of nothing. The doctors were under a lot of strain with the new service and Monday night didn't help any. There was no reason to go suspecting them – either of them – of anything.

It was showing on both, she thought, as she trotted along to the tram stop to catch a car up to Holy Corner. Dr Deuchar had been short with her a couple of times. He'd not liked her. . . what was it though? She remembered feeling foolish and being scared that her eyes would fill but she couldn't remember in the jumble of all the new experiences she'd been having what it was she had done to annoy him. Either of the two times she was sure it had happened.

She was still puzzling, trying to pull the memories back into focus, when the tram swung up and over the Tollcross junction, the wheels clacking as they found the tracks on the other side of the points. Helen was looking determinedly to one side; she hated seeing the car shake and resettle like you could if you faced the front. It didn't matter how sternly she told herself that dozens of trams crossed these points every day. Once you'd seen one miss and tip over and heard the screams of the passengers you never forgot it.

So it was that her eyes passed over the row of shops and, seeing the name Yarrow above the newsagents, she remembered baby Gordon, perhaps already safely arrived,. How glad his parents would be to greet him! Then fast on the heels of the happy thought came the one she had been chasing. *That* was what had upset Dr Deuchar; something to do with a newsagent. He'd been angry with her until he heard it was Yarrow she'd been speaking to and not some other man who sold papers and flake in the city. That was definitely one of the times. And the other was. . .

Helen sat bolt upright and gasped. There was a girl, out on the street, almost at Yarrow's shop, actually putting her hand to Yarrow's door as Helen watched. And *that* was the other time Dr Deuchar was angry. Monday morning, when Helen was just settled in her new office, and that bumptious girl, dressed for a factory but talking like a guest at a tennis party, had come looking for Miss Anderson. Helen leapt up and pulled the bell chain.

'That's a waste of a penny fare,' the conductor said. 'You've only been two stops.'

But Helen paid him no heed. She jumped off the platform as soon as the car slowed and hit the pavement already running.

'Miss?' she said, dodging a stout man with a small dog and a pair of girls walking arm in arm. 'Here, you! You in the brown hat! You've dropped something!'

The girl turned in the doorway to see who was shouting and Helen rushed up beside her.

'Me?' she said. 'Wait, do I know you?' She let the door swing shut and stepped away.

'I work at the Gardner's Crescent surgery,' Helen said. 'We met on Monday when you were looking for Miss Anderson.'

'She's disappeared off the face of the earth,' the girl said. 'Taking my hopes with her.'

'Hopes of what?' said Helen. 'Why was it you needed to see her? Could I help?'

'You?' The scorn was as clear as could be and it made Helen blush. 'No, dear. I wouldn't think so.'

'Are you in some kind of trouble?' Helen said.

'Am I "in trouble"?' The girl was laughing at her, Helen was sure.

'I didn't mean that.' Which of course she had. She had meant exactly that, because an idea was forming in her mind about Miss Anderson, sacked and sent packing, and a wee secret door to a wee secret place with three cubicles, and a girl sobbing and another girl – this one – as pert as you like, and Dr Deuchar furious to see her.

The girl was waiting for Helen to speak, one eyebrow lifted. But as she groped for something to say, the bell on the shop door behind them dinged and she turned, half-expecting to see Mrs Yarrow with baby Gordon in her arms, come to show him off. The smile died on her lips as she saw *Mr* Yarrow, glowering a blacker look than any she had yet seen upon his face and barrelling towards them.

'I told you to get!' he said. 'Take yourself away and don't come back!'

The pert young woman grabbed Helen by the arm and scurried off, dragging her whether she wanted to follow or not.

'Don't worry,' Helen said, when they were well up the street and out of sight behind a lavish display of fruit and vegetables ranged on racks outside a greengrocer. 'He's an odd sort of man. But he's harmless, I'm sure.'

'Easy for you to say! It's not *you* he's coming at like a bull.'

Helen blinked. 'Haud on,' she said. 'You think that was for *you*?'

'Of course it was for me,' the girl said. 'He's sent me packing twice this week and now he's watching for me.'

'Why?' Helen asked. 'What is it about you that makes you so unpopular?'

The girl reared back. 'That's a nice way to put it, I don't think.'

'Well, Dr Deuchar put you out of the surgery too, when you were looking for Miss Anderson. You must have done something to make everyone take a broom to you.'

'I wasn't "looking for Miss Anderson",' the girl said. 'I've had a belly full of her. Enough to last me the rest of my life. I was looking for my pal.'

'At the surgery and the newsagents?' said Helen. 'Why would you look for her there?'

The girl rolled her eyes and then glanced away, letting her gaze travel over the pears and peaches in the nearest baskets. 'Trusting sort, isn't he?' she said. 'If it was me, I'd put onions and tatties out here and keep the good stuff where wee boys couldn't pinch it.' And, indeed, Helen did notice the greengrocer standing inside the shop, keeping a close eye on the pair of them. She picked a brown paper bag off the hook and began to fill it with big red gooseberries; not too expensive, and fiddly enough to take plenty of time if she selected them one by one.

As she had hoped, the girl started talking again, once Helen was safely looking away. 'I knew she wouldn't *be* either of those two places,' she said. 'I just thought they might know where she was. I didn't know Yarrow had moved on to the new Mrs, and I didn't know Anderson was away. I don't know where to try next, if I'm honest.'

'Has your friend gone missing?' Helen said, glancing up. She saw the look of scorn and went back to perusing the gooseberries.

'What is it I'm standing here telling you? I said we should go together. I said it wasn't safe. But she was adamant she could talk them round better without me tagging along, annoying them. And now look.'

'Annoying who?' Helen said. The girl didn't answer. 'Look, if someone's missing and you're worried, why not go to the polis?'

The girl gave a hollow laugh. 'Aye right. Tell the police, or your doctor, or a lawyer or a priest. Tell someone you can trust, eh?' Her scorn had melted as she spoke and she ended sounding bleak, to match the look of misery spreading over her face. She looked, Helen, thought, grief-stricken. But her words didn't seem to match the pain it took to say them.

Helen set the half-filled paper bag back down on top of the tray of berries and took hold of the girl's arm. Doctors, lawyers, judges and priests. Where had she heard that list? She gasped, as the revelation broke over her. And all of a sudden she knew where a missing friend might be.

'Is she about your age?' she said. 'Lovely skin, thick golden wavy hair, nice-kept hands.'

'You've seen her?' Hope leapt in the girl's face. 'Where is she? Is she all right?'

'I've seen her,' Helen said. 'And I'm so sorry, but she's not all right.'

'She's dead?'

'Here!' It was the greengrocer. 'Are youse shopping or are youse hiding my display from my real customers and bruising my good fruit for your own entertainment?'

'Sorry,' Helen said to him. She took the girl by the arm. 'What's her name?' she said, as the girl twisted out of her grip.

'I don't even know her name. It was me that found her and I want—'

But she was off.

'How can I find you again?' Helen called after her, as the girl sped away up the street, dodging pedestrians. 'Hey!' She'd never shouted so loud since the days she'd yell up to Greet to throw down a jeely piece to the back green, but she bellowed now at the receding back. 'I'm trying to help you! Trust me! At least tell me her *name!*'

The girl gave Helen one last wild glance over her shoulder and said a word, drowned out by the squealing brakes of a bus near her and the clop-clop of a coal-cart pony near Helen, then she hopped onto the bus as it pulled away and was gone.

Helen stood, stunned. She hadn't really believed she was right, had she? She hadn't really and truly expected to have all her worst suspicions confirmed. But there was no mistaking it. She had read the girl's lips even if she hadn't fully heard the word. And there was no arguing it away. She'd said 'Sinclair'.

She was going to be late for tea, but she needed the thinking time. So instead of getting on another tram Helen walked, slow and steady, looking at the pavement and trying to catch up with her racing thoughts, all the way to Merchiston.

Mrs Sinclair had known it wasn't Fiona. She had been exasperated when Helen said it was. But as soon as the idea came up that it was Carolyn, she fainted. Then she was told it wasn't either of them and off she went to London to gather her chicks under her bosom again.

But it was, it was, it was. Helen had always known it was. And that scared girl knew it too. She said 'Sinclair'. The dead body in the mortuary was Carolyn Sinclair, even though Duncan Pyne played his wee game and said 'Maggie Dickson', even though the attendants had her down as 'Jane Bloggs'.

But why did the dead girl's friend think Miss Anderson or the Yarrows would know where Carolyn Sinclair had disappeared to?

And how could Mrs Sinclair have been so relieved and certain that both her daughters were safe unless she'd actually spoken to each of them? Which she couldn't have. Because one was dead.

Helen didn't understand any of it. But she knew what she was walking into. As she neared the stone gateposts, she steeled herself for Mrs Sinclair, grieving and broken, mourning her firstborn. However she had made such a terrible mistake on Monday night – whatever mix-up or mischief had led her to think her girls were all right – she would have learned the truth long before now. Helen wondered briefly why Dr Strasser hadn't seemed to know. Maybe Mrs Sinclair couldn't bear to tell him. But then how could she bear to have Helen come to tea?

It had never gone this badly wrong for Helen when she tried to pull the wool over Greet and Mack's eyes. Once or twice she'd said she was at her pals' when she was nowhere like it, but she had always come home again. That's how it must have been with Carolyn. Mrs Sinclair rang up where her daughter was supposed to be, and a friend spun a tale to cover the truth, thinking the truth was Carolyn had a fellow who was a wrong 'un, or she had gone away somewhere not respectable, or – this was it! – had sneaked back to Edinburgh for reasons of her own, with no plans to see her mother. That was definitely it. She had *been* in Edinburgh, after all. She had ended up in Helen's Anderson shelter.

What a cruel wee twist for a mother. Her daughter was dead and, when alive, she had lied to escape visiting. What a small, nasty thing to know. It made Helen want to see Greet, run her a bath and set her hair for her on Friday, forgive her for being the besom she was, because you only get one mammy and you might as well love her.

238

Helen pulled the bell and waited. After a moment, the stained-glass inner door opened and there was... she would have sworn Carolyn Sinclair. She gaped, unable not to.

'Helen,' the girl said, cooing in more friendly tones than she had ever used before. 'Come in, come in. You're just in time. We're all in the summer sitting room. Go through and I'll tell the daily woman to bring the tray.'

Helen nodded dumbly and went towards the back of the house where the 'summer sitting room' faced the long garden. She knew she had paled. She had just seen what looked like the dead girl sprung back to life. Trying to smile, she pushed open the door and saw, first, Mrs Sinclair in a pink blouse and a linen skirt, looking not at all like her usual self and definitely not like a woman in mourning. Sitting beside her on the little sofa with the gold legs was Fiona. She had a flowery dress on and no stockings, her bare feet in tennis shoes. She stood and came forward.

'Helen!' she said. 'It's been ages. How are you now you've taken on Mummy's yoke?'

'Fine,' Helen managed to say. 'Well, you know, busy and still getting sorted. I'm glad to have a chance to ask you a few things, actually, Mrs Sinclair. I've missed having you to turn to.'

'And I've missed you, Nelly,' Mrs Sinclair said. 'Sit yourself down and tell me all about it.'

The 'daily woman' arrived with a laden tray just then and Carolyn followed with a large teapot. Helen looked from one sister to the other and back again. They both had their hair swept up and pinned and Helen could see those thin earlobes, looking like rind with the afternoon sun shining behind them.

Before either of the girls could ask why she was staring she wrenched her eyes away and, for somewhere to look, settled on the teapot. It wasn't the one Mrs Sinclair usually used for guests. That one was half the size and so spindly Helen was always scared to lift it by its delicate handle. The plates looked different too. Instead of the snowy-white narrow sandwiches and the dainties so small it was an effort to make two bites of them and not just put them in whole like sweeties, today there were slices of ham-and-egg pie, fruit scones taller than they were wide, looking like battered top hats, and a whole sponge cake, filled with jam and cream and dredged with sugar. Mrs Sinclair hadn't just invited Helen for tea; she had laid on a tea specially. She had bought what she thought Helen would like to eat and spread it out.

The question was why.

'Ha— Have you moved home?' Helen said to Carolyn, when she was served with a cup of tea and a slice of pie. 'That's nice for you, Mrs Sinclair, to have them near again.'

'Yes, we've been prevailed upon,' said Fiona. 'All manner of concessions. . . conceded.'

'I was getting tired of London anyway,' said Carolyn. 'No matter what the good doctor said.'

'Which doctor was that?' said Helen. They tittered, all three of them, and she knew that she had missed something, the way she so often did.

'They're teasing, Helen,' Mrs Sinclair said, although she still had a smile on her lips. 'Ignore them.'

Maybe it was that that made her speak more boldly than she had meant to. Between Greet and Teen mocking her for getting uppity and this lot mocking her for still being what she was, added to everything else pressing on her, she was in no mood to tiptoe.

'I'm glad,' she said. 'Your mother had a terrible shock on. . . Mighty, was it only Monday night? You weren't here, Misses Sinclair, but it was awful.'

'Perhaps it wouldn't have been had you not made such a silly mistake,' Fiona said. 'After all, you were responsible for the shock when we get right down to it.'

'Fifi,' said Mrs Sinclair, warningly. 'Nelly is our guest, dear.' She looked down at her plate with distaste and set it aside on a little table, the slice of pie untouched. Again, Helen was struck by the pandering going on. She decided to test it and see how far it went.

'I didn't make a mistake,' she said. 'Or at least, you would have made it too. Do you know they still haven't put a name to that poor girl? Jane Bloggs, she is, at the mortuary.'

'No, no,' Mrs Sinclair said. 'I can set your mind at rest on that score, Nell. Her name is Maggie Dickson and she was a very bad sort of woman while she lived.'

'I don't like to contradict you, Mrs Sinclair,' Helen said, then she took a good big bite out of her own slice of pie. She was hungry and it looked delicious, brown pastry and pink ham with a thick layer of jelly sparkling like jewels. Helen couldn't have resisted it any longer without her stomach beginning to make noises. As she chewed, she saw that she had the three of them on the edges of their seats, even though she'd intended no such thing.

'Mr Pyne – Duncan Pyne, this is,' she said, when she had swallowed. 'Do you know him? – gave the poor girl that name as a joke, I think. Not a very kind thing to do, but maybe he's seen so many dead bodies it's blunted him. Maggie Dickson is someone from history. And Edinburgh history too. She's nothing to do with Glasgow.'

'He had to choose a name and so he called her after half-hangit Maggie?' Carolyn said. She sounded troubled. 'That's a rotten little twist, isn't it? I'm not sure what I think of that when all's said and done—'

'And it's hardly accurate,' Fiona added. 'Wasn't the creature you found hanged well and truly, Helen?'

'Don't be such a ghoul!' Carolyn said. 'How can you be so cold about someone who, after all, is—'

But her mother and sister had both rounded on her. Helen couldn't see Fiona's face but Mrs Sinclair's eyes flashed, in either anger or warning.

'What. . . um, what was that other thing you said, Nelly?' Carolyn asked, picking words out of the air in haste as if to

241

cover up her blunder. 'You didn't make a mistake? What on earth do you mean?'

'Just that she was your double. Your spitting image. Both of you. Have you cousins in Edinburgh? I'm quite serious! Are there members of your family you could ring up and just check that nothing's wrong?'

All three Sinclairs looked a bit sick now. Carolyn spoke first and it was a low murmur. 'We'd have heard if a relation died.'

'Or disappeared?' Helen said. 'Because, this is what I'm telling you, Miss Sinclair. She hasn't been identified. Jane Bloggs, she is, down there on her slab.'

'Nelly!' said Mrs Sinclair, sharp as a knife. 'You must stop this. You've never been a silly girl and you mustn't entertain silliness now. It was dark and you were upset. You had one look at a poor dead girl and thought she resembled one of my daughters. I have forgiven you for the great shock your mistake caused me. But you should be apologising, not carrying on.'

'But it wasn't, Mrs Sinclair,' said Helen. 'It wasn't a quick look in the dark, all upset. I went to the morgue, you see. I had a long look at her under bright lights. And I would have staked my life on who she was.'

'You went to the morgue?' said Mrs Sinclair. 'When?'

Carolyn and Fiona were looking green about the gills again. Their plates had been laid aside too and Helen thought that a lot of good food was going to be wasted in this house today. She wondered if she would be offered a parcel to take away as she had been sometimes after garden parties and other treats.

'I'm sorry to speak so plainly,' she said, then took another bite of pie to gain some time. Fiona regarded her with a kind of horror. Which didn't make any sense; they had done war work and they shouldn't be so easily shocked. 'I went yesterday,' she said, after a mouthful of tea to wash it down. 'And I thought somehow you'd been misled into thinking your daughters safe, Mrs Sinclair.'

'And yet it took you this long to pay a visit of condolence?' said Carolyn.

'But then I told myself it couldn't be true,' Helen said. 'Wouldn't Mr Pyne have met you both? At parties and things? Didn't he know your father? Oh!' With a flash behind her eyes so bright she might have sworn the others could see it too, Helen remembered the photograph, both photographs: the men alone, captured for the proceedings of their society and the men with the girls, snapped and put in the social club's private album. That familiar face leaning against the mantel who had made her think of Jane Bloggs? That was Mr Sinclair. There in the same room with Duncan Pyne and the rest of them.

'Oh what?' Fiona said. She sounded very uneasy.

'Nothing,' Helen stammered. 'I've just remembered something at work. I forgot to do something. I should get back to it.'

'Wait, wait, wait, though,' said Carolyn. 'You haven't explained. If you told yourself it couldn't be true, then why are you bringing it up now?'

'I have to say, Nelly,' her mother chipped in, 'this isn't like you.'

'Well,' Helen said, 'it's just that I'm not the only one now. Not the only one who made the same mistake, I mean.'

'Someone else looked at the corpse on the slab and said, "Why, isn't that one of the Sinclair girls"?' said Fiona.

Helen hesitated. It was so much worse than that. Another person might well make the same mistake when the likeness was undeniable. But the girl running away on Earl Grey Street just now had come at it from the other end. Helen had found a dead girl who looked like the Sinclairs and who'd come from nowhere. And someone was worrying because a Miss Sinclair had vanished. The two ends had joined up.

But should she tell them? The three of them were waiting like hungry weans watching their daddy cut up a joint of meat, dying to know which bit was coming their way. 'More or less,' she said. She couldn't have squared away why she was lying, but it felt right as the words left her mouth and even more right when she saw the three of them sit back and breathe out.

'And who was this person making silly mistakes?' Mrs Sinclair said.

Helen took another drink of tea and thought hard. She couldn't give the girl away because she had no idea who she was. On the other hand, if she described her maybe one of the Sinclairs would recognise her.

'I wasn't introduced to her,' Helen said. 'She's a young woman, about my age I would say. Twenties. And not from the top drawer, I don't think. But she's got a sort of a. . . How would I put it. . . a confident way with her. She's very free with herself, if you know what I mean.'

'Oh my God!' said Carolyn a split second before her sister clamped a hand on her arm and hissed at her to shut up.

'Do you think you know who it might be?' said Helen.

'Where did you meet this person?' Mrs Sinclair said, with a glare at both her daughters.

'At the mortuary, Mummy,' said Fiona. 'Nelly already said so.'

Helen nodded, thanking her stars she hadn't been forced to think up a lie, for she couldn't have come up with that one, and it was perfect.

'Disgraceful,' said Mrs Sinclair. 'Are they selling tickets at the door? Are they doing tours? That sort of nastiness was supposed to be over a century ago. I'm surprised at you, Helen, for being so ghoulish. I've been grievously taken in by you all these years, I must say. I think I shall have to speak to the doctors about this.'

As recently as yesterday, Helen would have laughed at the idea of the doctors listening. But now she wasn't so sure. That girl she met had annoyed Dr Deuchar just by her presence in the surgery. And it was right from the outset too. As soon as he set eyes on her, when she could have been there

244

for anything. She could have been ill or in pain and needing help but Dr Deuchar jumped down her throat. And why did Dr Strasser not know whether they'd burned files or handed them over? Whatever they'd done with them, she had to face one last uncomfortable fact: it was nonsense that all her furniture and curtains and the rest of it had been cleared out of his attic to make space for paperwork, for there were three deep stores, only a step from the office the files were leaving. No one in their right mind would lug heavy boxes up four flights instead of along that short passageway.

Those rugs and lamps, those plates and clothes brushes and velvety bath towels weren't going spare and needing someone to use them. They were the same as these slices of pie and wedges of cake. The same as this big brown teapot that had never before been used in Mrs Sinclair's summer sitting room. They were sops to Helen to keep her quiet.

The only question was, what was she keeping quiet about? She still didn't know who the dead girl was, or why she had been killed. She only had the thinnest thread to hold onto: that one word 'Sinclair' thrown over the shoulder of another girl who could be anyone, as far as Helen was concerned, even if Mr Yarrow and Dr Deuchar and these three women who were watching Helen so closely knew the stranger well enough to hate and despise and fear her.

'Please don't tell the doctors,' Helen said. 'I know it was silly to think I could make sense of it when the police can't. I'll put it out of my mind now and won't be so daft again.'

Mrs Sinclair looked at her out of narrowed eyes for a good long minute, then decided to believe what she was hearing.

'Good girl,' she said, and picked up her teacup again.

Carolyn and Fiona shared a smile. They were far too easy to convince, Helen thought to herself. They truly believed she was chastened and meant only to do her job and stop all the silliness. They had underestimated her. She was wilier than they imagined. She was nobody's fool.

Chapter 18

But she was so alone with it all. She had no one to talk to unless she turned to Sandy again, burdening him with it, no idea how it would take him. Teen was right; Helen *had* pulled away from her pals after her wedding; them as hadn't dropped her when she set out on her studies. And somehow she hadn't made any new ones.

She had seen others hanging back after classes, asking the teachers questions and favours, but Helen couldn't get out quick enough. She kept her head bent during the lectures, writing her notes as neat as she could get them, then scurried away. She couldn't join them in teashops and plan cycling trips out to the hills for Saturday, so she kept herself to herself until they stopped asking. If they thought she was snooty, that was better than knowing she didn't have the price of a cuppa or a bike to ride. But maybe she'd been daft to be so proud, now that she needed someone.

An idea was growing about a motive for a murder and she couldn't resist it. Maybe if she was going to talk it through, she should take it right into the lion's den. Maybe she should turn to the doctors and tell them what she knew. Or rather she should tell the one doctor who was definitely involved in all of this. The one who owned the wee house and the furniture that were Helen's bribe. The one who undoubtedly had something pressing on him. The one with the name that made Yarrow, the Torphichen Street girls, and even Greet distrust him. And give him the chance to do the right thing. Maybe he wouldn't want his partner to know all his secrets and maybe Helen could get round him that way.

'Doc?' she said, putting her head round his door after listening to make sure there were no patients in there.

'Helen!' said Dr Strasser. 'You're a busy bee, aren't you? We never see you.'

'I like making myself useful,' Helen said. 'I'd just as soon be out doing rounds as sitting in my office waiting for folk to turn up.' She was just too late to bite her lip, only realising after she'd spoken that it sounded like she was criticising the doctor, calling him lazy. She took a quick panicked glance about herself, hoping to see something he was very busy indeed with in here. But all she saw was the wee table by his armchair, with a book open and face-down, the pipe-rack and all his doings sitting ready.

'Don't worry about me, Nelly,' he said, with a sad smile. 'I'm not setting myself up as any kind of hero and one of the boons of my life is that I'm terribly hard to offend. Other more thrusting chaps take it poorly when the halo slips. But not me.'

'I'm glad to hear it, Doc,' Helen said. 'Because I've got something to tell you that's not going to be welcome.' She was lying. If Dr Strasser didn't mind what people thought of him she was in trouble, trying to get some purchase. But she was committed now. After what she'd just said there was no way she could leave it and walk away.

He smiled at her with that familiar distant look and spread a lordly hand out towards the patient's chair.

'I found the wee place out the front,' she said.

Dr Strasser frowned and hooked his head up to one side.

'The three bays, through the passage from Miss Anderson's office.'

Helen would have sworn his look of surprise was genuine. His eyes opened wide and his mouth broke into a beaming

247

smile. 'Well, I never!' he said. 'I'd quite forgotten about that. Can you believe it?' Then he grunted. 'What a waste of space to have it just sitting there. We could use it for storage.' He smacked himself in the forehead and laughed again. 'We could have used it for the odds and ends Miss Anderson left behind. Instead of lugging it all up to the attics or burning it.'

'I was thinking I could use it as a waiting room. If we opened one of the bolted doors. Or storage, like you said,' she added, in case she was being pushy.

'And why would you think I'd see red at any of this?'

Helen took a deep breath to gather her thoughts. 'Well, Doc, because, you see, I think I know what they were used for. Those three bays. I worked it out. See?'

'I highly doubt that, Nelly.'

'It was to help out girls who'd got themselves in trouble.'

'Well, well, well,' said Dr Strasser. 'And what brings you to that – might I say, rather startling – conclusion?'

'Because there was a girl in Miss Anderson's office on Monday morning, sobbing. And another girl – very pert – who came looking for someone. I think the first one came for help, but she couldn't get it because Miss Anderson was all packed up to go.'

'Margery Anderson?' said Dr Strasser. 'Helping girls who'd strayed? Oh I hardly think so, Helen. Good heavens, no. What on earth made you think so?'

'I don't know,' Helen said, feeling witless and confused. 'It doesn't make any sense, Doc. I thought the sobbing girl was the same one who died in our shelter. But she can't be.'

'Why not?' He pushed his chair back from his desk on its little wheels and stretched for his pipe, letting out a hearty sigh. 'If she was desperate enough to come here years too late, then perhaps she was desperate enough to take a drastic way out. What a rotten thing it was to happen to Sandy and you, just when you were settling in.'

Helen shook her head. 'No, that's not it,' she said. 'I went back to the mortuary, see? Because I wanted another look at her. And the attendant there said she wasn't... in trouble and she had never done anything to get herself in trouble. If you understand me, Doc.' Helen willed herself not to blush. This was a medical matter and she would have to learn to discuss it calmly. It was something they looked for in a post-mortem. Nothing more.

'She was a "good girl"?' said Dr Strasser. Somehow, him choosing a euphemism made it worse and Helen felt her cheeks warming after all. 'In which case, what makes you think she's mixed up in that old business?'

'Well,' said Helen slowly, 'one possibility I've been considering is maybe she was trying to blackmail someone. And she ended up where blackmailers end up, sometimes.'

'Trying to blackmail whom?' Dr Strasser had stopped filling his pipe, mid plug, and was staring at her.

'Miss Anderson sprang to mind,' Helen said. 'But you're sure that's not right.' She frowned. 'Why did you call it "old business" and say the sobbing girl was years too late?'

'Because, Helen, it was my dear papa who provided that particular service. I'm sure Miss Anderson would have run a mile if she'd dreamed of such things going on.'

'Old Dr Strasser?' said Helen. '*He* did that?'

'My father took a very practical view of what "kindness" meant.' Dr Strasser's face softened as he remembered. 'And believe it or not, Helen, he was far from alone.'

'But it's not still. . .?' Helen said. 'You don't. . .?'

'Not I,' said Dr Strasser.

'So you didn't give me and Sandy our house and fittings 'as a' – She couldn't say 'bribe' – 'way to keep me quiet?'

'Did I. . .?' Dr Strasser said. 'You're asking if I bribed you with champagne glasses and Turkey carpets to turn a blind eye to my abortion clinic?'

Helen blushed the blush of her life. She could feel her heart beating in her ears.

'No, Helen,' Dr Strasser said. 'I let you have the house for all the reasons I explained. And because I have no need of it. Re. the clinic, things have moved on from that rather ad hoc arrangement, thankfully.'

As was so often the case, Helen didn't understand him. For once she didn't nod and let it pass. 'What do you mean?' she said.

But he shook his head. 'I think not. I wouldn't want to alarm you. Especially given the flair for imaginative leaps you've just displayed. But let me say again if the girl you mentioned was trying to blackmail someone, she might not have got as far as she hoped. You'd be surprised.'

'Maybe not as surprised as all that,' Helen said quietly. 'Doctors and judges and lawyers and priests.'

'What's that?'

'Nothing,' Helen said, and sniffed. Her deep flush had left her nose running 'That's that then,' she went on. 'If it's *not* blackmail, *and* she died pure – like Billy at the morgue said – I don't see how else she could be mixed up in. . . what old Dr Strasser used to do. I was wrong.'

'Perhaps the mortuary attendant was being chivalrous,' Dr Strasser said. 'What good would it do to blacken her name after she'd died? If she had a name to blacken. We shan't know until someone identifies the poor child.'

'Blacken her name,' Helen repeated. 'If she *had* a name.' Then she sat up very straight. 'That's what it is! Doc, I really think that's what it is. She's got a name that means something in Edinburgh and so there's a lot of people trying to sweep what happened to her under the carpet. Maybe she tried here, not knowing that there was no one here doing those things any more and then she got desperate, like you said. Duncan Pyne gave her a false name, to spare the family, and the family aren't going to claim her body. And the attendant was just being nice. He *is* nice. Funny, eh? You don't expect nice folk to do that job.'

'You went to the morgue looking for Ygor, did you, Helen?'

'That film gave me nightmares, Doc,' Helen said.

'Me too,' said Dr Strasser.

'What film is this?' Dr Deuchar entered the room. 'I smelled the baccy,' he said. 'I'm out and I can't be fashed going to get more in this weather.'

Helen glanced out of the window. While she had been sitting there, the sky had darkened until the beech trees at the end of the garden looked pale against it. The air had changed too, feeling heavy and close. A yellow day, she had always called them when she was wee, from the warm air and the damp dust when the rain hit it, that Helen thought smelled like egg yolks boiled too long until they'd gone powdery.

'*Frankenstein*,' said Dr Strasser.

Dr Deuchar gave an elaborate shudder. 'That young lady has a lot to answer for,' he said.

'I'll get your baccy,' said Helen. 'From the Yarrows.' She watched Dr Deuchar as she spoke, thinking of his outburst when she mentioned their name and the hasty way he tried to cover it, thinking about his coldness to the pert girl on Monday morning. She hadn't imagined *that*.

Dr Deuchar was smiling and holding out a ten-shilling note.

Helen smiled back and nodded at Dr Strasser too. 'I won't be long,' she said. 'Although I might take my bag and see if I can't reel them in, like you said, Doc.'

'The famous nurse's bag,' said Dr Strasser.

'Almoner's bag now,' said Dr Deuchar.

And there was *another* memory, Helen thought as she hurried away, of something bothering her about that bag. It wasn't the swank she felt she hadn't earned. It wasn't Dr Strasser forgetting the woman while Dr Deuchar remembered her. It was something so small she had overlooked it, like one nit in a headful of hair. Now, just like that one nit, it was itching.

251

There was no time to scratch it though. Because she'd arrived.

'I haven't come to pry!' she said, as Mr Yarrow glared at her. She shut the shop door at her back. 'Look, I don't know what you think is wrong with me, but—'

'You've got poor taste in friends,' he said. 'I'll tell you that for free.'

'That girl outside earlier?' Helen said. 'She's not my friend. I'm an almoner. A welfare officer,' she added at his puzzled look. 'And that kind of girl is the sort that needs a lot of help.'

'I'd leave them to reap what they sowed,' said Mr Yarrow.

'Aye well,' Helen said, but bit her tongue on the rest of what she was thinking: that it wasn't the girls that *sowed* anything. 'I was just wondering how the bairn's settling in. Not for work, just being nosy. I love babies.'

'It's none of your business,' Mr Yarrow said. 'If you love babies you should be at home having them instead of marching about sticking your neb in. So, if you've no reason to be here—'

'A quarter ounce of Virginia flake, please,' Helen said. 'And not everyone's lucky enough to have a baby, Mr Yarrow, as you well know. So don't go flinging that at me.'

'You—You—You—' he said, spluttering over it..

Helen could have kicked herself. It was true but it wasn't professional to say so. 'I apol—' she began, but Mr Yarrow had found his voice.

'You take your filthy mouth, and your dirty ways and get out of my shop. There's laws against women like you.'

'What in the devil's name are you talking about?' Helen said, astonishment making her bolder than she would have been without it.

'My wife's a decent woman. You'll not get round *her*. But I want to know who sent you.'

'I have no idea what you're on about,' Helen said. She was shaking, but she made herself speak up. 'Are you feeling all right? I know you've been through some hard—'

'Who've you been talking to?' He leaned right over the counter and stared hard at Helen, his eyes wide and his chest heaving. 'You all look the same to me, when you're guised as good girls.' He would have said more if he hadn't been checked by a sudden cry behind him.

Helen looked up and saw Mrs Yarrow, a soft blue blanket held against her shoulder, young Gordon in evidence only as a bump and a quiet grizzling.

'What's to do?' she said.

'Your husband's not feeling well,' Helen said.

'Get out!' he yelled, loud enough to set the baby crying in earnest. 'Don't you dare come here trying to poison my life with your stain. You made your bed and I hope you die in it.'

'Robert,' said his wife. 'Stop shouting. You're upsetting the baby.'

'For two pins,' said Mr Yarrow, quietly now, staring coldly at Helen. 'Just try me, because I'm telling you: for two pins!'

Helen caught Mrs Yarrow's eye and mouthed, 'Be careful.' The woman gave a ghost of a nod as Helen opened the shop door and sped away.

She was almost back at the crescent before she thought of it, but when she looked down she was relieved to see the quarter of baccy clutched in her hand. She opened her fist and smoothed the paper. What was all that about? Poison his life? With her stain? The stain of women 'like her'? He knew nothing about her. *Nothing*. Only that she had no children and was an almoner. Maybe it was no more than him knowing what old Doc Strasser did in those three basement bays. Childless himself, humiliated by what he saw as his failure, maybe he was incensed at the very thought. It couldn't be more than that. Dr Strasser had just said it was all done with years ago, better ways of handling things now.

She dropped the baccy on the hall table and shouted through to the doctors that it was there but that she was leaving. She couldn't face them again. Then she set off, in a drizzle that matched her mood to a T, all the way up through Tollcross to the King's and then down as far as the Usher Hall – she was sure Sandy had said something this morning about ice cream tubs leaving the pavements sticky. She checked carefully round by the picture house, but him and George hadn't been near the place, that was for sure. There were wisps of straw washed up in the gutter from some mishap with a cart and, right enough, dark sticky patches with all manner of grit and chaff and scraps of this and that stuck to them, only now beginning to loosen again as the drizzle gathered itself to turn to a proper shower of rain. She made a circle of Castle Street and Cambridge Street and then struck out through the goods station towards Morrison Street in case it wasn't a theatre he'd been on about at all, but maybe the big Italian down at the Haymarket end, although as to who would pay the price of those ice-creams and then let any of it splodge onto the ground to make a mess for the street sweepers, Helen couldn't fathom.

She was all the way to the corner of Grove Street and not a whisker of him, when two things struck her. First, that she was half drifting homewards as well as half-looking for Sandy, but the home she was drifting to was still Greet and Mack's. It would take a while before that changed. The other startling thought to creep into her mind and make her stop walking was that if she didn't turn off towards her old home, or double back for her new one, she'd soon be at Haymarket, or – more to the point – at the back of Haymarket where, if she could summon the courage, she might just be able to learn something.

Chapter 19

It would have been miserable in any weather, Helen was sure, but in this determined summer rain it was bleak indeed. She pulled her hat brim down, turned her coat collar up, and stayed in the middle of the lane to keep her good shoes on the ridge of cobbles, out of the runnels to either edge, and to keep as far from the doorways and overhangs as she could too.

'The back of Haymarket' was bandied around in whispers up at Fountainbridge, sometimes wheeled out in jokes by the coarser neighbours. Once at night she'd heard a man, his words thick with the drink, shout it at a woman who was crying in the street. She'd never forgotten the contempt in his voice. Greet had come into their room and banged the window down, then hung over her bed to see if she was sleeping. She'd kept her eyes tight shut. Teenie was sleeping for real, snoring with wee popping sounds like she always did. 'The back of Haymarket,' Helen had repeated to herself once she was alone again.

She'd had a picture in her mind of a hidden bit of the city, maybe through an arch into a street no one used for anything else. Only now did she see that this was a child's view, like a dark fairytale where the wrong things are down a rabbit hole, through a looking glass, or at least in the middle of a thick forest. It turned out, to Helen's surprise and embarrassment at her younger self, that the girls in the doorways, women as old as Greet some of them, looked out over porters taking barrows of parcels from the platforms to the waiting carts, weans playing in puddles, making the most of the sudden downpour before their mammies cried them in and leathered them for getting soaked. There was even a man in banker's stripes, his umbrella unfolded for once and held down low over his head. He strolled up the middle of the cobbles, same as Helen, bold as you like, headed somewhere or other and not even caring that his route took him this way.

It was only when he glanced back for the second time that she finally cottoned on. He *wasn't* taking a shortcut through here on his way to some banker's business. He was here for the business being done here, with his brolly low to hide his face, and she was stopping him, her with her wee hat and her nurse's bag. She drew to a halt and looked to either side, suddenly wanting to be anywhere else. She wasn't equal to this after all.

'You lost, hen?' came a voice from the darkest corner of an alcove formed by an outside stair leading up to a goods loft.

'No,' Helen said, stepping closer. 'I'm hoping to have a word with someone.'

'Are you a nun?'

Helen laughed and moved closer. 'Me?' she said. 'Naw. But I might need to get some new claes if you thought I was, eh?'

'Ocht they're aye in mufti when they come roon us,' the woman said. 'Here, step in oot the watter. It's no' getting any better, is it?'

She had moved aside to let Helen join her in her shelter. This was one of the oldest women. Her hair was jet black but the rain had put some of the black on her forehead and running down her cheeks. She had a pretty dimpled face and very white china teeth that sparkled as she smiled. 'Whae is it you're looking for?' she said.

'Anyone really,' said Helen. 'I've got a couple of questions, see?'

'But whae sent you?' the woman said. 'The kirk, the cooncil, or the polis?'

'The other ones,' said Helen, shivering to hear that echo again. 'The doctors. I work at Gardner's Crescent.'

'Oh,' said the woman, with an arch look. 'Do you now?'

This time it made sense, in a way it hadn't when the two youngsters at Torphichen Street had laughed at the mention of the place. 'Aye,' Helen said. 'So you remember when old Dr Strasser was working, do you?'

'A lovely man. Since he stopped you've to go all the way over to Leith Street to a right old butcher that charges the earth. And so this is you saying it's starting up again and a nice young lass like you is taking care of the girls, is it?'

Helen only just managed not to yelp. She swallowed hard. 'I'm sorry. I'm afraid not, no. I've just got some questions, is all.'

'So you keep saying.'

Helen smiled in recognition of a point well-made. Her heart was going like a rabbit and her mouth was sour, she was that scared of where she'd found herself and who she was speaking to, but she had to admit she liked this woman. If she'd met her in a back court or on a tram, she'd have taken to her easily. 'It's about parties,' she said. 'Maybe still going on, or maybe during the war, just. But they were held at the St Andrew's Social Club.'

'That was just pure evil, that was.'

'I don't know what you mean,' Helen said. 'But I want to. Can you tell me?'

'Don't get mixed up in it,' the woman said. 'I'll tell you *this*. I'll tell you what happened to the last one that tried. She's on a slab in the Cowgate.' Helen gasped. 'So you leave well alone.'

'Is her name Sinclair?' Helen said.

The woman shot out from under the overhang and turned a horrified face Helen's way. Her voice shook. 'You never heard that fae me!' she said and was gone.

Without her protection, Helen wished she was gone too. The rain didn't seem to stop the business of the street and, now it was five o'clock and men were off their work, there was a steady stream of them, strolling up the lane, looking into

257

the dark corners. If one of them saw her and came over! She stole a quick glance at the opening onto Haymarket Terrace and when there was a lull she fled, running like she hadn't run since she was a girl. She was still running when she saw, a shout ahead of her, the blessed outline of the dustcart, broom bristles glistening in the rain, and the mismatched pair of them – tall, gaunt Sandy and wee round George – both with their oilskin capes on and looking like witch hats on legs.

'Sandy!' she shouted as loud as she could. The people closest to her, hurrying into the station or dashing out of it to get to their trams, gave her sidelong glances. It must sound in her voice that she wasn't all right, but none of them wanted trouble to keep them out in this rain. Sandy and George heard nothing, what with the raindrops battering their cape hoods and the noise of the buses at their side.

Before she caught up with them, George took himself away up Morrison Street with the barrow and Sandy, a fresh purpose in his step it seemed to her, set off in the other direction. He flung his hood back and raked his fingers through his hair, although the rain was as heavy as ever. This time he heard her calling and stopped dead, turning with a look of astonishment.

'Where are you off to?' she said.

'Wh—What are you doing doon here?' Sandy said.

'I've been up the back of Haymarket,' said Helen, then dug him in the ribs with her elbow. 'Talking to the girls, you daftie. For work. And, Sandy, there really is something going on. I've been ae way and yon way on it, telling myself I'm making up stories and then telling myself it's too much to be nothing. But now I know for sure.'

'Know whit?'

'Aye, well that's where it runs oot,' Helen said. 'But I know where to look for more. There must be an answer and I think it's no' far off. Maybe I could just march in and. . .'

'March in *where*?' Sandy said.

258

'St Andrew's Society,' Helen told him. 'Doon the New Town somewhere.' She drew back and gave Sandy a hard look. 'Ken what? When you're in your work claes there's no mistaking it, but as long as the rain keeps on, in that cape you could be anyone. Will you come with me and see if we can get past the door? Try and get answers?' Sandy screwed his face up and it seemed to Helen that he glanced away to the side. 'Where *were* you going anyway?' she said. 'Did you say? I'm that keyed up with all this.'

'Aye, I'll come with you,' Sandy said. 'But I'll need to take my oiler off in the lobby and then I'll be what I am for the world to see again.'

'But once we're in,' Helen said. 'I just need to hit on the right question. It's about the parties. Or maybe about Dr Strasser. Or the Sinclairs. Or Mr Pyne. Or maybe it *is* Miss Anderson. I don't know what end to pull to unravel it.'

'You're not making much sense, Nelly.' Sandy took her arm to hurry her across the wide expanse at the end of Atholl Place. 'And which bit of the New Town are we after? Because it's starts about here.'

He was right. One way led back to Fountainbridge, the police station and the breweries, the dairies and stables and coal yards. But turn the other way and you were in crescents and circles with gardens locked against strangers, squares of tall houses, broad streets of deep pavements and fancy lamp-posts. And there was miles of it.

'If you want to know something,' Helen said, pointing ahead to where a policeman in a cape not that different from Sandy's was pacing along on his beat.

'Och, dinnae go pestering the polis,' Sandy said.

'That's what they're there for,' said Helen. 'What else is he doing? He should be where I've just been, not out here looking in the nice shop windows at his own reflection.' She broke into a trot and hailed the man.

'Do you know where the St Andrew's Society is?' she asked him. 'We're looking for it but we're lost.'

The policeman stared first at Helen and then at Sandy. Rain was dripping off the peak of his helmet and getting caught in his moustache, which was so bushy and luxuriant it stuck out too far to be sheltered. 'What are you going there for?' he said.

'Work,' said Sandy.

It was a good answer and it should have set the policeman down, but instead his eyes flared and he gave both of them an even closer look. 'The baith of youse?' he said.

'Just me,' said Helen, on a hunch that this was the answer that would flush out a useful reaction. She was right.

'Oh, is that right?' the constable said. 'You're going for a job at the St Ant— St Andrew's Club, are you?' He turned on Sandy. 'And what does that make *you*?'

Sandy couldn't frame an answer, but Helen had been ready for it. 'He's my husband,' she said. 'And it's only a wee cleaning job a few hours a week. Why? Are they shut doon or something?'

The policeman looked at her hat and her shoes and then caught sight of her big nurse's bag. 'What's that?' he said. 'Your dusters? Get on out of it, before I take youse both in.'

'What the hang are y—?' Sandy began.

'I've seen you before,' the policeman said, taking a step forward. 'Years since but I never forget a face.'

Sandy had been holding Helen's arm, and now he squeezed it hard enough and in just the place to make her wince. 'Let's go,' he said. 'We'll find it on our own.'

When they were a good long way off from the policeman, he finally let go and shook his hand to get the cramp out. 'I'll have marks on me,' Helen said. 'What's wrong, for crying out loud?'

'What have you got yourself mixed up in?' Sandy said.

'A brothel,' said Helen. 'Definitely. Maybe the rooms were up at Rosebank, but it was run from doon here. And when the girls got in trouble they used to go to old Dr Strasser.'

'Aye, I'd heard as much,' said Sandy. 'Not about working girls, mind. But just about Doc Strasser helping whoever needed helped.'

'Does everybody ken except me?' said Helen. 'Is that why my mammy didnae want me working there?'

'Mebbes,' said Sandy. 'And mebbes that's why Mrs Sinclair took a fit over it too.'

'Except Old Doc Strasser has been deid ten years and this was still going on two years back just. Nineteen-forty-six. I've seen pictures.'

She stopped walking. They were halfway along Princes Street now, outside an ornate doorway between two posh shops. Helen had seen it before and registered vaguely what it said there, without ever thinking of what the words might mean.

'Look,' she said.

'The Royal Overseas League,' Sandy read. 'What of it?'

'I've got an idea,' Helen said. She was halfway up the steps and tugging at that big brass handle on one of the double doors. They didn't get two foot in the place, which was just what she'd been hoping.

'Here!' came the cry from a glassed-in cubby off to one side of the vestibule. 'The trade entrance is off Rose Street Lane. Get away round and ring.'

'Oh,' Helen said. 'Sorry. They told us just to come in.'

'Who's this?' said the man. When they stepped closer, they could see him, as fat as a tick and wedged into his wee cubby as if it had been built around him.

'Mr Pyne. Was that not his name?' Helen said. Sandy said nothing.

'Mr Pyne told youse to come tramping up our front steps?' said the man. 'He's not a member here. So he's no grounds to be saying anything.'

'Is this not the St Andrew's Club?' said Helen, making her eyes wide to match the sweet voice she was using.

'It is *not*,' the man said. 'It is most *certainly* not. You sound like a local. So how's this you've mixed up our beautiful Princes Street with that dingy Drummond Street, even if you can't tell the difference between the Royal Overseas and the St Antics. Go on with you, before I ring the bell and get you booted.'

The rain had stopped. Out on the street, Helen took her hat off, wrung it out and put it back on again. 'That's what that policeman was going to say too,' she said. 'The St *Antics*. I'm telling you, Sandy. It's a club for those and such as those and none of them are what they're making out to be.'

'Ocht, Helen,' Sandy said. 'There's more to life than what you learn in Sunday school. So what if it is what it sounds like? Better that than those girls you just saw on the street, eh no? And if they look after them when it all goes the way it goes, where's the harm?'

'Where's the *harm*?' Helen said. 'How about a girl deid in oor shelter and now everyone lying about who she is till she ends in a parish grave because her family's disowned her? How about that, Sandy Crowther?' With anger to spur her, she was off up a side street. Who knew which one; she could never remember, since they all went the same way, up and over the spine of George Street and down the other side to the gardens. But she knew if she turned to the east, Drummond Place was one of the big, deep crescents over there somewhere. She would find it.

And find it she did. There was nothing dingy about the crescent, no matter what that fat doorman had said. The houses around the gardens were as stately as any in the city and the fresh look of it as the sun peeked out again was almost enough to make Helen doubt everything she'd been thinking. Even the club itself, with its crest above the door and its balconies in front of the upstairs windows, looked like something off the films.

'I didnae mean it was all fine,' Sandy said. He'd been silent since she'd turned the sharp edge of her tongue on him. She didn't usually speak to him that way. 'Just that it happens and you'll never stop it, Nelly. I d'ae want *you* to end up the way she did.'

'What?' said Helen. 'How could I? *I'm* no' blackmailing anyone. *I've* no' been at their parties and seen who's there. All I did was open a box I shouldn't have.' Her voice had slowed and now she chewed her lip, thinking. Was that a way to poke a stick in the hole and see what stuck to it?

'What are you thinking?' Sandy said.

'Watch me,' said Helen, and crossed the road.

There was another doorman here, in another cubbyhole, and the same-looking hall beyond him, with a high fire crackling in a grate and armchairs to either side of it, newspapers laid on a table for the taking. Helen could smell the unmistakable lingering odour of suet, as if there had been a good hot dinner on such a miserable day, for all it was summer.

'Now then, how can I help you?' said this new doorman. He was Irish, Helen thought, and just as fat as the Princes Street one, with a shiny red face and a deep hitch when he breathed. If he'd come into the surgery the doctors would have had plenty to say to him.

'I think I can help *you*,' Helen said. 'Or help Mr Pyne and Mr Grossart and all them.'

'All. . .?' the doorman said. His breath ran out but he tried again. 'All. . . them?'

'Rev. Warner, was it? I'm trying to remember. Mr Yarrow.'

'Who's Mr Yarrow?'

'I know Mr Sinclair's dead now,' Helen said.

'What are you talking about?' the doorman said, but there was no force behind it. He sounded sick and his red face was blotched suddenly.

'I've found all the stuff that was stored up at Fountainbridge,' Helen said. 'You know, the stuff Dr Strasser put by.'

'Fountainbridge?' the man said, even more faintly. 'What stuff?'

'And I was wondering if the gents would like it back again,' Helen went on. 'If maybe you had room down here for it at the Society, now the Social Club's closed.'

'What *stuff?*' the doorman said, with a bit more vehemence.

'Glasses and costumes,' Helen said. She closed her eyes, trying to remember everything she'd found in that box in the attic. 'And photos, of course.'

'Oh, try telling them not to take photos!' said the doorman.

'And a roll of tickets,' said Helen. 'Did they really sell tickets?'

'Raffle,' he said. 'It was all a big joke. Raffling hampers like Christmas at the golf club.'

'But it's stopped now?'

'Couple of years since.'

'Do you know why?' said Helen.

The doorman was wriggling about on his stool as he spoke, as if to scratch himself, and Helen looked away, feeling embarrassed for him. It was only when Sandy said, 'What's that for?' that she turned back. The man was holding out a folded banknote. It looked like a pound.

'That's to go away and not come back or, if you do come back, come when I'm not here,' he said. 'I knew this would happen. Sooner or later. Come in the morning. I'm never on till after dinner.'

'*What* would happen?' Helen said, as she took the note. Sandy had been staring at it but she wasn't too proud. This would put fresh nets at her windows or fill the shelves of her larder. 'Do you mean the dead girl?'

She had thought him far too ruddy to turn properly pale, but he was the colour of raw dough now. 'Don't say that,' he whispered. 'You've no inkling what stone you've lifted there. I've got it buried so deep I'd forgotten till you just said it again. For the love of Mike, don't repeat that name.'

Then the three of them turned at the sound of a door opening somewhere inside the house. There was a burst of a plummy voice, muffled and strange-sounding.

'That's the news starting on the radio,' the doorman said. 'Cue for half of them to leave and go home. You should scarper 'fore somebody sees you.'

'Are you happy now?' Sandy said as, hand-in-hand, they made a run for it, turning onto the long street that climbed and climbed all the way up and around the castle rock to home.

'You're kidding, aren't you?' Helen said. 'Sandy, slow doon, I'm getting a stitch. Of course I'm not "happy".'

'But you'll leave it? You've got your answer. The girls went to parties at a club. They got in trouble, got tooken care of, until this one time it went wrong and a girl died. But it's over, Helen. You said it yourself, it's done. The glasses and whatnot are packed away.'

'Aye,' Helen said. 'Boxed up and years of dust. But that makes no sense, does it? Because she died – Maggie, Jane Bloggs, Miss Sinclair, or whoever she is – on Monday. It makes no sense.'

'Do you want to lose your job?' said Sandy. 'And lose our nice wee hoose to boot? You heard what that doorman said. You mention a deid woman and he says, "Don't repeat that name". What if he meant old Dr Strasser, who was in this up to his oxters? Do you want the surgery shut and us on the streets?'

'Mammy would have us back,' Helen said. 'And I don't think he *did* mean old Dr Strasser, you know. Wait till I try and get it straight what I said and what he said back. He knew Pyne and Grossart, didn't he? When I mentioned Dr Strasser having the boxes, he said "what boxes". He didn't say "Who's Dr Strasser?" That's not the forgotten name.'

'You're right,' Sandy said, interested again. 'No more it is. What name was it buried away deep down? It's harder for me because I know none of them. But you should be able to—'

'Yarrow,' said Helen. 'He said "Who's Yarrow?" And right enough, Sandy, he's not like the others. He's a nice enough wee shop there on the main road at Tollcross but he'd hardly be at a party with a bishop or a judge.'

'Maybe he gave the hamper,' Sandy said.

'It's a newsagents.'

'Or the tickets.' Sandy was joking and Helen smiled, as a wife should.

'Aye, that's more like it,' she said. 'He's no' oot the same drawer as the rest of them but he knows something about it. Tickets, it could be.' She stopped and put her knuckles into the small of her back, feeling the weight of her big nurse's bag solid against her hip. 'Let's move to Amsterdam,' she said. 'These hills are a killer.'

'Never,' said Sandy. 'You'll not catch me anywhere over there again in this life.'

Helen had turned and was gazing away from the streets and shops, all the way down towards the river and the hazy Fife hills in the distance. Looking a long way off always helped when something was bothering her. 'Tickets,' she said again. Then registering that Sandy had spoken she went on, 'Holland was neutral.'

'And a gey sight good it did them,' Sandy retorted. 'Tell it to Anne Frank.'

'Who?' Helen said.

Sandy shrugged. 'You're right,' he said. 'Nae point going back over all that, eh?'

'I'm no' saying that,' Helen said. 'Dinnae put words in my mouth then take the huff about them. I'm just saying there's this going on here and now and we cannae just watch it.'

'Aye but it's not,' said Sandy. 'It's over and done. Glasses packed away. Wee howff lying empty. And the girls are fine. Nae bairns to shame them, nae scandal aboot them. I'm no' saying it was nice but it's over, Nelly. If anything, it's a shame it is over. For if yon could have got herself sorted out she'd be alive today instead of in the morgue, wouldn't she?'

'She didn't kill herself!' Helen said. 'Billy at the morgue told me.'

'Billy at the morgue said she was a virgin, too,' Sandy reminded her. 'Billy at the morgue was trying not to upset you.'

Helen started walking again. She felt the pull of what he was saying. She would have liked nothing more than to settle for that explanation and get on with her job and her home and her life. Only trouble being, it wasn't true.

Chapter 20

They walked the rest of the way home in silence; Sandy's usual morose silence, Helen's silence coming from thinking hard and trying to catch up with a shoal of memories that were flitting across her mind, winking in and out of the light as she chased them. It wasn't until they were nearly at their own gate that she came back to the outside world again.

'Look at that!' she said, pointing. 'Were you back at dinner-time?' For the bathroom window was propped wide.

'Naw,' Sandy said. 'You must have—' But he stopped at her look. 'It'll be fine, quiet as it is away back here. Dinnae fash.' Helen was hurrying up the steps and fumbling with her key. 'Nelly, for the love! What acrobat's going to climb out over they banisters and slither in a top window. Will you calm down, will you?'

Helen was inside now and had banged open the bathroom door. She let her breath go and turned to meet him as he arrived beside her. 'I'll calm down about burglars,' she said. 'Seeing as whoever heard of a burglar breaking in to have a bath!'

It was unmistakable. The air was still soft from the steam and the distemper showed the tracks of water running down the walls. The bath was wet too, although scoured clean, with not a hint of a tide-mark.

'And burglars'd not wipe the bath over,' Sandy said. 'But someone's—' He stopped speaking.

'What?' Helen said. 'Did you hear something?'

'Naw,' said Sandy. 'I just thought on who it was.'

'Oh I *know* who it was!' Helen said. She sighed and it turned into a laugh. 'Did I dare tell Greet Downie what night she was getting her bath? Fool that I am.' She made her way to the kitchen to fill the kettle. 'Only how did she get in? Picking locks now, is she?'

'Ocht, that was me,' Sandy said. 'She came and found me and got my key off me. I should have told you but it flew out my mind.'

'I'll key *her*!' said Helen, going through to the other room to check for disturbance there. 'What a cheek. And look!' She toed the edge of the nice Turkey carpet. 'She's been meddling with this too.'

'What?' Sandy said.

'She's shifted this rug. She cannae seen green cheese but her een reel.'

'Why would even your maw shift a carpet?' Sandy said.

'Mercy knows!' Helen said. 'Because I put it down in the wrong place according to her? Because she wanted to take it roon by for herself but it was too heavy to carry? Maybe she just wanted to show me she could. I'd not put it past her.'

'Leave her to me,' Sandy said. 'I gave her the keys. I'll get them back. And I'll tell her to leave *oor* stuff, in *oor* house, alone from now on. How about that, eh?'

'Aye,' Helen said. 'That'll do. Thanks, Sandy.'

'Ach, you're a wee smasher,' Sandy said. 'You're worth getting the wrong side of Greet, easy.' He smiled and took a step towards her, then his face clouded and instead of the touch she was sure was coming he went to the sink and poured a drink of water into the mug they kept there. 'I might go now, if I've time,' he said. 'What's for tea anyway?'

Helen ran over the options briefly then laughed. 'It'll need to be egg and chips,' she said. 'Don't tell my mammy. I'll get to the shops tomorrow, maybe.'

Sandy left and Helen watched him go, but she didn't follow him to the stairs or look out the window after him. If he wasn't really going to Greet and Mack's – and she suspected he wasn't, for he never could lie to her and have it take – at least she didn't have to witness him going in that shelter and locking the chain behind himself again.

Helen peeled the tatties, sliced them up and set them in a bowl of water to clear. Then, with her tea, she sat at the big room table, still annoyed at the way the carpet was wrong now, fringes all up against the fireplace and getting caught under the press door instead of neat at the window end and the bed end, but she wasn't hauling it back again on her own. Instead she opened her bag. She still thought it was wrong to have it, but she couldn't deny it was rare and handy, the size of it. She pulled out her notepad and a pencil and set them in front of her.

Haymarket woman scared of name 'Sinclair'
Girl said 'Sinclair'
Duncan Pyne, Old man Sinclair, Rev. Warner, Rev. ?
  Mr Grossart
Sinclairs all spooked
Parties at St Antics club well known. Doormen. Rose-
  bank? New Town?
Miss Anderson.
Three bays.
Old Doc Strasser.
Girl – doc angry
Yarrow – doc angry
Yarrow angry with me/doctors/wife Why???? Member?
  Tickets?
Sinclair relative – suicide, murder?????
Virgin/pregnant???? Ask Bill at morgue????

'Or is Sandy right?' she asked herself out loud, when she had been staring at it for a good while. 'Think it through, girl.' She turned the notepad over so's it wouldn't distract her and put her head in her hands. The girls who went to the parties at

270

the Social Club got taken care of when the usual happened. Then the Sinclair relative – call her Jane – found herself the same way again and asked her pal – the pert girl from Monday – to help. But old Dr Strasser was long gone, the three wee bays were empty and there was no help to be had. So she killed herself and they hushed it up, the bigwigs and the family. Pride and shame.

Except, how hard would it be to find someone else to help? Like the 'butcher' who charged too much, over Leith Street way. Why wouldn't she go where she had to go to take care of herself?

Helen stood up and stared out the window, puzzling over that question. Why wouldn't she? Maybe. . . if she couldn't get away, from home or work. From prying family. Only why wouldn't she use the same excuse girls always had for being away and not being well after.

Helen felt an idea beginning to form inside her. Being away for a bit and not being well after. She repeated it to herself as if she could make the thought come clear. There had been enough girls 'off to their aunties a while' in Freer Street and Grove Place, coming back plump and sad, saying they'd been ill—

Helen took hold of the sill to keep herself steady as the wave crashed over her at long, long last. 'Appendicitis!' she said out loud. She heard a noise from below, from what had to be the bottom of the stairs, and she went to the front door to meet Sandy and share it with him. But she must have been mistaken. There was no sign of him on the steps, in the garden, or even coming along the street. Well, she couldn't wait. She wheeled back, stuffed her notepad and pencil back in her nurse's bag, snapped it shut and headed out into the late sun, feeling as light and washed as the city after the good cleansing rain.

Appendicitis! Teenie's friend's cousin who had the champagne glass without its base to sip her Lucozade out of? She had just had her appendix out and it went wrong and she kept having to go back. And Mrs McIrnie's daughter, Betty, who knew more than a bride should and had shocked her bridegroom? Hadn't her mother said she'd aye been healthy except for tonsils and her appendix. So maybe she'd had two visits to the three bays under the area. And then there was a string of mysterious check-ups. So maybe it was more than two. And what was the other one? Helen was reaching and reaching. She knew it was there and yes! Hallelujah! The first Mrs Yarrow. Healthy enough except for her appendix, the new wife had said. And 'all those tests'.

Helen could well imagine what happened. Bewildered by month after month of no happy news, maybe the first Mrs Yarrow told her husband she knew it wasn't her, because she'd fallen multiple times before. And so he put her out and... it all fell into place now... he went to Glasgow for the next one. Too many folk in Edinburgh knew his wife's tale. Glasgow. The same place they said 'Maggie Dickson' had been taken away to. The other city, so close in this tiny country nipped at the waist by estuaries, but it might as well be East and West Berlin.

She was on Cally Place now, nearly back at the McIrnies'. *My first follow-up visit,* she thought, and could have wept for poor Betty, who couldn't fall, and couldn't tell her mother or her husband why not. Couldn't tell anyone what she must know by now. She'd been unlucky; Dr Strasser, as experienced as he was, had botched it that one time and left her to ache.

She knocked smartly on the door and arranged a smile on her face, as Mrs McIrnie opened it. 'Mrs Crowther, isn't it?' she said. 'What brings you back?'

'I'm needing a wee quick word with your Betty,' Helen said. 'If she's in.'

'Aye aye, she's at the ironing, come away through.'

Helen set her bag on the floor by the deep press and followed Mrs McIrnie to the kitchen. Then she turned and gave the woman a firm smile. 'I'll not be long,' she said.

'I'm her mother!' Mrs McIrnie pulled her mouth down as her colour rose, but Helen kept smiling and waited until the woman flounced out with a click of her teeth.

'Evening, Betty,' Helen said. She looked around. 'Naebody in the box bed?'

'It's just you and me,' Betty said. 'What are you after this time?'

'I want to set your mind at rest if I can,' said Helen. 'And ask you to clear up a few wee bits and that for me.'

'Only the stork can set my mind at rest.' She spoke bitterly and Helen thought, as she changed one iron for another, that the spit on the new one fresh from the hearth was more vicious than need be. Betty pressed the hot foot on the yoke of the shirt she had smoothed on her table and looked up.

'What about adopting?' Helen said. 'Would your man go for that? There's a wean coming any day that's mammy's not the least bit fussed for having it. You could be ironing wee frills on a christening robe this time next month.'

Betty blinked and snatched the iron up off the shirt. She'd all but forgotten it. 'So it's right enough, then?' she said. There were tears in her eyes. 'If I tell him, he'll put me out. He'll blacken my name.'

'You might be surprised,' Helen said. 'Give him a chance anyway.'

'But it's right enough?' Betty said again, and her chest jerked as she sobbed. 'That I can't fall? That I never will?'

'I'm sorry. I think so. So – between you and me – can I just ask you? Or I'll say it and you just nod. Mm?' The first nod came and Helen pressed on. 'The St Andrew's Club?' Another nod. 'Parties?' Nod. 'And Dr Strasser, was it?' A shrug at that. 'But at Dr Strasser's surgery?' Helen said.

Betty shrugged again. 'I d'ae ken,' she said. 'It was dark. All I can tell you is it was a wee place just across the way from the doctor's bit, doon the steps.'

273

Helen nodded now. A wee place down the steps, across the area flags from the surgery to the three curtained bays. 'I'm sorry you've been so unlucky,' she said. 'And I'm sorry I'm bringing it back. But can I just ask one more question and then I'll be done?' Betty nodded. 'Was someone else here asking you things? Maybe a week ago?'

'Not "things",' Betty said. 'One thing. Was I willing to speak up and—' Before she could finish, though, the front door of the house opened and segged boots came along the passageway, stopping a minute and then carrying on to the kitchen. It was Betty's husband. He held up the nurse's bag and said, 'Whae's is this?' and then 'Oh!' as he saw Helen standing there.

Betty sank down to sit on the fender. Her eyes were glued to the big brown bag and her lip trembled.

'Lass?' said Stanley. 'Are you no' weel? What's to do?'

'My fault,' Helen said. 'I've sprung something on your wife, I'm afraid, and she's not had a minute to get used to it before here you are too.'

'Sprung what?' he said. He was taking the iron out of Betty's hand and leading her to a chair. Kind, Helen thought, and decided to chance it.

'A bairn,' she said. 'Not even born. Next week more than likely. But needing a good home. And I thought of you two.' She paused but when they both kept staring dumbly, she pressed on. 'I'll let youse mull it over. And I'll come back once it's here, will I?' She stopped at the door. 'What would you be hoping for? Boy or girl?'

Betty said nothing but her husband thought a minute and said, 'I d'ae care, as long as it's got its fingers and toes. Eh no, Betty hen?'

Helen stopped out in the close and scrabbled in her bag. Betty had nearly fainted when she saw it and she knew why. That was the tiny little thing! She opened the flap of a compartment and slid out the ticket. This ticket, she thought,

274

holding it up to the light, matched the roll in the box of costumes and photos up in the doctors' attic. Somehow it was terrible to imagine old Dr Strasser's nurse, at the Social Club, maybe all set up in a back room, doing check-ups and seeing which girls needed attention, and buying a raffle ticket while she was at it, not a care in the world. Sandy might call it kindness, the things the old doctor did for the girls, and whatever his son did now that was better, but it wasn't memories of kindness that had made Betty gasp when she caught sight of a bag. Helen would park it in a corner of her office in the morning and get a nice wee canvas cross-over satchel for taking around. She'd never wanted it anyway.

If anything, Mrs Shields' kitchen had gone downhill a bit further since Helen had left on Tuesday, despite all the warnings. They'd been living out the chippie for a day or two; that much was clear, because the papers were crumpled in the cold fire-place, greasy and reeking, and the pots from the last home-cooked meal were growing fur coats in the sink. In the midst of it all, Mrs Shields sat glum and unmoving, watching the wee boy play at chuckies with what looked – when Helen stole a glance – like oxtail bones, but tiny. Tail bones of something, they were.

'How are you feeling?' Helen said. Mrs Shields raised her eyes slowly and gazed back. Was she drunk? Helen sniffed the air for another note in the grease and fish and sour-cloth stink but detected nothing.

'He's no' been back,' Mrs Shields said. 'I've no' heard a word.'

'How long have you been sitting?' Helen asked, not liking the look of the woman's ankles any better than last time. Mrs Shields shrugged. 'Well at least get your feet up, eh? Have you a creepie?' Helen looked around, to see if maybe one of the piles of clothes or newspaper was on top of a footstool that she could use. Then she realised she could use a pile of newspapers just as easy. 'What have you got all this paper for?' she said. 'It's gey dusty.'

Mrs Shields bowed her head and Helen had to bend close to hear what she was saying. 'I bought a wee thing you can make briquettes with. Just old paper and water and you press them in it and then you don't need coal. But it doesnae work. I was gonny make them and sell them round the doors, get a few coppers to myself.'

'They should be strung up,' Helen said. She hadn't heard of the briquette machine, but there was always someone selling something that would make you a nice wee nest egg – a knitting machine or a dyeing kit or a set of transfers that would turn an old sheet into a dress length with the touch of an iron. Greet never fell for it and she'd made sure Helen knew better too. But the junk shop on Semple Street was full of the knitters, and the rag and bone man got sick of picking transfers off the cotton in his bales for a while there.

Helen, thinking the last thing Mrs Shields needed was to watch a visitor hefting around the paper that must be making her feel daft every time she looked at it, twitched an eiderdown off the box bed and laid it on the floor. She was careful not to look too closely at the sheets she'd uncovered. 'Here,' she said. 'Get down and lie flat and get your feet up on the chair. You'll be better for it. Look, I'll put a cushion under your head, see?'

Mrs Shields moved at last, unleashing a blast of rank sweat from inside her dress, and lowered herself to the bare boards.

'Mammy!' said the wee boy. 'Uppa down! Uppa down!' He abandoned his chuckies and came to nuzzle in beside her on the eiderdown. Mrs Shields smiled and twitched the edge of it over him. He plugged his thumb into his mouth and closed his eyes.

'Now,' said Helen. 'I've got an idea I just want to tell you. You can say no.'

'Is it a magic wand?' Mrs Shields said. 'Is it a train ticket hame?'

'I can get you the train ticket,' Helen said. She would pawn those blessed champagne glasses. If she never saw them again it would be too soon. 'What would you want a magic wand for?'

Mrs Shields opened one eye and gave Helen a ghost of her old cheeky look. Then she waved a hand over her belly.

'Then yes, I've got that too,' Helen said. Mrs Shields opened her other eye. 'A couple who're desperate for a wean and cannae have one. They'll take yours.'

'But just the one?' said Mrs Shields, clutching the wee boy close to her.

'Aye, aye just the one. And I'll keep an eye on him. Or her. Me and the doctors.'

'Are they here?'

'Just round the corner,' Helen said.

'And I'll be in Glasgow.' Helen nodded. Off to West Berlin, gone forever. 'I'll be away to Glasgow and I'll never know.'

The sentence had started one way and ended another, Helen reckoned, sliding from hope to regret in a few short words. 'You don't need to make your mind up right now,' she said. 'You have a wee think, and I'll get some of these pots washed, eh?' She stepped over Mrs Shields' legs to get the kettle off the cold fire and lit the gas ring to boil up some water.

She scraped the worst of the scum and scraps into a sheet of newspaper and set it on the floor to fling in the midden when she left. 'Have you soap?' she asked, but when no answer came she turned to see Mrs Shields, eyes closed and mouth open, sleeping soundly. There was an open box of borax on the windowsill that would have to do. She would rinse them thoroughly.

They were done and draining on a cleanish cloth by the time the woman stirred. Helen had looked under the sink and found a full mouse-trap, a trail of ants and a wee nest of weevils living in an old sponge. She was happy to pull the curtain back over and fill the kettle again for tea instead of tackling that.

'How would it work, like?' Mrs Shields said.

'Easy as anything,' Helen said. 'If you're going into the Simpson, I can pick up the bairn from there. Or if you're getting a Queen's nurse fae Castle Terrace, send word to me once she's gone.'

'You thought you were threatening me,' Mrs Shields said. She wasn't quite laughing. 'Warning me you'd have my wean off me. Shows what you know.'

'I ken,' Helen said. 'Sorry.'

'Dinnae be,' said Mrs Shields. 'You've flang me a rope. I was getting sick of the guddle but I thought if I tidied up I'd be stuck, and if I sat in my muck you'd save me.'

Helen said nothing. If that was the story she needed to tell herself, where was the harm.

'I mean it,' said Mrs Shields, as if reading her thoughts. 'I've not been right since it happened. Like I'm inside a cloud, ken how they look when you see them, like wool, like if you were in them you'd be wrapped in like wool off a sheep on a fence. Not like knitted wool. Ken?'

She was struggling hard to say something she didn't have words for.

'It sounds like depression,' Helen said.

'Whit?'

'Melancholy it used to be cried.'

'What have I got to be melancholy about?' said Mrs Shields, as a single fat tear slid down her cheek and into her hair.

'Nothing,' Helen said. She went over and knelt at the woman's side. 'You've a lovely wee boy, and a mammy back in Glasgow. The man that didn't trust you and doesn't deserve you is over here and here he'll stay. That devil that hurt you is long gone and you don't need to look at what he left you. And you're helping a sad pair have a happy ending of their own.'

278

'Are they nice?' Mrs Shields said. She was wriggling out from her son's grip, and rolling over to clamber to her feet again. Helen nodded. 'So will they no' mind what they're gettin' then?'

'They won't know,' Helen said. 'I'll not tell them.'

'They'll soon know if it comes out in him. If he's bad too.'

'Naw,' Helen said. 'That's all over now. Mercy, we've all fought hard enough to be done with that, haven't we?' She hoped Mrs Shields understood because she was far from sure she could explain it. It was just one bit of that one class with the wee foreign man and his funny accent, telling the class there was no such thing as some notion they'd never heard of anyway. But telling them with passion in his voice and reminding them that 'our boys' were fighting it even as he stood there.

'Aye,' said Mrs Shields. 'I suppose so.'

Helen left then, with her paper parcel of rotten food, hoping she had done the right thing. Thinking she had. She scrubbed her hands on a dock leaf growing by the wash house in the back green and then smoothed her hair behind her ears, wondering what she looked like, soaked and dried and scared and sad. All she wanted was home, a bite, a bath and her bed. And for once she was happy it was hers alone, so she could cry there.

Sandy was back. She could see the lamplight before she was in the gate. It still made her happy – or happy on the heels of a flare of alarm, anyway – to see a light shine with no black-out. At least he'd managed to get the key from Greet, she thought. Else he'd never have been able to let himself in again.

'Only me!' she sang out as she entered. There was no answer. 'Sandy?' she said, pushing open the big room door. He was sitting at the table, with his hands spread flat on the oilcloth. His chest rose and fell as if he'd been running and his face was as stark and drawn as she'd ever seen it, even when he woke from nightmares. 'What is it?' she said. 'Is it my daddy? Is it my mammy? Oh God, is Teenie all right? I ken what I say about her but—'

Sandy held up a hand. 'I've no' been to your maw's,' he said. 'That's no' where the key was.' He took a breath and let it go. And then another one. 'I've got to tell you some things, Nell. And I don't know how to begin.'

Chapter 21

'What's it about?' Helen said. 'The girl in the shelter? Or the parties? Or. . . closer to home?'

'Baith,' said Sandy. 'All three.'

'Well, just start,' Helen said. 'So long as you get round it all, it doesn't matter what order.'

She waited, expecting Sandy to speak, but instead he stood and grasped one end of the table, nodding at her to take the other. Together they lifted it and set it beside the back wall. Then Sandy knelt and started rolling the carpet.

'What are you doing?' Helen said.

When it was rolled aside he shuffled over on his knees to the square of ugly board that spoiled the nice polished planks. He was scrabbling at it, cursing. 'Goan stand on the other edge, Nell,' he said. 'It's easier with two.'

Helen, frowning, set her feet one behind the other as if she was walking a tightrope, just at the join between the board and the right floor, and she felt it give. Gasping, she jumped away, but it had been enough to let Sandy get his fingers under and he lifted the board, like a trap-door, letting a billow of foul air rise into the room.

Helen put her nose in the crook of her arm. 'Uff,' she said. 'So it really is mouldy and rotten down there? I thought that was a lie.'

Sandy was staring at her over the edge of the board. 'Come and see,' he said. 'It's not a brothel.'

Helen stepped closer and saw, not quite a staircase but more than a ladder. 'Is it the fever hospital right enough, then?'

'You've seen things, eh no, Nell?' Sandy said. 'You were all right when you saw her in the shelter, and at the morgue, weren't you? Only, I need you to tell me what you think. And tell me what to do. I need your help, Nelly.'

Helen put her hand on his shoulder to steady herself and set one foot on the top rung, testing the strength.

'Oh, it's sturdy enough,' said Sandy. 'We've been up and down it.'

'We?' said Helen. She looked down into the darkness. Were there people down there?

'I'm right behind you,' Sandy said, and Helen waited until she could take his hand. She wasn't scared of the dark but she was scared of whatever *this* was.

Once they were both on solid ground again, standing on what felt like a stone floor, Sandy fumbled in his pocket and struck a match. 'I brought a lamp down,' he said. 'Earlier.'

When it was lit, a strange sight sprang into being, flickering and skirling as the lamp flared and settled. The floor *was* stone, big flags painted white and white walls all around. The room was empty but for a high, narrow bed over by the back wall and a clothes horse Helen thought it was. No, not a clothes horse. And not a bed. It was an operating theatre table and that tall thing was a tank.

'Ether,' she said. 'Chloroform.' She frowned. 'For *fevers*?'

'They've tooken the wee stuff away,' Sandy said. 'Instruments and that. But it must be gey hard to wheel a bed up the street, or a big tank of gas, without the neighbours noticing. Once the black-out was lifted, like.'

Helen was thinking hard, trying to fit this new information into what she'd settled for herself already. 'Right then,' she said. 'All right. Well, it makes sense really. I mean, ether's kind to the girls and a better room, more like an operating theatre, must be safer. One went wrong, when they were doing them in the wee bays across the—' She stopped, as a flash of insight hit her. '*That's* what Betty meant. Downstairs across from the surgery. She meant here. Across the gardens. It was here she was done and it went so badly wrong she cannae fall for a wean even now she wants to.'

Sandy was looking over her shoulder, but he blinked and fastened his eyes on her again now. 'Helen, hen,' he said. 'This is not abortions, this. Come on. You must know that now.'

Helen shook her head.

'Why would anyone be tracking down doctors and black-mailing them over that?' Sandy said. 'They'd be thanking them, wouldn't they? Think, Nelly. You know deep down. I ken you do.'

Helen felt a wave of sickness. Some of it was the smell down here. That was rubbish about the mould and rot, but the air was foul with something. She let out a small moan. 'You're right,' she said. 'Of course you're right.' Why would anyone say the girls had appendicitis, unless to account for a scar? And what kind of operation leaves a girl dying for a baby in her arms and never a chance of getting one? A hysterectomy. 'You're right, Sandy,' she said again. 'Oh, the wickedness of them! All so they could have their fun and never have to worry about a by-blow.' Now there was more than sickness. As the new truth crashed over her, she all but swooned. For their rotten and selfish reasons, the members of the St Andrew's Social Club had stopped old Doc Strasser taking babies out once they were started and moved on to letting young Doc Strasser make sure they never started at all. 'Devils!' she said. 'Monsters!' Then she stopped. 'It can't be true!'

'You know it is,' Sandy said. 'You're looking at it.'

'You don't understand me,' said Helen. 'I'm not wringing my hands. I meant it can't be true. Because it wasn't once each. The three girls I know about had to keep going back. I thought it was more abortions and "tests" was just the excuse. But why would there be tests and check-ups after a hysterectomy?'

'Because a baby's not the only worry,' Sandy said. Helen frowned, not following, and he smiled at her. 'You'd know if you'd been in the army. Syphilis and gonorrhea, Nelly. Even once the girls were barren the gents would still need to make sure they were clean.'

'Clean?' Helen cried out. '*Gents?* It was those smirking pigs in their bow ties that were filthy. Just the *same* as the bloody army. Blame the women, eh?'

'I'm sorry,' Sandy said. He put out a hand and Helen grasped it, feeling his skin as sweaty as her own. It was so close and airless down here. She looked at the stairs leading back to her sweet, lucky life and wondered if she could simply climb them, pull the carpet over and carry on living it.

'There's more,' Sandy said.

Of course there was, because he'd said he didn't know where to start. There had to be more. Gently, Sandy put a hand under her elbow and led her out into the passageway, through to the other room. 'Be strong,' he said, and lifted the lantern.

Helen didn't know what she was looking at, except to say it was some kind of box or tank, made of concrete with a lid of dull metal. It sat in the middle of the floor like a. . . Helen groped for the memory it was stirring in her. It wasn't like a cow lying down in a field, for it was bigger. And it wasn't like one of those standing stones you find out on the hills for no reason, for it was longer than it was tall and it was squatter, bulkier, than any boulder she'd ever seen. Why was she thinking about days out, though? About treats and picnics? Then it came to her. The way this tank sat proud in the middle of an empty floor made her think of rainy days inside the Chamber Street Museum, because what it looked like was a. . .

'Sarcophagus,' she whispered.

'Nay,' said Sandy. 'It's a bomb-proof store for medical supplies, is what it is. But you've hit the nail on the head about what it's been turned to. That you have, Nell.'

'Have you opened it?' she said. 'Have you seen?'

284

Sandy was nodding. 'And I'm not opening it again. Her own mother wouldn't recognise her now. There's no point putting the sight in your mind.'

'Her, though?' Helen said. 'Definitely "her"?'

Sandy was pointing at the sharp edge of the box, where the lead cover was bent over and sheared off. Helen stepped forward. There was a hair caught on the ragged metal. It was long and dark and, as Sandy held the lantern even closer, Helen could see that it was still shiny.

'As black as coal,' Helen said. 'To go with her skin as white as snow.'

'You know who she is?' Sandy said. 'Was.'

'Aye,' Helen said. 'Wee soul. Wee darlin'. I know who she was. Oh Sandy, what a crying shame.'

'Who?' Sandy said and his voice was unsteady. 'How do you know about a thing like this?'

'I cannae mind of her first name,' said Helen, 'but she was a Mrs Yarrow. Oh the silly wee fool. She telt her husband. Telt him what was wrong. And he killed her. Two years since. That's when the parties stopped. At least that's when the photo albums stopped anyway. He must have gone to them – the members – and threatened to let it all out.'

'Did he kill the girl in the shelter too?'

'Could have,' Helen said. 'She was going round asking questions. I know that much. She went to the McIrnies' and questioned Betty. Betty as good as said so to me. So who knows who else she stirred up. Who else she angered.' Briefly, Helen laid her hand on the lead cover of the box, then she stepped away. 'I hope it *was* Mr Yarrow killed the other one,' she said. 'The girl in the huttie. The Sinclair cousin, she must be.'

'Why?' said Sandy.

'But I don't see how he could have.'

'How no'?'

'Because it wasn't just a rope, and how would a newsagent get chloroform?'

'He couldn't,' Sandy said. 'It would have to be someone...'

'Medical,' Helen finished for him, when it seemed he would never say it on his own, and for a moment they stared at each other.

'But then why would they gie us this place?' said Sandy at last. 'Gie the upstairs of it anyway. Because I never did understand that, not properly. And with this sitting down here, it's even stranger.'

'Not them,' she said. 'Him. Either to make it look like there was nothing amiss – just a wee house for a young couple. Or to make it look like we knew what was what. Like it was all me and none of it would stick to him. Like the bag too. Miss Anderson's bloomin' nurse's bag that she took round when she was checking the girls. He pretended he knew nothing about that bag, you know. All to make it look as if I knew about his dirty work.'

'Strasser?'

Helen nodded.

'And Doc Deuchar kens nothin'?'

'No,' Helen said. 'Not quite. He kens there's a cloud over the Yarrows and he wisnae happy to see that girl in the surgery on Monday.'

'But he. . . whit? He trusts his partner? Or is he getting fooled, same as us?'

'Hangin' by a thread, I think,' Helen said. 'Suspects and hopes he's wrong. I need to speak to him. He *cannae* know Mrs Yarrow's deid in here. He *cannae*. I'll tell him and then we'll go to the polis the pair of us. I've got nothing to hide. Nothing beyond getting in the back door of the mortuary with a tray of pies. We're going to lose our hoose, Sandy, but *we've* nothing to hide either. We're lucky. Let's get out of here, eh? Back upstairs.'

'You're sure?' Sandy said. 'Sure you can stand up to Strasser and to Mrs Sinclair too?'

'Mrs Sinclair?' said Helen.

'Of course! If the girl in the shelter's a Sinclair cousin or something, that found out what went on here, she'd have telt her auntie first, eh no?'

Helen squeezed her eyes shut, as if understanding could be forced that way, but she had to give up and breathe out before any of the Sinclair angle made any sense at all.

'I'm going over to talk to Doc Deuchar,' she said. 'Him and me together will sort this out. He was there Monday night, and then at the morgue and up at Mrs Sinclair's too. He'll be more able than me to get it straight. And, like I said, I've nothing to hide. Nothing to fear except working in the bottlin' hall and livin' back at my mammy's.'

Helen took a step towards the staircase, but Sandy didn't move.

'Do you want to come with me?' she said. 'You can if it'll make you happy.'

'It's not that,' said Sandy. 'It's just there's something else I need to tell you. One more thing.'

'Can you tell me upstairs?' Helen said. 'I need a sit down and a cuppy tea. I need out of here.'

Sandy nodded, then looked over her shoulder. Helen whirled round, hearing a sound behind her, and let out a scream at the sight. A bone-white, rake-thin man, with the light of Sandy's lantern shining on his high bald head, was standing in the doorway. He took a lurching step into the room, and Helen shrank back.

'Don't be frightened,' he said. He was English and sounded tired; more than tired – worn through.

'Y– You're the man that banged on the door and hid in the shelter,' Helen said. She was pressed against Sandy's side now, wishing he would put an arm round her.

'This is Gavin Gregson, Nelly,' Sandy said. 'We were in the same hut, over there. He's been campin' in our Anderson shelter a couple of nights.'

287

Helen breathed out and took a step away from Sandy, ashamed of huddling against him, cringing like a wean. Especially when he'd made her look stupid by keeping his hands at his sides.

'Well, why didn't you let him in the house?' she said. 'I'm sorry, Mr Gregson. You didn't need to be kipping out in the shelter and creepi' round. We've loads of space. You can stay as long as you like. If you're visiting. Or maybe we could even have a lodger. Could we not, Sandy?'

Gavin Gregson was staring at Sandy over Helen's head. She turned to look at her husband and then faced front again. 'What am I missing?' she said. 'Are youse not pals? Have you come here to make trouble, Mr Gregson? Have you got a grudge and you've come to settle it?'

'We're not "pals", no,' the man said. 'But I haven't come to make trouble. Exactly. I didn't have a grudge when I set out. And I hope we can settle everything.'

Helen shook her head and shrugged. 'I'm not with you.'

'Nell,' said Sandy. 'I want you to tell Gavin. . . Tell him about us.'

Helen looked over her shoulder again. 'What about us?' she said.

'Tell him about our marriage,' Sandy said. 'The truth, mind.'

'Why?' said Helen.

'Please!' Sandy said and there was real pain in his voice.

'I don't know what this is,' said Helen. 'But however it's come to be *your* business, Mr Gregson, we're *not* married, except in name. We had a wedding and we share a house. That's it. I don't know why, so don't ask me. And I don't want to talk about it any more because I'm mortified.'

'I can tell you why,' Sandy said. He took a deep breath. 'I promised Gavin I'd be faithful till he was free and came to find me.'

288

Chapter 22

It was late. Clouds had come with the dark and there were no streetlamps on the wee lane that led along to the back of Rosebank. Even through her shock, Helen could see now what a perfect spot it was for what had been done here. She kept her eyes trained on the lamplight glowing from the crescent and thought about what she was going to say.

If she ever got a chance to say it. Because how could she get to Dr Deuchar without seeing Dr Strasser too? Maybe she could think up an excuse if the wrong one came to open the door. She pressed on anyway, plan or no plan. What else could she do?

As it happened, she got lucky. She rounded the bottom of the gardens and met Dr Deuchar coming up the other way.

'Caught me!' he said. 'Perfectly good whisky and soda in the house, but I can't resist the 80 shilling at the Haymarket. Where are you off to, Nell? A port and lemon at the. . . Are you all right?'

'Not really,' Helen said. 'I was coming to see you, Doc. If it's not too late.'

'Never,' Dr Deuchar said, climbing the stairs to the front door with a solicitous arm behind her. Helen remembered wondering why Sandy wouldn't do the same when that Gavin Gregson had scared her. She felt fresh tears threaten, although she'd been sure ten minutes before that she'd cried herself dry and would never shed another tear again.

'Is Doc Strasser in?' she said.

'No,' said Dr Deuchar. 'I can ring him up if you need both of us, though. I know where he is.'

'No!' Helen said. 'I'm glad it's just you. I need to talk to you.'

He took her to the drawing room and poured her a measure of something she thought might be brandy. It was horrible but she felt it doing good after just one mouthful. So she took another.

'Now then, Nelly,' he said.

'Can I just say it all?' said Helen. 'And you listen?' Dr Deuchar waved his brandy glass in agreement. 'I know it won't come as a shock. I know you suspect something. Right,' she said. 'Old Dr Strasser did abortions.'

Dr Deuchar had just taken a drink and spluttered lavishly as his gasp got in the way of him swallowing. 'Sorry,' he said. 'Carry on.'

'He did them in the three bays across the area. Downstairs. But our Dr Strasser thought of something better than abortions as and when, and maybe sometimes the girl wouldn't agree and then there would be all kinds of trouble. So what he did, instead, was diagnose appendicitis where there was none and take everything out. Hysterectomies. He even told me. He said he had better ways of dealing with things than his father in the old days. I'm not saying everyone. I'm not saying that.' She had seen the doc's face fall and pale. 'But there were parties, see? There's a club, down in the New Town where they have – or had – these parties. All the high heid yins went along. Really high-up people like Mr Grossart and even Mr Pyne. Mr Sinclair used to go when he was alive.' Dr Deuchar took another drink and Helen heard the glass clink against his teeth as if maybe his hand was shaking.

'So you, see, Doc, that was what our wee house and the downstairs house at Rosebank were for. It was never a fever hospital. *That's* what they did there. And the worst of it is the girls didn't know. Mrs McIrnie – mind her you brought to see me on Monday – her daughter's been done and now she's wanting a baby and she doesn't understand why she can't fall. And there's another one I know of. Leastways, my sister's chums with her cousin. She's definitely one of them, though. "Had her appendix out" and pinched a glass from one of the parties. They don't know they're barren now, just like they didn't know that their "check-ups" were looking for every nasty disease they might have caught off those so-called gentlemen. And then there's Mrs Yarrow – not the one married to him now. You suspected Yarrow was no good, didn't you?' Helen took a breath. 'Well, you're right. He's no good at all. The first Mrs Yarrow was done too, you see. And she told her husband. Maybe she took pity on him hoping for good news, month after month, and came clean. Or maybe he beat it out of her. I wouldn't put it past him. And he killed her, Doc. To get rid of her and start again with another wife. He killed her. But there! He had no better luck next time and they've gone and adopted a wee boy now. I worry for them both. Mrs Yarrow and the baby. *He's* not right in his head. From pride or shame or remorse, or fear that he'll be caught, I couldn't tell you. But he's stewing for something bad.'

You're telling me,' Dr Deuchar said, 'that Yarrow the newsagent murdered his wife? Are you sure? Maybe she left him.'

'He murdered her, or someone else did,' Helen said. 'And then out it all came. That's when the parties stopped. Mrs McIrnie's daughter got married. Bessie McNulty's cousin stopped having to go for checks. And there were no more photo albums. 1946 is the last one.'

'But do you have any proof that she died? Perhaps the poor woman left the brute.'

'Her body's in a lead box in the downstairs at our bit,' Helen said. 'I think it's been there the whole time.'

'Good God! But—'

'Doc, you said you'd listen. Because then there was Monday. That dead girl's a Sinclair. I *knew* she was. She was like a triplet with Fiona and Carolyn, but she must be a cousin or something, I think now. And I don't know if she was a party girl or if she just found out about it, but she was making trouble, going the rounds trying to get other party girls to talk to her, and now she's dead too. And her family won't own her and even Mr Pyne's been lying about who she is. And I wondered if it was Mr Yarrow killed her, except for the chloroform. Because where would he get it? So, this is what I'm saying, Doc. I think it was Dr Strasser. I think he killed the Sinclair girl to keep it all from coming out.'

'And hid her in the Anderson shelter in your garden?' Dr Deuchar said faintly.

'He must have had a plan to get rid of her,' Helen said, 'and maybe get rid of Mrs Yarrow too, even after all this time.'

'It's not so easy as all that to "get rid of" dead bodies, Helen,' said Dr Deuchar. 'Not these days.'

Helen shuddered. 'Don't,' she said. 'All those old dark stories have been haunting me. But even if it's hard to make a body disappear, what choice did he have? That story about the rot and mould downstairs wouldn't last for ever.'

'Rot and. . .'

'Yes, he... Helen said, frowning. 'I think he told me that.' She tried to remember hearing about it. The downstairs flat empty because of mould and bad timber. She had been standing in the empty house and she was talking to. . . 'Mrs Sinclair! I *knew* she was part of it.'

'Mrs *Sinclair*?'

'Maybe she didn't know all along. Maybe not as bad as all that. Maybe the cousin told her first and tried to get her to help. But Mrs Sinclair couldn't bring herself to say all that about Grossart and Pyne and even a bishop. And her husband, although he's dead. Shame doesn't die, does it?'

'Or maybe,' said Dr Deuchar sadly, 'she couldn't *bear* to know. She suspected, but couldn't face it. You'd be surprised, Helen, at the human capacity to lie to oneself.'

Helen gave a hollow laugh. 'Oh, would I? I've learned more about what you can *not* see even when it's under your nose. . .' But she had to turn away from that, before tears overtook her.

'Why do you think Strasser let you move in?' Dr Deuchar ran his hand over his mouth and looked at his empty glass as if he wished there was another good glug left there.

'Maybe it was to have a. . . what do you call it?. . . a stooge?'

'A scape-goat?'

'Aye, that's it. And the job too. No one would believe I didn't know what was going on, see? All the war years I worked with Mrs Sinclair. She could say whatever she liked about me, and who'd believe me over her? Who'd believe I got this job fair and square? Not even my own family. You wouldn't credit the things *they've* said to me. And who'd believe we lived in a house with a dead body downstairs and didn't know that either? Or that we'd *taken* a free house and all that lovely furniture except because I had the doc over a barrel with what I could tell about him.'

Dr Deuchar slumped in his chair and let his head fall back.

'Can I get you some more, Doc?' Helen said. He held his glass out. 'You know,' she went on as she poured, 'the only thing I don't really understand is how a Sinclair relation first got mixed up in it. The other party girls are right ordinary. Girls like me. But if it's not that, how did she end up trying to get Betty McIrnie to speak up? Going looking for Mrs Yarrow. How?'

'You said it yourself, Nelly,' said Dr Deuchar. 'Mr Sinclair was in the club.'

Helen shrugged. 'And. . . he told her about it? Why would a man tell a niece or a cousin the likes of that?'

'Oh come along, Helen,' Dr Deuchar said. 'You're a good girl but not a stupid one. It's not nieces and pretty young cousins that a family keeps quiet, now, is it?'

293

Helen gasped. 'She—That poor soul in our Anderson shelter was Mr Sinclair's *child*?'

'Clever girl,' said Dr Deuchar. 'Yes, that poor girl in the mortuary is not a cousin. She's a sister. She's Mr Sinclair's daughter. She's the reason the St Andrew's Social Club came up with a better plan.'

'Oh my heavens,' said Helen. 'Her mother was a party girl away way back and she wouldn't get seen to when she fell?'

Dr Deuchar nodded. 'There had been a couple of. . .'

'. . . girls died,' Helen said. 'And Duncan Pyne took them to the morgue. I'd heard as much. Or nearly.' She sighed. 'And so that's what got her killed? She knew who she was and she wouldn't keep quiet about it?'

Dr Deuchar nodded.

'Doc, on Monday night, did *you* know who she was?'

He shook his head. 'I thought, like you, that it was Fiona. It was when you said to Mrs Sinclair that perhaps it was "her sister" and that made her faint. I did wonder then. And then the "Maggie Dickson" story confirmed it. But I kept quiet. Powerful men, Helen. They could ruin me and my courage failed.'

'How could any of them ruin *you*?' Helen said.

'Helen,' said Dr Deuchar. 'You of all people should understand that. I wasn't supposed to be a doctor. Perhaps a schoolmaster if I was lucky. A clerk, more likely. Until I got a scholarship to the school where old Dr Strasser sent his boy. We were two outsiders together and became fast friends. If it weren't for the Strassers, I don't know where I'd be.' He had dropped forward to rest his elbows on his knees and he looked up at her beseechingly. 'I mean, that's why you're round here telling all this to me instead of down at Torphichen Street telling the bobbies, isn't it? Because you know your word alone isn't enough. Well, neither is mine. Not in this city.'

Helen hesitated, but she couldn't lie. 'I suppose so,' she said.

'Have you told anyone else?' he said. 'Or am I the first?'

'No one,' she said. 'Not a soul.' Dr Deuchar sat up and put his glass down on the side table. 'Well, Sandy,' she added. 'But that doesn't count, because we're married.'

For a long moment Dr Deuchar said nothing. 'Except we're not real—' Helen began, then bit her lip as the door downstairs opened and shut. They both heard the bolt shooting home and then Dr Strasser's feet climbing the stairs.

'Night, Deuchar,' he called as he passed the drawing room and kept going to the bedroom floor.

'What will we do?' Helen said.

'Leave it to me,' Dr Deuchar said. 'Stay here and keep quiet, Nelly.'

He slipped out onto the landing and Helen only heard his feet on the stairs because she was listening. When all was still again, she sat back and closed her eyes. There, behind her eyelids, where she guessed it would be for the rest of her life, was the one image from this terrible night that had felled her. Not Mrs Yarrow's single black hair; not the hole in her floor with the steps leading down; not the doctor's pale face as she wrecked his practice for him with all her news. What she saw when she closed her eyes was Sandy taking hold of Gavin Gregson's hand and squeezing it tight. And Gavin Gregson smiling, with tears shining in his eyes.

'Why did you marry me?' she had screamed at Sandy. Howled at him.

'So nobody would ask why I didn't,' Sandy said. 'I didn't think you were bothered, the way you fought me off before.'

'I was being good,' said Helen. 'Being careful. Don't you dare make out you didn't know that's all it was. Don't you dare blame me!'

'No one's going to blame you,' Sandy said.

'No one? Like who?' said Helen, a new horror leaping in her. 'Who knows, besides you and me and. . . *him*?'

'Don't be like that, Nelly,' Sandy said. 'George knows. And the doc knew.'

'Old Dr Strasser?' Helen said. 'How could you? He'll have told his son. This is it. This is what they reckon they've got over us to keep us quiet. Well, they can think again. They might have it over you but it's none of my doing!'

She could still hear the sound of the door slamming as she went tearing out and down the steps to sit on the damp grass in her garden – her wee garden she was so excited about! – and cry herself sore.

She shivered again now. It was a warm enough night, but she was tired and hungry and she felt as if she'd been sitting here in the drawing room for an hour. She cocked her head and listened: to the silence of the old house, the tick of a clock, an owl in the trees outside the window. What if Dr Deuchar had come to harm? What if they had fought and Dr Strasser, right now, was packing a bag to run away? Where would he go? Did he have a club he could go to? Or would he go to a hotel? Or catch a train? Or a boat? How far would he—?

Club, Helen thought. Now why had her mind snagged on that? Anyway, what did it matter where he went? The main thing was that he should leave without knowing she was in here. But what if he came into this room to fetch something? On her tiptoes, she crept to the door and eased it open. The streetlamp shining in downstairs gave just enough dim light to see that there was no one on the landing. Helen stole across to the head of the stairs and stopped there. It was truly silent upstairs. They weren't arguing. What were they doing?

As she stood there, a door opened and footsteps crossed the landing above. 'Doc?' she called softly. The footsteps halted, then a head appeared over the banisters, staring down at her.

'Helen?' Dr Strasser said. Helen fled. She took the turn in the stairs, feeling as if she was flying through the air, but she knew Dr Strasser was gaining on her. 'Helen, what's wrong?' he called as he galloped down behind her. 'What are you doing here? What's happened?'

She was fumbling with the bolt on the big front door when he finally caught up.

'Nell?' he said, taking hold of her arms. 'What's the matter? You look. . .You look terrified. What on earth's going on?'

'Where's Doc Deuchar?' she said.

'In bed,' he said. At least he had let go of her arms and stepped back. 'I heard him come up and go into his room half an hour ago. Why? Can't *I* help you?'

'I – I don't understand,' Helen said. 'Why would he just go to bed and not come to talk to you? He said he was going to talk to you.'

'About what?'

But when Helen spoke again she wasn't really answering. 'He said "St Andrew's Club",' she murmured to herself. 'How did he know it was that one? I never told him.'

'Well, whatever this is about, it's easily fixed,' Dr Strasser said. He crossed the hall and bounded up the stairs. Helen could have worked the bolt free and gone out into the night, but she found herself following him. He was at Dr Deuchar's bedroom door when she got to the top of the stairs.

'You awake, old man?' he said, knocking gently and then a bit more firmly. 'Deuchar? Are you there?'

'Maybe he left,' Helen said. But deep inside she already knew.

Dr Strasser turned the knob and pushed the door open. Helen heard him cry out and got just a glimpse of Dr Deuchar's feet a yard off the floor swinging a little as the rope creaked.

'He sat and listened,' Helen said. 'He just sat there and listened to me laying it all out. He asked me if I'd told anyone. He was going to—. But I had told Sandy. So he came upstairs and. . .' She sank to the floor and let her head drop to her knees. Dr Strasser would have to cut him down, or ring the police, or do whatever he was going to do, without her.

Postscript

'Where have you been?' Dr Strasser said to Helen, as she came in the front door of the surgery. 'You're. . . what's that wonderful word?'

'Ploatin',' Helen said. 'I am.' Dr Strasser – she kept asking Helen to call her Dr Sarah; she said it was less confusing – was 'trying to learn Scottish'. Helen was trying not to laugh at her. 'I've been to see Mrs Yarrow. She's so brave. The muck she gets flang over that shop counter every day and she just stands there and takes it.' Helen headed downstairs to her office to put her bag away.

'It's only going to get worse during the trial and up until they hang him,' the doc said, following. 'Perhaps after that it'll die down.'

She didn't believe in hanging, Dr Sarah. She didn't believe in a lot of things.

'I went to see Betty too,' Helen said. 'They go together in my head. Doc, that is the fattest baby I've ever seen in my life. He's like a bunch of balloons.'

'I'll have a word when she brings him to the clinic,' Dr Sarah said. 'But all well, otherwise?'

'Aye, fine,' Helen said. 'And there's new folk in Mrs Shields' house. Poor things. They'll need all the Lysol in the Store warehouse to get it clean.'

'I wish I'd seen it,' said Dr Sarah. 'I have a horrid fascination for filth, so long as I don't have to deal with it.'

'You're a one, Doc,' Helen said.

'That makes two of us,' Dr Sarah said. 'Ah!' she added, cocking her head. 'Here's Sam. Let's have some coffee. Out in the garden since it's such a lovely day.' Dr Sarah believed in fresh air and flowers. She took flowers on her rounds and left posies at bedsides.

'Tea,' Helen said. 'I'll get it.' She couldn't thole the way the two Dr Strassers greeted each other when one had been out on rounds. Too much kissing and cooing, and she got enough of that at home.

Except that wasn't fair. Gavin lived downstairs and she lived upstairs and Sandy. . . well, Sandy was upstairs when Greet and Mack came round and was always there to help with heavy jobs. And he'd never held Gavin's hand again in front of her. But she heard the low voices and soft laughter sometimes and she always put the wireless on to drown it out.

'I know it can't go on like this forever,' she had said to Dr Sarah, the first time the two women had a proper talk. It was Christmastime and they were tucked up by the fireside, drinking cocoa.

'Why not?' the doctor had asked.

'The things you say!' Helen had burst out.

'Is it because you want a baby? Because I daresay you could get one. Oh, don't look at me like that!'

Helen wasn't as easily shocked as she used to be, but Dr Sarah usually found a way. 'I think,' she said, after taking a bit of time, 'I think I'd rather care for the weans that are here already than make more.'

'Quite right,' said Dr Sarah. 'Me too! What a team we make, Helen. But. . . forgive me . . . don't you want a husband as a. . .?'

'Partner in all of life's travails,' said Helen. Dr Sarah looked startled but nodded. Again Helen took some time to think. 'I'd rather have pals,' she said in the end. She paused for a while before continuing. 'I think. . .'

'What?'

299

'It's hard to put words to it, but I think it was my pride that took the worst of the blow, not my heart. I did love Sandy, when we were both at the school and walking out together. But all those years he was away didn't only change *him*. Do you see? When he came back, I know I fell back in with it all, the way it was, the way it was supposed to be. . . but once I'd got over the shock – of Gavin – and stopped being angry, stopped feeling foolish for being tricked, once my pride had mended. I think I was. . .'

'Relieved?'

'It sounds awful to say it. But yes.' Then she laughed. 'Maybe it *can* go on like this forever. Gavin's happy. Sandy's better all the time. And I've just got so much work to do.'

Dr Sarah beamed. 'There have been many such arrangements. Not all in Bloomsbury. And the cottage is so very quietly situated. It's ideal for this, as it was rather too horribly ideal before.' She shot Helen a worried look.

'I keep telling you, Doc,' Helen said. 'None of us mind. When you've lived in a room and kitchen with your family. . . Or a hut in a stalag with thirty other men.' It wasn't that she never thought of Mrs Yarrow or the Sinclair girl, but she loved her wee house no less for the memory of getting them justice.

Helen smiled as she took the tea-tray out into the garden. It was even better now, with another six months gone by, and the long days filling the upstairs rooms with light. What a way she had come since that Sunday last summer when she served tea to Greet and Mrs Sinclair.

Dr Strasser had his arm along the back of Dr Sarah's deckchair and both of them had kicked off their shoes to wriggle their toes in the unkempt grass. 'Well, Nelly?' he called out, when he caught sight of her. 'Did you reel them in for us?' Then he bit his tongue. She bit her tongue quite often too, whenever she heard herself quoting Dr Deuchar.

'I set my line,' Helen told him. 'They were thon suspicious way, still talking about charity and standing on their own two feet. Not looking for hand-outs. It vexes me, Doc. It's been nearly a year and they're that stubborn, some of them.'

Dr Strasser tutted. 'Making more work in the end.' He gave Helen an innocent look, eyes wide and brows raised. 'Did you apply the magic formula?'

'I know you're laughing at me, Doc,' Helen said, 'but it really does work.' She paused. 'And yes I did.' She was proud of it now she had finally plucked up the courage to say it out loud. *Help Yourself To Health.* It wasn't *Dig For Victory*, but she had seen too many people square their shoulders and lift their chins to doubt that it was something.

She had even shared the words with her fellow almoners the night they all met in the snug at Deacon Brodie's to compare notes and pool wisdom. Deacon Brodie's wasn't Helen's choice, but it was central and right handy for whatever buses and trams the other women were coming in on.

'I'm not too proud to admit I'm wrong,' said one of the Leithers, when they were all settled with their drinks and they'd seen off a couple of working men who'd looked like pestering them.

'About the welfare?' Helen asked.

'About the service,' said the Leither. 'The whole thing. I thought it would unravel like a ball of wool. Or maybe blow up like bad ginger. It was the size of it. The number of. . .'

'Hydra heads?' said the Southsider.

'Well, cogs, I was meaning.'

The Southsider had been a lady almoner in the old days, but she had no side; sitting there with a half of shandy quite the thing and not minding that the rest of them were tittering at her. Hydra heads, Helen thought, and laughed again.

'We're war-trained,' said the other Leither. 'That's what it is. Efter we got all that up and running in '39, this was easy.'

'But we can't relax,' Helen said. 'There's plenty watching to see it fail. As if it's hurting them to be helping others!'

'It'll not fail,' said the lady almoner. 'It's a snowball rolling down a roof now. Of course we won't see the proof in rows of figures, black and white, for a year or two, but we know already, don't we, ladies?'

'That we do,' said both Leithers in unison.

'So,' said the lady almoner. 'To business.' She snapped the cover back on her notepad, with a twang that clearly satisfied her greatly. 'Round the table.'

'Lollipops,' said a quiet woman from the Holyrood ward. 'They're my new secret weapon. Give the bairns a lolly each the first time you get a foot over the door and you'll be sure of a welcome anytime.'

'I give out wee chamoises when I send folk for an eye-test,' said one of the Leithers. 'They're that soft and they smell that good, the patients are champing to get their specs, just so's they can polish them.'

'Did you know you can fit a hand-towel in a thermos if you roll it up tight?' said the almoner from Abbeyhill. 'Wring it out in hot water and keep it in case you're somewhere clarty and they've not got a slip of soap to their name.'

'There's a new convalescent home opening at the foot of the Pentlands,' the lady almoner said. 'They'll take anyone for a week on our say-so. Johnston Terrace has the forms. Five pages, I'm afraid. But worth it.'

Helen sat listening, wondering if there were gaggles of women gathered around tables all over the country talking about spectacles and thermoses, nursing homes and lollipops, and a hundred other things big and small that were going to play their part just as much as the surgeon's knife and the chemist's mixture.

When it was her turn she shared her slogan, trying not to blush as every single one of the others jotted it down.

'You're miles away, Nelly,' Dr Strasser said, making her blink. 'Your tea's getting cold. Everything all right?'

'Fine,' Helen said, taking a hasty sip that turned into a gulp when she realised he was right. She must have been day-dreaming for a good while. 'Fine,' she said again. She meant it. Life was better than she could have dared to hope a year ago. And the reason was a startling one.

She had told Dr Sarah she'd rather have her pals, but it was one pal really. She had started going to the pictures every week, and then the odd lunchtime concert, with Carolyn Sinclair, who needed a friend as badly as did Helen. A friend who wouldn't whisper and mock and judge on account of her mother and sister. They were barricaded into that mausoleum of a house in Merchiston, supposedly without a stain upon their characters – for Duncan Pyne was a chivalrous man – but shunned by all their old acquaintance and a delicious scandal for the rest of the city.

'No more than they deserve,' Carolyn had said the first time she spoke to Helen about it. 'I knew about Daddy's by-blow and I knew that it had happened at that awful club he was a member of. Those poor girls dressed up like Wild West floozies. But not the rest of it, Helen. Not the operations. Not murder!'

'But *she* knew?' Helen said. 'Your mother.'

'She knew about Mrs Yarrow being murdered,' Carolyn said. 'She didn't know about Frances until you found her.'

'Frances,' Helen said. Not Maggie Dickson. Not Jane Bloggs. Frances Sinclair. At least there was something to put on her headstone, once the earth had settled over her grave.

'The mother had kept it quiet her whole life, for a stipend,' Carolyn said. 'A stipend which *my* mother kept on paying after Daddy died. But the thing is, Daddy's mistress, I suppose we should call her, left a letter to be read after her death. And then Frances came to the house to have it out with us. As soon as we saw her, of course, there was no denying who she was.'

'No,' said Helen. 'I thought it was you – one or the other of you – the minute I laid eyes on her.'

'Mummy and Fiona thought they'd shut her down, seen her off. But I think Mummy let something slip. God knows

303

what. And it only served to set the girl off on a quest, you see. To uncover what the hell was going on at the St Andrew's Society. She found three of the new girls, the girls who would never get pregnant and cause trouble—'

'Bessie McNulty's cousin, Betty McIrnie, and that one who came looking?' Helen said.

Carolyn nodded. 'Frances began to put it together and deduced the truth about the operations. Then she made the mistake of confronting Deuchar. And he killed her.'

'And stripped her clothes off to hide who she was and hid her body in the Anderson shelter...'

'Presumably overnight until he could stash it in beside Mrs Yarrow.'

'Only Dr Strasser gave me the keys to the house that very day and the whole thing started to go wrong.'

'You can almost feel sorry for Deuchar about that particular little irony,' Carolyn said.

Helen twisted her face up, unable to agree. 'Although,' she conceded, 'the funny thing is, he was a good doctor. We're struggling without him.'

They didn't struggle for long. Dr Strasser was married in the spring and there were two doctors at the Gardner's Crescent surgery once more.

Helen smiled at them both, sitting in their deckchairs in the dappled sunshine, not quite holding hands but with the backs of their fingers touching. Her tea was clap cold now.

'Don't look so worried, Doc,' she said. 'I really am fine. Honestly.'

'And, uhhh, Sarah tells me things are settled down all right at home?' Dr Strasser asked, in a strangulated sort of voice that made Dr Sarah bite her lips.

'That's one thing I've always meant to ask you,' Helen said. 'About home. Why did you suddenly give me the house that first Monday of the new service? I mean, out of the blue like that?'

'Thank God I did,' said Dr Strasser. 'Or you might be living above two corpses even now.'

Helen shuddered. 'Oh no,' Dr Sarah said. 'I wouldn't have let that dreadful Mrs Sinclair say "mould and rot" and leave it at that. I'd have found the women.'

'Well, Gavin would have found them anyway,' Helen said. 'He found Mrs Yarrow quick enough. But can you tell me, Doc? Why you gave me a house and an atticful of furniture all of a sudden?'

He gave his bride an arch look and said, 'Shall I tell or would you rather?'

'Oh, that's right. Blame me,' said Dr Sarah. 'He had proposed once before, you see, Helen. And I asked for time to think it over. Then he proposed again, that Sunday before the service started up. "Come north, my love, and tend the sick of Fountainbridge." I don't like being pestered when I've asked for time. And so I refused. And so *he*…What's that wonderful expression for throwing a monstrous huff like a toddler?'

'Went and ate worms?' Helen said. 'Flang his toys out his pram?'

'Such an expressive dialect,' Dr Sarah said. 'Yes, exactly.'

'I've owned the building as long as I've owned the surgery,' Dr Strasser said. 'I inherited it from my father and I didn't ask too much about what went on there, more's the pity. But when I set my cap at Sarah I fitted the upstairs flat out for Dr Deuchar, planning to move my bride in here, of course. When she turned me down, and there was no need for Deuchar to move out, I suppose I did…'

'Flang your toys out your pram,' said Dr Sarah.

'Fling,' said Helen. 'Flang is the past tense.' She blushed a bit. They were so easy with her now she sometimes forgot they were her bosses, but she really shouldn't be going around correcting their grammar. 'Thanks for clearing that up, Doc,' she said. 'It was niggling at me.'

'But otherwise,' said Dr Strasser, 'things at home are fine?'

'Absolutely,' Helen said. She hadn't pegged Doc Strasser for one of those people who would take to married life so completely they stopped believing anything else was possible. 'Or leastways,' she said, thinking to convince him by shading her answer, 'they *would* be fine if my mother didn't ask me every Friday night if she needs to start knitting.'

'Refer her to me,' said Dr Sarah. 'I'll shock her into silence.'

Helen could well believe it. This was the better idea Dr Strasser had had. So much better than girls waiting till they were in trouble then traipsing round the back streets. Dutch caps, French letters, Irish intervals. 'It's like a Grand Tour,' Dr Sarah said laughing. She laughed a lot and she made Dr Strasser laugh a wee bit now, from time to time.

He hadn't been laughing when he first spoke to Helen a week or two after Dr Deuchar died. 'I would never have operated on someone without her consent,' he had said. 'I of all people.'

'See now, Doc. I didn't know that,' Helen had said. 'I don't think anyone in Fountainbridge ever guessed you're...'

'Jewish,' he said. 'It's not a rude word, Nelly.'

'Old Dr Strasser never said,' she pointed out.

'He probably thought it was obvious.'

'How?' said Helen. 'It's not like you wear yon wee hats or ocht.'

'Only in Edinburgh!' said Dr Strasser, shaking his head. 'I should really warn my Sarah what she's getting into. But I don't want to put her off from coming.'

'She'll be glad to get out of that Manchester,' said Helen.

'When were *you* ever in Manchester?' said Dr Strasser. 'That's what I thought. *Typical* Edinburgh.' He did laugh then.

Dr Sarah had settled so well into what she called the frozen north that she didn't have a cardigan around her shoulders to sit in the garden today. And her legs were bare above her strange brown sandals. Not that she tried to 'fit in' exactly; she meant what she said about shocking Greet and not caring one whit that she had done so. She wouldn't be happy, Helen reckoned, till every woman in Fountainbridge had a wee box on her bedside table and every man had a wee box in his jacket pocket. She was mortifying to talk to about it and she managed to turn more conversations in that direction than Helen could believe.

'I'll put the Simpson out of business before I'm done,' Dr Sarah was sometimes heard to say. 'And we'll have a city full of girls and women doing exactly what they jolly well please.'

'Some of them "jolly well" want a bairn in their arms,' Helen said. She was just as fierce for the mothers needing help as for the girls needing not to be mothers. Just as fierce for the grubby or angry or grasping as she was for the neat or the calm or the grateful. They were all trying to get by and they needed wee Nelly Downie fae Freer Street to balance 'that English lady doctor with nae stockings on and never a hat', as Mrs Suttie described her. 'Ten minutes in the door and saying things that would make a sailor faint,' said Mrs Bonny, fanning herself. 'Likes to call a spade a bloody shovel,' Mack said.

Helen couldn't argue. But she couldn't deny that their patient list was growing. She could have used all three of the basement bays for her own waiting line. Not that she could get them, for Dr Sarah had turned one into a wee bit for bairns to play in while their mammies were being seen to.

'Easier to talk without little ears flapping,' she said.

307

It wasn't ears flapping that worried Helen. It was tongues wagging. The mortuary van at her door twice in one week, and at her work too. Dr Deuchar buried on the parish like a common criminal – 'Which he is,' Dr Strasser said, grimly, about his old friend – Mr Pyne sacked, Mr Grossart struck off, Mr Warner de-frocked. Edinburgh had never seen—

Helen stopped herself. Edinburgh had seen things *exactly* like it. Worse even. And would again. She just hoped she never had to deal with them. A quiet life would do.

Acknowledgements

I would like to thank: Lisa Moylett, Zoe Apostolides, Elena Langtry and Jamie McLean at CMM Literary Agency; Francine Toon, Jo Dickinson, Sarah Christie, Kate Keehan, Ilona Jasiewicz, and all at Hodder and Stoughton; my family and friends for patience and kindness, especially my mum, Jean McPherson, who helped me with details of domestic life in 1948 – from divvy numbers to bubblegum. *She is not Greet.* None of my sisters is Teenie either.

Laura Dawes' *Fighting Fit: the wartime battle for Britain's health* (Weidenfield and Nicolson, 2016) was invaluable in allowing me to read my way back to how things were just before the big change in 1948. Aneurin Bevan's *In Place of Fear* (1952, Kessinger Legacy reprints, 2010) was like a siren song; I had to hold hard against it to stick to the story and resist too much philosophy. (And I still can't believe no one else has re-used the title before me.) Chris Nottingham and Rona Dougall's paper "A Close and Practical Association with the Medical Profession; Scottish Medical Social Workers and Social Medicine" in *Medical History*, Alberts, Suzuki, Chakraborty & Yasuda eds. (Cambridge UP, 2012) was an ongoing inspiration. I take full responsibility for any departure from their careful scholarship. The story is the boss of me. That story would have been much the poorer without the treasure trove of *Waters Under the Bridge: 20th century Tollcross, Fountainbridge and the West Port,* Tollcross

Local History Project (Aberdeen UP, 1990) which let me hang out in the back green and meet the neighbours.

Last but immensely not least I would like to thank the NHS: cleaners, porters, orderlies, auxiliaries, therapists, administrators, technicians, paramedics, nurses, doctors, volunteers, and of course medical social workers. I dreamed this book up in 2019. I wrote it in 2020. Getting to compose a love-letter to the NHS was one of the few bright bits in that dreadful year.

Glossary

Baffies – slippers
Bahookey – bottom
Bairn – baby, child
Beel – blush
Besom – lit. broom, fig. woman
Boak – retch, vomit
Bogey – go-cart, small wagon
Braw – good
Breenge – plunge, rush in
Buddy – person
Bunker – draining board
Caw – turn a skipping rope for others
Chuckies – marbles, jacks,
Clart – dirt, slovenly person
Cloot – cloth or small fabric article
Close – the common entrance and stairs of a tenement
Clout – hit, slap
Clype – tell tales, snitch
Creepie – footstool
Fash – bother
Flit – move house
Gey – very
Grue – shudder, express disgust
Haddie – lit. haddock, fig. unhandy person
High heid yins – social elites, bosses
Howf – den, small shelter

Humph – lug, carry
Jeely piece – bread and jam
Keek – peep
Ken – know
Killy-code – piggy-back
Midden – lit. refuse heap, fig, any messy or dirty place or person
Neb – be nosy
Oxters – armpits
Pan-loaf – posh, affected
Perjink – natty
Piece – sandwich
Ploating – sweating, uncomfortably hot
Poke – paper bag
Press – cupboard
Rare – good
Segs – bootnails
Skelp – smack
Sleekit – sly, devious
Sowel – lit. soul (affectionate)
Swither – weigh up otions
Tablet – confection similar to fudge
Thole – endure
Thrawn – stubborn, contrary
Toorie bunnet – cloth cap with no peak
Wame – stomach
Wean – lit. wee one, child
Wersh – savourless, insipid
Wheen – a quantity

An invitation from the publisher

Join us at www.hodder.co.uk, or follow us
on Twitter @hodderbooks to be a part of
our community of people who love the very
best in books and reading.

Whether you want to discover more about a book
or an author, watch trailers and interviews, have the
chance to win early limited editions, or simply browse
our expert readers' selection of the very best books,
we think you'll find what you're looking for.

And if you don't, that's the place to tell us what's missing.

We love what we do, and we'd love you to be a part of it.

www.hodder.co.uk

@hodderbooks

HodderBooks

HodderBooks